MW00563427

To Rose,

Our amazing instrumentalist on the viola. Thank you for your music.

With love,
Bill & Charlotte

Xmas 2024

100 YEARS

SIMON & SCHUSTER

THE INSTRUMENTALIST

Harriet Constable

Simon & Schuster

NEW YORK   LONDON   SYDNEY
TORONTO   NEW DELHI

100 YEARS
SIMON & SCHUSTER

1230 Avenue of the Americas
New York, NY 10020

This book is a work of fiction. Any references to historical events, real people, or real places are used fictitiously. Other names, characters, places, and events are products of the author's imagination, and any resemblance to actual events or places or persons, living or dead, is entirely coincidental.

Copyright © 2024 by Harriet Constable and Kubuni Ltd.

All rights reserved, including the right to reproduce this book or portions thereof in any form whatsoever. For information, address Simon & Schuster Subsidiary Rights Department, 1230 Avenue of the Americas, New York, NY 10020.

First Simon & Schuster hardcover edition August 2024

SIMON & SCHUSTER and colophon are registered trademarks of Simon & Schuster, LLC

Simon & Schuster: Celebrating 100 Years of Publishing in 2024

For information about special discounts for bulk purchases, please contact Simon & Schuster Special Sales at 1-866-506-1949 or business@simonandschuster.com.

The Simon & Schuster Speakers Bureau can bring authors to your live event. For more information or to book an event, contact the Simon & Schuster Speakers Bureau at 1-866-248-3049 or visit our website at www.simonspeakers.com.

Manufactured in the United States of America

1   3   5   7   9   10   8   6   4   2

Library of Congress Cataloging-in-Publication Data is available on file.

ISBN 978-1-6680-3582-5
ISBN 978-1-6680-3584-9 (ebook)

To my mum and dad,
who raised me with love,
and let me be
bold and curious.

Historical Note

In 1696 a baby was posted through the wall of the Ospedale della Pietà, an orphanage in Venice. She was named Anna Maria della Pietà and became one of the greatest violinists of the eighteenth century. Her teacher was Antonio Vivaldi.

UNO

I

VENICE 1695

Dusk, and the Marangona bell tolls in the Piazza San Marco. The chimes shiver out from the bronze mouth, glide over the domed roof of the Basilica, lick the cockles lining the mud-drenched canal, and filter through a gap between pavement and wooden door. Behind it, a girl standing in a narrow, dimly lit passageway looks up.

To some, the bell indicates the time. To others, it notes holy days, gatherings of the council, public executions. But to her, it is a signal that she and her fellow workers may take to the streets for the night. Now is the time for business.

She wraps her yellow scarf around her neck, a light wool that signifies her trade, and walks outside. Her home is a brothel in the San Polo district, tucked away behind the Ruga dei Oresi, the main thoroughfare for travelers and locals crossing the bridge to San Marco each day. A strategic location: this is where the work is.

The clip of her heels echoes off the cobbles as she turns. Left out of the brothel door, left again at the corner where the butcher sells entrails, and straight on until she reaches her usual spot on the edge of the Rialto Bridge. She nods to a woman who has arrived moments before and is setting up. Then she folds her cloak and scarf and places them on the cobbles beneath the bridge. There is a silent understanding—*we keep our things here, neatly, while we work.*

Hers is a green linen dress with a high waist. A ribbon weaves around the deep, square neck. Her fingers find the collar and she tugs the shoulders down until her breasts are naked to the night, perches on some pale brickwork, and waits for the next customer. This person is usually male, usually alone, often with a whiff of wine about them.

Her heart pounds, sitting here, but less than it used to. At seventeen she feels she can handle most things. Three a day, on average. Six months, nearly six hundred clients. She taps her foot to the beat of her mind. It's just another night's work.

He's not a regular. Male, yes. Alone, yes. But she's never seen him before. He's businesslike, she doesn't mind that, but he must be forty years her senior with eyes as dark as the devil.

"Let's go," he says, looking over his shoulder as if worried about being caught. He smells of woodsmoke, tobacco. His voice is gravelly and low.

She leads him back to the brothel, up the wooden stairs that creak under his weight. He grunts and crouches to avoid hitting his head as they enter the room. His red cap and tin-buttoned coat suggest a position at the naval yard. She's heard they can build a warship in a day there.

There's a large bed with dark wooden posts and a few candles burning down to the stub. Their shadows flicker and tremble against the walls. She takes a deep breath, and the door clicks shut behind her.

Nine months later her stomach is swollen and tight. She wakes before daybreak because a pain, electric and astounding, has begun to pulse through her. Following the plan, she gathers her matted yellow scarf around her and tucks the fabric she's been embroidering into her pocket.

The first challenge is the stairs. The pain throbs scarlet. There's a hot, tearing feeling somewhere deep and low inside, buckling her legs as she clings to the splintered wooden banister. She makes it to the street but then drops to her knees, clutching her stomach on all fours. Is she going to make it in time? It's not far from here, but in her condition . . .

You can't stop, she tells herself. You can make it, she decides.

She struggles to her feet and continues down the street, body sliding along the brick walls for support. Beneath her shoes, puddles split, reflections shattered in two. The journey is just a few streets but it seems endless. The pain is breathtaking, so much worse than even fifteen minutes ago.

Three knocks, some shuffling, and a midwife, wrinkled and gray, cracks the door open an inch. Her eyes drop to the stomach, where a younger hand clutches taut skin. The midwife's face changes from frustration to concern. The door opens wide.

"Between your teeth," the midwife says, wrestling a bone from her small black and white dog and handing it to her.

The dog growls. The girl growls back. She bites down, more animal than she's ever been. The pain becomes spectacular, a vivid red, like she is being torn apart from inside.

It's her last waking thought. Spectacular.

Two days have passed in the darkness of this small room in the midwife's house. It's nowhere near long enough for her ripped body to recover, but the bed is needed. Another girl is screaming now.

"Time to go," the midwife says.

"But where?" the girl asks. She hadn't expected to survive the labor.

The midwife hands back her yellow scarf, and she's surprised to find a wriggling creature wrapped inside. She'd almost forgotten about that. It is blotched, wrinkled, blue-veined. The midwife holds up a spoon, feeds it the last drips of sugar water. The girl wrestles with its squirming limbs, unable to focus, unable to think, until her eyes roll back in her head and pain begins to spasm through her thighs. Her tears drip onto its face. The creature screams in anger.

The girl walks for a while, turning through the maze of backstreets and bridges with little direction. She is so tired, her body still bleeding and raw. All through the night she has battled the penetrating screams, but there is quiet now at last.

Dawn approaches, a thick fog snaking down the canal. She just has to keep walking. Just keep walking and this thing will stay quiet. She reaches an opening where ornate buildings with peaked windows back onto the jade-green canal. Four steps lead down to the water. It laps against them enticingly.

Come to me, it calls. *Come to me.*

The water is cool, but even this early on a spring morning it's refreshing. She clutches the creature to her body and wades in deeper, deeper.

This. Of course this is the solution. It is so peaceful, so calm. The girl leans back and, simple as breathing, sinks both their bodies beneath the surface.

But the creature, shocked by the chill, by the wet, by the lack of oxygen, erupts. It's angry and alive and real again all of a sudden, struggling against her grip.

Just stop, just shush, she begs. Not much longer. Not much longer now.

But it is a raging firestorm of a thing, and she cannot hold it back. Their heads tear above the surface as both of them scream for breath, for life.

The creature grips her hand harder now. It's not screaming, it's begging her as, somewhere in the distance, a single note, elegant and long, pierces the air. She slings the creature out of the water, folds it into her sodden cloak, and runs.

The giant, carved doors of the Santa Maria della Fava are open, awaiting the first attendees to Mass. The girl is dripping wet, her teeth chattering, the creature quiet in her arms as she staggers in. She is met by the swift steps of the priest, the click, click, clack of his feet down the aisle.

"No whores allowed," he says, shoving her back toward the tall wooden doors. His embroidered silk robes billow in the breeze.

"Please . . . Brother," she begs, tugging back her cloak to reveal the creature in her arms.

His face turns from disapproval to disgust. He shoves her again. She feels the whip of air as the door slams in her face. She sinks down to the ground, her legs splayed out in front of her. Breathes in, breathes out, another jolt of pain quivering through her thighs.

The air, she realizes as she grimaces against her own body, smells sweet. A blend of butter, sugar, and flour drifting from the pastry shop nearby.

Her breasts are throbbing; the creature starts to scream again. The solution is simple. It's animal. She already knows what to do. With a listless hand she peels down her dress, exposing a bare breast. It latches on and starts to suck.

The woman who finds her was once a *cortigna lume* too, a hustler who lost her looks but kept her resilience. The girl wakes in the hustler's humble home, on the floor surrounded by a few cushions and a blanket. There is a slim table against the wall, and on it a box filled with playing cards. She's handed a cup of coffee, steam winding from its surface. She brings it to her lips, blows gently, and then sips. The warmth sinking into her body is almost enough to draw tears.

The hustler is bent down, talking now. One hand nurses her lower back, the other collects an empty plate and cup off the ground next to her. She doesn't catch the girl's eye when she speaks. "You can stay here until you're recovered, and then you'll pay me back by month end. I can get you work at my old brothel. They'll like the look of you, once your snatch is healed."

The plate and cup clink together as she straightens up. The hustler points with the cup. "You'll take her to the Pietà. Two weeks from now, once you're stronger. But not a moment longer. If she gets much bigger, she won't fit in the hole."

"What's the Pietà?" the girl says quietly.

"They'll raise her there, give her a good life. She'll get an education, opportunities. They even teach them instruments." It's not a conversation, the hustler doesn't wait for a response. She turns and leaves the room.

The girl blinks, watching her go. Then there's a gentle cooing, a wriggle. She feels a swelling inside and braces herself. But pain does not come. In its place is something stronger, something enduring, something good. She looks down to see what has caused it. And for the first time, she realizes she has a baby girl in her arms.

The next week or so is the sweetest of her life. She watches the baby start to focus, locking onto her eyes and learning this is her mother. The girl feeds her, cuddles her, strokes her cheeks, and wipes the spittle from her mouth. And although they are not of the same body anymore, there is a fundamental understanding. They are, and will always be, part of one another.

She breathes in the warm milk smell of her and thinks of what she wants to say to her one day. Things she wishes someone once said to her.

She will tell her to run. She will tell her to dream. She will tell her to let what is inside pour out. And when her daughter asks what she might do with her life one day, what she might be, she will tell her: Anything. Anything that ignites your world in multicolor.

Three days before it is time the girl takes her daughter and her coins and walks across the city. She will buy paper, beautiful Venetian paper, paper fit for a queen, with the little money she's saved.

The shopkeeper sniffs his disapproval at her as she selects the finest she can afford—a thick cream sheet marbled with flecks of green. She hands over more coins than she'll spend on three days' food, but that doesn't stop her.

A sign above the next door reads "*Scriba*." A rope hangs from the center of a black metal bell. She clanks it against the edge three times, and a handsome man with ink-stained hands answers to its chime.

"Write this," she says once inside, and he transforms her words into beautiful loops on the paper. She folds it carefully and tucks it beneath her cloak.

Back at the hustler's house, she slips a playing card from the deck on the side table and, using a small knife from the kitchen, slices it diagonally in two. She slides one piece into the folds of her corset.

It is dawn again, a time which will forever mean pain to her now.

"It has to be today," the hustler says.

The girl bundles her baby into her yellow scarf and takes to the streets once more, stirring a thick layer of fog at her feet. Her skirts slap against her ankles as she hurries through the dizzying maze, her heart strumming in her chest. Gold masks in the windows jeer at her as she passes. The animal inside her is alert, prey anticipating an attack. Her ears are more attuned to every twitch and whistle, her hands wrapped protectively around the child beneath the cloak.

Get there fast, don't dawdle, pay attention. Left, right, right, left, right. At the first sound of danger, run, she tells herself. Run.

But the journey is silent, and as she approaches the Pietà from the alley to the side, she feels herself slow. How long it takes to make those final steps she will never know.

She stares at the grate, at the hole in the wall where she will lay her baby, this part of her, this bundle of fire and energy that makes her flare with pride. This creature which begged her to live.

She can't do it. She staggers back, clutching her daughter tighter to her chest, when a whimper distracts her attention.

On the ground beneath the hole in the wall there are boxes. They look to be filled with snags of material, discarded food, and rubbish, but a noise coming from one of them draws her closer. She peels back the lid of the box and stifles a scream.

Inside, a child blue with cold and covered with the scratches of an animal takes its final breath. The baby looks large, too large to fit in the hole in the wall.

She takes a deep breath and places her fingers to its neck, but the beat is gone. She closes its eyelids and, ever so gently, lifts some fabric over its face.

It is everything she needs to see.

She stands up, takes one last look at her daughter, and slides her carefully into the hole in the wall. She slips the folded note and the other half of the playing card into the bundle of blankets. She kisses her on the head, stands back, and rings the bell. Then she turns and, not bearing to look back, disappears forever.

Go now gentle babe, the note says, *and know that you were loved.*

On the other side of the wall, the tempo is different.

"First one of the day," Sister Clara calls as the metal clapper dings against the mouth of the bell. She rushes out into the courtyard and from the hole pulls a wriggling baby girl.

"Fifteenth April 1696," she instructs Sister Madalena, who is jotting down the details into a huge string-bound book filled with names.

Chiara della Pietà, arrived 20th February 1687, with a stamped coin and a note from the mother. Paulina della Pietà, arrived 29th April 1695, with an embroidered cloth. Agata della Pietà, arrived 4th May 1695, with a poem and a head wound from the box.

The baby is unwrapped, taken to a basin, and washed. Her skin is checked for infections, the little hair she has for lice. A rod is placed in the fire. There's a sizzling, the iron smell of flesh, and a fierce scream. In the rod's place there is now a "P," angry and raw, on her upper left arm. The wound is bandaged. A priest baptizes her. And then they return to the file.

The baby's breath is short, staggered: she is suffering with pain. But there is a look in her eye. A furious determination.

"And what shall we call her?" Sister Madalena asks.

Sister Clara looks down at the child, who takes her finger in her tiny hand. She squints in concentration.

"Anna Maria della Pietà," she announces, as the baby squeezes tight. "I have a feeling about this one."

She is standing on a podium, poised for the moment. The moment of her lifetime. Soon she will accept the certificate of *maestro*. She will be, officially, a Master of Music.

It feels like every second Anna Maria has breathed has led to this. Like every choice, every beat, is connected. The lights blind her, heat radiates from the audience. She feels thousands of adoring eyes, all of them fixed on her. And the respect. It has a weight to it. It moves through the air, thick and alive and glorious. She sucks it into her lungs.

Then, a giggle.

She frowns, snaps from her imagination and into her dormitory, where her podium is a single wooden bed, her certificate a handkerchief.

"It is my duty, and my honor," Paulina, a thin girl with a pointed chin, bellows in a mock-low voice, "to . . . to . . ." Her focus shifts, the moment almost gone.

"Bestow," Anna Maria whispers out of the corner of her mouth.

Paulina swallows the laugh bubbling up inside.

This may seem like child's play to some, but not to Anna Maria. Because there are some things that girls just know. Some know their spirit can rage like a fire. Some know that power is up for the taking. Some know that death comes early and cruel. And some know that they are destined for greatness.

Anna Maria della Pietà is destined for greatness.

At eight, she knows this as surely as string knows bow, as

lightning knows storm, as water knows sky. She *knows*, like she knows that one of her toes sticks out at an angle, that the meat on Wednesdays tastes like fish, and that the note *C* is green. It, like so many things, is a certainty. So standing on this stage, hands on her hips, accepting her title, is as natural as dreaming.

She gives a cough, encouraging her friend to continue.

Paulina's smile drops. She nods. Serious. "To *bestow* this title upon the one, the only, Anna Maria della Pietà," she cries.

Anna Maria smiles, throws her hands out to the crowd, and then, reaching forward from her podium, takes the certificate graciously.

The crowd goes wild. She leaps from the chair in the corner of the room, beaming as she applauds. Because today, like every day, the crowd is Anna Maria's other best friend, Agata. She is dark-haired like Anna Maria, but shorter, softer. There are whoops and cheers as Anna Maria bows, again and again, her mess of short curls bouncing into her eyes. She steps down from her podium and takes the hands of her fan.

"All my life I have worked for this honor. *Grazie, grazie, grazie*," Anna Maria says.

Paulina is giggling, cheeks flushed with two pink dots. One piercing blue eye meets Anna Maria's. In the space of the other is a sunken hole, the lid badly stitched, the flesh bunched and red. "My turn, my turn," she begs.

"One more go," Anna Maria says, climbing back onto her podium, thinking about how she can improve her speech, "and then you'll have your chance."

At daybreak, the bells clang in the Piazza San Marco. It is not five minutes' walk from the imposing Ospedale della Pietà building, which overlooks the lagoon. Behind the green-shuttered windows, three hundred orphaned girls are already awake and working. They form a repetitive stream, one after the other, moving through the hallways, wearing white.

On the fifth of five floors, Anna Maria is stripping her bed as the deep purple bongs flood her senses.

B flat, she thinks.

Sliding her hand through the bars, she cracks open the small dormitory window. Cool morning air floods through. She breathes in deeply, peering out over the terra-cotta tiles to listen to the new day. Far below, someone is running along the cobbles. There's the rumble of a cart being pulled, the shriek of a baby, the bark of a dog. But the crescendo will come in about an hour, when the world will pour out onto the streets and canals and Venice will be alive once again.

First comes Mass, taken in the chapel. The girls drone devotions back to the sisters.

Next comes gruel, taken in the refectory. Anna Maria slaps her spoon against the gritty lumps in protest. Then there are the chores. Washing and scrubbing and sewing and steaming, chopping and boiling and scraping and cleaning. Freedom comes after noon prayers each day.

When the sisters are practicing their hymns and psalms, Anna Maria sneaks away. Takes the curving stone staircase two steps at a time, crashes into the attic dormitory.

The bed screeches as she pulls it to the right. She clambers up, fidgeting for the latch between the shutters behind. A scraping sound and it submits as she crawls forward onto a small wooden platform. Once they hung washing here. But when a storm left it splintered and cracked it was forgotten. Now they use the bigger platform on the other side of the building. Now it is all hers.

Sunshine floods Anna Maria's face; the planks creak under her feet. She takes her position, gathering her stained cotton smock beneath her and crossing her legs over the hot wood. Satisfied, she surveys her kingdom.

In her city, the roads are made of water. Life breathes from every direction, energetic, colorful, and loud.

She raises her hands to the orchestra, ready to conduct. Cue the gondoliers, who hum a sprightly tune as they glide through narrow streets. Cue the fruit sellers in the square chanting, "Dates for a *denari*, lemons for a *lira*!" Cue the combmakers, knife sharpeners, wood-carvers, and more, each faction singing a tune of their making. Cue the crowd who applaud the dance of the jokers, the gulls who cry out as they soar through the sky. Cue the spinners who tap to the whirl of their looms, the shoeshiners who buff overlooking the lagoon. Cue the milkmen who tinkle glass bottles together, and her friends in the courtyard who scream round the tree. Cue the man singing opera from the tunnel on her left, and the bells clanging *midday!* from the tower on her right.

And now, cue the colors. The blues and yellows and greens and reds, the purples and oranges and whites and browns. A kaleidoscope of a world explodes before her eyes. Tones and hues float up, high above the city, hanging like notes on a stave, matching the sounds below. Then they blend and swirl, a shoal of fish, as a smile lights up her face.

This girl had notes before she had words, and those notes have always had color.

Behind her, Paulina and Agata scramble out, scooting close on either side.

"Sorry we're late," Paulina says. "We had to repeat our blessings."

Agata nods and rolls her eyes.

"Welcome to the party," Anna Maria says, looking straight ahead. "Welcome to my Republic of Music."

In 1704, life at the Pietà is one of contrast. Gut a fish, pluck a harp. Crush a toe, string a symphony. Where there is pain and brutality, there is music and song. And there is Anna Maria, Paulina, and Agata.

There was no moment of inception, no specific act that drew them together. It is just as it would be for a sibling. They are simply there, present, always.

Anna Maria's head sinks into the nook of Paulina's neck. She slides Agata's arm into hers. When Agata turns her head, a dent the size of a palm is revealed. It is on the right, just above the neck, and concave like a cupped hand. A few strands of her straight hair fall across it; the patch itself is bald.

"One day we will rule over this," Anna Maria says, looking out at her city. "Really, truly rule it. Not like now. Not like pretending. We'll be the musical kings of Venice. Crowds will fall at our feet."

"We'll be covered in jewels!" Paulina squeaks.

"We'll journey to Paris and Rome," Anna Maria says.

"We'll eat cream *frittelle* all day long!"

"And no one will be able to say what we do but us."

Agata lets out a little moan.

Anna Maria nudges her. "It was the *frittelle*, wasn't it?"

Agata's face breaks into a lopsided smile. She nods.

They'd been allowed the fried balls of pastry only once, a donation to the Pietà during *carnevale*. They arrived in a ribbon-bound basket, the smell of lemon peel and sweet dough seeping through the wicker. The other girls had snarled over them like stray pups, but Anna Maria managed to snatch three before they were gone. She, Paulina, and Agata scoffed them right here on this rooftop, grinning through their sugar-flaked lips.

Anna Maria sighs, remembering the taste. Leans back as Agata and Paulina follow. They lie staring into the sky as clouds flit overhead.

The sun moves behind a cloud now, shading Anna Maria's blemished face. Scars, from the pox two years back. "You'll grow out of them and into yourself," Sister Clara says. But Anna Maria already feels like herself. Always has. And anyway, looks hardly interest her. Everyone has something here.

Paulina rearranges her smock, ironing out the creases that have formed there. Agata looks at Anna Maria, waiting for what comes next. A gull swoops by and Anna Maria calls out to it, until Agata is laughing and Paulina is joining in with the caws.

Paulina rolls over, takes Anna Maria's hand. "Twins," she says, as their palms connect.

She is so slight, sometimes Anna Maria wonders if the wind might blow in from across the lagoon and carry her away. Wisps of pale blond hair flutter about her face in the breeze. Agata leans across Anna Maria and pokes Paulina.

"Fine, triplets," Paulina says, laughing now.

The bells chime one, and Anna Maria leaps to her feet. It is, finally, the afternoon. They have their music lessons.

"What's that?" Anna Maria asks, storming into the room where Signore Conti is leaning against a large instrument with a pitched roof and slim legs. It's made of wood and decorated with elegant swirls. She likes the black and white of the keys. But it's not a harpsichord, she's played one of those before. It's bigger.

"Good afternoon to you too, Anna Maria," he says, pushing back his long golden curls. He is tall and slim, with a square-set jaw and a dimple in his chin. People say he's elegant; some of the older girls say they want to *have him*. Anna Maria isn't certain what they mean, has little interest in finding out.

"It's called a *fortepiano*. It is the latest invention from Signore Cristofori. Instead of a plucking mechanism inside, the strings are tapped with a hammer. It gives the player far greater control of the volume, see?"

Anna Maria lifts onto her toes and, clutching the wooden edges, pokes her head into the instrument's bowels. She notes the little wooden tabs hovering above the strings, ready to strike.

"Signore Cristofori has kindly donated this one to us. We must be very grateful."

"I want to try it," Anna Maria says, hands on her hips, stomach jutting out.

Signore Conti considers her for a moment. "You will get your turn once we finish with the flute if you are good. But first, sit."

After class she loiters, pestering until Signore Conti gives up and lets her try the *fortepiano*. She runs her fingers over the smooth keys and he teaches her a line of melody that she samples a few times over.

Pleasant, she thinks. But this isn't it.

Like the flute and the oboe, both of which she's spent the last year learning, the colors of her mind are there, but they're dull, muddled. It won't work for her plan.

Anna Maria della Pietà will be the youngest ever member of the *figlie di coro*, the orphanage's world-famous orchestra, and a *maestro* by eighteen. The world will know her. They will know her as the greatest musician that ever lived.

The corridors are quiet when Anna Maria leaves Signore Conti's class finally. He tells her to go straight to supper, that he will inform the sisters why she is late once again.

She hurries along the third floor, the pads of her scuffed boots slapping the stone tiles with speed. The walls are gray, cracked, the ceilings low. There is one barred window at the end, daylight rapidly fading. She skids and turns, reaching the spiral staircase, when a sound, piercing and rich, stops her sharp.

She follows the noise, edging back the way she came until she finds a door ajar. Squinting through the gap, she sees a man, not far from his teens, with a gasp of curling, shoulder-length red hair.

He is facing a fireplace, dressed in a simple brown coat with short tails and cream breeches, lit by the glow of the flames.

In one arm he holds a violin, in the other a bow. He races it across the strings, twitching and jolting, aggressive and rigid. Possessed, surely. Anna Maria should fetch the *medico*. This man needs a priest. But her feet are paralyzed—the sound holds her still.

Instead she studies his fingers, the movement of his hands. The bow flies back and forth as the colors of her mind start to flow. Amber, gold, citrus, and white, silver and ocher and puce. The shades blast past her eyes. She has to hold the doorframe to steady herself. She has never seen this instrument played in this way. Never heard it speak with a voice so clear and bright it could be singing her very name. Like another element, she thinks. Earth, air, fire, water. And now this.

But the twists, the turns. It's too much. It's frightening. She considers running, hurling her body from this moment. And yet, somewhere deep inside, a tension is ebbing. These notes feel familiar, the sound one she knows. The colors begin to layer until a landscape forms—green mountains and purple flowers, orange sunlight, bursts of white. It moves and sways in front of her eyes. Without knowing quite why, she wipes tears from her cheeks.

Now she knows something else for certain. She must get her hands on this instrument.

She hides in the small cupboard opposite the room he is in, back pressed up against a shelf of crusted ink bottles, toe in the gap to stop the door from locking shut. Breathes in the dust. Waits until he stops. Hears the click of the locks on the case, the creak of the door, the clack of heels diminishing. She explodes from the darkness.

The violin is there, the man is not.

She edges toward it slowly, steadily. Clicks open the clips, reveals the contents of this treasure chest. The glossy body, the long sleek bow, perfectly encased in velvet. Her breath eases as a feeling, warm and sweet as melted sugar, runs through her.

She reaches out a hand, trails her small fingers across its body. The wood is smooth and cool like a pebble. She leans closer, breathes in the smell of varnish, old books. Her mouth fills with saliva.

She tucks her hand beneath the neck and eases it out. Raises it importantly to her chin, just like he had it.

Her fingers meet strings, try to mimic his clutch. With great drama, she drags the bow from left to right.

A terrible screech echoes around the room, followed by a series of short screeches as the bow bumps its way down the strings.

Unexquisite, she tells herself. But try and try again.

She readjusts her position as—

"What *are* you thinking?" A sharp voice from behind.

Her stomach clenches. Slowly, she looks over her shoulder.

He is standing in the doorframe, his hair red as fire.

"Put that back, child," he says quietly, "and get out before I make you."

———

Supper. They sit in the refectory, an arched stone room on the bottom floor of the Pietà, set with three long wooden tables. Beneath the benches, hundreds of pairs of feet in black mended boots, curtained by white cotton skirts. There is the clatter of plates, the hum of conversation ("I'll swap the ribbon but that's it"; "Slow down, you'll choke").

Paulina is poking at something brown and spongelike on her plate before touching it, suspiciously, to her tongue.

"What can this be?" she says, pulling the spoon back and inspecting its contents once again.

Anna Maria does not hear her. She is thinking about him standing there, watching her as she rushed to place his violin back in its case. Her knee judders beneath the table.

"Anna Maria?"

She blinks, places a hand on her leg to calm it. Then she leans across, sniffs the spoon Paulina is now holding out, pulls a face.

"Boiled brains?" she offers.

Agata nudges her, shaking her head in warning. But too late—Paulina lets out a howl, and the whole refectory, a hundred or more students, turns to look at them.

"Silence, foolish girl." Sister Madalena scowls, marching over from her wooden stool in the corner. A large woman with a bulging back and calloused hands, she looks upon each of the orphans with a perfected disdain, aged like an old wine over the years she has been here.

Paulina should hush. But she can't help it. She starts to retch. She leaps from her chair and runs through a stone archway into the kitchen. Just makes it to the large wooden box in the corner where they deposit the peelings and scraps, heaving into it. Its contents, brown and pungent, will be emptied onto the waste barges this evening and sailed to the farms beyond the city for manure. Anna Maria will hear the horn from her bed, see its color, know the note.

Anna Maria and Agata burst into laughter, but Sister Madalena delivers an *I am warning you* stare and they stifle it. Quickly.

When Paulina returns she is paler than usual. On her plate

now there is a portion twice the size. Her hand moves, slowly, to cover her mouth.

"You will eat it all," Sister Madalena says, looming over her like a bad smell. Tears form in Paulina's eyes. "Or it will be the whip. I'll be back to check."

As soon as she is gone, Agata leans across the table, pulls Paulina's plate toward her. Then she turns to Anna Maria, widens her big hazel eyes, mouths, *"Please?"*

Anna Maria purses her lips, looks at the sludge on the plate. Something seems to be wriggling in it. But then she sees Paulina. Wet-faced, breath shuddering in and out.

Anna Maria huffs out, "We'll split it."

Agata nods and, taking a deep breath, picks up a spoon. Paulina stands, rushes around the table, and plants a kiss on both their cheeks.

Anna Maria begins to chew slowly, grimacing at something gristly and fibrous on her tongue. She tunes into a conversation between two girls sitting behind her.

"Another one?" one girl whispers.

"Yesterday," her friend responds. "That's three this year."

"Do you think it was . . . the raven?"

Anna Maria lowers her spoon, looks to Paulina. "What are they talking about?"

Paulina fixes her with a stare for a moment. "There is a story . . ." She stops, looks down the table, checks they are not being watched. "That there is a man. A creature. That he comes for the Pietà girls in the night."

"A creature?" Anna Maria breathes.

Agata, chewing stoically, shakes her head. She swallows before she mouths, *"Not true."*

"I said it is a story," Paulina says defensively. "Some of the girls were whispering about it in the dormitory. No doubt they're trying to frighten us." Her eyes flick down the table again.

"What happens when he comes?" Anna Maria asks.

Paulina has a glimmer in her eyes. She shifts. Anna Maria leans closer.

21

"The fog arrives first. It curls down the canal, submerging everything in its path. Then there is a sound. A suck, suck, suck. It is a noise only the older girls can hear. They say it gets into their bones."

Horror is spreading across Anna Maria's face. Paulina's eyes grow wider.

"They wake, risen in a half-dream state, and walk barefoot toward the sound. When they reach the doors to the canal they stand there, frozen, staring out at the water until he comes. He stands on a gondola with one lantern rocking at its prow. His body is human but he has the head of . . ." She takes a breath, frightened, it seems, by her own story. "The head of a raven. Beady black eyes, a long dark beak."

Anna Maria is clutching the bench beneath her.

"He moves closer, silent but for the suck, suck, suck of his oar in the water. The girls are pulled to it. They take the hand of the creature, step a foot onto his boat, and then—"

There is a shriek next to them—a girl laughing at something her friend has said.

"What?" Anna Maria demands. "What happens then?"

"And then he takes her. The fog folds in on them, and when it clears, there is no one to be seen. The last thing anyone hears is her scream."

Anna Maria pushes out a breath, realizing that she has been holding it for some time.

Agata is tapping Anna Maria's forearm again now. *"It's just a story."*

Just a story, Anna Maria repeats to herself, trying to smile now. But her knee begins to judder beneath the table again. It is not normally the sort of thing that would rattle her. She must be more on edge after being caught with the violin. She lets out a sound, an attempt at a laugh. But as she does so her eyes flick to the window, to the canal that lies beyond. And it takes every ounce of her effort not to slam her palms to her ears, to refuse to ever hear the noise of the gondola in the mist.

3

Moonlight settles over Anna Maria from the square in the roof above the beams. She lies listening to the sounds, fidgeting with her froth of dark curls, the ends tickling her ears. Her hair used to reach her shoulders, same as the other under-fourteens, but the sisters clipped it fingernail-short when she got sick and it became too matted to brush. Sister Clara sighs at it daily, complains it is ruffled as a crow's feather.

Three this year, Anna Maria thinks, remembering the conversation at supper. She feels a chill run through her, tugs her blankets a little higher.

Sister Madalena is pacing through the dormitory, checking each girl is asleep, cracking her knuckles in a bid to ease the swelling. Anna Maria hates the sound, wants to lift her hands to her ears but knows doing so will reveal she is still awake. She snaps her eyes closed as the clicks get louder.

She feels large hands gripping the wooden bedframe. A body leaning forward. Covers shifting. She tenses.

But then the hands are gone, the footsteps are fading away. Anna Maria breathes out, allows herself to open her eyes once again.

Now Sister Madalena and Sister Clara are in the corner. They look funny next to one another—Sister Madalena being so large and Sister Clara so small. They scratch some notes into a thick pad, the same every night. Which ones are in trouble, which ones are ill, what chores they'll each face tomorrow.

Not laundry, Anna Maria thinks, not laundry.

Next to her, Paulina whistles through her nose, sleeping as if mummified. On her back, arms snapped to her sides, the white of her remaining eye eerily visible. Anna Maria smiles, watching her now. Little Paulina Rabbit. A nickname given because of the way she holds her hands clutched to her chest when she speaks, the delicate way she nibbles at her food.

Sister Clara once told Anna Maria that palaces in the countryside have whole islands full of rabbits. Hundreds of the velvety creatures live on small grassy nooks surrounded by moats. Anna Maria thought it sounded like heaven, was desperate to visit and have them bounce into her lap. Then she learned they keep them there only until they are ready to be eaten. She's seen Cook lifting a box of live rabbits into the Pietà kitchen, dragging them out one by one, pinning them down. Watched their legs kick out, just before the snap.

Agata lies in the bed on the other side of Anna Maria, her limbs splayed over the edges of her mattress. Anna Maria's stomach turns, seeing the back of her head. Sister Madalena says that she was too big to fit in the donation box. That they must have forced her in. That this is why she has never been able to speak.

Beyond Anna Maria are a hundred more girls, twisting and turning and snoring and snuffling.

A curl of breath leaves her mouth and she shivers. She does not want to think of the gondola, of the man with the raven head at its stern. She forces the thought of him away, decides instead to run through the events of the day.

Her pitch was off in singing class, that will need addressing. And she couldn't achieve the resonance she was hoping for with the flute. She tries some breathing exercises like Signore Conti taught her. In for three, out for five, in for three, out for . . . Her eyelids droop.

She leans back, but instead of her body hitting the mattress, her stomach lurches and she crashes through ice-cold water. The shock pierces her body. Though she wrestles, she floats further into the depths. Her eyes open. Colorful buildings shudder

above, swaying to music that is slowed down, warped. She grabs for the rippling surface but still she is pulled down . . . down. She screams, bubbles erupting from her mouth, drifting up above her. She screams and screams and screams and screams and—

She's clutching her throat, gasping for breath, sitting up.

"Calm, breathe." Paulina is next to her, stroking her arm. "It's only another nightmare. That's five this week."

Paulina guides her toward her own bed, lifts up the scratchy, moth-eaten blankets. Anna Maria feels her thin body scoop around hers like a mold.

The darkness in the dormitory feels icy, sinister, like some-thing lingers near them. The gondola floats into Anna Maria's mind, the single lamp rocking at its prow.

"Will he come for us too?" she whispers, clutching the covers tight.

"Hmm?" Paulina asks.

"The raven man. Does he take all the girls?"

"They say it is just a few. And that music . . ." She pauses, checking Sister Madalena is not moving closer. "That music offers protection."

"How?"

"I don't know. Perhaps those with skill are spared."

Anna Maria holds this idea, grips it tight. Those with the most skill are in the orphanage's orchestra. She will find her place there, just as she has planned it, and she will be safe from this monster in the dark.

Those with skill are spared, she repeats.

She slips her hand into the soft, small palm of her friend, heart slowing at her touch. And tonight, like every night, it is here that she finally falls into a restless sleep.

A warm breeze filters in through the window of the smallest music room on the third-floor corridor. It is large enough to fit a desk, a line of cushioned wooden chairs, and a scattering of music stands. Anna Maria sits in the middle, legs crossed beneath her chair, first to class as always. To her right, a fireplace with a

stone surround. Behind her, the window, cracked open an inch, set with latticed iron bars.

A shadow looms across the floor. Paulina and Agata should be here by now. She wants to tell them how she tripped on the way up here and—

Anna Maria feels her stomach clench. Standing in the doorway is the man with the red hair and the brown tailcoat.

"Where's Signore Conti?" she says before she can stop herself. It is Wednesday, midafternoon. They have their flute lesson now.

He steps into the room, his movement fast and rigid. He flicks back his tails, places his case on a side table, clicks open the locks. He doesn't turn, doesn't look at her, doesn't answer her at all. Anna Maria's palms become clammy. She's certain punishment awaits her for sneaking into his room, touching what wasn't hers. But what kind? And how long will he make her wait, squirming, to find out?

The rest of her classmates start to filter in. Paulina sees that the teacher has arrived already and lets out a little squeak, hurries across to Anna Maria. Agata comes moments later, wiping her hands on her skirts, leaving grubby prints on the cotton. She is followed by Candida and Cecilia, twins who were left together when they were just a few hours old. They are, like always, linking arms. The class settle in their seats, copies in white smocks that are long, concealing. Every girl stares curiously at the intruder.

"I am your new teacher," he says, moving toward the chalkboard in front of them. There is a strange tone to his voice. The pitch wobbles, like he's trying to make it sound deeper than it is. "We will be learning the violin."

Agata and Paulina look at Anna Maria. Only the over-twelves have been learning this instrument. They have not been given the chance until now.

He writes his name, tiny pieces of chalk dust drifting to the floor as he underlines it twice.

Anna Maria feels her breath catch. She has heard of him, of

course. Everyone has heard of him. He is a *maestro*, renowned for his virtuosic violin playing throughout the Republic. Venice's one to watch. Hotshot, arrogant, she's heard the other teachers whisper. Anna Maria grips the edge of her chair. She has angered one of the greats.

But he is not what she expected. In her mind he'd been taller, more handsome. Instead, his shoulders slouch like he's in some kind of pain, and there's a weakness to his hands without his violin. He seems unsure what to do with them.

She looks down at her own hands, then back at him. She raises a palm to her pox-scarred cheek.

"Today we will . . ." He stops, wheezing for breath, and then coughs several times into a plain handkerchief before continuing. "Today we will master the basics. How to hold the violin, how to stand, how to play open strings."

So he is a little odd. It hardly matters. Anna Maria has heard him play. The astonishing speed, the spectacle of colors he can conjure. This man deserves her respect. She feels it with the same certainty, the same intensity, as the beat throbbing in the pale blue veins in her wrist.

She sits upright, focusing now. When he says "how to stand," she cracks her spine, brings her shoulders back, sucks in her stomach.

Her eyes flick to the case where his violin lies. Snug, elegant, waiting.

There's a scuffle as everyone rushes to the cupboard to collect an instrument. Twenty or so cases are scattered on the shelves inside. They are battered and grazed, the instruments donations from wealthy benefactors who have used and then discarded them. She lurches for the least damaged one but it's tugged away before she can grip it.

"One at a time, no pushing."

She settles for one from the middle shelf before those are gone too. This violin is paler than his, and a few of the horsehairs on the bow are sticking out, but she still likes the way it feels when her fingers close around its neck.

Now they are back in a line, and he marches along in front of them. She breathes in the smell of pine and incense. Like a priest, she thinks. She knows the smell from chapel.

Reaching Anna Maria he slows, lingering just inches from her. The pulse in her wrist quickens.

He curves his head toward her and, not meeting her eye, says, "Place your violin down."

Next to Anna Maria, Paulina moves to do so. He claps, hard, once, and she bolts back upright. "Not you," he says.

Anna Maria looks up at him. "Signore?"

"Down. Now."

Her heart slides into her throat. She turns, places her violin on the seat behind her. The room falls silent.

"Hands," he says, motioning for her to move, to stand behind her chair and clutch the bar at the top.

She's going to get the whip, she knows it. She can feel the air swell, the way the leather cuts through it, the raw sting on her knuckles.

He looks at her, his eyes cool and gray as frost. "This girl believes she is above the rules. That she may touch, may take, what is not hers."

Her jaw clenches. The class watches. Not a breath cracks the air between them.

"You will stand there," he says, "and you will learn your place."

She does not speak, but she will not look away from him, will not be the one to break the stare.

He moves through the group, ignoring Anna Maria now, tightening the pegs of a few of the violins until he is satisfied.

"Now," he says to the rest of the class, "lift your instruments to your chins, being mindful to keep your cores—that is, your stomach muscles—strong, and place your hands like mine."

He lifts his violin, glides his bow downward across the thickest string. It emits a rich green sound, raising the hair on Anna Maria's arms.

The class is shaken, a nervousness in the air. A few eyes flick to Anna Maria before they follow, replicating his movement. The violins meld together into a warbling, uncertain tone.

"Take your time with the bow, draw it across the strings smoothly, like a paintbrush to a canvas. No jolting movements."

The green grows more vibrant. Warm and fresh, it ripples through Anna Maria's mind.

"Good. Now place your index finger on the thinnest string. This is called the *E* string. Then, holding the bow delicately, like it is a bird's beak, draw it across."

The class follows this instruction.

"Use the tips of your fingers, don't let them blend across the strings," he says, adjusting some of the girls' hands as he weaves between them.

Anna Maria looks to her right. Next to her, the thin strings are cutting grooves into Paulina's fingers. But Paulina only pushes down harder, and Anna Maria realizes that with this one small adjustment she gets a cleaner sound. The movement brings different shades—one luminous, one pale, one dark like olives.

Anna Maria's breath is becoming heavier, deeper. She is focusing only on these instructions, on the intricate rules of the instrument.

The teacher explains that if they place their index finger at the scroll end of the thickest string it plays an *A* note, which glows yellow in Anna Maria's mind, but when they place their second finger about an inch lower on the same string it plays one note higher, *B*. The fourth finger on the same string of the instrument plays *D*, which is violet as a berry.

In that instant Anna Maria realizes the endless possibilities. She watches as Paulina runs her finger up and down the string, thrilling as the multicolor stream pours out.

"Very nice," he says, walking between them.

Anna Maria is locked in, concentrating on Paulina's fingers, her instrument, her sound. Her knuckles are whitening across the back of the chair.

"Very nice indeed. Soon, if you keep it up, you will be able to do this."

Standing in front of them, he raises his violin to his chin and rushes the bow back and forth across one string. He follows with an intense flourish of notes, his elbow cutting angles in the air.

And Anna Maria can hold it no longer. She lunges for the violin in front of her, lifts the sleek wooden form beneath her chin. Pleasure shivers through her at the feeling. An extension of her own body.

She fumbles to find the hand position, presses hard on the strings. Her nostrils are flared, her lips clenched with focus as she traces the color trail he has left. Reds, yellows, greens, and blues. Red, red, blue, green, blue, green, blue. There is no violin anymore. No Anna Maria anymore. Simply color, sound, and a feeling, something calm and certain, of a body finding its soul.

"How dare you . . ." he is saying, but she cannot stop for him.

Two steps to her chair. He grips her by the shoulder, his palm ready to strike. Anna Maria stumbles, the violin slips from her neck. But she is raising it again, she is playing because this is right. The violin sings for her with a sound that is warm and smooth as balm. He must know it. He must hear it.

The colors scream through the room. The fleshy part of Anna Maria's forearm aches, and for the first time in her life she is conscious of the fine tendons that run from her middle finger down the back of her hand. She grimaces. But she will not submit. She will not give in.

She braces herself. But the blow does not come. Finally, as if pulled from a trance, she stops. She lowers the violin, slowly, to her side. The silence is thick and throbbing around her. She looks to her left, to her right. Every classmate is staring. And then her eyes snag upon her teacher's.

The world seems to dissolve in that moment. Scale, shadow, and space slip away until there is nothing but him and her, frozen in time. His chest is heaving, but his face is blank. Is it anger, surprise? She realizes the tension feels good. Excitement is trembling, deep in her soul.

His words are tight, strained as he breathes, "Enough. Class dismissed."

With these words she is wrenched back to the room. And now fear bites. She is running for the cabinet, heart pounding in her chest.

What will he do to her? What will he take from her?

She is stashing her instrument among the frenzy of classmates when a clicking makes her stop.

And the anticipation as she turns, as she waits, could be sliced up, chewed, swallowed whole.

"Not you," he says quietly. "You stay."

4

At the Rialto fish market the gulls are insatiable. They swoop and sway, diving like pellets of hail toward the stalls, greedy for the last morsels of bream, the slithers of sardine. Shoppers duck, flinging hands over heads.

"Back, get back," the fishmongers cry. They swipe the air with wooden brooms. Movements met by furious flutters, indignant squawks. The racket ripples through the arches and into an alleyway beyond, where one bird, hungry and irritable, decides upon a different tactic.

Liftoff. White wings beat, higher and higher through the shaft between buildings, from coolness to heat, darkness to light, feathers rustling in the breeze. The air up here is smoother, cleaner.

The bird erupts into the piercing blue sky overhead, sunlight shattering across its back. It soars for a moment, basking in the afternoon warmth, until the salt waft of fish dictates its new direction. It adjusts its wings. Southwest.

It soars across the Grand Canal, red hats of gondoliers glowing below. Over terra-cotta roofs, domed churches, lines of washing and snaking canals, until it spots the perfect vantage point to spy its next meal. It circles and descends, yellow feet landing on the curving, moss-flecked tiles of a building overlooking the lagoon.

Two floors below, Anna Maria stands, violin in hand, her heart thudding.

"Again," he says.

"Signore?"

"Play that again for me, now."

"I'm sorry, Signore, I shouldn't have—"

"Just do it," he snaps.

The feel of his grip still lingers on her shoulder. She raises the violin, envisages the colors, and she plays.

His cheeks are pinched when she finishes.

"You have clearly had lessons before. Who was your teacher?"

"Before, Signore?"

"Yes, before."

"I haven't, Signore."

"Stop saying 'Signore' like that!"

She gulps, flinches. A curl of his red hair springs out of place. Her eyes dart to it. His hand shoots up and smooths it back down.

The tap, tap, tap of a beat being drummed on a desk filters through from the music room next door. It feels like it is inside her, like it is trying to get out.

She takes a breath, tries again.

"I haven't had lessons before. Not on the violin. Today is my first. I play the flute and oboe well, I have lessons each afternoon. I have tried the *fortepiano* and I sing, although Sister Madalena says I should really stop. It's giving her an earache."

His lip twitches. He's an adult, but only just. Something about the way he holds himself makes him seem younger. Concentration lines are starting to settle on his forehead, two sharp parallels facing off between the eyebrows. But nothing around the eyes. No history of a smile.

"How old are you?" he asks.

Her chin juts forward. "Eight."

He takes a step closer. "Do you think that you are sharper than I am, Eight?"

"No, Signore. I mean . . . no."

"Do you think you can outwit me?" he says, his cheeks flushing now.

She shakes her head, her voice small. "I don't think that."

He considers her for a second, seems satisfied with this response.

"Repeat this," he says.

Long red and pink notes follow, separated by playful tangles which make his fingers flutter up and down. She watches intently, tries to map the movements, the order of the shades. By the time it ends, on a high *D*, the color is so bright she feels her eyes widen.

He nods stiffly. Her turn.

She lifts the violin once again, connects it to her body. Closes her eyes and lets the bow lead the way as the sound vibrates through her.

Anna Maria understood tempo, pitch, and tune before she could speak. Music is her blood and bones and everything besides. But it has never been like this. It's like she has cracked open another layer, found something deeper inside herself.

She draws the bow back across the strings and looks up at him.

"Another," he says.

He tests her three more times, each phrase becoming faster, more aggressive, more intense. She tries to follow, but the colors are too much. They billow and rush and clash. She grits her teeth, barely blinks for focus. But her fingers are tripping over themselves, they stumble on her determination.

"I'm sorry," she says. "I'm trying to keep up but—"

He holds up a hand. She swallows her last words.

"I have never known a girl to play like this. Not any so young as you."

Anna Maria frowns. Being a girl is not something she has given much thought to. She opens her mouth to say something in response, but then he turns, moves toward his case. Plucks a cube of rosin from it and begins to rub it, slowly, against the hairs on his bow.

The silence roars in her ears. What is happening? Should she leave?

He looks up at her suddenly. "Tell me, do girls have ambitions in this place?"

"Yes," she says, taken aback. "I want to be a violin player like you."

She almost adds she wants to be the greatest violin player in the world, but something makes her think better of it. The other girls laugh at her for saying things like this.

He lets out a short laugh. "I am not merely a violinist, Eight. I am a composer. Instrumentalists are forgotten."

Her cheeks burn. "Players are remembered too," she says.

"For a matter of years, perhaps. But it is not the same. Composers are remembered forever."

She shifts her feet again. What she wants to say, she probably shouldn't say. She can still feel his palm raised an inch from her face, but the words burst out anyway.

"I want to learn. I want you to teach me."

He flicks around, snaps his violin case closed, and marches toward the door.

And at the edge of the room, on the precipice of dreams being made and dreams being shattered, he turns his head ever so slightly back toward her.

"Tuesday, two o'clock, come alone," he says.

A rumor circulates in the Pietà the next morning like a feather on the wind. Hushed, excited tones: "The king of Spain is visiting!"

The sisters were speaking of it at morning meal. Saying that he wishes to see the famous orchestra of orphans as the finale to his Grand Tour.

So Anna Maria is at the chapel window in the courtyard, standing on her tiptoes, hands pressed to the mottled stained glass. A candle flickers inside. The doors are shut—she cannot sneak in. But the sound of the *figlie di coro* finds its way to her through the cracks in the brickwork, the space between the window and the frame. A triumphant song, with bold colors: fuchsia, turquoise, white. She shifts, hoping for a glimpse of the king, but she can see only movement, blurred figures, her crisp green eyes staring back.

She leans so close her breath catches on the glass, leaves a misty circle like fog on the lagoon. She raises a hand to the center and draws her initials, carefully, tongue between her teeth. Then her name is called. A barbed, curt tone. She hisses, tears herself from the view. Runs, skidding, back into the main Pietà building.

Soon, she tells herself.

Inside, she finds Paulina and Agata in the dormitory, screeching with laughter. Paulina is wearing a long navy cloak, several sizes too large for her.

"May the Lord bless you," she is saying to Agata, who is knelt down as if in prayer. Agata crosses herself solemnly. They do not see Anna Maria approaching.

"And may the Lord bless your abundant coat," Anna Maria whispers in Paulina's ear.

Paulina practically leaps from her skin. Anna Maria is laughing, tugging the folds of gold-embroidered fabric from her shoulders to try it for herself, saying, "Where did you get this from?"

"Ahem."

The three girls turn, wide-eyed.

Sister Clara is kinder than she looks. Like an icicle. Small, pointed, cold.

"What is the matter with you three?" She is walking toward them, tutting as she goes. "You don't say, you scream; you don't walk, you leap."

"We do not leap!" Anna Maria says.

"And you're never simply angry, you're enraged." Sister Clara holds her hands out. Anna Maria, begrudgingly, places the cloak into them.

"Whose is this?"

Paulina glances at the floor as she mumbles, "Signore Conti's, Sister Clara."

Sister Clara sighs. "Return this at once."

They are already hurtling through the door together as she calls, "You three must learn to be good girls! I will send Sister Madalena next time!"

That night, Anna Maria lies in her small bed, not dreaming of drowning, not running through the events of the day with a knot in her stomach, not frustrated by the noises of the girls and the sisters. Tonight she is focused on one thing only. She needs to become a composer.

It is so obvious, now that she thinks of it. She had got only as far as planning her succession to *maestro* by eighteen. But what is the point of being extraordinary if you won't be remembered? To be remembered is imperative. It is everything.

This she has known since the pox.

Anna Maria was six. It started with a patch of tiny red spots on her chest. Livid as hot tongs, the itch kept her awake, scratching through the night. The next morning her whole torso was enraged. She was taken to the *infermeria*, kept away from the other patients. She'd wake sporadically, ripped from her nightmares by the unbearable sting. The rash crawled across her shoulders and up her face, her body growing weak and feverish. She lay there, breath shallowing, as a shape appeared at the end of her bed. Like a veil or sheet, billowing, rippled not by a breeze but by the breath of something dark, other. Something waiting for her.

She clutched the edges of the mattress, slammed her eyes shut. The squeak of the door sent out a bolt of blue, the tweeting of a bird a dash of white. And as the colors moved through her mind, tears rolled down her cheeks. She was terrified of the veil, of being alone forever somewhere dark and unknown. But it was more than that. It was the pain of knowing she had something special within her that would never see the light.

Then one evening she woke, her heart a drum. She looked down, certain it would pound straight out of her chest. Lying there, moved up and down by the staggered effort of her breathing, was her playing card. The Queen of Hearts, sliced diagonally. Her half, the top half, showing the left eye and cheek of a colorful carnival mask, decorated with gold dots and curls.

She reached down, surprised, for she normally kept it in the cabinet by her bed and had no recollection of placing it here. She held it tight, watched the eye that stared back at her. It was like it was telling her to fight. And so she clutched it closer, rubbed the sharp, sliced line, feeling something potent run through her. This thing, this energy and force, this creativity within her. It must find air. It must live on.

In the days that followed, the boils started to blister and drain. And as scars took their place, a new itch began to grow. Ambition had always been a part of her but now it was vivid, alive like never before. It prickled her thighs, tingled in her joints. She would never be alone if she was remembered. She launched herself from the *infermeria* and back to her friends with one thought in her mind above all others: she would not fade quietly into the abyss.

There is a rustling next to her and a soft thud. She turns her head to see that Agata is awake, her arm stretched across from her bed, her palm on Anna Maria's mattress. She is lit by the moonlight streaming in from the square in the roof.

"Another nightmare?" Agata mouths, bunching her other hand into a fist and pressing it against her forehead to demonstrate what she means.

"No," Anna Maria whispers, turning so the pair are curled up facing one another. "I've been thinking."

Agata tilts her head to ask, *"About what?"*

"Composers."

Agata frowns.

"Composers are remembered forever," Anna Maria says.

Agata raises her eyebrows, smiles. She takes Anna Maria's hand in hers, weaving their fingers together.

"Yes," Anna Maria says, "I know it now, Agata. I know it's what I want to do."

Agata squeezes Anna Maria's hand tighter, then rubs her thumb gently across Anna Maria's wrist. She lifts her other arm into the air and stares up at it, a fist punching the sky.

Anna Maria watches, smiling.

The click of the dormitory door opening, and the shadow of Sister Madalena in its frame.

"*Good night,*" Agata mouths, and Anna Maria mouths it back. Within moments Agata's lids are shut, her eyes beneath flicking from side to side, descended into dreams. Anna Maria returns to her thoughts.

She won't be able to publish until she's named *maestro*. That's at least ten years from now. If she's going to get good enough to publish by then, she needs to begin practicing immediately. Her foot begins to jig beneath the sheet. She needs to start composing right away.

"I'm told you show great promise at the violin," Sister Madalena says, looking Anna Maria up and down as if no information has ever given her less pleasure. Her white coif and veil draw attention to her aging skin, the dark puffy bags hanging under her eyes.

It is the next morning and they are sitting in her office. A small windowless room on the first floor, with just enough space for a desk and chair. The shelves are filled with large leather-bound books. A candle flickers in a mount on top of them.

Great promise, Anna Maria thinks. Her chest swells. She is on her podium again, violin by her side. *Maestro*, the crowd cheers. *Maestro!*

"You look ill. Are you ill?"

The sharp clap of Sister Madalena's hands in front of her face brings her back into the room.

"Are. You. Ill?" she repeats, slowly and more loudly.

It's hard for Anna Maria to hide her irritation. She had the same from Sister Madalena last week, and from Sister Clara on the way to this meeting.

"No, I'm not ill. My lips are just pale." Milk-pale, with skin to match. Always have been.

Sister Madalena tuts. She starts scribbling something in the big notebook on the desk in front of her.

"You were saying about the violin . . . ?"

"Yes," Sister Madalena says, not looking up. "You will continue your private lessons every afternoon and your other music classes will cease."

Anna Maria considers this for a moment.

"So I won't have classes with Paulina and Agata anymore?"

The desk jolts; a few strands of parchment flutter to the floor. Sister Madalena has slammed her palm on the desk.

"One of Venice's most promising musicians is offering to give you private tuition and you are worried about not seeing your friends? It is time to grow up, girl. It is high time indeed."

Anna Maria is nodding before she even realizes it. "I'll do it. Yes."

"Good. Keep your hair combed and tidy and do as he says. At the first whiff of trouble, this opportunity will be taken from you. Understand?"

Anna Maria reaches up and tugs her fingers through her mess of curls. Tries to flatten them with her palm.

"I understand."

That afternoon Anna Maria's senses are alight. They tune in to the click of the lock, the shriek of the iron gate pulling back, the power and potential of her small foot stepping across the boundary of the dark, cold Pietà building to the great world beyond. She has landed the best job of all: fetching the water for Cook.

She turns off the main promenade and weaves slowly into the square, savoring every step. The day is bright, the air cold. She tugs her shawl closer as she walks toward the well in the center, icicles glittering at the edges of its marble head. It is one of more than a thousand in the city, capturing rainwater through the grates which pierce the surrounding stone.

Waiting in line, she soaks up the energy, the pomp. Boys in velvet blazers run and cheer, chasing after a ball made of twine. They kick it high into the sky, where it soars through an open window. An old man pokes his head out, grumbling something, but the boys begin to chant and soon he is chuckling, tossing it back down.

Pigeons bathe in the puddles around the well, ruffling their feathers and cooing. Tall women in lace collars and long cloaks walk with their small dogs, leads matching their gloves. A man with white curls, his hair freshly powdered, tucks a silk handkerchief into the pocket of his embroidered jacket and then steps onto a gondola. Out just to be seen.

He is a Somebody, Anna Maria thinks as she pulls the bucket up. It bangs against the bricks, some water sloshing back down into the depths.

One day, not long from now, Anna Maria della Pietà will be a Somebody.

There are four music rooms at the Pietà. Lined up one next to the other on the third floor, they smell of trees and resin. It is the afternoon, and a melancholy tune drifts through the cracked walls of one of them toward Anna Maria, standing out in the hall. She tiptoes toward its source.

Agata sits at the *fortepiano*, fingers gliding across the black and white keys, her body swaying with the music. Her hair is loose and parted at the center, the dent in her head shaded from the light.

The sound is dark, muted, plum. But it flourishes and ripples like a velvet cloak.

Anna Maria sneaks closer, closer, and—

"Rah!" She jabs two fingers into her friend's rib cage. Agata leaps from her seat and flips around. Half laughing, half incandescent, Agata mouths a selection of words they are not supposed to use, flinging her arms out in fury. Anna Maria holds up her hands to surrender.

But Agata shakes her head, her large eyes filled with revenge. She presses a low key on the *fortepiano*, a warning of what is to come. Then she lunges forward. Anna Maria leaps out of the way, tearing around the side of the instrument. They skid around the *fortepiano* in a game of cat and mouse until Anna Maria slips and Agata crashes into her. They find themselves back-to-back on the floor, the instrument a cave above them, laughing and heaving for breath.

A pigeon lands on the stone windowsill, ruffling its feathers, nestling into its perch in the sun.

"That's sounding better, by the way. You're improving fast," Anna Maria says once she has gathered her breath. In only months, Agata has gone from playing basic chords and scales with one hand to performing simple pieces with fluidity and grace.

She feels Agata reach round, squeeze her arm in thanks.

Everything is just as it should be. Anna Maria has been selected for lessons on the violin, Agata is developing her *forte-piano* skills, Paulina is becoming known for her singing and aptitude with the oboe. Anna Maria breathes deeply, her back pressing into Agata's.

Moments pass like this. Then she feels her friend's body sliding against her back. She smiles, thinks the game is starting up again. But there is a thump. The sound of a head hitting the ground.

"Agata?" Anna Maria twists back. "Agata?" she says, faster, louder now.

The edges of Anna Maria's vision crackle. The whites of Agata's eyes are visible, lids rolling back into her skull.

Anna Maria scrambles up, runs to the corridor, yells for help.

Agata is slipped onto a stretcher, lifted by two sisters whose last words as they leave are: "Get back to your class."

The *infermeria* is a cavernous space in the courtyard behind the Pietà building. Anna Maria stands at the thick black doors, her palm against one, fingers pink from the cool morning air. She needs to push it open, but the screams of babies from the nursery next door hum in the air and there is a smell seeping out: sour and metallic, of pain and fear. It sets something quivering in her stomach. It is Paulina who clutches Anna Maria's elbow, who leads the way forward.

There are three lines in total, ten beds per row. One is surrounded by a thick ring of curtains. Mumbled prayers drift from behind it. In a bed in the middle row a girl is curled up, blanket pulled up to her neck, sleeping quietly. All the other beds are empty today—apart from one.

There, at the far end, is their friend.

Agata is sitting on the edge of her bed, dressed to leave. She looks sheepish, her face more flushed than usual, her smock skimming the floor.

Relief rushes through Anna Maria's veins.

"Did you miss me?" Agata mouths, moving her hands to her heart and then cracking them apart.

"Not really," Anna Maria says with a sly smile.

At the same time Paulina chides, "Anna Maria!"

But Agata is smiling too now.

Anna Maria takes a seat on the bed next to her, clutches her hand tight. "Of course we did," she says.

"How are you?" Agata asks.

"Don't worry about us! How are you?" Paulina is inspecting her face, pressing her cheeks.

The sister appears from behind the curtain. She is a small woman, hands on her hips when she speaks. "Aren't you supposed to be in prayer?"

"Sister Madalena sent us to collect her," Anna Maria says quickly.

The sister makes a face but does not push the matter.

"Is she going to be all right?" Paulina asks.

"Nothing wrong with her. It'll have been a bad bit of meat. Off with the lot of you, then. Quick now." She fans them away.

Agata stands, linking arms with them both so that they form a line. They set off, clanging into a few beds on the way, refusing to be parted. By the time they reach the door and try to squeeze through it as one, they are in a fit of snorts and giggles once again.

5

On Tuesday, her teacher is by the window, violin raised, staring out through the bars to the Riva degli Schiavoni waterfront. He is dressed today in a faded waistcoat and white shirt, his hair freshly powdered so that the ends are still flame-red but the center parting fades to gray.

The sounds of other lessons dance under the door and meld in the air. An oboe from one room, a flute from another.

The other girls in her class whisper about him, call him forbidding, harsh. But Anna Maria does not agree. *Maestros* cannot worry about insignificances like other people's feelings. They must prioritize sound, expression, perfecting each note. It is how they come to be great, how they come to be adored by the crowd. So much so that one day one of them calls out, *Maestro!* And the rest of the crowd stands, joins them too. The crowd decides who wins in this world. The crowd chooses the *maestro*. The musician can think only of them.

Anna Maria looks down at her scuffed boots, the splashes of dirty water on her white smock. She touches a hand to her wet hair, Sister Clara's solution to the combing mess, pats a few of the curls back down.

He is not so fancy, Anna Maria decides. The waistcoat is faded and looks to have been made for someone larger than him. She tilts her chin up and marches forward.

He does not turn, does not greet her. There is a thrill, and a terror, in not knowing what will come next.

"Today we will return to the basics," he says, still facing the window. "Any player must master how to hold the instrument and bow, how to tighten and tune, how to rosin and mend before they can play."

Fear fizzes up inside. She doesn't have time for all that. No time at all. She must be in the *figlie di coro* by fourteen for her plan. And for that she needs to be pushed.

"But—"

"You will do as I say." His words are sharp as a blade.

She has to hold her tongue. Literally hold it, between her teeth. She feels a strong urge to kick him.

He turns to look at her now. "And you can wipe that look from your face. When I complained about my father's methods he used to pinch my arms until they were purple. Would you like the same treatment?"

She shifts, shakes her head. The soft flesh beneath her armpit tingles.

He begins to tweak and fuss over the most menial of things. She is permitted to ask a few questions: that little curve of wood beneath the strings is called the bridge, the twist at the top of the neck is named the scroll. She enjoys tuning, that makes the color brighter, but now they are halfway through their session and her cheeks are hot with frustration.

There is a tap at the door. He turns his attention to it. "Enter."

Standing in the doorway is a girl close to Anna Maria's age. She wears a gray cloak, a velvet that shifts with the light. Her hair is curled into tight ringlets which hang about her face, and at her neck sits a tight loop of pearls. She is no orphan.

"Ah, yes, come in."

Anna Maria looks sharp toward her teacher, mouth opened to say no, to say it is her time, that this impostor has no place—

"You may leave, Eight," he says.

She grits her teeth, walks slowly to stow the violin. On her way out she gives the impostor a look of pure venom.

"Girls," Anna Maria announces, "are pigs."

Using two wooden spoons held at arm's length, she pulls a soiled cotton robe from a large woven basket. It is Wednesday morning and she, Paulina, and Agata have landed the worst chore of the day.

Laundry is done in the room next to the kitchen. A rancid perfume of decomposing fish from the kitchen cloths and sweat from the older girls' shifts hangs in the warm air. Wooden sideboards jut up against damp stone walls. There are piles of soap, jugs for water, and double doors opening out onto the canal. All food comes into the Pietà through these, all waste goes out.

Anna Maria stood a moment at those doors earlier, watching the water lap against the building. Had to step back when she looked down the canal and envisaged the gondola creeping out from the mist.

Just a story, she told herself, as her heart pricked at her ribs.

"Guzzlers and hogs, all of them," Paulina agrees, wringing out a deeply stained shift over the canal. Her voice is muffled by the cloth she has tied to her face to mask the smell.

Next to her, Agata tugs a line that stretches from the Pietà building across the canal and pegs clean clothes to it to dry in the breeze.

Anna Maria flings the robe into a dark soup of water and starts to bash at it with a wooden paddle. Water splashes her smock, scattering little brown flecks across the white cotton. She sucks her displeasure through her teeth.

This drudgery is infectious. If she wastes enough hours here she will surely never escape. Will spend her days wringing other people's grimy stockings, tending to dull ailments, cleaning up after whining infants. It is mindless, banal, stinky work. Work for people with no skill or talent. There is, she thinks as she slaps another smock into the pail, no place for her here.

"Today we will learn about the character of sound," he says, instead of a greeting.

It is their second lesson. A violin and bow from the cupboard await her, laid on the chair by the empty fireplace. There is a battered leather satchel stuffed with parchment on the floor.

Finally, she thinks. All her senses tune in to focus.

"When we play a piece of music, we must consider who we need to *become* to play it. Consider Alberti's Sonata Number One, for example." He lifts his violin, emits a tune that is light and cheerful and yellow. "What character do you see?"

Oh, this is a good game. The challenge tingles in Anna Maria's fingertips.

Listening closely, she decides, "It's a boy, skipping to the market with an apple in his hand."

For the first time, her teacher laughs. It's a rattly sound, ending up in a cough. She blinks and smiles in surprise.

"Very good, Eight, very good. And what about if I play you Albinoni's Adagio in G minor, who do you see now?"

The sound is beautiful, but it's sadder than before. Blues and purples. It's someone older, more complex.

"I see a lady, tending to her garden. She's old with gray hair. She's sniffing roses and remembering her life."

Her teacher is staring at her.

"Am I wrong?" she says quickly.

"No," he says, "it is just . . . you continue to surprise me." He stands up, walks toward the window. "And now what if I play you something . . . invented?" His shoulders slump as he drags his bow from left to right, left to right, a muddy sort of brown.

"I see an ugly old dog with a scowl on its face," she says.

His laugh comes out as a bark. He is wheezing into his handkerchief until the coughs become gasps and Anna Maria is moving closer, saying—

"Are you all right?" She wants to add "Signore" but stops herself at the last second. What comes out instead is "*Maestro?*"

"I need"—he staggers between coughs—"a moment."

She hears his footsteps fading down the corridor and the creak of a distant door. The shutters rattle on their hinges; the excited scream of a child floats through the window from the prome-nade below.

There is a beat, and then her eyes grow wide. She, the all-powerful Anna Maria, has broken her great teacher. Reduced him to a pile of stutters and coughs.

She jumps up, deciding to practice the elements he's just played her, to impress him when he returns. She starts to glide around the room as she plays.

She imagines she is a dancer. No, a skater, sliding across the lagoon to the pale tremor of her notes. She lets one foot glide forward, then the other, creating a slow scuff, scuff, scuff of blades marking ice. Whites and blues start to flow from the instrument, frozen and glistening. She speeds up, chasing them into the sky. She swirls and she spins, faster and faster, leaping over ruts in the frozen ground, sliding between skaters when—

Smack. She crashes to the floor, her chin thudding on the wooden boards. The violin and bow skid out of her hand and under the cupboard.

Dazed, she pulls herself up, shakes her head, looks back. What villain has tripped her?

In the middle of the room her teacher's satchel lies open, kicked to its side. Several leather-bound books and quills are scattered across the floor, and a pot of ink has spilled. Its dark blue blood is dripping into the grooves of wood beneath the instrument cupboard.

A clench in her gut. She is a silly fool! His things are broken, spilled about, because she was not paying attention.

She leaps to her feet. Fast as a mouse about to be trod on, she scampers around the room. Grabs the bottle off the floor, a drop of ink seeping onto her fingers. Scans for the lid, sees it cowering by the curtains. *Get back here, pesky little thing.*

She collects the books, one after the other, starts ramming them into the bag.

And then she looks down at the items she is holding.

Manuscript book. Quill. Ink.

Desire shoots through her body, vibrant and hot. She should put them back. They are expensive, and not hers to take. Instead her eyes flick to the door. She tunes in to her ears. More shrieks from the children playing outside. But no footsteps. So she slides one leather-bound book from the bag, begins to flip through. And now a thrill of fear. She could get the cane if she's caught.

But the pages are so deliciously pale, empty and yet full of opportunity. She plunges her arm back for a quill and the ink and then runs to the cupboard, sliding them underneath next to the hiding violin.

The clip of low heels against stone, and he is standing in the doorway.

"*Maestro*, then, is it?" he says, leaning against the frame.

She is standing again, violin and bow in hand, heart slamming against her ribs.

"If you like," she says, coolly as possible, blowing a loosened brown curl from over her eye. "And I'm not Eight. I'm Anna Maria."

He nods graciously and, stepping forward, holds out his hand.

"Anna Maria della Pietà, I am delighted to make your acquaintance."

The cupboard opposite the music room is pitch-black and freezing. She waits, the air close, her legs hugged to her chest, for the sound of him leaving.

Into the room as the bells chime one, tugging the contraband from under the cupboard as they strike three, out again when the bells chime five. By the time they strike seven, she is at the stairs. She runs for the dormitory, stashes the manuscript book, quill, and ink beneath her mattress, and now she is tearing back down toward supper.

Early the next morning Anna Maria and Agata are sitting up in Anna Maria's bed, a crisp dawn light starting to stream through the square in the roof, the scratchy blanket covering them both.

The stolen manuscript book is still hidden beneath her mattress. Anna Maria can practically feel it there, throbbing, so resolved is she to get it out. But Sister Madalena was prowling last night. She will have to wait for the right moment to begin her work.

She looks down at her hands, rubs her thumb over the note she holds, soft like tissue from being folded and unfolded countless times. From inside it she pulls her sliced playing card.

She doesn't know who left her. Doesn't know why. Sometimes she thinks she should ask, but always changes her mind.

Agata lets out a breath. She is holding a poem, scrawled in messy handwriting on the back of a crinkled newssheet from May 1695.

> *You have my heart*
> *Tho' wee must part*
> *I will return for you*

Over a thousand items have passed through the hole in the wall. Tokens of love and loss, slipped between blankets, clutched in small hands in the cold dark of night. A reminder to every girl who has been given away, of every person who whispered "goodbye." It has become a ritual—Anna Maria and Agata waking early, unable to sleep, finding themselves next to one another, staring at the items they were left.

Agata strokes the final line of the poem with her finger, then looks at Anna Maria. *"What is she waiting for?"* she mouths.

Anna Maria sighs, tilts her head back until it comes to rest on the wooden bars of her bed. Nine years Agata has waited. But there has never been a murmur of a return.

"Would you really want her to come?" Anna Maria whispers, repeating lines she's said before. "She might put you to work. And she won't have a *fortepiano* for you to play. And you'd be taken away from us." Anna Maria motions to Paulina sleeping silently in the bed next to them.

Agata shakes her head. *"She wouldn't. She'd take us all."*

"But I don't want to leave. Not until I am *maestro*."

"Not even if someone comes for you?"

Anna Maria looks at the sliced card in her hand. She's never heard of any girl being collected from this place. Her voice is flat, certain, as she says, "No one is coming for me."

Agata pulls back, begins to fold up her newssheet. She sniffs quietly, trying to hide her tears.

Suddenly it is like Anna Maria is glass and a crack is working its way through her. She reaches out, places a hand on Agata's. There is a pause before she says, "We'll soon discover why she waited so long. No doubt she'll have her reasons."

Agata's eyes crinkle at the edges, her nose a little pinker. *"Do you think she'll look like me?"*

Anna Maria takes in Agata's wide nose, the crooked smile, her big hazel eyes. The crack running through her widens. But there is no time to respond. There is a noise from the hallway and Agata leaps from Anna Maria's bed and into her own, pulling the blankets up high. Anna Maria slides down flat. They wait, ears twitching.

When the door does not open Anna Maria rolls onto her side, facing Agata's bed.

"I know she's coming," Agata mouths.

All Anna Maria can offer is a feeble smile. Then a shadow cuts through the ray of dawn streaming in, a gull's cry curling overhead.

"We should get some sleep," Anna Maria whispers. "We still have an hour, at least."

Agata nods her agreement and rolls over, pulling the blankets close. Anna Maria inspects her slice of playing card once again. The left eye of the carnival mask stares back at her.

No one is coming, she thinks.

The season slides from summer to autumn. Some days the lagoon invades, creeping so high it vanishes streets, soaks feet.

Anna Maria's mind is dazzling today, bright with mustard and honey notes that blow and sway like the leaves. She is learning a simple piece which consists of plucking and bowing.

Though the instrument is old, overused, a few of the strings worn thin, she likes the way the vibrations shudder through her body.

He sits opposite her, one knee folded across the other, chin in his hand, forehead wrinkled in the middle. He has been like this for some time.

"How are you doing it?" he says eventually.

"Doing what?" she says, as the vivid yellow morphs into shades of syrup and butter before her eyes.

"How are you remembering? You haven't looked at the sheet of music once since you first glanced at it. You never do."

She lowers the violin. The room is glittering this afternoon, the sun shooting bolts across the floor.

Anna Maria can't explain it, the colors and the notes. She's known for years now that it is something unique to her, but she keeps it to herself. Seeing things that others don't can get you in trouble here. Last year, during oboe practice, a girl called Francesca said she saw a horse galloping on the lagoon. Her eyes glazed over and she started to shake. Signore Conti told the sisters, and they put her in the Correction for three nights, bread and water only. That just made her more delirious, and when she told them the horse cantered right into her cell, they bled her.

Anna Maria shivers. She doesn't want to be bled. "I don't know, I just am," she says.

He shrugs out of his position. "Very well, keep your secrets. I have mine too."

She doesn't like this. She wants to know all his secrets. But she keeps quiet for now.

He stands, begins pacing back and forth in front of the window, his silhouette rippling the light. "This morning I was informed that the Pietà will be honored with a visit next month from Lorenzo Ciuvan, one of the school governors. I have been asked to create a short concert for him, selecting some of the most promising students from each year."

He stops, looks at her. If eyes could burn, hers would blaze right through him.

"It will require a lot of practice on your part. It will mean—"

"I can do it," she says before he can utter another word.

"Yes?" he asks, his mouth stretching into a grin. He looks young, excited.

"Yes!"

She wants to leap into the sky, to grab something and throw it. But there is another girl in the doorway now, a ribboned bonnet on her head. Anna Maria seethes as she has to swallow the thrill, pack up quietly, and leave.

6

Winter is a thick blanket which settles across the city. Fog disappears the streets, the buildings, the people. Gondolas on the lagoon rock up and down, slapping the icy water. Steel gray and menacing, no one can tell where sea ends and sky begins.

Anna Maria's breath is a silver current in the air, her nose running and numb. She hates days like this, when the water churns and rises and the canal looks like a long jade snake slithering into oblivion. Who's out there? she wonders. What's waiting in the fog?

Thunder rumbles above, a gull shrieks on the roof. Anna Maria shrinks down, pulls the blankets over her head. Her fingers find the "P" which has stretched and warped on her upper arm, scarred skin softer, more fragile now.

She should be sleeping still; an important day lies ahead. But the nightmare came back, and she cannot let herself close her eyes again. She decides, instead, to put her mind to use.

The air around her grows humid and warm. She listens closely to the sounds of the girls dreaming. The whistle of Paulina's nose. The snuffle from Agata. She brings her hands to her nose, rubbing until it tingles with warmth. Then she listens for a noise of the sisters coming to check on them. When she is certain it is silent, she rolls onto her front.

Quietly, carefully, she slides the manuscript book from under her pillow. Gulps down the guilt that tries to distract her. Into its folds she has slipped some of the music they've been practicing. She tugs one sheet free and studies it. The notes rush up at an angle in triplets at the start, three of them connected at the bottom by a line. There are words like *moderato* and *lento* in places; the *ff* means to play it LOUDLY. She likes when she sees the *ff* in a piece. It makes the colors brighter.

Her pale arm shoots out from under the blanket and, stretching down, she unstoppers the ink bottle beneath her bed, dunks the quill nib in.

At the end of five bars, on the left-hand side, she practices the treble clef. She's careful to move fast so the ink doesn't spot. Tongue between her teeth, she makes the symbol swirl out from the center and curve upward before shooting down the middle and ending with the flick.

Above her, a shard of ice slips from the Pietà roof, falls, and smashes, glittering on the promenade.

Anna Maria huffs, makes a face. The treble clef she has drawn is a little too big, and it's leaning at an angle. She slides out a sheet behind, where hundreds of imperfect treble clefs line up next to one another. She compares them. They are getting smaller, daintier, but they still need work.

She returns to the clean parchment. Next to her latest treble clef, she draws a note. A simple black pebble, sitting horizontally on the middle line, with a straight tail jutting down from the left. She smiles now: it is perfect. She sees and hears it in her mind. Whitish-blue. *B.*

She tugs the copy closer and starts to replicate the notes exactly into her book, just as she has been doing in the quiet dark for months.

To be a composer, she must learn how to write.

It is Friday, one week until the concert. For the first time, he has brought all the students who will perform together to practice.

They are in one of the larger music rooms today. There is a semicircle of velvet-padded chairs, a fire crackling quietly. Six of them in total, they represent the most promising students from every year. Next to her is Vittoria, from the class above, with a square face and straight black hair, who plays the harpsichord.

Then there's Anneta, who's twelve, holding her bow like a wet rag, and Christina, who's fourteen, with long dark arm hair. They both play the cello, the large, curved instruments resting patiently between their legs. Second from the end is Vincenta, fifteen, with a mole on her cheek and a violin in her hand.

But it's the girl on the end who Anna Maria is staring at. Jealousy is a living, breathing thing. An animal that crawls through her veins and pokes out, hissing, from her eyes.

Chiara della Pietà is sixteen, a violinist, and she is in the *figlie di coro*. The older girls are allowed to grow their hair out and pin it up; hers is combed into a sleek knot at the base of her neck. Her eyelashes are so thick and dark it looks like they have been painted.

He is talking to her, his hair tied with a simple black string, his arm resting on the back of her chair. She laughs softly at what he is saying.

Anna Maria wants to punch her, taking up all the attention like that. It doesn't help that she hardly slept last night. She feels her bow hand tremble, shifts about on her seat.

She peers down at her legs, sees her feet hanging off the ground. The other girls' are all firmly on the floor. She sits up a little straighter, shuffles forward until her leather shoes squeak against the wood floor. Tilts her chin up. She might be the smallest, but she's the one who wants it most.

"Anna Maria, a moment."

Her teacher beckons her. She stands, surprised, and follows him out into the corridor.

The sound of the girls warming up flows through the gap between the door and the stone floor like smoke.

"This is your first opportunity of this sort?"

Anna Maria nods.

"Good." He smiles at her. "I want you to enjoy yourself. Have fun today."

She readjusts her face. Hadn't realized she was frowning.

"Better," he says.

"Yes, *maestro*. Thank you."

She takes her seat once again, eyeing him like a hawk. She can feel the other girls glare, wondering what was said in the corridor.

"Chiara, let us start with your solo."

Chiara smiles, reveals a set of straight teeth. Tucks a wisp of hair behind her ear before she picks up her instrument. Anna Maria tongues the gap in the back of her mouth where three of her teeth rotted and came out last year. The bitter taste of iron.

But then Chiara begins to play. The sound is so crisp that Anna Maria shifts, sits up straighter. The colors are luminous. They rush out from the instrument's body toward her. Anna Maria leans closer. Crystalline, magnificent, cut diamonds before her eyes. They tremble and shoot, unexpected and rare. The world falls silent, there is nothing but the trail. It guides her from her seat. *Come closer, come closer.*

She's moving, she's reaching, she leans out to touch them—

"No," she whispers.

The colors start to fade. The sound diminishes. For a second there is silence. And then comes the laughter.

The real world snaps back into focus. Anna Maria is standing not two feet from Chiara, her hand reaching out in front of her. The other girls are looking at her, eyebrows raised, smirking.

"She's so strange," someone whispers.

Heat throbs up Anna Maria's neck. She closes her hand, pulls it back to her side.

"Enough," he says to their sniggers. "I thought you were serious musicians."

And, instantly, silence.

Anna Maria looks to him, stuck, unsteady.

He nods. *Take your seat.*

At the end of the class he asks her to stay back. She moves toward him slowly, shoulders slouched. She has got it wrong; he must think her a fool.

He looks her deep in the eyes, holds her gaze so long she feels her pulse quicken. When he speaks, his words are slow, deliberate.

"You are here for a reason," he says, and the words grip her like a fist. "I want you to hold on to that."

The girl with the gray velvet cloak is back, waiting in the hallway when Anna Maria leaves rehearsal. The cloak is pulled close around her body. Her eyes are dark with shadows, her cheeks look tight and pinched.

Anna Maria would scowl at her, tell her she has no place coming here. But standing by the girl's side is a woman. Her mother, Anna Maria assumes. She is tall and large, fine wrinkles around the eyes, one eyebrow arching higher than the other. She wears an apple-green dress with a lace trim, and a musky, expensive smell wraps around her. Against the dull, damp corridors of the Pietà, she is vibrant as a rare bird. She does not notice Anna Maria look up at her, take her in.

"Off you go," she says to the girl. Her tone is deep and calm.

The girl nods silently and walks, head bowed, into the room.

Anna Maria is about to ask the woman why she is here when she is stopped by a voice behind her.

"You played well today."

Anna Maria turns to see Chiara in the middle of the corridor. She frowns, looks over her shoulder, certain she must be addressing someone else. Beyond them, the girl's mother is walking away.

Chiara lets out a soft laugh. "I mean it, Anna. Governor Ciuvan is going to be impressed."

Words do not come. Anna Maria smiles stiffly, nods, watches as Chiara passes her.

She could follow. She could ask questions, try to make conversation. But instead, at the last second, just as Chiara is about to round the corner and disappear from sight, she shouts after her, "It's Anna Maria!"

She turns now, heading for the smallest music room, down the corridor. Inside, she opens the instrument cupboard doors, pulls out a case, places.it on a chair, and creaks it open. The locks are battered, one hanging off at the hinges. The violin inside is a mousy brown. And though its structures and curves are still beautiful in form, it bears the markings of a lifetime of abuse. Anna Maria walks toward the window, inspecting it more closely. The body is covered in scratches and dents. It hurts her, to see a violin like this. But it is the best of the bunch. It will have to do.

She raises the instrument to her neck, summons the colors to her mind. She is away, chasing reds and blues, tumbling with the speed of the greens and grays, until a howl pierces the air. She stops instantly, tries the note again. But the violin protests, a wolf in conversation with the moon. It is not her playing that is the issue. This instrument has been unloved, uncared for. The violin is in pain. She grits her teeth, trying to move past it. She adjusts her bow pressure, enough to reduce the howl to some-thing fuzzy instead. Not a good solution, but the best she can muster.

She practices until the sun has sunk, until the candlewicks have burned to the stub, until she is plunged into darkness.

The next morning the lagoon looks bare, exposed, a low fog clinging to the surface of the water beneath a barren sky.

"Pietà girls say please," Sister Clara says, tapping these four words on the chalkboard with a narrow wooden stick. The class drones them back to her.

Anna Maria stretches up, stifles a yawn. For an hour every week they are schooled in ways to smile and thank, to bow and praise and compliment.

"Why thank you, Signore," Sister Clara demonstrates.

Anna Maria crosses her arms, foot jiggling in frustration. This class is a pest. Decorum has nothing to do with her composi-tions, with her skill. And she would sooner skin a rat, she thinks, than be considered demure.

Another yawn threatens to erupt when there is a knock at the door. Then feet shuffling, a stern voice calling her name.

Anna Maria follows, confused, as Sister Madalena marches into the corridor and up the spiral staircase. When they reach the attic dormitory the confusion fades, and in its place comes dread.

Sister Madalena arches her large body over Anna Maria's small wooden bed. Rips back the frayed blankets. Reveals several guilty blobs of ink.

"Explain yourself," Sister Madalena says, her small dark eyes meeting Anna Maria's.

Anna Maria should say something, anything. But she can't speak, can't move.

"Open the cupboard."

Anna Maria shakes her head.

"Open it." Sister Madalena steps closer. Anna Maria can smell last night's supper on her breath.

She leans down, pulls it open, tries to maneuver her body so Sister Madalena can't properly see in. But, fast as anything, Sister Madalena is tugging out the manuscript book, the quill, the ink. She cradles them in her arms for a moment, looks down at them like an unwanted baby.

"Come with me," she growls.

The desk jolts, knocked in his rush.

"What the . . . what's the meaning of this?" he asks, standing as Anna Maria is dragged by the scruff of her neck into the largest music room. The fire spits; the air smells of burning.

"We have a thief in our ranks." Sister Madalena slams the items down in front of him.

Anna Maria must speak. She must explain.

"I need them!" she blurts out. "To practice . . . to . . . help with my playing."

He flicks through the pages, sees her copied-out notes. He knows the pieces, of course, he knows they're not hers.

Anna Maria feels a breeze as her dress is pulled up, gasps, tries to tug it back down. This cannot happen here, not in front of him. But then a sharp whack across the back legs.

The blows come, stunning and fast, again and again. She is shaking. She won't cry. She will not cry.

One day, she thinks, I will whack you right back.

She flicks only one look at her teacher. She watches him turn away.

"Correction immediately, and no violin for a week," Sister Madalena says once her legs are red and raw.

"No!" Anna Maria screams, now beating and kicking back.

Correction she can handle; she's spent nights there before. But the concert is in less than a week.

"Please"—she squirms, looking at him—"don't let them do this."

On his face there is confusion, surprise. But he makes no protest. He stands by and watches as Anna Maria is dragged away.

Pesky dark hole of doom.

Anna Maria kicks at the rats that scuttle in and out between the bars. The scrape of her leather boot across the floor echoes off the stonework. She sits in one of three freezing cells that make up Correction, a block behind the *infermeria* where students are sent for punishment. Her cell is so narrow there is barely enough space to turn. A barred window hangs out of reach, a high ceiling above it. The smell is dank, cold, one of misery and mold.

Her stomach grumbles, an individual creature as dissatisfied with this situation as she is. She hisses at the empty plate lying in the corner.

Then a creak, a grunt, and a patter of feet.

"Quiet! Hurry, quick, close it behind you."

Anna Maria kneels, left cheek pressed against the cold metal bars, peering to the right to see Paulina and Agata pulling the heavy wooden door closed. A grin spreads across her face.

"What are you doing here?" Anna Maria whispers as Agata skids toward the bars, mischief glittering in her eyes.

"Wait for it," Agata mouths, holding a finger to the air. Then she shoves her hands into the folds of her skirt and plucks out a small, squashed package. She slides it through the bars. It is

warm, the sweet waft of fennel leaching through the cotton. Anna Maria unwraps it quickly, hungrily, to find a *pinsa*, a round ball of dough dotted with raisins, figs, and seeds.

She is biting into it already, asking, "How did you . . . ?" through her stuffed mouth.

Paulina, who is guarding the door, her face illuminated by a crack of light, looks toward them both. "Cook left them on the side for the *figlie* girls after practice—we snuck one for you before they came out."

Agata nods, gleeful.

"Thank you," Anna Maria whispers, swallowing the last bite. But as the food hits her stomach she feels a sickness that has nothing to do with hunger.

Agata must notice, because she taps the bar to get Anna Maria's attention, mouths, *"What is it?"*

Anna Maria thuds back, crosses her legs in front of her. "It's over," she says, the words heavy in her mouth. "He's never going to forgive me for this."

Agata shuffles closer, grasps Anna Maria's hand through the bars. *"No,"* she is mouthing, shaking her head.

But Agata is wrong, and the truth of it tugs deep in her chest. Anna Maria drops her head, watches a cockroach scuttle across the floor.

There is another tap now, faster, harder against the metal. Paulina whispers, "Someone's coming," and Anna Maria looks up again just in time to catch Agata's last words.

"You will make it," she mouths, her knuckles white, clutching the bars. *"You will make it."*

The door screeches open, a chill breeze rushes in, and Paulina hisses, "Run!"

Three nights pass in Correction, Anna Maria's mood darker than the ink she stole. Finally the iron doors open once again.

Daylight. Beautiful, shimmering daylight awaits her in the courtyard. The air is crisp, cool on her skin. She stretches up, feels her spine click and adjust while watching the clouds dart overhead. Then she realizes she is being watched.

He is standing by the doors to the main Pietà building in his familiar brown tailcoat, his curls neatly framing his face.

She edges closer, feels her hand begin to tremble at her side. It is not just the concert that she will miss. He will withdraw her lessons, give her the cane, or worse.

"I do not expect you to steal, Anna Maria," he says when she stops.

She nods. Won't speak, won't take her eyes off her boots.

"The concert," she says, "I am sorry, I—"

"You will be allowed to take part still, I have seen to it."

She snaps her head up. Is he lying? Joking? Tricking her somehow? But his expression is calm. He is not, she decides, and the feeling is honey-sweet.

"Why did you do it?" he asks, his voice cooler now.

She takes a breath, heart quickening. What to say?

"I wanted to improve. I wanted to impress you."

He surveys her for a moment, then sighs.

"I see the drive in you, Anna Maria, but you will not succeed like this." He places a hand on her shoulder, squeezes, his face serious. "You can trust me. If there are things you need, simply ask."

A beat before she speaks. And then she nods, stiffly, once.

"I need a quill, some ink, and some paper," she says. Then she thinks of the music cupboard, of the scratched, bruised instruments, the wolf howling to the moon. "And I need my own violin."

He is laughing, coughing, pulling his handkerchief from his pocket.

"Very well, then," he says once his breath has returned to normal. He digs into the bag by his side and holds out a tattered feather quill, a small glass bottle, and a few sheets of parchment. "These will have to do for now. A violin is expensive, but I shall put in a request."

7

The day of the concert, and Anna Maria is charging up the spiral staircase. There have been more rumors circulating about some of the girls in their dormitory, the ones who are not showing promise with an instrument. That eventually, the gondola will come for them.

The thought pushes her forward, a rapid beat in her chest. In two hours she is required at the chapel. She will spend every second until then ensuring she is prepared.

She runs, hand grabbing the banister, launching herself through the archway to the third-floor corridor. And there, standing outside the smallest music room, is Paulina.

The skin around her eye socket is red today. She must have been rubbing it. Anna Maria remembers the day that the *medico* had to be called to remove the eyeball, after it became milky like the lagoon, after she stopped being able to see.

"There you are." Paulina runs closer, her cheeks flushed. She takes Anna Maria's hand in hers. "Agata is unwell."

Anna Maria feels herself being tugged back the way she came. "Wait, hold on just a moment."

"They're not sure what's wrong with her," Paulina says. "She passed out again. She's in the *infermeria*."

Anna Maria feels her stomach drop. Her mind flicks back to the pair of them sitting beneath the cave of the *fortepiano*. "But it's been months since—"

"I know." Paulina is staring down the corridor now. "Still," she says, "we have to check."

Anna Maria looks at Paulina, then toward the music room. She is on the brink of everything. And she is already walking on thin ice for her behavior. If she leaves now, everything will be ruined. Besides, she and Agata were awake and whispering at dawn this morning. She was fine.

"I can't, I need to prepare for tonight. But I'll visit straight after."

There is a flicker of surprise on Paulina's face. "You're not coming?"

"I'll be there straight after," Anna Maria repeats.

"After practice?"

"After the concert tonight."

Another flicker across Paulina's face. "They won't let you in then."

No visitors after sundown, Anna Maria had forgotten. But she cannot leave. Not now.

"Fine, then first thing tomorrow."

Paulina shifts. She seems to want to say more, but after a pause she releases Anna Maria's hand. "Well then, I suppose . . . good luck."

Anna Maria watches her go. Then she turns, a hand on the doorframe, and steps into the room. Her music is already on the stand. She stares at it, not blinking, barely moving, until a stream begins to flow. Until she is off, away with the colors of her mind.

Sundown. Anna Maria should be at the concert already, warming up, but she had stumbled on a few bars of a piece, got caught up perfecting them. She is panting, hurrying through the entrance hall, when a hammering makes her stop.

The wooden double doors are open, but the gates beyond them are locked. Standing on the promenade tapping the bars is a man in a black coat, with a wide-brimmed hat and a leather bag at his feet.

He has not seen Anna Maria; she has already turned toward the corridor that leads to the courtyard and chapel. But now she is looking back. The man is calling out, saying something about the key. She could fetch Sister Madalena, ask her to see to him. But she is late, she tells herself. This is not the priority.

She does not look back as she runs.

The hubbub of a small crowd arriving drifts under the door and into the room off the chapel. A statue of the Virgin Mary stands in the corner, palms pressed together. It is like she is one of them, getting ready to go onstage.

Each of the girls is focused and quiet, tuning their instruments, glancing through their sheets of music. It's all anticipation, little noise. Apart from Anna Maria's groans. Behind her, Sister Clara is tugging at her hair again, wetting it down by dunking her hand into a small pail of water on the desk and then smoothing from the parting. A few freezing drips find their way down Anna Maria's neck.

"It's the best I can do." Sister Clara sighs, standing back to consider her efforts. She dries her hands on a piece of cloth and then, reaching into the cupboard behind her, she says, "You may wear this, it's—"

It's a brand-new smock made of crisp white linen. Anna Maria is tugging it on before she can finish. She stands before the mirror in the cupboard door, her pupils dark and wide, her stance strong.

This is it, the beginning.

"Very smart. Now remember," Sister Clara says, peeling a stray hair off Vittoria's robe, "first impressions are everything. Happy governors mean more gold for the music program. So heads up, smile. Make your Republic proud."

A tap at the door, her teacher's voice muffled behind it.

"Enter," Sister Clara says.

His hair is tied back with a white ribbon, and he is dressed today not in his usual brown or black but in a blue velvet suit. It is still too large for him, but he looks smart, elegant.

He scans them all, nods approvingly.

"Gather around," he says, and they form a semicircle. He makes eye contact with each of them as he speaks. Is it Anna Maria's imagination, or does his attention flick most often toward her?

"I could wish you luck tonight, but luck is not what you need. You have the skill, the talent. We have practiced. We are ready. So I ask only this: when you pass through those doors, think of it not as the space that you pray in daily, but as a stage in one of the finest palaces in Venice. Play with your utmost energy. Let us give the audience what they want. Let us give them a performance to remember."

Chiara leads the way, stepping out into the chapel. Anna Maria grips her bow firmly, tilts her chin up, and follows Chiara out. She leaves reality behind in that side room. She enters, instead, the world of the concert.

A modest but beautiful space, the chapel has a colorful floor made from patterned marble and wooden beams which arch high above their heads. But it is the audience that holds Anna Maria's attention. There are at least thirty attendees she's never seen, sitting in rows, talking quietly.

Governor Ciuvan is immediately obvious. He is in the middle of the front row, being fussed over by two of the sisters. He's not a handsome man, tufty graying eyebrows protruding beneath his curled white wig. But with his broad shoulders and straight back, he has a certain authority. He wears a pale blue knee-length coat adorned with gold buttons, his black tricorn hat resting in his lap. Anna Maria hums with energy and excitement, just to be this close to the power.

In the chancel there is a small raised wooden stage. The three violinists face the cellists, the harpsichordist behind. Chiara leads them, taking the chair closest to the front of the stage. Vincenta sits next to her, and then Anna Maria. She tucks her new smock under her legs, lingering a moment on the folds of clean, crisp linen. Pulls her shoulders back, sucks her stomach in.

Their teacher takes his position at the front of the stage. He looks more confident, more mature, than she's seen him before. He begins his introduction.

"She's a Marcini," Vincenta whispers from the corner of her mouth, motioning to the woman a few seats from the governor, her dress adorned with feathers. Anna Maria narrows her focus. She was the woman standing in the corridor in the apple-green dress the other day, the mother of the rich girl.

But Anna Maria did not realize, did not know who she was looking at then. The Marcinis are one of Venice's oldest and wealthiest families. At least one of them has been a doge in the past. And Elisabetta Marcini's name is famous around the Pietà. Anna Maria has heard she sometimes takes a shine to the girls, buys them instruments of their own.

"Does she have a daughter?" Anna Maria asks.

Vincenta shakes her head. "No children, I don't think."

Anna Maria's forehead creases. Supporting orphans is simple charity, she understands as much. But if she is not the rich girl's mother, why help so?

"And the man sitting behind her is the governor's son," Vincenta adds.

Anna Maria scans the row. It is a crowd of dignitaries, noblemen and -women of Venice. In this chapel, here, waiting to see her perform. The beat in her chest grows louder.

Her teacher begins his solo. He stands with his feet pressed together, pert in his lace-edged cuffs. That alarming speed, the twists and turns. She has to close her mouth, imagine invisible knots around her legs to stop from standing. His body is rigid, she can feel his concentration. Excitement gathers and crashes through her body.

One day that will be me. I will have that talent and more.

He finishes to polite applause from the crowd. Then he lifts his arms, looks into each of their eyes.

"Energy," he mouths, widening his eyes so they all smile.

Chiara's solo is elegant and refined. The governor nods approvingly.

Then the cellos, and then Anna Maria and Vincenta join them, following Chiara's lead.

The notes come, splashing and luminous. A bolt of orange

here, a dash of magenta there. The instruments frolic and leap, connecting and skipping with one another. Anna Maria is not sure whether it's the audience, the excitement, the pressure, or something else, but this feels different than before. On this stage, the world is alive with the multicolor of Anna Maria's mind. It is like a delicious extra ingredient has been added. It makes everything glimmer and glow.

Her solo comes now. She will give them something to remember. She is dancing with the notes on her stage. She looks to the crowd, feels herself smile and sway.

But then her eyes are drawn to the back corner of the chapel. She is certain she sees a shift, a shape. Something is lingering there in the darkness.

Now she notices the sound. It is slurping, repetitive, feeding through the open doors that lead from the edge of the chapel straight out onto the canal.

The colors become a blur, racing before her eyes. The shadow ripples like cold skin. The bow slips in her hand but she grabs for it, clasps it tighter in her grip. She will not let it loose; the raven will not come for her.

She looks to the governor, sees him nodding along. At the back of the room the sisters are rocking gently, joining in.

And then there is her teacher, conducting at the front of the stage, eyebrows raised. She finishes, fear skipping in her stomach as he mouths, *"Bravo."*

The world grows silent for a moment, and the noise is gone. But the feeling still ebbs through her. The suck and draw of the deep.

Applause echoes around the chapel, delicious and addictive, plucking Anna Maria to this moment. She watches the governor's wife lean across, whisper something in his ear, and then point at her and nod. The governor turns his attention toward Anna Maria. He raises his hands higher, directs his applause at her.

She feels a sting of pleasure. She does not look back to the darkness.

Anna Maria della Pietà has arrived.

After the concert, the girls are asked to wait at the gates, to shake the hands of the guests as they depart and collect donations in the wicker baskets at their feet. Anna Maria watches Elisabetta Marcini approach. Anna Maria will stop her, make herself known, ask her directly to donate for her own instrument.

But as Anna Maria reaches out, Elisabetta looks up, over her, to Vincenta, who stands by her side. It is she Elisabetta moves toward; she Elisabetta stops to praise.

Anna Maria's forehead knots. Her teacher said "Bravo"; the governor clapped for her and her alone. Surely Elisabetta has made a mistake.

"Excuse me," Anna Maria says. But her voice is louder than she intended. It comes out as an affront.

Elisabetta looks at her, eyebrow raised, lips thin. "Can you not see that we are talking, girl?" She turns her back, fluttering the feathers on her dress. Anna Maria is left standing on the outside, looking in.

There is a single hackberry tree in the courtyard. Leaves having curled yellow and drifted away on the autumn breeze, it is now a skeleton, bare arms reaching into the sky.

On the topmost branch a black crow beats its tail. Perches here watching, waiting, until the church bells ring nine times through the air. Now the bird swoops down, oil-black wings thrumming past the *infermeria* doors, and then upward, where it disappears into the bleak sky overhead.

Inside, Anna Maria is motionless, hunched over, hands in her lap. Her breath is shallow. It shudders in and out of her chest, visible in the chill. In the distance there are words, noises.

"Happened quickly . . . nothing we could do . . . you have five minutes."

There is a hand on her shoulder. There are footsteps. There is silence.

Next to her lies the body of her friend. Arms by her sides, hair skimming her shoulders. She could be sleeping.

Anna Maria takes her hand, ice-cold and hardening.

"Agata?" she whispers. Half expects her to snap open her eyes. Half expects to see them crease at the edges, the way they always do when she smiles.

But there is no response, no movement. Just a child on a bed. A child far too small for this.

Anna Maria cannot make sense of it. Where is her friend? Where has she gone?

Anna Maria looks around her at the other girls lying in the *infermeria*. A few beds away there is a girl curled up, dark hair splayed out over her pillow. For a moment her heart skips. This must be Agata. Turned away, hiding, a joke for them to share.

But then she looks back down at the hand she holds in hers, at the small, transparent nails, at the thin white scar that runs across her palm.

She remembers that day, when Agata slipped running down the stairs, tumbled forward, sent her hand right through the stained-glass window at the bottom trying to stop herself. How Paulina howled. But Agata was cool, calm. She stuck her hand straight into the air, a shard of glass sticking from it, and marched herself to the *infermeria* as the blood dripped onto her shoulder.

Anna Maria strokes the scar with her thumb. These hands, she thinks, that played the *fortepiano*, teased gentle tunes from a silent block of wood and strings. Brought it to life, made sense of it, gave it meaning.

Anna Maria did not come. She didn't see Agata grow dizzy yesterday. Didn't see the seizure, the way she screamed out in the night, how she struggled to stand, to walk these past hours. The nuns said something about the dent in her head. They said it was too much.

Triplets, she thinks urgently, pressing her palm against Agata's now. They had a plan. What about Rome? What about Paris? What about cream *frittelle* and growing old and being the greatest musicians in the world?

She does not feel the warm tears rolling down her face, does not hear the footsteps of the nurse passing her by. She is staring at her friend. The closest thing she'll ever have to a sister. Watching the stillness of her chest.

She was alone. The thought hollows her out, takes the air from her lungs.

Anna Maria knows what it is to be here, isolated, on the brink of darkness. To see the black, lingering, festering thing in the shadows and know the end is near. Agata would have been frightened to see she was at the edge. She would have wanted Anna Maria to hold her hand, to say she must wait just a little bit longer. She would have liked to have looked into the faces of her sisters and know that she was loved.

Anna Maria closes her eyes, touches a hand to Agata's cheek. It is still soft, the skin translucent like the wing of a chick.

The edges of this world fold in on themselves at her touch, and for a moment she is walking in some place she does not know. A place that is blank, blurred at the edges. It is cold: so cold Anna Maria brings her hands around her body. It is not for them, not for someone as small and warm as Agata. It is not a place of light.

The blank moves like a snowstorm, a blizzard. Anna Maria wants to scream. But there is a movement ahead. In the distance stands a figure with brown hair. She is walking away from her slowly, certainly. Anna Maria hurries forward, willing her to turn, to look back.

"Agata!" she cries as the wind and snow roar. "Agata," she calls again.

Where is she going? There is nothing out there, nothing but endless, glaring white. She will not make it. Anna Maria is running, tripping against the snow, staggering, trying to keep up. *Stop, wait*, she wants to say, but Agata moves forward still.

"Turn back," Anna Maria demands. "Turn back now!"

Because this death, this thing, this presence that draws her, that tries to take Agata from her, it has not met Anna Maria's will. She will not have it. She will force Agata back to life with the very essence of her being. Her friend must live. She shall live. She screams out now. "Turn back, Agata!"

But the wind, the snow, it is too much, her voice is drowned.

The whiteness is closing in. Anna Maria thinks she has lost her. It is too cold. She cannot stand the bite of it much longer.

But then the figure pauses, just for a moment, her head turned an inch to the left.

Her words float through the air toward Anna Maria. Ember-warm and flowing. Liquid pine.

You will make it, she whispers. *You will make it.*

The blizzard fades in that instant; the sky glows golden, effervescent. It illuminates the back of Agata's head, concave like a cupped hand. Anna Maria has to raise her arm to the blinding light.

And then she opens her eyes.

She drags in a breath. She squeezes Agata's hand harder.

"Come back." Her voice is cracked, splintered, strained by the tears across her cheeks. "Agata, come back. Someone is coming. Someone is coming for you."

But there is just a body, cold, hardening on the bed in front of her. The skin pinched and glossy.

There is no coming back from this.

The world is suddenly too warm. It swells, clinging to Anna Maria's skin. Her mind seems to crack, she is tumbling back, drowning. And suddenly it is her on this bed, staring lifeless at the ceiling, and Agata in the chair, clutching her frozen hand.

Then comes the thought, the worst of all.

At least it wasn't me.

And now she hears the voices behind her, the nurses and sisters whispering at the end of the bed.

"He was waiting for an hour."

"Who?"

"The *medico*. Locked outside the main gates."

A claw twists in Anna Maria's stomach. Last night, before the concert. The man tapping at the bars, asking to get in. Anna Maria had stopped. But then she kept running, because she was late, because she was due at the concert.

"No one knew he was there," the nurse whispers. "By the time someone saw to him, it was too late."

Anna Maria drops Agata's hand. She reaches the doors, tries to fling them open, but finds her path is blocked.

"Where were you?" Paulina's face is blotchy and red. Two dents in the tops of her cheeks mark the sleepless night.

Anna Maria recoils. "I can't . . ." she says, trying to get past, but Paulina stands firmly in her way.

"I was alone," Paulina says.

The shriek of a metal bed being dragged across the floor sends white bolts past Anna Maria's eyes. The world is too loud, too much.

"It's not . . . I didn't—"

"Didn't what, didn't know? I told you, Anna Maria. There was time for you to come."

"Stop, don't." Anna Maria pushes out into the courtyard, where the cold air smacks her face. The crow circles in the sky overhead.

"Where are you going?" Paulina says, close behind her. "You can't leave, not now!"

The world is spinning, trees and sky and buildings warping into one grotesque whirl. She needs to get away, far away from this place of pain and death, but Paulina's voice drags her back once again.

"Are you listening to me? Anna Maria? Anna Maria! Some things are more important than music, you know!"

At these words something deep inside Anna Maria snaps.

"No, they're not!" The words explode from her chest. "It is the reason. It is everything."

Paulina is shaking her head, trembling.

"Don't look at me like that. I'm going to be the best. This is what it takes."

Anna Maria turns back toward the Pietà building. But after a few steps Paulina speaks again. "If this is what it takes, then I want nothing to do with you."

Anna Maria does not look back. She runs, before Paulina can see that her vision is blurred by tears, before Paulina can say another word. Down the corridor of the Pietà building, into the room at the far end. The door slams shut behind her.

Two steps toward the hole in the ground. She barely makes it before the vomit comes. She retches until there is nothing left.

Shivering, she lifts her skirt, wipes her mouth with it. Crawls back into the corner of the small room, knees to her chest, breath heaving in and out. Her head falls into her hands, the noises of Venice rippling in through the tiny window beside her.

Gradually, the light outside fades, until the square of yellow on the wall becomes a small oblong close to the floor.

It is some time before the gull shrieks outside, before it snaps Anna Maria back to this world, to this life.

She looks up, blinking. Splintered and numb. Her body empty like a cave or a shell. She lets out a sound. It is that of a wounded animal: a bottomless, aching pain. And then she takes the image of Agata, her friend, her sister, and forces it somewhere deep, somewhere primal, somewhere black.

The city grows darker still, the oblong dissolves into the night. Her breath slows, until her pulse is a dull thud at her wrist. Her sliced playing card floats into her mind, the eye watching her silently. She follows it, clinging to the sill of the window, pulling herself into a standing position. And finally, to no one but herself, she says, "I will be remembered. My life will mean something."

DUE

8

Light splits across her face, making her squint and recoil. The creak of shutters folding open.

"Up," Sister Madalena says, tugging back the blankets on her bed.

Anna Maria groans, stretches out, her eyes still squeezed shut. At thirteen, her limbs have grown slender and long. Her dark curls splay out across her pillow, matted from a night of twisting in her sleep. She plucks open an eye, her head facing the bed where Paulina used to sleep. Before she asked to be moved. To the other end of the dormitory. Away from Anna Maria.

Sara sleeps in Paulina's old bed now. She is already up, pinning her auburn hair, folding her sheets back. Most nights she cries herself to sleep, freckly face wet and blotchy. Anna Maria doesn't get involved.

Sara's big eyes keep flicking across to her, disapprovingly, as she folds.

"Stop staring at me," Anna Maria snaps, pulling the blankets closer. Sara squeaks, a caught mouse, then hurries away.

Anna Maria's time is precious. In the five years since the governor and his wife took notice of her at the concert, she has focused, incessantly, on her instrument. Each afternoon, and often well into the night, she can be found in the smallest music room on the third-floor corridor, testing out a new skill or refining one she's newly learned. She can't sit around and dream anymore. There's work to be done to make it into the orchestra, and that work takes effort.

She hardly even watches Paulina now, from her bed, when she's laughing with the other girls before they go to sleep. Or through the door when Paulina is in oboe class, playing Scarlatti's concerto with such grace. Hardly watches her at all.

Anna Maria sits up. The bed creaks, in need of repair. She tugs the itchy woolen blanket higher. It is the same one she has used since she was five years old, rubbed thin, scattered with holes.

Then comes the familiar sinking feeling when she remembers her teacher is still gone. Six months it's been. Ill health. Something to do with the cough, his breathing. Signore Conti has taken over, but it's different, like trying to run in a pair of boots that are far too small. Signore Conti doesn't have the skill, the speed. Signore Conti cannot understand her.

She extricates herself from the tangle of sheets and stands. Removes her night shift, tugs on her smock awkwardly, trying to hide her body from the other girls as she dresses. Sister Clara rushes over, starts tutting and fiddling with her hem.

Moments like this make Anna Maria want to scream.

"It's fine," she says, jerking a loose thread out of Sister Clara's hands, "I have it."

The bubbles catch the light, tiny rainbow orbs that slosh across the floor to the scrub, scrub, scrub. Anna Maria dunks her brush back into the pail, wincing as her fingers meet the dirty frozen water. She tugs it back and forth across the stonework with red, chapped hands, blistered fingers ready to burst.

She knows she must endure it, but it is intolerable. It is preposterous, to be on her hands and knees, soaked apron dragging along the entrance hall floor. Her skill on the violin is known throughout the Pietà now, but still she is required to scrub, to work, as average as the rest of the girls in this place.

She sits back on her heels, knees digging into the stone floor. The walls seem to have inched closer, the ceilings lower in these past years. The building is like a weight on her chest.

From the corner of her eye, a figure emerges. Paulina is

walking toward the spiral staircase holding an oboe. Headed to class.

Her blond hair has grown long, darkened somewhat, but her frame is still small compared to others their age. The skin around her missing eye is uneven, but the scarring is no longer red and raised.

Anna Maria smiles, tries to smile, but Paulina snaps her head down, quickens her pace, doesn't look back.

Agata swims into her mind, grinning, mouthing, *"Triplets."*

Anna Maria rubs the tear away with a frozen hand, forces the image back down. Her reflection stares back at her from the wet floor. A grubby stain is all that remains on her pox-marked cheek.

In the afternoon Anna Maria sits in the corner of the smallest music room, the bars from the window casting shadows across her face. Someone has slid a hand through, managed to crack the window an inch to let in some air. But still the room feels small, hot for September.

A fruit ship is moored in the lagoon. Merchants have disembarked and laid their goods on carpets and rugs along the promenade; the sweet smell of basil and peaches floats through the gap.

She is studying the work of Giuseppe Tartini, a Venetian composer she discovered in a stack of donated pieces in one of the music rooms.

Violin poised, she stares at the middle section of a score titled *The Devil's Trill.* Her left hand contorts, fingers extending as far as they can reach across the strings to match the notes he has written, but it is not enough. Her smallest finger is flickering. Her tendons are becoming hot and alive, her blistered fingertips nipping at her attention.

She takes her hand off the strings, stretches it out, releasing some of the tension that has built up there. She tries again, and again, circling back a few bars and then arriving at this point, until her hand cramps into an awkward shape, unwilling to continue.

She growls, urging her fingers to submit until her tendons scream and, with a sharp intake of breath, her hand jolts out of position. She lunges before the violin is dropped. From her other hand the bow slips, clatters to the floor.

She clenches her jaw. Sits down abruptly, listening to the chatter in the street below, until it melds with the tap of feet in the corridor, the swish of a violin case rubbing back and forth against a coat.

She does not turn, does not greet Signore Conti when he enters.

Let's just get on with it, she thinks.

"Have you missed me, Anna Maria?" A sharp voice: not the one she was expecting.

She snaps around, breathes in the familiar smell of pine and incense. She wants to open her arms and embrace him.

He holds his violin case in his left hand, a manuscript book in his right. His handkerchief is folded into a triangle, tucked into the pocket of his faded waistcoat, and there is a freckle on his cheek that she has never noticed before. She is, she realizes, now nearly as tall as him.

He takes her in, scanning up and down. It is a look she cannot interpret easily. She stares down at her skirt, moves a hand to hide a stain that is left there from the scrubbing. Then—

"Let us not waste time, it has already been too long. Show me where you have reached in practice." He strides over to her stand, where *The Devil's Trill* manuscript is perched. He raises an eyebrow, nods his approval. Now he lifts his palm, a signal for her to begin.

Her whole body focuses on the notes, on the language of dots, lines, and curves that paint her way. She plays a little slower than it should be, but she is able to move through the sections smoothly, carefully maneuvering her fingers to avoid the blistered patches, until she reaches the middle, when her hand contorts into a claw again and her tendons rage in protest. She emits a sound, of two physical things connecting with a thud.

"You always stumble at this point," he says, as if he has been here to witness it.

She nods. He plucks his violin from its case. The gloss of it. The deep red. How she wishes she could play it.

"Hands are tricksy things. They seem to want to move in some directions and not others. But tricksy things can be tricked." He looks at her. She leans a little closer, her gaze intent on him. "Try stretching backward."

He demonstrates, placing his smallest finger in the farthest position first, and then working back down the fingerboard until the rest of his hand is in place.

The sound that flows out of his violin is petal-soft, delicate as a spring breeze across her neck. She aches for it in the depths of her stomach. To play, to own an instrument that can thread the air with song.

Anna Maria follows, mimicking his positioning, starting in this strange way, and finds that she is smiling. Her hand feels different. Freed, somehow, to reach all the notes. There is more space for her middle fingers to move, no ache from her pesky tendons. She does not even feel a stretch. She draws the bow across the strings and finds the sound to be complex, alluring. Just as Tartini intended it.

"That's it," her teacher says, nodding now. "That's it."

They reach the final section, the most advanced of the whole piece.

"That bar is faster," he says, showing her on his instrument. And then he does something she doesn't expect. He continues, elaborating on the notes written on the page, creating something of his own.

"I don't understand," she says as soon as he is finished.

"A *cadenza*. It is an opportunity for the player to add their own expression to a piece, a little part of themselves. This is mine."

She has heard of *cadenzas* but never known the meaning of the word until now. It is an opportunity to compose within the bounds of Tartini's own world. She is lifting her instrument before he can say, "Give it a try."

The preceding section is stuffed with maroons and yellows, the music leaping between the two. She follows the passage of color, letting the bow and her fingers guide her as she invents. It is but a couple of bars, but to her it feels life-giving, energizing, like she is discovering a whole new part of her mind.

There is a pause when she finishes. He is looking at her again, his eyebrows arched in surprise.

"Well," he says finally. "Yes, that was very good. Let's try it again, faster this time."

She nods, grits her teeth, sets her fingers in position, but at this pace she cannot avoid the pressure on her blisters. He stops her with a raised hand.

"What is that look? That tension in your jaw?"

"It's nothing," she says quickly, lifting her instrument to try again.

"You are not there, with Tartini. Are you in some kind of pain?"

Her heart beats a warning. She does not want to tell him; he might not let her play.

He moves closer, takes her hand from the violin, turns it over in his. He inhales abruptly, scanning the blisters, the redness, the cracks. There is a dark look in his eyes when he says, "I will take care of this."

"Please," she says quickly. "I don't want to stop."

His brow furrows. "You are certain?"

"Absolutely, yes."

He looks toward the window for a moment, toward the calls of the fruit sellers below. "Very well."

They focus on feeling, on expression rather than pace, and by the end of the lesson they are having fun with the piece, finding new shape and shades where she has not seen them before. It has taken one hour with him to achieve what Signore Conti could not help her with in over six months.

She is grinning, packing away her violin when he asks, "Is it helping still, your exercise in copying down music?"

"Oh, yes," she lies, "it's helping very much."

He knows only that he supplies her with paper and ink. She will tell him about her compositions eventually. When they are ready. But not now, not yet, when they are but child's play to his genius.

He nods, satisfied.

That evening Anna Maria passes Sister Madalena's office. A flame trembles on the mount outside the door. Her teacher's voice drifts from inside. She slows, moves closer.

"She has work hands," he is saying.

Sister Madalena's voice is flat. "All the girls have to work."

"And how would you have her play? With hands that are blistered and red? Give me this, Madalena, give me this one thing at least."

Anna Maria cannot see her response; the next words she hears are his.

"Thank you," he says, "I appreciate it."

In the distance, the campanile bell tolls once, twice. And Anna Maria is grinning, running, her shadow flickering against the cracked corridor walls.

Agata, nine years old, sitting at the *fortepiano*.

Anna Maria and Paulina are in the corner below the window, legs entwined, watching her play. Three notes, in a minor key, repeated and then developed into melody. Scarlet, bronze, honey brown.

Anna Maria can feel the warmth of it moving through her veins. Though the sound is melancholy, there is a comfort to it, a release. It is like being embraced when you are sobbing. Like crying until the sadness has found a crack—a way out.

Paulina holds Anna Maria's hand, stroking her thumb with her own. And Agata is looking up now, her eyes creasing into a smile, mouthing, *What do you think?*

The snap of thunder jerks Anna Maria back to the present.

She is standing in the refectory, rain pelting the windows, waiting for her food at morning meal. She stiffens when she realizes where her mind was, pushes the memory away.

Already the news is out. The twins, Candida and Cecilia, are scowling at her, along with a few other girls. They know she has escaped, for now at least, the horror of chores.

"She thinks she is so special," she hears them whisper.

Anna Maria looks away. She focuses her attention instead on the five girls waiting in front of her. They wear different uniforms than the usual grubby white smocks. Instead they are sleek, in black cotton dresses with square necks and long sleeves. Some of them are wearing colorful brooches, their hair tied back in low buns with ribbons. They laugh and chat, edging closer to the food.

Cook, a sister with muscular arms and a tomato-stained linen cap over her hair, is standing in front of a large vat of something that is thick and spluttering. She ladles it into terra-cotta bowls as if both have somehow wronged her.

But now, seeing the girls in black, Cook stops. She hurries out into the kitchen. Returns with a basket full of fresh bread, cheeses, and fruits. Hands them over to a chorus of polite thanks.

Anna Maria watches, tracking all this intently.

Here's what she knows. The *figlie di coro* is considered the greatest orchestra in the world. There are other orchestras in the Republic and beyond, but the Pietà's one is unsurpassed. There are about forty members, and most girls are auditioned at sixteen. The *figlie* play lots of concerts, and they make money. Real money, of their own. They get nicer clothes, more regular baths, better food.

Most of the members are in their late teens, early twenties. Girls can choose to stay in the orchestra their entire career, so getting a spot is tough. But places do become available every year. The pestilence killed half the orchestra once. That would have been a good year to audition.

Of the forty members, about eight are violinists. Then there are singers and wind instrument players, cellists, organists, harpsichordists. Some also play the lute and mandolin. There might be one new violin place per year. And if you're not in the *figlie* by seventeen, you're put to work—lace-making or dishwashing or something else awful.

Anna Maria picks up her bowl and marches across the refectory to a gap on the wooden bench. She looks down at the food, lumpy and brown. Takes a spoonful, feels it congeal in her mouth. Candida and Cecilia watch her from the end of the table.

Her eyes meet the girls in black again.

Soon she will be the one with the fruit and the ribbons.

Every evening the sisters check the beds for red stains. Some of the girls are given clean cotton rags to stuff under their shift each month. They curl up, groaning in the dark, clutching their lower stomach like they need to be held in place.

Anna Maria knows something happens. Something that will happen to her too one day, maybe soon. It looks awful and painful and like it should be avoided at all costs. But the only stains she's ever had in her bed are blue ink. And she's smarter about that now.

The changes that are happening to Anna Maria are different. And they are miraculous and fascinating, a wick flaring into flame.

Music, sometimes fully formed pieces, has started arriving in her sleep.

The night is like so many nights. She wakes, tries to sit up, but then the world trembles and blends and she realizes she is underwater. Instantly her hands reach for her throat, as if clutching it will give her breath.

It's a dream, she tells herself. Just a dream. But she is stuck, paralyzed, her lungs screaming for air. Sometimes hours go past this way, with her frozen in time. But tonight, instead, the music comes.

A melody, wistful and alluring. It is calm, slow, minimal. One note drifts through the water toward her, a leafy green, then another, paler and yet more bright. Beneath is something richer, darker, lower. The notes rise and fall together like ribbons in the wind. At first she thought it was just one violin, but now she realizes it is two. The violins start to mimic one another. Small variations of the tune, tossed back and forth, a question and answer. Her limbs begin to unlock. Her stomach is unclenching. Her feet meet the soft, muddy bottom and she kicks off, pulls her hands through the water, and starts to swim.

At dawn she erupts from the surface. Tosses back her blankets and creeps out of the dormitory. By the time she hits the stone corridor she is running, the floor freezing against her toes, her long shift flapping in the wind tunnel her movement is creating. She slams to a halt outside the cupboard opposite the largest music room. Slides the lock across, pulls open the double wooden doors. Snatches the candle from the shelf, lights it from the lantern burning in the corridor. Then she crawls in, shuts the doors behind. Breathes in the smell of dust and parchment.

Light shoots across the small space, illuminating a stack of manuscript books, several quills, and some bottles of dried ink. She spreads them out in front of her on the floor, crosses her legs. She begins to scribble, colors pouring from her, her hand moving so quickly it could be possessed. The vibrations of the Republic waking ripple through her body. The rumble of a cart, the toll of bells, the cut of a boat through the water. The sound unbinds her. A snake shedding its skin.

By the time Sister Madalena comes to wake them, she is back in bed, her blanket pulled up high, her composition hidden in the space between her mattress and the slats of the bed, on top of tens of other compositions. And her heart is thumping to the beat of her song.

On Sundays the *figlie di coro* put on a concert in the Pietà chapel. Sister Clara says it brings in lots of gold for the orphanage.

About half the orchestra members will play, and sometimes other students get to go and watch. Anna Maria is on collections duty, standing at the doors while imagining herself on the stage. There is the thud of coins chinking into her basket as locals wander in. It is mainly men, finely dressed in wigs and lace collars. A rich, low tone hums in the air, of conversation before the concert begins. The chatter and energy remind her there is life beyond these gates. They make the cold, dark Pietà feel alive.

One day, she thinks. One day not long from now.

Her eyes flick to the side doors, opening onto the canal. The sound of water sucking at the brickwork. Next to them Paulina is sitting in the back row, her hands clutched together.

Anna Maria's heart leaps a little, spotting her so close. Her face has widened these past years, her lips now rose pink and rounded, her nose a little longer. A single curl hangs over her shoulder. Anna Maria would like nothing more than to take it in her palm, to feel the silky softness of it between her fingers.

She watches a moment longer, gathering her nerves, then decides she will go over. She will say something like "hello." Something like "I miss you." She takes a step forward, reaches out her arm . . .

But Paulina does not see. She shifts toward the girl next to her, laughing at something. Anna Maria steps back, leans against the wall.

The *figlie* take to the stage; she counts twenty in total. There is Chiara with her glossy hair and even glossier violin, who is twenty-one now. The years have only made her more beautiful. Her frame is a little more rounded, her face a little more defined. With her are some of the girls Anna Maria sees in the refectory. There is Lucietta, who takes her position at the organ at the back, and Teresa, who she's heard practicing in the music room next to her sometimes. She makes the flute sing, a sound that shivers through Anna Maria's bones. Between them there are the ailments—the missing fingers, the burn marks, the scars from accidents. But none of that matters when they play. All that matters is that they are in the *figlie di coro* and she is not. As she watches them on her stage, the feeling burns. A want so strong it could surely light a fire.

Signore Conti steps out to polite applause, smoothing down his blond curls and then fluttering his fingers in a wave to the audience. He takes his position at the front of the orchestra.

Anna Maria holds her breath, waiting for the colors to come. Her hands begin to flicker, like it is her up there, fingers pressing strings, and her teacher watching, saying, "Very nice, Anna Maria, very nice."

But then something shifts her attention. Three men at the back are pointing at girls in the audience. One takes out a small string-bound notebook and pencil from his coat pocket and starts scribbling something down.

The music has begun, but there is more whispering around the room now. More pointing at the girls, more men turning to one another.

Stop, she wants to tell them, feeling the blood rise in her face. Stop that at once.

She looks toward Sister Clara, who is standing in the corner. But Sister Clara doesn't move, doesn't even blink. She's noticed the men talking—it's impossible not to—but is acting as if this is normal.

Now one of the men in the back row turns and looks at Paulina. She blushes. He leans across, whispers something in her ear. Paulina is barely moving, her eye glassy and frozen, like she gets when she is scared. The man turns to his friend, looks back at Paulina, and then they write something else in their book.

"Who do you think they'll select?" the girl standing next to Anna Maria whispers with a lisp.

"What are you talking about?" Anna Maria hisses, not taking her eyes off Paulina.

"Which will become wives? That's what they're here for."

Anna Maria shoots her a look, until the girl edges away from her. Suddenly the suck of the canal is deafening, roaring in her ears. The gondola floats from the mist into her mind, the lamp at its helm, the creature that steered it. A childish ghost story, yes. But not completely wrong. Girls are married off sometimes, she knows this much now. It is the ones without talent, skill, those who have no future ahead. But she has never seen it happen, never felt it closing in.

Anna Maria stomps forward, grabs Paulina by the hand.

"What are you doing?" Paulina whispers as she is tugged up from her seat.

There's a tut from the audience, a "shh." Sister Clara has not noticed; she is busy surveying the pointing men.

"Trust me." Anna Maria tugs harder.

Paulina allows herself to be led into the courtyard, then plucks her arm free. "What's this about?"

The sunlight glares down on them. Anna Maria has to lift her forearm, shade her eyes.

"They were picking you. For a *wife*! They looked at you and then wrote you down in their book. I had to do something, I had to get you out."

Paulina's face shifts from irritation to horror. "Was that what he was saying? He whispered something about . . . well, I don't want to repeat it."

"What? What did he whisper?"

Paulina squirms, then says, "About my menses. He asked if they had started."

Anna Maria can feel her heartbeat thudding through her body. They could have been picking a fish out of a basket. Just sitting there, as if they owned it all.

"Well," Paulina says, looking down at her shoes now, "I suppose you need to get back to practice."

Anna Maria opens her mouth, but the words don't come. She stares as Paulina walks across the courtyard and out of sight.

She places a hand on the hackberry tree to steady herself, its bark rippled beneath her palm. She will not go back into that concert. Will not stand by, waiting to be offered up like cattle in a pen.

She waits a moment, then straightens up, her eyes moving to the doors that lead back into the Pietà building.

Pulling it open, stepping inside, is a little girl. She looks back at Anna Maria, just for a second, as the doors to the chapel open onto the courtyard, as the crowd of students and visitors pours out.

Anna Maria blinks, but the figure is gone. She runs to the doors, pulls them back. The girl is at the other end of the corridor now, turning into the entrance hall. Her straight dark hair sways behind her.

"Wait!" Anna Maria breathes, hurrying after her. "Come back."

She sees a flick of hair, a body moving up the spiral staircase. Her heart pounds faster, faster as she sprints up the stairs, as she runs. The girl is heading into one of the music rooms now. Three notes flow from one of them, a repeated pattern, slow, in the minor key. Scarlet, bronze, honey brown.

Anna Maria grabs for the doorway, clutching the frame. The *fortepiano* lies in front of her. She stands, barely breathing, listening for the notes, for the rustling of a dress moved by hands signing their speech, for the snuffle that she made when she would sleep.

But no. There is silence. There is no one here.

Nighttime. Anna Maria is lying in bed, listening to Sister Madalena shuffle through the room. The door creaks and Sister Clara enters. Their whispers carry across the beds.

"Any offers today?" Sister Clara asks. "Many of them are bleeding now, the choice is wide, at least."

"There is a concern, from many, that the girls are too . . . sophisticated. Too intelligent."

"Too intelligent? To be married?"

"They don't want wives who are sharper than they are."

Anna Maria feels a tremor pass through her. At the Pietà they have always been schooled in many subjects, taught that intelligence is a good thing.

She rolls over, frowning, urging her menses never to come. To marry would be the death of everything she holds dear. She cannot be considered for that fate. Not when she has so far to go. She must get into the *figlie*, quick as she can. The *figlie* is for life. The *figlie* can protect her.

The thought churns into her mind, until her eyes are dark shadows and the moon hangs bright in the sky. Until the water comes for her.

9

The next day Anna Maria is stopped by Sister Madalena after noon prayers, told to go to the kitchen.

"Kitchen?" It is a dirty word in her mouth. "But I have my lesson. I am exempt from chores, I thought my teacher had—"

"Now." Sister Madalena's lips are a flat line.

Anna Maria grinds her teeth as she stomps there, but at the doorway she slows. He is standing behind the central wooden counter, a stock-stained apron tied around his neck, his face flushed with something that might be mischief.

"*Maestro?*"

He holds out an apron.

On the counter in front of them she sees various ingredients. A bowl of eggs, a square of butter, a sack of flour. There is a little pot of honey, amber like a gem. She looks at him.

"My mother taught me to cook," he says, pulling a large mixing bowl toward him, adding a mound of flour. Some of it puffs upward, falling like snow upon his red hair.

"The *fugassa* was our favorite recipe, made once a year when my father was away. The ingredients were dear for a family like ours. We could only make it once." He looks at her now. "Pass me the eggs."

She does not know why they are here, in the kitchen, pouring flour. But he is telling her things about himself, he is sharing with her his secrets. The feeling flutters inside her like a wing.

She takes an egg from the bowl; he cracks it on the edge. A luminous gloss of yolk and white pour out. He folds them gently into the flour.

"The leaven," he says, pointing to a white liquid in a small wooden bowl. He pours it into the mix, tells her it will help the dough rise.

"It has taken me a long time to perfect this," he says, beginning to knead. "I never asked for the recipe, you see, and when I wanted to," he pauses for a moment, his hand hovering above the dough, "when I wanted to, it was too late."

"Too late?" she says quietly.

He does not meet her gaze. "The sugar." He nods toward a large sack in the corner, hands her a glass. "You remind me of her somewhat. She too had little interest in the rules." He flicks a look at her, his mouth inching up at the corner. "Quickly now, fill the cup."

A few granules flutter onto the floor as she returns, mesmerized. A whole glass of sugar, held in her hands.

He takes it from her, pours it into the dough, begins to knead again. "Cooking is, in some ways, like composition. You need just the right ingredients, combined in the right way, to create a masterpiece."

Composition. Her ears prick at the word. She looks at him more intently.

"A composer is a translator, connecting people to that which they cannot voice, that which they may not even know. It is a bridge between sound and emotion, mere humans and God." He looks at her again. "What would you add now?"

She feels her stomach clench. Her eyes flick to all the ingredients, the pots and cups and bowls on the counter. She does not know.

He points to the butter. She slides it closer to him.

"The ultimate product, the final piece, may be spectacular. What we play will have speed, energy, fizz. It will rouse people from their seats. But to create this, there must be a solid base.

And for that, we must learn the language of those who came before us."

He lifts the dough from the bowl, places it on the floured worktop. "Only then can we create something new. A language of our own."

He folds in lemon and orange peel, chopped almonds and honey. The dough is becoming soft, elastic. He slices it into two, begins to braid the pieces together like hair.

Anna Maria is watching, focused. The wing inside her flickers more fiercely. She has never seen an adult be so gentle, so careful, with anything.

"How do you know when it is ready?"

He smiles. "A master knows when it is ready."

Heat billows out of the oven door when she opens it, dousing them in warmth. He slides the pleated dough in.

She has spent so much of her life in this kitchen, chopping and peeling, scrubbing and cleaning. But never this. Never folding these expensive ingredients into one another as if they are paints to a canvas, never creating something beautiful and new.

Within minutes, the tender smell of bread is filtering through the kitchen. Is it, she wonders, what a home smells like?

He tilts his head back a little, seems relaxed by it. "Smell has power. It can conjure a person back to a time, a place. Would you agree?"

The comment plucks Anna Maria away, and for a moment she is waking up in her dormitory bed, just eight years old. Agata is laughing, telling her to hurry up, to roll over so she can show her something. Anna Maria feels the rain of Agata's small fingers on her back. She is showing her the latest piece she has learned, showing her without the *fortepiano*.

Agata had a smell. Pillowy, soft, like rising from sleep.

It catches Anna Maria in the throat. She has to grip the floured work surface.

He is speaking slowly. "Music has the same potential. The ability to control the emotion, the will, the memory of the audience."

He comes to stand by her side. "What do you want to make people feel? What do you want to make them do for you?"

She is looking at him now, holding his gaze. She notices his pale gray eyes are flecked with hazel.

"Your time is up." Cook is at the door.

He looks from Anna Maria toward her. "We are nearly finished."

Cook folds her irritation into her arms. "You think it is easy catering for three hundred hungry girls each day? You've had more than an hour. I need my kitchen back before supper. And you'll share that when it's done." She nods toward the oven.

Anna Maria feels the air in the room cool around them.

"Very well," he says eventually, his voice tight.

Anna Maria is sent away. She can smell the loaf as she walks from the kitchen alone. She can smell it at supper, though it cannot be in the oven any longer. And she can smell it that night, when she reaches the dormitory before the other girls, when there is something wrapped with paper and string waiting for her on her bed.

She unfolds it quickly. The crust is silk-smooth, sprinkled with chunks of sugar. She looks up, gleefully, holding it in her palms.

But no, of course. She has no one to share it with.

Then she sees the note attached to it. Two words, scribbled in looping black ink.

Our masterpiece.

It is a week before she sees him again, in the smallest music room as usual. He is hunched over the desk, examining a piece of music. The paper blazes, lit by jagged sunlight. Seeing her in the doorway, he holds it a moment longer, as if considering his next move. Then he lays it on the desk, beckons her over to take a seat next to him.

"Corelli's violin sonata, the first three movements. What do you see?"

It is made up solely of semiquavers, a note which is played for a quarter of a beat. She knows only one other composer who has used them this way.

"*The Devil's Trill*, the second movement." She looks, incredulous, at her teacher. "He has stolen this idea from Tartini!"

He smiles. "And yet Corelli's piece was written before Tartini's *Devil's Trill*."

"But . . . no." She cannot accept it. "Tartini is a master. He would not take from someone else."

"Do you find the overall effect of *The Devil's Trill* to be the same as this piece?"

After a moment she shakes her head. The two pieces sound nothing alike.

"Tartini was Corelli's student," he explains. "*The Devil's Trill* took the essence of Corelli's idea and did something new with it. He learned the language and then added fresh ingredients. Not necessarily better, but different."

She looks at him. Tastes the sugar-sweet bread on her lips.

There is a beat, and then, "You may take this." He hands the manuscript to her. "Study it, find the places where Tartini has deferred from the expected. Learn the rules so you can break them."

She takes the sheet slowly, watching him, wanting more. Is he telling her to compose? Is he giving her permission?

They spend the remainder of the lesson playing the Corelli piece. She is packing up, planning to run to her dormitory, to study the two manuscripts side by side as soon as they are done here, when her teacher hands her something else.

"What's this?" Anna Maria holds a piece of thick cream paper that was lying on the desk. It feels heavy in her hand.

"Why not read it and see?"

At the top are names, men's names. Two sets of six in columns next to each other. She recognizes one. Wasn't that the governor who came to see her play once?

Her eyes gloss across the paper, past a couple of brown spots. Coffee stains, perhaps. Until . . .

One violin. Anna Maria della Pietà. 20 ducats. Permission granted.

A noise, somewhere between a gasp and a moan, shoots out. She opens her mouth. But she can't speak. Just nods, her throat swollen, her eyes suddenly blurred.

She had almost forgotten. Almost given up hope.

"I'm sorry it has taken so long," he says quietly.

He puts a hand on her shoulder. Squeezes gently. A warm sensation floods through her from the site of his touch. She looks at his faded jacket, his curled red hair, his collar folded up on one side. She wonders, for a moment, what it would have been like to have a father. Would he have squeezed her shoulder so? Would he have helped her to play?

She flings a tear away with a clenched fist.

"It took a lot of convincing to get the governors to make such a costly purchase. But I told them you'll be needing it. For your audition."

"My audition?" she asks quickly.

"For the *figlie*, in the spring."

It is everything she's dreamed of. Yet still she says, "But I'm only thirteen."

"It is six months away. I think we can prepare you by then. And you'll be almost fourteen by that time, if I am correct. Either way, you will be the youngest ever member if you get it. I'll be considered for promotion at the same time. The Master of Music role. It will mean they will publish my compositions, there will be performances." His excitement is infectious, humming through the room. It sets her pulse ticking faster. "I want to do big things, Anna Maria. I want to create music that moves people from their seats, that sends them into the sky. I want you there for it all. What do you think?"

Not even looking at him now, but onward, to six months, to the future, she says, "I think I'm going to be the youngest ever member of the *figlie di coro*."

One week later there is a woman with Sister Madalena, sitting by the small brick-lined fireplace in a classroom on the first floor. Anna Maria slows as she approaches, watching them from the dark corridor through the cracked-open door. Their chairs face one another. Anna Maria can see the slick black back of Sister Madalena's veil. Specks of dust glitter through the room, lit by the sun pouring in.

The woman with her is hunched forward, her shoulders rounded, dark gray hair pulled back and flecked with strands of white. There is a brown shawl around her shoulders; her dress is long and simple, high at the neck like one of the nuns'.

Her words rise up, flow toward Anna Maria.

"It was a scandal, you understand, at my age . . . I couldn't . . . there was nothing—"

Sister Madalena leans forward, places a calloused hand on the woman's knee. "No need to explain."

Anna Maria moves to enter, but there is a breath behind her, and she turns, surprised, to see Paulina by her side. Her cheeks are flushed like she has been rushing. Her smock has a green stain on the shoulder, perhaps from the kitchen. Anna Maria feels a stab of excitement, seeing her so close. She moves to say hello, to ask her about the stain, but Paulina's brows fold together. "What are you doing here?"

Anna Maria stiffens. "I was summoned."

"So was I."

The door creaks as Paulina slips past and pushes it open.

"Girls," Sister Madalena says, twisting back to look at them. "Good. Take a seat." She motions to the desks in front of them. Her voice is quieter, kinder than usual. It is strange.

Anna Maria looks at the woman now. She is smiling softly, though her cheeks are damp with tears. It makes the corners of her eyes crinkle. Just the same way that they did for—

"Tell her about Agata," Sister Madalena is saying.

A fist clenches itself around Anna Maria's heart. Her eyes shoot to Sister Madalena, then back to the woman who sits opposite. It can't be. It cannot be. But then Anna Maria looks to the woman's hands, sees what she is clutching. The newssheet is folded, dripped with tears. But she can just make out the poem still, the line—*I will return for you.*

And suddenly Agata's crooked smile swims into her mind, holding that same sheet, tucked up in bed by her side, their bodies warm beneath the blanket.

The world in that instant becomes black, cold. Anna Maria feels herself shift, her chair screeches against the floor.

Paulina is looking at her. There is a crease between her eyebrows, one of sadness, concern. She has not looked at Anna Maria like this, not in the years since Agata died.

Paulina turns her attention to the woman. "She was . . . she was our dearest friend."

She talks for some moments, of the jokes they would play on one another, of the way Agata would eat Paulina's food so she wouldn't get in trouble, of the way she snuffled in her sleep. When she tells her of Agata's gift for the *fortepiano* the woman lets out a small noise. Quiet, pain-filled, tender like a kiss. "I had hoped music would be a comfort to her."

Anna Maria cannot speak, cannot move. Sister Madalena is looking at her, a question on her face. But she does not ask for more.

"She was nine when"—Paulina looks at Anna Maria—"when it happened." She takes a breath, lets it out slowly. "She used to speak of you." She points to the crumpled paper clutched in the woman's hands. "She believed that you would come."

The woman stares down, her thumb rubbing the final line of the note. "I am too late," she whispers.

Anna Maria does not hear when Sister Madalena says, "You may leave now, girls."

It is Paulina who taps her, who brings her back to the room. They stand as a soft hum of prayer leaves Sister Madalena's lips, as she takes the woman's hands in hers.

When they are at the door the woman looks up, before Anna Maria can run. "Thank you," she says finally. "Thank you for being her friends."

———

In the dormitory, Anna Maria draws the bow slowly across the strings. She watches her half playing card, laid on the bed in front of her, her note beneath it. She does not understand how she knows what to play, how she can place fingers to strings and transform sadness and love into colors, into notes. She knows only that it is right, that it is all she can do, that it is the only place she can be.

The piece is tender, plucked from somewhere soft, somewhere fleshy, somewhere deep. There are honeys and golds pouring out, and among them black, gray, a piercing, luminous white. And it is this note she holds. She holds and she holds and she holds it, for as long as her arm will allow, until the bow falls, until her breath is a gasp, until the tears flow, shuddering out. Until there is a hand at her shoulder.

Anna Maria does not have to turn. She felt that hand every day for eight years.

"I hadn't realized you were hurting so," Paulina says.

But Anna Maria cannot take her eyes off the card, off the message that lies beneath.

"What is it?" Paulina whispers.

Anna Maria has to gather her breath before she can speak. When she does, her voice is quiet, small. "Why was my note so final?"

"What do you mean?"

"The other . . . the . . ."

"Agata's?"

Anna Maria nods, just once. "Her mother said she would return, and she did."

Know that you were loved stares up at them from the parchment. Past tense. Final.

Paulina grips her shoulder tighter. Eventually she says, "You were left here to make something of yourself."

For the first time all year, the lagoon is fizzing with life. A hundred gondolas dot the water, their curved ends casting shadows on the surface. A tall ship cuts between them, a tower of red sails billowing in the breeze. At the edge of the promenade, where hefty wooden piles shoot up and gondoliers tie their boats, merchants have laid rugs and wares. There are spices and silk cloths and salts and carved woods, feathers and carnival masks and cottons and colored wools. And then there is the wonder on the faces of those stepping onto shore. Venice is made from moments like this: starry-eyed dreamers first touching foot to land. Every person brings something new. The fresh goods of merchants who are here to make a fortune, the fresh scrawls of thinkers here to make their name, the fresh tunes of musicians come from faraway lands. Every step is a movement, every beat marks a change.

In the Pietà dormitory, Anna Maria is woken early by Sister Madalena.

"Whatisit?" she says, eyes bleary, hands grabbing for the sheets as they are wrenched from her grip.

"You are needed. Get changed and go down to the music rooms immediately."

Anna Maria starts to extract herself from the tangle of bedding. The crackle of paper makes her turn, lift the blankets, tug out the note and playing card inside. She had been staring at them late into the night. Must have drifted off and let them fall.

She stands slowly, turns to her side table, and places them on top of it. She stares at them for a moment, palm pressed to the card. Then she nods, silently, just once.

Ten minutes later she is at the door. The morning sun shoots through the window, silhouetting his frame, making his hair look like it is on fire.

"I am visiting an old friend this morning to see about your instrument. I wondered if you would like to join me," he says.

An opportunity to go outside, into the world, to people and energy and life. She doesn't need to speak. Her eyes grow wider and her lips break into a smile.

It is the furthest from the Pietà she has ever been in her life. Her heart pounds, eyes flitting back and forth trying to take every-thing in.

Out here, at street level, the colors are overwhelming. Music pours from the windows, rolls off the boats, flows from the mouth of every passing worker. She feels as if she could leap into the air, clutch the notes in her hands.

They walk toward the far end of Venice along the waterfront, past merchants selling piles of tea from golden plates and women who have laid out rugs, lace fabrics, glass beads for sale. Men pass them, humming as they carry buckets of dried fish, sacks of fresh vegetables, a knife grinder in a wheelbarrow. Cobblers hold small toolboxes, singing as they walk. On the rooftops, servants waft laundry and lay it out to catch the cool winter sun. The air smells of fish and salt and spices from the passing ships.

She licks her lips, savoring the taste of the city. Takes a deep breath, then another, to remind herself she is awake. She is really here, walking through Venice to find her violin.

Her teacher looks at her, smiles briefly.

"What?"

"No matter," he says, smiling wider.

"What!" she demands.

He is laughing now. "It is simply . . . your wonder is infec-tious, I suppose."

She thinks back to her first lesson, all those years ago. Him so angry, her so determined. Two bolts of clashing lightning. Yet she has worked hard, and she has impressed him, and every day since, his affection for her seems to grow.

"People are intrigued by you," her teacher says, an eyebrow raised as a woman passing them looks twice.

Anna Maria looks at her, then a man who is passing too. He takes her in—the messy hair, the Pietà white smock.

"It is rare, of course, to see one of you out in the Republic. They must realize that you are special."

Thrill kicks in Anna Maria's chest.

They turn now, into a narrow alleyway flanked by a huge brick wall. She cranes her neck, tracking it all the way to the top.

"The arsenal," he says as she follows him. His breath wheezes a little. He tugs out his handkerchief and coughs.

She knows this is where they build the ships, but she's never seen it, never imagined what a monstrous space it could be. They pass an open yard with piles of logs stacked on top of one another. The sounds of men heaving heavy objects and the clunk of metal drift over the top of the wall. She wonders about the huge swaths of red and orange fabric they use for the sails, if the walls inside are lined with it, if giant colorful bolts of cloth tower behind the brickwork.

But they are slowing, and her attention shifts. He knocks three times on a sleek black door.

It isn't a shop. It is a palace. The wide entrance hall is hung with ornate paintings and a huge mirror with golden edges, and through it is a large room set with an oval table. It could be a dining room, if you were eating violins for supper. The table is covered in them. Glossy, spectacular, curvaceous. She feels her stomach rumble. Behind them, more violins are hanging in a tall glass cabinet like clothes on a rail. To her right there is an archway—she can see a *fortepiano*, an ornate rug, some cellos sitting up like people at a concert, and a line of chairs.

Forget Venice. Forget streets and people and sky, spices and glass beads and masks. She has arrived in heaven itself.

"Take a seat," her teacher says, pointing to one of the leather-padded chairs in the salon through the archway. "We will be seen to soon."

Anna Maria sits with her hands clapped between her legs, afraid that if she lets them loose even for a second they will touch every single glorious thing in this place.

"Good to see you again, Antonio."

A man with a short white beard and a heavily creased forehead hobbles in. He runs his hands over his dark blue apron, then takes her teacher's hands in his. Something about his sun-kissed face and his long gray eyebrows remind Anna Maria of a fisherman.

"How is your father?" he asks, his voice husky and soft.

It's like her teacher is younger in here. Despite the fact that he is about a foot taller than the man, he seems to slouch. He flicks his red curls out from beneath his collar, shifts a little, and says, "Fine, fine, thank you, Nicolò. I'll tell him you asked."

The man is nodding, warmth in his eyes. "An excellent violinist, your father. Most impressive indeed."

"Yes," her teacher says, "I've heard." He crosses the room, places his hand on the back of her chair. His chest puffs up as he speaks. "I am here to introduce you to another fine player, though. This is Anna Maria, from the Pietà."

It is her moment. She springs up.

"Anna Maria," the man says, shuffling closer.

She likes the way he says it, like her name is a lyric. The "r" rolls across his tongue.

"My name is Signore Selles, but you may call me Nicolò. I hear good things about you. I will be proud to serve you."

She is nodding. Serve you, she thinks. She likes the sound of that. And calling an adult by his first name, that makes them equals.

Her eyes shift to the glass cabinet. To the jewels that lie within it.

Nicolò smiles, seeing this. "A violin is perfection. Every detail has a function." He walks to the table, picks an instrument up. "You see the shape? It is a self-supporting structure, so thin but so strong. The edging," he points now, "looks decorative, but it prevents cracking, and these f-shaped holes," Anna Maria looks hungrily at the dark swirls set in the front of the instrument, "allow the warm tone to be released. There is nothing you could change. Nothing at all."

Her heart is skipping. She wants desperately to touch it, to play it.

"Do you know what this part is called?" Nicolò asks, pointing to the largest piece of wood at the front. Anna Maria shakes her head. "This is the soundboard, made only from the finest alpine spruce, trees from the northeast which grow into the sky for nearly two hundred years. The winters are long and cold, so the growth is slow and regular."

He turns now to her teacher. "Perhaps she would like to see a little of the workshop, understand how they are made?"

"Yes," she is saying before he can reply. "I'd like that very much."

Her teacher nods, bows slightly. "Go ahead. I need to speak to Marco about my bow."

She is led down a dark narrow corridor toward the smell of dust and wood. A chunky table stands in the middle of the workshop. Another man in an apron, tall and skinny with a bald patch in his thinning hair, is hunched over it, drawing a small metal tool across what looks like the neck of a violin. Curls of wood are gently shaved off, dropping on the floor.

A bank of chisels and blades sits patiently in a row at the end of the room. Next to it is a noticeboard, and on it there are blueprints and drawings mapping the thickness of the woods, the parts of the instrument, a list of planned restorations, and a timetable for completion. And she looks up now, following the scent of maple, to see ready-to-varnish models, pale and naked, hanging above her head, swaying in the breeze.

She has come to the land where instruments are born.

"We are luthiers. Violin makers. But each one of us has our own skill. Alberto here specializes in woodwork, I in varnish. We have specialist staff to make the bows."

She reaches forward to touch her slim fingers against a plate, perhaps a back plate, that hangs up on the wall. It has been roughly carved.

"This piece is made of maple," Nicolò says, watching her. "It needs to be smoothed; the edges will be rounded. Do you see the way it glows? The way the grains of the wood are only a hair-width apart?" He plucks it from the hook and moves it back and forth so that it catches the light streaming in through the window. "This is a sign of a fine piece of wood."

"What about the strings?"

"Catgut."

"Catgut!" she cries, imagining Cook slicing open the cat that sneaks into the Pietà kitchen at suppertime and plucking out its insides.

"Not actual cats," he chuckles, "but intestines, yes, from sheep, mainly. And the bow hair comes from horse tails—only the finest, most perfect strands are selected."

She is nodding slowly. Then a new thought bubbles up. "How do you know what it will sound like when it's finished?"

The glow from the window makes his eyes sparkle. "That, my dear, is part of the charm. Every violin is different, just as every person is different. There is some magic inside it, I like to think. Something we cannot predict or know. At the end, when it is ready, you simply have to play it and see."

The small hairs on the back of her neck lift and tingle.

Behind them there is a yap, a shriek, a burst of laughter. Thumping into the workshop comes a girl of perhaps five or six years. She is giggling, her long red hair tied back with a velvet bow which bounces in her haste. She is pursued by a little dog with a matching ribbon around its neck. The girl knocks into Anna Maria.

Nicolò tuts. "Sofia, what have I—"

But he is interrupted by a smack. The worktable shakes. Sofia—in her whirlwind of excitement and rushing and chase—has hit her head against its corner.

Nicolò winces. He rushes to her, and her tears are instant,

appalled. He places a hand at her head, starts gently to rub. "*Dolce bambina*, are you all right?"

Sofia's breath stutters. The dog is circling them, front legs bouncing up. *Play?* it is saying. *Play?*

But Anna Maria is not watching the dog. She is staring at Nicolò, at the girl. At the way he attends to her, at his concern for her head, at how he soothes the bump with his hand. For a second she is reminded of the curve of Paulina's body against hers, from the nights they'd sleep together in her bed. Envy sparkles up in her, sharp and brilliant. She would like to rip Sofia out of his hands, she finds, to stand in her place instead.

"What have I told you about playing in the workshop?" he is saying, drying Sofia's eyes with a cloth. And Sofia's sobs are quietening, her shocked breath calming. Soon she is laughing again, the dog yapping with joy. She is running from the room, calling, "Thank you, *Papà*, sorry, *Papà*!"

Nicolò chuckles to himself, shaking his head, watching her go. "My apologies, *cara*," he says, turning to Anna Maria.

Cara, she thinks, feeling her chest flit. He called her *cara*.

It is something said by fathers to daughters. But no one has ever used it for her. The word is warm in her mind. She looks at him. His kind, creased eyes. His soft gray hair. An apron dusted with wood shavings, flecks of red and brown. She has the urge, for a moment, to take his hand and hold it.

"Where were we, where were we?" he is saying. "Ah, yes." He pulls a long band of cloth marked with lines from a drawer in the table. "You are thirteen, correct?"

She nods.

"Very good. Then I believe you will need a full-size violin—but to be sure, I will take a small measurement."

She stands perfectly still as he lifts her left arm and draws the material from the base of her neck to the middle of her palm. She closes her eyes and imagines herself holding her violin. She is ravenous to touch a finished model, to feel the way the notes glide under her skin.

"As I thought," he says, rolling the cloth back up and writing down the measurements in a small string-bound pad on the table next to him. "You are ready. Come."

He leads her through to a smaller room off the workshop that looks like an artist's den. On one wall a wooden shelf is stuffed with mismatched glass pots. They are labeled with pigment numbers and filled with a thick liquid in shades of amber, maple, and wine. There is a desk in front of them, on it a large leather-bound book scribbled with chemicals and quantities. A collection of stained paintbrushes stick out of a cream jug, and around it are more liquids in jars. Clear varnish and lime water, extracts of parsley seed, a large tub of roots jutting out of murky brown water.

"Choosing a violin is like choosing a spouse. Musicians spend months making the right decision. They will return time and again to try out all our options and decide which one perfectly suits them."

"I want to try one," she says quickly, then adds, "please, if I may."

Nicolò smiles, deep lines in his cheeks. "You will not need to pick. For you, *cara*, we will craft one from scratch."

He shifts now to reveal a violin which is perched upright in a stand on the windowsill, naked and raw. Its body is still pale, unvarnished. It has a fingerboard but no bridge, no strings.

It is in the process of becoming.

The breath catches in her throat. She reaches forward to touch it. "Is this—?"

"Yes." Nicolò lifts it in its stand onto the desk and takes a seat in front of it. "This will be yours soon."

She clutches the desk. Surely it cannot cost twenty ducats alone. "Can the Pietà afford such a sum?"

"Not just the Pietà—your teacher insisted upon a custom instrument and has donated his own gold. This will be something very special, something perfected just for you."

A deep, warm feeling builds in her chest. Not only will she have her own violin, but her teacher believes in her enough to gift his own money. For this she can wait. For this, it feels, she has already waited a lifetime.

The hubbub of chiseling and cutting and sanding and scraping flows through from the workshop. Nicolò gestures to a small wooden stool in the corner of the room. Anna Maria pulls it across. Rolls her shoulders back so she's sitting upright.

"Today I will begin varnishing." He slides open the desk drawer to reveal more glass pots, these thinner and taller than the ones on the shelf. Each is filled with powders in shades of reddish-brown.

"Pigment," he says, selecting one and removing the lid. He taps a small amount of the dry, crumbly mixture onto a glass plate on the desk.

He pours a dot of what looks like treacle onto the dry mix, then takes a glass tool with a flat bottom and starts to rub them together.

A deep, autumnal shade of red appears on the glass as he rubs in a circular motion. Then he takes a paintbrush, dabs it into the mixture, and raises it to the instrument.

Gently, ever so gently, he draws the brush across the front of the violin. And Anna Maria watches as something deeper, more complex and beautiful, starts to grow.

That night she lies in bed, replaying every moment from the workshop. The sweet smell of maple in the air; the violins dangling, suspended from the roof; the way the wood glowed as if lit from within. And the girl, Sofia. Her little dog. Her bumped head. The way Nicolò soothed her, cared for her, dried her tears.

Eyes closed, Anna Maria brings a flat palm to her own head. Begins, carefully, to stroke the knotted curls.

And as she does so, her teacher swims into her mind. It is his hand at her head, stroking, soothing her now. The thought sends a warmth through her, a smile spreads across her lips.

"Hush, *cara*," he is saying, tugging the blankets higher, tucking them snug about her body. "Sleep now, *dolce cara*."

On Saturday they have a delivery. It arrives in the entrance hall in a large wicker box. About thirty girls are crowded around, exchanging whispers.

"What is it?"

"What's inside?"

"Open it, open it."

Sister Clara slips off the wide blue ribbon and creaks open the lid. The hay stuffing leaves a trail across the floor, revealing five wooden dolls with red lips and silk gowns. There are moans of delight, cheers, and a scuffle. Some of the girls push closer, try to grab for them. Anna Maria watches, eagle-eyed, until she realizes there isn't a new instrument inside.

In the afternoon, as the dolls are being tugged and yanked around the dormitory, Anna Maria runs to her cupboard and slides out Tartini's manuscript. Next to it she places a clean piece of manuscript paper. She studies the music and thinks about the word *cadenza*. An opportunity for her own expression. She closes her eyes, sits in silence, concentrating, allowing the memories from the violin workshop yesterday to flood her senses, until the notes are pouring from her like she is ink itself.

The months roll into one another. Anna Maria spends most nights in the music rooms alone, preparing for her audition, studying the work of Tartini and Vandini, Marcello and Corelli, Lotti and Biffi and Porta. She pores over their music, learns a little something more about them. The ways they have inspired and adapted from one another, the depths of their minds, the surprises of their notes.

Life beyond the Pietà is muffled by thick walls, iron bars, panes of glass. She itches to get back out there and run with the breeze in her hair. To run for her violin.

Sometimes she wonders where her teacher goes after classes each day. She watches him through the barred windows, leaving the Pietà building, emerging into the open expanse of the promenade, getting smaller, moving away. She imagines him alone, sitting at a small wooden table with a single candle for company. She wonders if she might pull up a chair, join him someday.

Sometimes she thinks of Paulina, imagines her in the corner, smiling, clapping after she finishes a piece.

Sometimes there is nothing but the color, guiding her way.

It is a quiet existence. Rehearsing, refining, watching, waiting. Just her, the instrument, and her mind.

"Can you go no faster?"

It is taking everything in her power not to break into a sprint. Across the bridges, down the canals. Four months have passed since her last visit to the workshop and today, finally, is the day. Her violin is finished. Yet he is heaving for breath, several steps behind, slowing her down.

"My chest condition is not serious, but it does make rushing somewhat impractical, Anna Maria. Much as I appreciate your enthusiasm, you are going to have to be patient with me."

She huffs.

"When I am master of the Pietà's music program I will take us in a gondola no matter the distance," he says, fixing her with a look.

She smiles at this, slows a little, watching the canal lap at the boats. The water is milky today. The way that the winter sun hits it makes it look like a deep, complex jewel.

Part of her wants to step out onto it, just to see if she might walk straight across its rippling surface. But she takes a step back. Then another. She must not get so close.

She focuses on the colors and noises of the city—the smell of coriander and basil from the window boxes they pass, the blues and greens of a song hummed from a passing child—until they are standing at the door. She raps her hand on it, feels it vibrate, like it is matching her excitement.

The wait. The click of the lock. Nicolò is beaming down at her, his eyes sparkling again.

"It is time, Anna Maria."

He leads her down the corridor. She springs, weightless, until she is standing next to the *fortepiano* in the salon.

The glass cabinet clicks open. She holds out her arms. And from the large, age-spotted hands of Nicolò to her slim, pale, young ones, he passes her instrument.

It is featherlight. She cradles it like a newborn, neck supported with one hand, body with the other. Stands there, for how long she does not know, feeling this violin in her hands. Its deep red hue, the smooth gloss, the slim neck, the perfect curves, the swirl of black at the tip. Her breath is slowing, becoming calmer, more gentle. She has been handed her missing limb.

She holds it up now, feels it slot into the nook beneath her chin as if here it has always belonged. Takes the bow, every single hair slick and in place, and raises it to the strings. She'll play an *F*, as deep and red as the instrument she holds. She draws the bow, feels the strings vibrate through her as the violin awakens, reveals its voice in song. The sound is liquid, gleaming, sublime. The red she had expected to see flows out in front of her. But then it does something different. It trembles and fragments before her eyes, no longer simply one color but a thousand shades of gold and auburn and maroon. A soul come to life.

Tears break from her eyes. It is the first thing, other than the playing card and the note, that has ever been truly hers.

Nicolò's voice brings her back to the salon.

"Violin making is a family business. My father and grandfather came before me. I made Antonio's father's violin, I made Antonio's violin, and now I have made your violin."

He takes her instrument from her for a moment, places it and the bow on the cabinet sideboard, and clutches her hands.

"You are a part of this now. I welcome you and your instrument to our family."

Family. It's not a word she has ever known. She looks across at the violin—her violin—and promises she will care for it and protect it and that now, together, they will achieve something remarkable.

"Thank you," she says, her throat thick.

A shadow and he is there too, leaning against the wall in the corner, smiling awkwardly.

"You helped pay for this?" she asks.

He looks away, shy. But he nods, almost imperceptibly, once.

She shakes her head in disbelief. "Thank you both."

"We should return," he says.

She feels her jaw tighten. She needs three pieces to audition. It's taken her over four months to perfect one; she hasn't even started on the other two. And there are only eight weeks to go.

The violin is eased into its case, handed to her carefully. She follows her teacher into the mirrored hallway, stops before the door.

Suddenly she feels the water at her feet, and it is too much, she cannot move.

He turns back. "What is wrong?"

She looks at the case in her hand. The expense, the perfection of it. Fear is like a bell tolling in her chest. But it is weak, and she hates it. She will not speak it, will not give voice to her thoughts.

Already he has read her. "Do you think I would be working at Venice's most prestigious musical establishment if I let doubt lead my way?"

Venice's most prestigious musical establishment. He did not call it an orphanage, and she could embrace him for it.

"Do you?" he repeats.

Her stomach jolts. She shakes her head.

"Precisely. Whatever that voice inside is telling you, I want you to ignore it. Focus your attention on this." He points to the violin in its case. "Show me that you deserve it."

She can see herself in the mirror behind him. She looks young, small for thirteen, her cheeks pink from tears. She is no one still. And yet she is here, with him, holding her own violin.

He comes closer, until he is only inches away. "You belong here," he says. "Do you hear me? You deserve this."

She feels the words powering her, from the edges of her body to her chest.

I belong here, she tells herself. I am Anna Maria della Pietà.

11

The stench of rotting waste wafts through the chapel doors from the canal. With it comes a warm spring breeze, the first of the year. It is Sunday afternoon. On the stage at the front, five members of the *figlie di coro* are singing a haunting choral tune. The sound rises up, thickening and rounding in the space above their heads, echoing off the stone pillars.

Anna Maria is at Mass, but she is not praying. Her audition is in one week, and she is running over her music in her mind. She's supposed to perform three separate pieces, each about five minutes long. For one, she'll play the final and most difficult section of *The Devil's Trill*, the only piece she is fairly confident with now. Next she will be playing the first two movements of Violin Sonata No. 1 in D major by Corelli. The phrasing in the second movement is hard. Like a sentence, a phrase has a start and finish. But sometimes she's been landing too abruptly on the notes, snapping the sentence up into ugly little chunks.

The girl next to her yawns, her head bobbing forward as her Bible slips off her lap and onto the floor.

Then there's the final piece. The Torelli. They've picked the first movement of the Concerto in E minor. It has a different character than the other two. It makes her feel powerful when she plays it. More like she's wielding a sword than a bow. But it's fast and complex, just like the others, and it has a lot of running notes. Her two hands have to move in vastly different ways, at great speed, at exactly the same time. That in itself is hard enough, and it's got to be in tune, and she's got to keep a steady pace.

She looks down at her hand, realizes she's been digging her fingernails into her palms. The dents are four sinister smiles staring back at her.

She'll discuss it all with him tomorrow; she has a two-hour lesson in the afternoon. But it's a long wait until then, and she's not allowed to practice on a Sunday.

A knot sits, tight and unmoving, in the base of her stomach as she watches the singers fold their music and take their seats. A priest replaces them, his gold-patterned vestment flowing up the steps like water over rocks.

She is not good enough. She is not ready.

On Monday, Anna Maria skids into practice as the campanile bells strike two. She puts down her case and opens it the same way she does every day, as if she doesn't believe a thing of such beauty could still be inside. She beams as it is revealed. The shine, the curves, the sheer perfection of this instrument.

She lifts it out, holds before her the potential to make molten that which is silent, static. She feels like she could shatter the earth, make it vibrate and flow. A girl, her hands, this instrument.

Light bounces off its surface, casting a glow on her face. Sister Clara was right, the scars on her cheeks are less obvious than when she was a child. But they're still there if you look closely.

She'll be a little rusty, she always is when she's had a day off from practicing. And she and her violin are still getting to know one another. Or rather, getting reacquainted. It's as if they've been separated, and now they must reconnect. Learn one another's quirks and preferences, how best to care for and protect one another, how to make the other shine. It's happening, but it takes time, and time is not something she has much of.

Five minutes pass, and now she is standing in the window, tapping her foot impatiently. She cranes her neck to see if she can spot him rushing down the promenade toward the Pietà building. When she cannot, she runs to check the corridor.

She collides with someone rushing into the room at the exact moment she is sprinting out of it. There is a thud, her head hitting the doorframe.

"Goodness, Anna Maria, are you all right?"

A faint gleam surrounds her vision.

"What . . . ?"

She focuses a little harder, until she sees the long golden curls, the handsome face. Until her stomach drops.

"Where is he?" she says.

Signore Conti steps briskly into the room and begins setting up.

"Unwell again, I'm afraid. You are aware of his chest condition and—"

"No," she breathes.

This cannot be happening. Not now, not so close to her audition.

The harpsichord lid snaps shut a little too loudly.

"I'm very sorry to disappoint you, Anna Maria, but you will just have to manage with another lesson from me for today."

She could punch something. She thinks of the chapel, the men sitting with their little notebooks.

Too intelligent to be married.

She feels herself go cold.

A trembling flame casts the only light on her, tiny globules of wax dripping onto the shelf. She is in a small room next to the kitchen, where a wooden tub has been filled with warm water and lined with a linen cloth. Outside, a line of girls wait their turn for their monthly bath.

The building whistles, cracks in the brickwork allowing the chill night air to seep through.

Anna Maria slips off her smock, shivering. She crosses her arms over her naked chest, shielding from the cold the mounds that have appeared there in recent months, and steps into the water. She used to be able to sit comfortably in it, but now that she is tall and skinny, she has to tuck her knees up to her chest to get as deep and warm as possible. Little bits of skin and dirt float up from the girls before. She was seventh in line tonight. Not the worst. No one wants to be at the end, when the water is cold and rancid and they make you wash anyway.

She plucks a wooden brush off the floor and starts on her arms. Flecks of dirt leave her skin to the scrub, scrub, slosh, scrub, scrub, slosh. The feeling that her time is running out makes her chest flicker with worry.

She finds herself thinking of him. Her teacher has told her his condition is not serious, but he is unwell so regularly. Who takes care of him? Does he manage all by himself? She does not like the thought of him suffering alone, and she hates that his illness interrupts their progress.

But as she scrubs her mind begins to drift, to water and beats and boats churning up the lagoon. To waves on the canal and sails shimmering in the sun. A feeling, a buildup. Stronger and stronger. And now: colors!

About half the water sloshes over the side of the tub as she leaps up, flooding the floor. She grabs the cotton robe folded over the chair in the corner, flings open the door, and runs past the startled girls waiting outside. Her feet slap against the stone floor, leaving liquid footprints as she chases down the notes. They blast past her, gold and blue and orange and gray, black and green and white. She is panting by the time she reaches her cupboard on the third floor. She's outrun them, she needs to turn back. She tries to remember, to hold them in her mind.

Lock. Lantern. Light. Write. She literally reaches out for the last strand of note—a bright yellow—and tugs it down onto the paper.

She is halfway through before she realizes something remarkable is happening. She has started at the bottom right corner of the manuscript and is working her way to the top left.

The piece is coming out backward.

Somehow it makes sense. She passed it in the hallway and now she is tugging it back, note by note, color by color, to the page. It pours from her body and into life, the beat of her heart keeping time. Minutes pass like this, vivid and ludicrous all at once, as if she can feel her mind expanding. Until she stops, sighs—relief a physical thing that leaves her in that moment. There are seventeen pages of song. A piece of her, transformed.

Tuesday, and he is unwell again. They tell her he will be for another day or more. It makes worry twist in her stomach.

She uncrosses her legs, leans over the scattered manuscripts splayed across the desk, and picks her violin out of its case. She cradles it in her arms, finds it soothes her somewhat.

The sun has changed from a tiny lemon high in the sky to a huge peach skimming the horizon. It casts its soft glow across the lagoon and through the windows into the room, bathing everything in gold.

She looks down at her instrument and sighs. They will have to keep going alone.

She shifts her attention to the Torelli piece she's been studying for some time now. She starts running the first few bars of music, but there is something wrong. The notes are correct, yet she is not feeling anything. She tries again, and again, until her back thuds against the chair, her eyes pressed closed in frustration.

Moments later, when she opens them, there is a figure standing in the doorway. Oboe case in her hand, a small smile on her pink lips. They have not spoken, not since the day Agata's mother came. Seeing her so close Anna Maria feels a charge of energy, like lightning over the lagoon.

"Hello?" Paulina says, like it is a question.

"Hello," Anna Maria offers back.

There is a pause, the air thin, and then—

"Are you struggling with that?" Paulina takes a step toward her, points to the manuscript on the desk.

Anna Maria does not hear the question. Paulina is here, standing at the door, saying something. She is speaking, and the words are directed at her.

"The Torelli," Paulina clarifies. But she shifts, looks uncertain. "Or perhaps I should . . . Never mind."

She is turning to leave and Anna Maria is standing, saying, "Wait. The Torelli. Yes, I am struggling with it, yes."

Warmth spreads across Paulina's face as she comes closer. She pulls a chair across, places it by Anna Maria's side, her oboe case at her feet. Concentrating, she pulls her hands into that rabbity clutch. Anna Maria wants to take them in hers, to fold her arms around her and lay her head on her shoulder.

"It's a fascinating piece," Paulina is saying, staring closer at the notes, her finger trailing the melody. Anna Maria is nodding, trying not to smile. Paulina has come. Paulina is speaking to her. "The way the violin climbs out above the orchestra and then swoops back down, weaving among it." She tucks a strand of pale hair behind her ear. "There are so many twists and turns, the notes pacing off in unexpected directions."

Anna Maria knows as much. It reminds her of the little metallic fish she sees darting back and forth in the canal, glinting in the sunlight. But to hear Paulina say it, so close, makes the hairs on her arms stand upright.

"The piece is bright, and there is so much variety," she agrees.

"Will you play it for me again, from here?" Paulina says, pointing to the first bars.

Anna Maria's fingers shiver as she brings the violin to her neck. There is a mixture of colors, just like usual, vivid and clear and—

Paulina touches her arm suddenly. "That's it, the way you are playing it. It is *all* bright—too bright. You're leaving yourself nowhere to go."

It's not something her teacher has ever suggested.

Anna Maria cracks a smile, looking at Paulina. The manuscript flutters to the ground but she does not notice. She begins more gently, easing the sound out like a bird from a nest. She touches the string so lightly that the beginning sounds more like someone breathing rather than strings being hit. Now she lets the sound grow and develop, until it is a fountain overflowing, expanding into the sky.

"Tease them out, that's it." Paulina nods, standing to leave. She is back at the door when she says, "Find the darkness in the light."

Anna Maria feels him before she sees him. It is Friday afternoon, three days until the audition, and she is waiting for her private lesson. He is leaning against the doorframe, standing, watching her. The smile that greets her is brief.

He walks into the room now, but his movement is slower than usual. She can hear the breath rattling in his chest.

"Are you feeling better, *maestro*?" she asks.

"Somewhat," he says, his mouth tight.

He takes a seat at his desk, instructs her to begin. She reaches the second movement of the Corelli piece and messes up a number of the notes. It makes her squint, the colors muddy in her mind.

He stands abruptly. She tries to mask her sharp intake of breath. "You're concentrating too hard there." He adjusts his face so that it is kinder. "Let the bow lead the way. And don't hesitate between movements, keep it fluid, your wrist flexible."

She grimaces.

"Bum bum ba," he says, tapping two fingers against the desk. "Keep time. You are rushing the final section."

Anna Maria feels her stomach clench. She's noticed that she speeds up toward the end, had told herself that much earlier this week. But it's one thing thinking something, it's another thing making her body do it.

He must see the worry flit across her face. "It is fine." He smiles. "It is fine. Try again."

But it is not fine. She is causing him dissatisfaction. She is getting it wrong.

"Too fast." He is starting to pace now, the rattle in his chest becoming more pronounced with the effort. "Again too fast, even in the *grave* section."

"I'm trying," she says, bringing her violin to her side. "But when I play it feels about right."

"It is not right." He stops suddenly. "It is much too fast. You need to show the audience you are not just playing it; you are feeling it. This is my reputation, Anna Maria. You understand that? If you are too immature, if you cannot grasp a simple piece, I should not be letting you audition so young."

Heat rises in her cheeks. She feels a surge, like she will cry.

"Again," he says, facing away from her now.

She grits her teeth, begins to play.

"No," he snaps, spinning back toward her.

She cannot stop them: the tears spill. And she is furious with herself for it. She wants to raise a hand to her face, to shock herself out of it with a slap. She wipes her cheeks roughly with the back of her hand, her fingers still clenching the bow.

He paces toward her, speaking as he goes. "You think I am putting you through hell, no doubt. But hell is everything else. Hell is the world without music, do you not see that?"

Of course she sees it.

"Would you prefer that I say well done, good job for trying? Would you like me to patronize you so?"

"No," she says, wiping her cheeks again. "But it's been hard to decipher." She pauses, then adds under her breath, "All on my own."

"You have had lessons with Signore Conti. There is no excuse for this mess."

"Actually, I haven't," she says, feeling defensive, argumentative.

"You haven't?"

"I have attended my lessons, but . . ." She should not say it, but the words insist upon it, they will be spoken. "Signore Conti is hopeless."

A muscle moves in her teacher's jaw. It could be anger or amusement. She is not sure if he's pleased she doesn't like Signore Conti or furious she hasn't benefited from his lessons.

"Still, I agree, it sounds monstrous," she adds. "I do not wish you to tell me otherwise."

He takes a deep breath, walks back to the window. She can hear gulls floating in the sky, cackling like madmen.

His voice is calmer when he speaks again. "My father was a violinist, and his father before him. Both of them famous in Venice and beyond. The instrument came just as naturally to me, but I was not allowed to play. Our *family*," the word is a bitter fruit, "was too large, and the responsibility to provide for them fell to me. Violin, though I was practically an heir to the throne, was not considered a reliable career. My music had to make way for religion."

"You weren't allowed to play?"

"Priesthood was my calling, or so I was told. It took many years, and many quarrels, to get to where I am now."

He beckons her with two fingers. She comes to stand by his side. Beyond the latticed bars of the window, the lagoon is a rippling silver blanket. The wind pushes it west, east, west again. The movement is endless, unstoppable.

"You too want to be great. I see that. I am merely trying to make it possible. I push people beyond what is expected of them. I push them into greatness because I had no one to help me."

She nods, hanging on his words, green eyes meeting gray. A soft silence wraps itself around them.

He leans closer now. Raises a hand to push back a stray hair which has fallen at her cheek. His voice is low as he says, "You are becoming quite captivating, you know."

She blinks, the words a surprise to which she has no response. She thinks of Nicolò for a moment, in the violin shop with his daughter. Is it something, she wonders, that he might say to her?

A breeze flows through the window and suddenly her teacher bristles, a shell snapping closed.

"So," he claps his hands together, "you understand what we must do here. Let us return to the second movement of Corelli later. Show me the Torelli now."

She fumbles as she tugs out the copy from her manuscript book. Then she plays, finding that her thoughts about easing out the sound are helpful. When she finishes he is facing away from her again.

"That one will work. But be mindful of your pace. When you rush, you lose clarity. The notes blend together like soup."

Soup? Something inside her shrinks back again.

"And now *The Devil's Trill*," he instructs.

They run it three more times. She had been excited to show him her *cadenza*, her own ideas for Tartini's piece, but the atmosphere is thick and tense as bone. She does not know what will happen if she tries to share this sacred part of her with him right now.

Finally they're back to the Corelli. He says very little as she plays, as the tendons in the fleshy part of her forearm begin to ache. She has barely lowered her instrument in over an hour. When she is finished he starts packing up his things. She thinks he is going to leave without another word, but at the last moment he looks up.

"Two of these pieces will work for the audition if you keep your focus. But the Corelli still needs attention. You will practice Saturday and Sunday too. I shall see that Sister Madalena allows it. Until Monday," he says. And he leaves.

Her spoon hits the surface again and again, metal plunging into the lumpy depths. Some of the liquid slops over the edge. The girl next to her pulls a face, edges away.

Anna Maria stares down at the bowl. A blend of beige and gray with a few mangled beans floating across the surface. Soup. She does not want her music to be compared to this monstrosity.

Across from her is a table filled with members of the *figlie di coro*. There's Chiara from her concert all those years ago, sitting with her head resting against her clutched palm, laughing at something Giulia, the girl next to her, is saying. Anna Maria has heard her singing—she produces a sound like a bird at dawn, crisp, pure, and bright. And there's Bianca, who plays the oboe as if it were pure gold, valuable and precious in her hands.

Anna Maria slurps up her food, watching them. She is within touching distance of the greats, of greatness. If she can just fix the Corelli in time.

The bowl is basically empty, but she slops a little more over the side so it is finished. A thrum begins in her chest. Rushing now, she stows her plate. She's about to leave when she hears her name. Gripping the doorframe, she turns.

Paulina is walking toward her, elbows pressed to her sides, her hands clutched together. She smiles. "I heard you have your audition on Monday. I wanted to say good luck."

There is a nervous flutter in Anna Maria's stomach. The corner of her lip edges up as she opens her mouth to respond.

But there is a creak, a slam. And then pain explodes across her hand.

12

"You're fortunate it's just the one finger," the nurse says cheer-fully, giving Anna Maria's hand a little shake to test the bones, which makes her scream out in pain. "Could have broken the lot of them from the sound of things."

Paulina is standing in the doorway, shaking her head.

"It wasn't your fault," Anna Maria says, grimacing.

"I distracted you, I'm so sorry, I'm—"

"Really," Anna Maria says, "it's not that bad."

"Off with you now." The nurse flicks her hand toward Paulina.

"But can I just—?"

"Out."

Paulina gives Anna Maria one last look before she leaves.

Anna Maria didn't know what had happened in the imme-diate aftermath, her mind sparkling with pain. The sister said one of the old bolts had been loose. It sent the large, heavy door slamming down onto the small finger of her bow hand while she was looking the other way.

A wave of pain spasms out from her knuckle and Anna Maria has to bite her cheek to stop from yelling out. But the nausea that follows is not about this physical feeling. More than pain, there is fear. Her audition is tomorrow.

The nurse turns, and from her metal rack of drawers she pulls a rigid wooden splint and a long spool of linen. She starts ban-daging Anna Maria's throbbing finger to the one next to it. A thin sweat forms across Anna Maria's forehead.

"Here." The nurse hands her a damp cloth. She turns to a table covered in little glass bottles, picks up one labeled "Laudanum" in tiny swirling writing. She then takes a larger, unlabeled bottle and unstoppers the cork, pours a few drops of the laudanum in. The liquid is reddish-brown. She hands the larger bottle to Anna Maria.

"One sip before bed and another every three hours tomorrow."

Anna Maria nods gravely. The nurse pats her on the shoulder and tells her to go back to the dormitory and rest.

The second she is out of the *infermeria*, Anna Maria drops the cloth on the courtyard stone and peels off the bandage. Pain shoots up her arm. There is a dent in the finger where the door hit it, below the knuckle, and the purple glow of a bruise taking shape. But the swelling isn't too severe. As long as she doesn't say anything, there's no need for anyone else to know. She tucks the bottle of medicine into her smock. She must save it for tomorrow before the audition. Then she scales the spiral staircase up to the music rooms, the shooting pain morphing into a throbbing ache. She grimaces, grits her teeth, and returns to practice.

The cracking sound doesn't wake her. Anna Maria is already wide-eyed, grimacing up at the rafters when Sister Madalena walks past her bed, tugging her fingers out of their joints one by one. Anna Maria flinches, bile rising in her throat at every click. Her right hand is under the blanket, hidden from inspection. She's certain it must be as big as a bucket by now and is terrified to look. The pain flashes across her hand in intermittent bursts and then pulsates around the knuckle. Her whole body is shivery and wet, her mattress soaking, her skin clammy and pale. And she is furious.

It must be at least three hours before dawn if Sister Madalena is doing her second round of the night, and Anna Maria hasn't slept a wink from the pain.

"Why?" she whispers to the ceiling.

She is on the cusp of everything. She needs rest and calm before her audition.

She rolls onto her side, carefully maneuvering herself so that she doesn't move or touch her hand. Starts grinding her teeth, the small muscles in her jaw tight and pulsing. She should have stayed later practicing this evening but the pain was too intense. It was hard to hold the bow, let alone run through all her pieces. She glances at her bedside cabinet, where the little glass bottle is lit by the moonlight.

Her eyes flick to her violin, snug and waiting by her bed. Should she give in? Should she? The case does not rock, gives no signal, no answer.

The throb pulses again.

"I can't," she says, leaning across for the bottle now. "I need to sleep."

She unscrews the cap with one hand and takes a long gulp. The grainy, bitter taste makes her sputter. She wipes her mouth with her forearm, lies back, and breathes. In, out, in, out, until pain and world blend into one. She drifts, above and out of them, as they fade into nothing.

She is in a tunnel, a tunnel made of colors. She flows through it like water down a pipe as they ebb and swirl around her. Each color is like a long thick string, but with its own individual texture. Some are silky and smooth, some are rutted like stone, some are spiked and sharp. She reaches out to touch one and the whole world shifts. No longer a tunnel but a circle, with her at the center. It spins, faster and faster now, the colors combining until she cannot tell one from the other. Below her, in the center of this whirlpool, a dark hole emerges. She takes a step forward, sees the water ripple beneath her, and she plunges in.

A feeling, warm and soft against her cheek. She leans closer, a purring cat, and listens to the sounds. Feet pattering on stone and sisters muttering about chores and—

She sits bolt upright. Paulina, next to her, flinches back in surprise.

"You're awake," she says, composing herself. "Good. I . . .

I came to check on you. The sisters said you had a fever in the night and were shaking and talking in your sleep. They let you lie in till noon. I'm so sorry about your hand, Anna Maria, it's all my fault, I shouldn't have—"

"*Noon?*" Anna Maria repeats, ripping back the covers. "My audition is in two hours! I was supposed to spend all morning preparing."

She stands up, then feeling like she might vomit from the dizziness, sits back down. She lifts her untroubled hand to her hair, roughly pushing back the strands that are stuck to her face, and then looks down. Although the pain is starting to return, her other hand is still a normal size, the purple bruise not much worse. But she won't take any more swigs from the little glass bottle. She can't risk going back to sleep.

"You still plan to audition today?" Paulina says, taken aback.

"Of course I plan to audition today," Anna Maria snaps. "If I could just find my . . ." She lurches forward for her shoes and Paulina grabs her shoulders to stop her rolling off the bed.

"Right," Paulina says. "Wait here. Just rest for a moment. I'll be back."

Anna Maria lies, helpless, rubbing her head with her left hand, cursing her right, until Paulina returns with a cup of something dark and sour and steaming.

"It's Cook's coffee. Apparently it helps—I've seen her taking it in the morning after too much wine at supper."

Paulina's cheeks are flushed with mischief. Anna Maria's stomach contracts. She has missed her so. But she doesn't say. Just gulps the liquid down, grimacing at the tart, acidic taste.

And they wait.

Anna Maria is sitting on the cold stone floor outside the largest music room, at the far end of the third-floor corridor, knees clutched to her chest, violin case by her side. Her heart is pounding. It could be from the bitter coffee, or the little bottle of medicine, or the fear.

The cool stone soothes her hand, so her palm is laid flat

against it. There are a few angry red lines starting to emerge from the purple bruise, but the pain is manageable for now.

A whisper makes her look to her left. Another girl is walking quickly toward her, a long brown plait swinging from side to side, a violin case in her hand.

Is her name Margot? Martinique? Anna Maria has seen her in lacework but didn't know she played violin, didn't know she would be auditioning. She's at least two years older.

"Is this the room for the *figlie* audition?" the girl says, pointing ahead.

Anna Maria nods.

The girl slides her back down the wall until she's on the floor next to Anna Maria. "Mind if I join you?"

Anna Maria does mind. She is about to start running through the music in her head. But for some reason, perhaps the tiredness or the lingering pain or the feeling in the depths of her stomach that she is about to fail, she says, "Fine."

The girl offers her a smile; it makes her eyes crease at the edges. Anna Maria is, momentarily, reminded of Agata. What might she look like by now? The thought makes her ribs contract. She pushes it out of her mind.

Sister Agostina, a thin woman with a face like a bird's, pokes her head out of the room. "Marta della Pietà," she says curtly.

"That's me." Marta gets back to her feet, looking excited. She glances at Anna Maria. "I'll be seeing you, then. Good luck!"

Anna Maria gives her a small nod. "You too," she says, while at the same time thinking, Fail. You will fail.

She tracks Marta's movements as she hurries into the room. A hunter stalking its prey. The door clicks shut. There is a pause, a few moments of mumbling, and then Marta begins to play.

Anna Maria groans, her head tilting back until it hits the wall. Marta is good. Really good. It's almost painful to listen to.

She does not want to go after this audition now. Not in her state. She plugs her fingers into her ears, closes her eyes, takes a deep breath.

You need this, she tells herself. Remember the podium, the

crowd. She hears the audience cry out in awe, "Anna Maria, Anna Maria!" And then she plucks her fingers from her ears.

"Anna Maria della Pietà," Sister Agostina says irritably. "It is time."

At the threshold between the corridor and the audition room Anna Maria pauses. She grips the handle of her violin case a little tighter, tilts her head up, and marches through the door.

Then she feels her stomach lurch.

Twelve men sit in a long line in front of her. She was expecting some of the music teachers and sisters, but not this. Not all these eyes, these men's eyes, staring back at her, judging her.

Each of them has a small wooden desk, a quill, some parchment, and a bottle of ink in front of them. They talk between themselves, not taking notice of her. She scans the line quickly, taking in their attire and features. Lace cuffs, buttons popping open over bellies. Sideburn length and hair color aside, it's like she has stepped into a room of the same person, multiplied.

Her eyes flick to the corner. He is near the window, arms crossed, back to the wall, legs jutting forward slightly. He looks plain, comparatively, in his simple brown coat, his cream breeches. But the sun makes his red hair glow the color of a violin. It does not matter that he does not have gold and lace. He has skill, she thinks proudly. He has talent.

He gives her a small nod, nothing more. Her finger twinges, sets off a wave of nausea that pulses through her body. When she looks down at her hand, she realizes it is shaking.

Sister Clara and Sister Madalena conclude the row of men, one on each side like white bookends.

In front of her there is a music stand and a wooden chair. She walks toward them.

"When you are ready, please begin," says a man on the far left, next to Sister Clara. His voice is higher than expected, nasal. Anna Maria recognizes the eyebrows. He is Governor Ciuvan, the one who watched her perform at just eight years old. She looks again at the row of men. They are all the governors of the Pietà.

She places her violin case down carefully on the chair, clicks it open, feels blood rising up in her cheeks. For some reason it's taking her longer than usual. She can hear every breath, every shifting foot. She tries to concentrate on her instrument.

She lifts it to her chin, connecting it to her body.

She raises her bow, the small finger of her right hand quivering. She is about to touch the strings for the very first time when there is a sharp tap on her shoulder.

"Child, you have forgotten your music. Get it out, quickly." Sister Agostina is by her side.

"I . . . um . . . I don't have any," Anna Maria says, her bow flopping back down.

"Well, go and get it," Sister Agostina hisses, turning to smile at the men, who are sitting silently. Staring.

"No, I meant . . . I don't need any. Thank you." Anna Maria shifts on her feet. Sister Agostina looks at her as if she has just fallen on her head. But she curtsies and scurries to the back of the room without another word. Governor Ciuvan frowns, doesn't say anything. Anna Maria looks to her teacher, who nods almost imperceptibly. *Continue.*

For a moment she is paralyzed. She was going to start with the Corelli, slow and steady, to ease her in. But *The Devil's Trill* is the piece she knows best. Maybe she should start there, try and get at least one good piece out of the audition. There is a cough, an impatient shuffle.

She must make a decision. She must hurry.

And then something clicks in her mind. What she wants to feel, more than anything in this moment, is powerful. The music can give her this. She will start with the Torelli.

She begins, waiting for the colors to emerge before her eyes, to guide her, but they do not come. It could be the nerves, the sick feeling rising in her throat. There is no time to know. She just has to focus on her hands, on the movement of the bow, on hitting the running notes quickly and accurately like she's practiced it. By the time she finishes the piece, she is sweating, and she realizes her broken finger has started to ache. She darts her gaze up to the judges, but their heads are all down, scribbling curling letters on their parchment pads.

"Next piece," Governor Ciuvan says without looking up.

The Corelli. She does everything in her power to start slow, to give the notes expression and depth, but her finger is distracting her, a constant flicker of pain. Again the colors do not come. She is rushing it; she knows she is. She grimaces, locks her jaw, strengthens her stand.

The second, faster movement is a blur. She tries to remember not to hit the notes too abruptly, to give the sentences a smooth shape, but her hand is throbbing now, it's hard to focus on anything else.

At least this is it. The last one, and then she can go back to the dormitory and hide under the blankets and cry. The world can swallow her up, for all she cares. Because what else is there? If she fails this, she faces the men with their notebooks. If she fails this, what is the point?

The Devil's Trill. She's saved it until last. As she raises her bow to her strings she imagines the devil standing in the corner of the room, red hair and a black mouth. He is watching her, possessing her. She stares him down, feels the notes quivering inside her before she has even started to play.

Colors. They burst from the devil's mouth and shoot around the room, quiver up through the floorboards and break free into the air. They tremble across the heads of the men watching her. They are playing with her, cajoling her. She submits to them, lets them inhabit every crevice of her mind. She is not playing her violin, she and it are simply pirouetting with the shades of yellow and blue and green that flow between them.

She reaches the *cadenza.* She could not stop if she wanted to. Her invented notes pulsate, flowing from her body into shades of blue, green, and gold.

Her teacher stands up straight, looking at her. Takes a step closer, then another. He knows this is her work, that this part belongs to her.

She draws the bow across the strings a final time. Flinches as a shooting pain fires from her finger up her arm. Then she looks at the governors.

They stare back.

There is not a smile, not a flicker of emotion between them. She packs and leaves in silence, feeling like she is tumbling, the water swallowing her up. At the door she slows, moves to the side, hurries out. Another girl passes her. She is older, taller, walking with more confidence. It is her audition now.

Eating is out of the question, as is sleeping. At midday today the names of those who have been accepted into the *figlie di coro* will be displayed in the music room corridor. There are three positions for singers, two for oboists, and one for violin. Just one. Anna Maria will not go, she's decided that much already. Cannot stand there willingly, seeing another name in her place.

She and Paulina have crept out onto the rooftop. It is smaller, more cracked than she remembered. Below them, carts carrying coffee beans and sacks of citrus fruits rumble along narrow alleyways, and sailors, fresh from their trip to the Indies, hum a sweet melody as they walk from the market to the ship.

Paulina's hand is resting on Anna Maria's leg as she looks out across the terra-cotta rooftops.

Anna Maria's face is turned away to hide her tears. Her hand is bandaged back up, a makeshift job she did herself. She couldn't go back to the nurse; she'd get the whip for taking it off in the first place.

Paulina shuffles a little closer. "You don't know you've failed, not yet."

"I do. I do know it."

She thinks of the colors of the first two pieces, how nothing ever emerged. It must have sounded terrible. She can hardly even remember now, so intense was the pain and the focus and the nerves.

"Let's say that you did. It would give you more time to spend with me again." Paulina turns Anna Maria's face toward her. "Would that be so bad?"

Anna Maria offers her a weak smile in return. But the feeling inside is so complex she doesn't know how to voice it, not without her violin. She cannot envisage a future without her music. How could she grieve for the career she never had? How could she look at her manuscripts and know that she didn't give them the chance to be heard? Then again, there is this ache inside her, a yearning, deep and strong. To be near Paulina, to make this friendship work. Why can't it be simple? Why can't she just want this and nothing else?

Paulina does not wait for an answer. Instead, gently, she pats Anna Maria's hand and says, "You have done all you can."

At one in the afternoon they clamber down from the rooftop. Anna Maria refuses to go to the third-floor hallway, so they pass through the second floor, where Sister Clara is leading a class. Anna Maria glances through the open door. Ten girls sit in a circle, small squares of delicate lace on their laps, pulling at thread with a needle. What bothers Anna Maria more than anything is the silence. No vibrations, no flowing hues, just people hunched over material, tugging quietly. She feels herself shudder.

Paulina leaves for oboe class, and Anna Maria finds herself alone. No practice today. He's been busy managing the governors as they make their decisions on the auditions. She should go and find Sister Madalena, put herself to some use. But there is a quiver in her stomach—anger, jealousy, and curiosity all mingled into one.

Who was it, then? Who took it from her?

The parchment is fluttering in the breeze. It is weighed down by an inkpot on a desk at the end of the corridor, a tiny cream square that grows bigger, bigger, bigger as Anna Maria approaches it.

There are two columns of names. She sees Chiara's, so this must be a list of members who are already in the *figlie*. In the right-hand column, at the bottom, it says "new additions." Three singers, two oboists, and one violinist.

And there, at the very bottom of the page, in the last spot on the list, are four words.

Anna Maria della Pietà.

She sinks to her knees, her fingertips pressing into the floor. Her tears cast dark flecks across the stonework.

Then, a voice behind.

"You stunned them, Anna Maria. There wasn't even a contest," he says.

She looks up, tries to steady her breath.

He offers her a hand, a handkerchief. She gets to her feet, dries her eyes, pushes the hair away from her face.

He continues, "And I have been promoted to Master of Music. I am now responsible for the entire music program at the Pietà. Thanks in part, no doubt, to the talent of my finest violin student." He nods at her and smiles. Then he takes the handkerchief back, folds it into a triangle, and slides it into his chest pocket.

A swell of relief moves through her.

"Things will start to move faster now," he is saying. "There will be expectations—concerts, events. It will mean more practice, even compositions."

"Compositions?" she says quickly.

"I want to do great things. I want to create music that will change the Republic, music the likes of which no one has ever heard." She is frozen, staring, hanging on his every word. "I have been tasked with composing something already, for the war effort against the Turks in Corfu. I will hold a competition among the *figlie* to help me with it. You will enter, of course. The final piece will be performed at a concert for General Schulenburg four months from now." He pauses, then adds, "With a *cadenza* like yours, no doubt you'll rise to the challenge."

She is screaming with joy on the inside. To him, she offers only a cool professional smile.

"Then we don't have a moment to spare," she says, marching past him, leading the way back into the music room.

13

Anna Maria sits up, shoulders rolled back, eyes and ears intently focused. She is in the front row of the bank of eight violinists in the largest music room, at the opposite end of the line to the subject of her attention. All other faces and instruments blur into the background. She watches a girl from several years above her, with small, protruding eyes and a large forehead. Anna Maria tracks her every movement.

It's been six weeks since she joined the *figlie di coro*, since she started to settle into this new routine. Mass, morning meal, arithmetic, then reading, writing, and noon prayers. These are followed by two hours of private classes with him, two hours of practice with the orchestra, and finally supper and bed.

Forehead is laughing now at something the girl next to her, with the legs that buckle inward, is saying. But the girl next to her does not matter. Forehead—Sanza della Pietà—is first violinist. Sanza della Pietà gets all the important solos. Sanza della Pietà is the one who must be crushed.

She is holding the bow as if it were the lightest of feathers. As if she may drop it at any moment. Anna Maria looks down at the bow in her own hand, tries to loosen her fingers, to soften her wrist in just the same way. The dent in her finger is still there from the break, but the pain is practically gone. Her hand remains a little stiff, though. She frowns at it, urging it to work the way she wants.

Of the eight violinists in the *figlie di coro*, there are three she has identified as her main competition. Sanza, yes, but also Chiara

138

and Prudenza, both of whom are far older and more experienced than her. Chiara has been in the orchestra ever since Anna Maria performed with her in the concert for the governors at eight years old, and Prudenza about the same. Chiara plays like she is painting the music. A flick here, a long smooth line there. And Prudenza is captivating, intense. She has a scar on her cheek that looks like she has been in a dagger fight, and her hair trembles as her slim arm moves the bow back and forth across the strings.

Anna Maria feels a pang of jealousy every time she watches them with their instruments. They probably both want the first violinist spot too. But she must be the one to stand out among this crowd. First violinist will be hers.

Their teacher stands at the front of the room, correcting the tuning on one of the violins.

Everything has changed in the past few weeks. The way girls look at her in the corridor, now that she is wearing the black cotton smock with long sleeves and a square neck—the one that signals she is a member of the *figlie*. As if she is a king. As if she is someone to be admired. As if she is someone at all.

The way food tastes in her mouth. Sweeter, more satiating.

The way her violin feels in her hand. More sturdy, more connected even than before.

The calm she feels, now that she is here, settled, forever safe from the possibility of marriage; from being taken from her music.

And her room. Her room!

Not much more than a box to some. Just a bed, a small barred window overlooking the courtyard, a little desk with a stub of candle, and a wooden chair. But the best part of all is the door. She can shut out the world, create her own space, hide away if she wants to. She can think and dream and compose late into the night without anyone knowing, without anyone telling her to stop. She sighs just thinking of it as he moves across the room, the little golden buckles on his shoes jingling to his step. Ever since he has become Master of Music his clothes are more decorated and elaborate. No more simple tails and faded waistcoats.

At this moment he is dressed in a green velvet suit adorned with silver edges.

"Today we will test the start of a piece I have been composing," he says.

There are murmurs around the room. He is energized, his hands shaking as he places the music on their stands. It is the first time he has given them work of his own to play.

There are three pages with many twists and turns. Not a complete number, but the beginning of something she can tell could be special. Anna Maria is reminded of the first time she ever heard him play. There is energy, intensity in the piece. But as she watches the notes become insects, black beetles crawling across the page, finding new positions. She would send that section higher, she would linger longer at the start. She watches, mesmerized, as her mind invents solutions for the ending.

"It may look different to what you are used to. Do not worry. We are here to practice, to learn." He looks directly at Anna Maria. "I simply ask that you try your best."

Standing in front of them now, he raises his arms and they begin to play.

They are a few lines in when he lifts a hand, revealing a lace-lined cuff. His direction for them to stop.

He moves toward the singers, asking them to adapt a few of the notes that are too high, scribbling new ones onto their sheets. Then—

"Sanza, bar thirty-one, if you please."

Sanza has a solo here. Anna Maria stares as Sanza begins to play, but then she stops. She brings her instrument to her lap, her fingers to the pegs at the neck of her violin.

She is retuning. Now, in the middle of a piece. Anna Maria rolls her eyes. Wants to shout, *You should have been ready*, but manages, just, to keep the words inside.

There is a tightness in her teacher's jaw, but he lets her continue.

Sanza begins again, and a couple of chairs down, Prudenza joins in too.

"Fine," he says, "fine. But crowds do not pay to see fine."
Prudenza's eyes shift nervously.

"No bother," he says, his mouth a tight smile. "Let us try that again, but this time I want you to build the volume as we reach bar thirty-four and keep it going through to bar thirty-five."

They do so, the *figlie* joining in with them, but as the orchestra plays he becomes more agitated, pacing back and forth. They have repeated the same section seven times when—

"Stop, stop." He stands behind the desk, head down, hands gripping the edges. There is silence but for the thump in Anna Maria's chest.

"Everyone stand," he says now. "Move your chairs against the wall."

The shuffle and creak of wooden chairs against the floor. He coughs into his handkerchief, takes a long, deep breath.

"Out into the corridor." The *figlie* exchange concerned looks. "You heard me correctly. All of you."

They stand in a line, backs to the cracked gray wall, the smell of stewing vegetables drifting up from the kitchen. He paces along in front of them.

"Each of you is focusing too hard. You are here, with me, in the Pietà. I need you to forget who you are, forget where you have come from. Great musicians do not simply play, they transform."

Anna Maria hangs on his every word.

"When you walk back into that room, walk not like you are walking into our rehearsal but"—he searches for an idea, seems to pluck one from the sky—"like you are entering a banquet, and you are the guests of honor. Inside lies a table, and upon it a feast. The plates are piled high with fried fish and roasted lamb, with cakes and cream and jam."

His energy has changed again, it glitters like broken glass.

"I want you to walk in there and stuff yourselves. Eat, and do not stop."

The girls are grinning at one another. Anna Maria is straight-faced, focused, hungry. She walks back toward the room, her core strong, her shoulders rolled back. She closes her eyes at the threshold. With her last step, she enters the feast.

They lift their instruments. Instantly the sound is deeper, stronger than before.

"Orphans." His fist hits the desk, making one of the girls jump. The sound becomes clearer, swelling in the room.

"Orphans," he says again, pacing between them, straightening their backs. "Is this what you want people to think? 'Poor girls. Let us clap along in pity, let us make them feel better.' I want you to play like you mean it. I want you to play like you are starving and only the music can make you full." His voice is faster now. "I want you to take who you were and say no more. Transform. I want you to obliterate yourselves."

Something happens in that moment. A shift, a snap. The *figlie* begin to move as one; the sound grows in shape, texture, and size. They look at one another. Their eyes are dark, hollow.

"Feast," he says now, "feast!"

Anna Maria sees the table, a blaze of purples and greens and golds. It is delicious, she is ravenous. She feasts until she is panting for breath, until her armpits are damp, until he raises a hand before them.

He takes a cloth from his jacket pocket. Anna Maria cannot believe it. He is wiping tears from his cheeks.

"Play like that from this day forward," he says, folding it, placing the cloth away, "and soon you will be hailed as masters."

Light cutting through water, casting shards of sun across the floor. A crushing pressure. A weight on her lungs. A deep, feral dread.

Anna Maria gasps, sits up, her breath shuddering in and out. She reaches for her violin, clutches it close, tugs the blanket up a little higher, so it's protected.

The curves are smooth beneath her hands. She focuses on them alone until her heart stops racing.

No matter what she tries, even when she practices well into the night, even when she is exhausted, she cannot shake these nightmares.

"Why do they haunt me still?" she asks, plucking at a string. It sends out a bolt of green.

She leans back, closes her eyes. Tries to block the water from her mind. She tosses and turns a few times, searching for sleep. Then, giving in, she drags herself off her mattress.

She lights a candle, pulls open her desk drawer, unfolds her note. The sliced playing card tumbles onto the floor. She places it back on the desk, her hand lingering on it for a moment. Then she returns to the note. It's been months since she's held the soft paper in her hands. She rubs it with her thumb, back and forth, back and forth.

Know that you were loved.

In that second there is a giggle behind her. She gasps, spins toward it. She rushes to the door, peers out into the dark hallway. It is empty, silent. But as she stands, breath held, she feels another body. Warm, pressed against her side, holding her crinkled newssheet.

A cold breeze moves through her room and she stiffens, shakes her head.

There is no one, she tells herself. There is nothing.

She closes the door. Folds the note without looking at it again, places it in the drawer.

The next afternoon Anna Maria can feel the itch to play crawling across her body. Her teacher stands before them in a maroon velvet waistcoat, the beginning of a new piece he has created on the music stands.

A rap on the door and Sister Madalena appears, her body filling the doorframe. Wordlessly, she enters, stomps to the back of the room. She stands there, watching him with her beady black eyes, as the class turns to look at her.

"Continue," she says, taking a seat.

His eyes shift to Sister Madalena, then to the girls, then back to Sister Madalena.

"Very good." He nods.

A few sheets of the parchment slip off his stand and onto the floor. One of the twins, Cecilia, is closest to him. She bends at the same moment he stoops to collect them.

"I have it," he hisses.

She retracts as if splashed by scalding water, takes her seat. Ducks her head to hide the tears.

Anna Maria looks at her. He is being tested: Sister Madalena has no doubt been sent by the governors to check his capabilities as the new Master of Music. Can Cecilia not see that she has flustered him? Made an already difficult situation worse?

There is a fine sweat on his forehead when he stands back up. He pauses, coughs quietly into his handkerchief before finding his place in the music.

But soon they are playing, and Sister Madalena's foot is begrudgingly tapping along. Over forty-five minutes he does not stumble, does not lose his way again. Anna Maria smiles, watching him impress like this. She never doubted that he would rise to the challenge.

Still, the relief when Sister Madalena leaves is palpable, a weight lifted from every shoulder in the room. The door clicks shut. He walks over and, peering through the glass panel for a moment, checks she is gone.

Then he turns back to the class.

"You," he says, pointing to Cecilia. Anna Maria feels her heart kick in her chest. "What is your name?"

The look on Cecilia's face is that of horror. She glances to her left, to her twin, Candida.

"Do you not know your name?" A laugh moves through the room.

Candida nudges her: *Speak.*

"Cecilia, Signore," she says quietly.

"Cecilia Signore. That's an odd kind of name." More laughter now. "Tell us, Cecilia Signore, why did you interrupt me today?"

"I . . ." There are tears forming in her eyes. "I didn't . . . I was trying to . . ."

"Did she not interrupt me?" He looks to the room.

"She did," someone calls. There is nodding, agreement.

He looks back to Cecilia. "Are you . . . crying?" he asks.

"I'm sorry!" She gasps, runs from the room. He does not react. Just stands and lets her go.

Anna Maria's hand, she realizes, is shaking by her side.

He respects you, she reminds herself. It is not the same for the others.

"Let her leave," he says to the class. "We have business to attend to. For our upcoming performance, I have been tasked with composing something to help our Republic in its defense against the Turks. Our forces have suffered badly in this most recent war, and now we understand that they have taken the island of Corfu."

There is some nervous muttering.

"A good deal of the last two centuries has been spent battling them, and our forces have not been conquered yet. But you are right to be concerned. Our music lives in the shadow of threat, and thus the piece must create a feeling of power and victory. There will be a competition to help me with it."

There are whispers, shuffling. The excitement dances through the room.

"You are each required to write a piece based solely on a title and a key signature. There are no restrictions as to instrumentation, style, or length as such, but bear in mind that I am one man with limited energy. I cannot study hundreds of hours of your work, no matter how masterful it is."

There's a polite murmur of laughter. Anna Maria flicks her eyes toward Candida, just for a moment. She is glassy-eyed, frozen, staring at the door. She would like, it seems, to stand and run after her sister.

"You will compose a piece invoking the feeling of war, of being challenged to fight. The key is G minor. The competition will close one week from now. Have your submissions to me by then."

Anna Maria's stomach jolts, her attention back on him. Just a week to prepare. She has so many ideas, she doesn't know which one to pick.

"We must think," he continues, "about what men need in the face of war, to carry their souls through. We must ask God for His favor through the music."

She wishes she had some parchment to write down what he is saying, but she's not allowed to bring it to class. Paper is expensive. If she has it, everyone will want some. She tries to commit what he is saying to her mind, but it's so much easier with notes. She listens to the tune of his speech. To carry their souls through, she thinks, eyes squeezed shut in concentration.

He continues, "The concert will be held in three months. The entire orchestra will perform at the Marcini Palace."

Anna Maria sucks in her breath. The Marcini Palace. It is better than she could have imagined. She will be outside the Pietà for the first time since she had her violin made, performing to Venice, to the world. Delight shudders through her. She cannot wait to tell Paulina after class. If she runs, she may be able to find her before supper ends.

"It is a substantial opportunity, a chance for our new members to prove themselves. We must make the Pietà proud."

He catches Anna Maria's eye.

"Finally," he says, "do not tell anyone outside of this room about the competition. Many at this institution do not believe you should be allowed to learn the art of composition. I disagree. So," he looks directly at her, "this will need to be our secret."

Anna Maria's chest slumps. If she cannot tell Paulina about the composing, perhaps she will not rush to her now. In fact, her attention could be better used entirely. She picks up her violin case and rushes out of class, toward her room, toward her manuscripts.

Cecilia's seat is empty the following day. Anna Maria does not ask why.

———

The moon is bright and round in the sky, illuminating the cathedral domes, the pillared chimneys.

Cool night air floods Anna Maria's face as she cracks open her bedroom window. It slides an inch before it hits the bars. She has been woken again by her nightmare. So she stands, peers down onto the courtyard, tries to calm the thrumming pulse in her ears. The courtyard seems so much smaller than it used to, the single tree in the middle no longer a giant but something sweet, scalable. Below, the streets are bathed in a deep shade of blue. Curving glass lamps throw a soft glow over the cobbled stones. It is silent but for the coo of pigeons nesting in the bricks below her room.

After a moment, footsteps break the calm. A *bolleghieri*, a lamplighter, emerges in the alleyway next to the courtyard, carrying a wooden ladder. He fixes it against the wall, clambers up, and extinguishes a flame. He is sprightly and muscular, his sleeves rolled up over strong, veined arms. He's probably just old enough to be called to the war in Corfu. How long until he must leave his family to fight? What strength will he need to face his mortal enemy and win?

Her body starts to ripple at the edges as she watches him. She rushes to her desk, pulls her candle closer, tugs her manuscript book open. Her soul, like a knot, begins to unfold. And out the notes pour.

After her private lesson the next day there are only a few minutes to spare. They pack away their things and then walk together to the biggest room at the far end of the corridor, where the orchestra rehearses.

A thought has been scratching at Anna Maria for the past hour. Moments before they reach *figlie* practice, the words burst out of her. "I want to be first violinist."

He looks at her, amused. "You remind me of myself," he says. "And I'm not surprised. You have the talent."

She sucks in the praise, feels it light up her chest.

"But there are no first violins before sixteen in the *figlie di coro*."

Two years from now. She will be average, normal. This cannot happen. This will not happen.

"That's too long," she says.

"I agree. But what to do? Every violinist in the *figlie* wants the role, and we have a fine first as it is. Besides, it is a highly responsible position. Are you sure you would want that much work?"

He has started walking again. She has to skid to catch up to him. "Yes, I'm sure. You said it yourself, I stunned at the audition. I've earned my place in this orchestra. If I can get into the *figlie* early, why not this too? I want to be the first."

His eyes meet hers. "Focus on your practice and compositions for now. If you keep improving . . . well, we shall see."

Friday, and her hands shake as she reaches for the door handle. She is clutching a piece of parchment. Her entry for the composing competition. She cannot wait until the deadline. Not when this music is in her grip. This piece which is so absurdly alive it threatens to leap off the page and roar.

"An early submission?" he says, looking impressed as she hands it to him.

"A draft," she lies, for it is as perfect as she can imagine. "I wanted to hear your initial feedback."

He lays the manuscript in front of him on the desk, bends toward it, hands splayed on either side.

The year is growing warmer, heat baking the pathways outside the Pietà, the fireplaces in the music rooms cleaned and emptied for the season.

His eyes rush from left to right at astonishing speed, taking in the tumbling scales, the golds and browns and greens. Reading it over his shoulder she has to close her eyes or risk lifting off into another world completely. Pride flows through her. This is her work, her notes. And for the first time ever, she is showing them to someone. Not just to someone. To him.

After several moments he looks up. He places his palms together on top of the parchment. It almost looks like he's praying.

"What do you think?" Anna Maria says.

The air stills. What is it? Why won't he speak?

"Anna Maria," he sighs, "this is a competition to work with me, on *my* compositions. I am not looking for originality or individual flair. You must find my voice and mimic it if you want to win."

Worry shifts deep in her stomach.

"I don't understand—"

"This sounds nothing like me," he says, smiling, handing it back now.

She frowns. Originality, she assumed, was a good thing. It is with originality that all music is created, surely.

"I can see what you are doing. The story of the young boy leaving his job as a *bolleghieri* that you have scribed in the margin is compelling, and the horns make it feel grand—they are a great signifier of war. But you must learn my language. You must find your way into me, beneath my skin."

He stands, comes closer. She feels a finger on her chin, her eyes brought up to his. It sends a shiver through her.

"I know you can do better."

Her heart is hammering, jolting from beat to beat. His palm is on her cheek now. It feels cold against her face.

"You will stay here tonight, study my work, my style, my intensity. Improve upon what you have shown me. It is not too late, Anna Maria; the competition closes on Wednesday."

She nods. It is all she can do.

When he is gone she breathes deeply. Her feelings are jumbled, sloshing around in her stomach. There is shame that she misunderstood the task, and confusion too. She stiffens at the feeling of his touch, which still ripples through her body.

The sun beats into the room, overwhelming and bright. She turns to the desk. She picks up the quill and draws long diagonal lines across the pages of composition she has shown him. Her stomach starts to growl with hunger but she ignores it. As the sun sets across the lagoon, she pulls his sheets of ideas from the back of her book, spreads them out before her, and starts to read.

The next three nights are torture. She doesn't sleep, hardly even eats. Last night she heard Paulina playing her oboe in the classroom next door. Stood against the wall for a moment, ear pressed to the brickwork, letting the sound engulf her. She wanted nothing more than to run down the hall, to sit with her and watch her play. But the secret cannot be shared, and this opportunity is so important. So she dragged herself back to the desk, to his music, willing herself to go on.

Tonight, the third night, she is starting to realize something. His music feels different every time she plays it. In the piece that she is currently studying, she starts to see he is building relationships between the instruments by using related keys—groups of notes that form the harmonic foundation of the piece. This helps to bring out the story, the character.

At first when she played the piece it seemed like there was just one character. She saw a girl dancing in a square. But yesterday when she studied the cello part more closely she realized it was actually two. There was a boy, with some flowers, waiting for her in the corner. The violin and cello started to converse. And now a whole cast is exploding out of it. There are more children, there are adults, and it is not a square but a ball, a grand dance between them all.

She pulls her teacher's work back toward her now. It's so . . . different. There's an anxiety to the music. It is frenetic, even crazed in places. He takes the notes on an unexpected journey, creating anguish rather than harmony, surprise rather than calm. She's never thought that compositions could be so liberated, so expressive. It's like he is from another century.

She lets the music wash through her mind, the colors lifting her off the floor, through the window, gliding her over the rooftops at great speed until she comes to the end of the section and there is no more.

Because these are snippets, pieces. More a collection of ideas than a full composition. They are in need of completion. She imagines herself in his gold-buckled shoes, his velvet blazer. Looks down and sees his body in place of hers.

Maestro, she thinks. Let's finish this.

14

Wednesday afternoon. The *figlie* have spent their practice running sections of his compositions while he has been hunched over the desk, scanning their work. The windows to their music room are cracked open in the heat. Sweat glistens on Anna Maria's neck, pools between her thighs.

The piece that she handed in this morning is on the top of his pile of papers. She can see the pattern of her notes, watch the way the colors lift off the page. But his expression gives nothing away.

"You will all stand." There's the creaking of chairs, the rustle of instruments being placed in their cases. "The following girls will step forward.

"Anastasia della Pietà," he says.

The girl a few seats down from Sanza shifts. Her violin clips the chair as she puts it down, steps forward.

"Bianca della Pietà."

Bianca is standing opposite, oboe clutched in her hands. She looks almost mythical with her white-blond hair and sharp features. She turns to place the instrument on her chair and steps forward confidently, but her hand moves to her neck, rubbing it as she stands and waits.

He does this sometimes, splits them up. But it can mean different things. You never know if he's calling because you've won or failed.

"Anna Maria della Pietà."

It's like a hand has clenched her insides.

She will not meet anyone else's stare. She steps forward slowly, as if onto the frozen lagoon, the water licking the ice beneath her feet.

He snaps the book he has been reading from shut, throwing up dust particles which dance in the air.

Only three names. Then could it be . . . surely this means . . .

"The three of you will work with me on the upcoming concert composition. Congratulations."

Victory shoots through Anna Maria's veins. She looks down, imagines his buckled shoes on her feet, and beams.

He has chosen a story from the Book of Judith as inspiration for the piece they are helping to compose. Judith represents Venice, and Holofernes represents the general of the Turkish army. The finished piece will be an oratorio, which is like an opera but intended for a concert instead of a theater.

In the story, General Holofernes is sent by the Assyrian king to Israel to besiege a town there. His army is about to conquer it when a young widow called Judith goes to him to ask for his mercy. Holofernes falls in love with Judith, which she indulges temporarily. But when, after a banquet, Holofernes drinks too much and falls asleep, Judith seizes her opportunity. She beheads Holofernes and returns victorious to her people.

Anna Maria loves the ending in particular.

For the past three weeks she, Anastasia, and Bianca have come to the music rooms every evening after classes end. The composing adds another two hours to their day, on top of four hours of practice. Anna Maria doesn't even think about food, about when she'll sleep. Her mind is in this world of battles, pushed beyond anything she's ever experienced.

Tonight the moon skims the sky, casting a rippling silver light across the lagoon. The campanile bells clang for the last time at midnight and fall into a silent slumber until morning.

Anna Maria is reviewing the recorder section they have just written. It is uncanny. With this instrument choice and these notes, they have been able to evoke a gentle breeze. Peace, moments before Holofernes will be killed.

They have decided they will use every tool that the *figlie* have in their arsenal for this piece: compose for an army of instruments. Some players will perform with more than one instrument on the night, as many of the *figlie* are competent in two or three. Anna Maria trembles just thinking about it, for it is sure to dazzle the audience.

Across the table from her their teacher is reviewing Bianca's work. The evening air is stiflingly hot. He tugs at the sweat-dampened collar of his shirt for the third time in less than a minute.

Across from Anna Maria, Bianca yawns widely, then her stomach grumbles so loudly it makes her laugh.

"This is a mess," he says, looking up abruptly.

Bianca's smile drops.

"This part in particular." The tip of his finger taps at the top bars on the page. "There is too much repetition, it isn't gripping enough. Not by far."

His face looks hot, flushed. Anna Maria wonders if she should run to the kitchen, find him something to drink, but knows better than to speak now.

"I'm sorry. I must be tired," Bianca says.

Irritation spasms at the corner of his mouth. Bianca is talking as if this is an everyday opportunity. Like the chance to compose with him is normal.

"Anna Maria." He turns to her now. "Bianca says she is too tired to play. What do you think? Are you too tired?"

"No," she says quickly.

"Anastasia?"

"No, Signore, not too tired," Anastasia says.

Bianca looks panicked, fidgets with her hair. "I didn't mean I am too tired, Signore. I'm simply a little hungry is all."

But his cheeks flush a deeper red. "You are splitting the solos far too equally. You are clearly striving for balance, some sort of equality. I am not interested in either. I want to startle; I want to dazzle. And this"—he taps the paper harder—"did you even consider changing the texture? Did you think about bringing more instruments in at all?"

"If I could run to the kitchen, return with a few rolls, perhaps," Bianca says.

"We will not leave this room until it is done!" His hand slams the desk. A sheet flutters to the floor. Anna Maria flinches. Does not bend to collect it.

She does not like Bianca—any other girl is competition and probably laughs at her behind her back. And she does not like Bianca's attitude toward this important task. But her teacher in this moment is a gale, spinning, gathering energy. She does not know what he might strike in his path. She wants it to be over. Wants to go back to a few moments ago, when all was silent but for the chiming of bells.

"Of course. I am sorry, Signore," Bianca says, bowing her head. A strand of her white-blond hair falls across her face, like a curtain closing.

But he paces across the room, wrenches open the desk drawer, and extracts a long, slim ruler. Anna Maria feels her heart slide into her throat.

The shock on Bianca's face as it breaks across her knuckles is the worst. Her eyes widen with every crack. Anna Maria has to look away. She tries to make herself smaller, invisible.

Not me, she thinks, flinching at the beat.

Crack. Crack. Crack. Crack. Crack.

"Stop, please!" Bianca is screaming.

"Leave, then," he shouts. "You do not have what it takes."

She runs, knocking her chair to the floor in her haste.

Anna Maria keeps her head down, her gaze a blur directed at the music. She has to put down the quill. Doesn't want him to see that she is shaking.

He stands, breathless for a moment. The air in the room could be snapped. He steps closer to her, comes to a stop with his palm across her manuscript.

She looks up slowly.

His voice is strained. "We cannot have an anchor about our necks. I am sure that you agree?"

"Of course," Anastasia says instantly, but his eyes remain on Anna Maria.

Anna Maria nods.

He softens at this, his shoulders lowering, the flush receding from his cheeks. "Precisely. This is far too important. You must be exhausted. Here." He bends down, slips a battered apple from his bag, holds it out. "Take this. I am sorry you missed supper. We shall continue this tomorrow."

Anna Maria's fingers glance over his hands as he passes her the fruit. He adds, "I insist, really. Get some sleep."

Anna Maria's eyes skip to Anastasia, sitting silently at the table, her hands empty.

"You may leave too," he says. But he does not reach into his bag, does not offer any more gifts.

Silently, the pair stand. On the other side of the door they do not look at one another, do not exchange any words. They both hurry silently to bed. Anna Maria's heart beats so loud it shivers the rest of her body. But then, lying on top of her blankets as the sweat pools around her lower back, she clutches the apple and feels a glow ripple through her.

The next afternoon as Anna Maria enters *figlie* practice she sees Elisabetta Marcini. She is standing in the corridor in a plum satin gown, whispering with Sister Clara. Anna Maria catches only snippets, enough to gather it is about the concert at her palace. Though years have passed since Elisabetta ignored her after that first concert, still Anna Maria scowls at her. She scans quickly for one of the rich girls usually in tow, but there is none today.

Once inside, Anna Maria takes her seat, leans forward, cranes her neck once everyone has arrived. One position is empty.

"Where's Bianca?" she says to Prudenza, who is sitting next to her today.

"Dropped," she answers, eyebrows raised. It makes the scar on her cheek wrinkle. "She was crying to Anastasia about it earlier. Refused to go to morning meal."

Anna Maria is staring. Prudenza adds, for clarity, "From the *figlie*."

"She's out of the *figlie*?" Anna Maria says in a tense whisper. "I thought once you were in the *figlie* you were here for life if you wanted?"

Prudenza snorts. "No. It depends on the Master of Music. Signore Gasparini dropped girls all the time. They were constantly holding new auditions."

It is like Anna Maria has been plunged headfirst into the canal. The room seems to close in on her, warping until it is black, endless. For a moment she hears a noise she has not heard since she was eight years old. A suck, suck, suck.

She had believed the *figlie* would protect her. That if you got this far . . . that those with skill were spared from a meaningless life, from the possibility of marriage. But now her mind is reaching back. Cecilia never returned either.

Dropped. The word thuds against her skull. And then a thought sends a shiver down her spine.

How was it, exactly, that her place became available?

She slumps back, silent. Shaking.

"Anna Maria?" Prudenza is saying.

But now he is here, unpacking his instrument, shuffling his music on the stand.

"I'm fine," she says, her voice as cold as she feels.

She looks at her teacher. She must do more, she must do everything in her power to protect her place here. She digs her feet into the floor, takes her instrument from its case, finds her focus, her resolve. Bianca sealed her fate with her poor work and careless words. One less member of the *figlie* is one less musician standing in her way.

"I have news," he says. "General Schulenburg sent word that last month our Republic has formed an alliance with Austria. Together we are overpowering the Turks. We expect Cyprus to fall any day now. By the night of our concert, we shall be victorious."

It is a fine summer's eve, the sky glowing lilac through the long stained-glass windows. As with the first *carnevale*—created in the twelfth century to celebrate the Republic's victory over Aquileia, a city in the northeast which was its enemy at the time—this is a jubilant night of disguise.

It seems like the whole of Venice has poured out, liquid from a golden chalice, into the Marcini ballroom. There is a buzz, an energy in the air. Silk dresses and velvet cloaks sweep the mottled marble floor. Elegant Murano glasses clink together. The waft of musk perfumes and sugared *frittelle* drifts around, and heads are topped with tightly ringleted wigs, adorned with lace and feathers and beads.

But who are these people? No one can tell. Every face is concealed, the masks so lavish that Anna Maria's eyes can barely take all of them in. Golden twigs and flowers curl over the eye of one, feathers in purple and blue adorn another. Some masks are slick and black with long dark beaks; others tinkle, bells dripping from the peaks above the eyes.

Anna Maria has seen *carnevale* from the windows of the Pietà, but she has never been part of it. It is decadent, majestic. It is everything she dreamed her first performance with the *figlie* would be.

The orchestra is positioned on the wide balcony that wraps around the ballroom from corner to corner. Their teacher stands at the north end of the room, on a small wooden box so they can all see him over the ornate balustrade. He wears a golden coat, his hair tied back in a matching ribbon, and a sleek black mask covers his eyes. He is rereading his music.

Anna Maria is with the violins and cellos; the singers are opposite them on the other side of the room and the woodwind players are at the south end of the balcony.

She drinks in the fabric-covered walls, the doors emblazoned with gold swirls, painted scenes. The room is a jewel box. It is wealth beyond which she could have ever imagined. And yet she is here with the elites. No longer a girl posted through a wall without a name, but Anna Maria della Pietà of the *figlie di coro*, performing music she has helped to write.

You belong here, she tells herself. This is your destiny.

Her eyes find the enormous chandelier in the center of the room, where more than two hundred candles flutter. It's adorned with multicolored glass flutes and tiny dangling orbs which chink together, shivering in the vibrations made by the chatter.

Up further now, until she's staring at the hand-painted ceiling. A girl has been drawn there. Blond curls, black eyes. She is holding a violin among a scene of clouds, the look on her face one Anna Maria instantly recognizes. Determination.

A hush ripples through the crowd, and General Schulenburg enters, cutting a line through the guests in his army attire. He wears a deep blue mask with silver edges. The audience fans out around him as he takes his position in the center of the room. He is greeted by Elisabetta Marcini, standing in a turquoise gown with a long train.

Anna Maria takes her seat, smooths out her black cotton dress. She is the smallest girl in the *figlie*, given that she is younger than everyone else. But she is growing fast, and in recent months it's like she's rediscovering her limbs. They are becoming so long, cumbersome. She's not always sure where to best place them.

She does the only thing she knows how to do. She concentrates on her instrument, the color of the music on the stand in front of her. When she picks up her violin and connects it to her body it all clicks into place. She is no longer simply human. She is something else, something more. She is complete.

Her eyes blur as the *figlie* start to warm up. The bows dance across the strings as if of their own accord. She starts running a passage, one of the most difficult in the piece. But as she does so her eyes catch on something that makes her left hand slip, makes her violin screech.

In the audience below, there is a girl with white-blond hair, a vivid red gown, and a crown of pearls on her head. She holds her mask in her hand, the ribbons trailing.

She is walking slowly, with effort, shoulders slouched as if something holds her back. She stops in the center of the room, near the general. Looks up in that moment. Looks directly at Anna Maria.

Her eyes are dark, sunken, shadowed with the purple of a grape. Anna Maria has to blink, shift forward to be sure. It is Bianca. In the audience, among the elites. What is she doing here, dressed like that?

Bianca looks to her right, flinches. There is a man at her side. A man too many years her senior. Large-bellied, gray-haired, a raven mask covering a black beard. He takes her wrist, pulls her toward him. He is holding up her mask, he is tying it too tight around her face.

"Bianca?" Anna Maria hears herself whisper.

Just days ago they were together, composing. And now she is here, being handled, touched, controlled by this man.

A wave of nausea pulses through Anna Maria as reality dawns. Bianca has been married off. Already. She is taken. Gone.

Anna Maria's heart starts to hammer, her grip tightening around her bow. She looks to her left, her right. The *figlie* are warming up still. She should play. She must play. She forces her hands down to hide the shaking.

There is no more time to think. Their teacher is raising his arms. The *figlie* hold their instruments. The audience looks up, seems to collectively inhale. And they begin.

Time becomes a blur. The audience gasps in delight when the girls put down one instrument for the first time and pick up another: violin to oboe, cello to lute. They build their defense, trumpets, clarinets, recorders, and bass joining the fight. An army of instruments, they march toward victory to the beat of the timpani.

The four voices—soprano, alto, tenor, and bass—are sung entirely by the girls, even though this is rare, even though females never normally sing these parts. A girl called Appolina takes the role of Holofernes, capturing the deep tones of the enemy though she is but sixteen.

The audience edges closer, hanging on every note.

Fear and excitement become one now. Anna Maria feels her body liquefying, blending with the violin. After these months of work every inch of her instrument seems to understand her, to bring to life her ideas, the tones and shapes she wishes to convey.

She draws her bow back and forth. She is in charge, controlling and emitting the emotions of these pieces with skill and precision.

Feel this, know this, she and her violin tell them. I will not fade quietly into the abyss.

The audience is moving, swaying. It is like the *figlie* have cast a spell. Five hundred of Venice's most rich and powerful submit. They freeze, entranced, for more than an hour as they perform. Until the last bow glides across strings.

The whole crowd stands in rapture, in applause. The feeling is headier even than a dose of laudanum. More potent by far. This love, this admiration. It is something Anna Maria has never felt, never known. It must continue.

Their teacher takes a small bow, then stretches out his arms, applauds his orchestra too. Pride swells in Anna Maria.

The applause gets louder and her teacher selects Sanza to stand now, her smile wide. It is hard for Anna Maria to watch her take a bow. Next he selects Appolina to stand, the cheer growing louder still. And then he does something unexpected.

He points to Anna Maria. His mouth inches into a smile.

Stand, he indicates, *stand*.

She is fumbling with her instrument; she shoves her chair back with a screech. And she is up, addressing the crowd, her fans, smiling at them, bowing, letting the glory wash over her skin and pour down her throat.

At the end she hangs over the balcony, sees his red hair weaving between the crowd.

"Thank you," he says. "The honor was all mine," he says. "That's most kind," he says. And beyond him a girl in a red dress is marched out, pearl crown askew. Anna Maria looks away as the man's fingers dig deep into Bianca's arm.

A *gazzetta* flutters in the breeze, threatening to escape the clutch of the boy who is running with it. He blows through the labyrinth of coffee shops and laceworks, past the churches and the butchers, until he is at the gates, panting, hanging on to the iron bars to gather his breath.

Sister Madalena holds out her hand. He slaps the *gazzetta* into it, accepts the silver coin in return, feels the gate smack his bottom as he rushes away. To his next hustle, his next chance to earn enough to buy his mother some bread, some medicine.

Their teacher is in the middle of his feedback on last night's performance when Sister Madalena walks in.

"It is here, the review," she says disapprovingly before stomping back out.

The air swells as they watch him read. Then a small smile ripples across his face. Anna Maria's heart pumps faster. He passes the *gazzetta* to Sanza, who takes so long reading that Anna Maria has to bite her cheeks, and then she passes it down the line. Anna Maria is craning her neck, reading over Prudenza's shoulder now because she cannot wait any longer.

It is written by a person called Jean-Jacques Rousseau, a writer from Geneva who says he has discovered a love of Venetian music during his time here. Her eyes focus on the following words.

The figlie di coro *have no equal, either in Italy or the rest of the world.*

Her heart hammers faster, she skids across the lines.

. . . music so voluptuous, so moving, it drove me to despair. I felt an amorous trembling, the likes of which I have never before experienced . . .

Is this real? Is he talking about her, her orchestra, her music? And then the last line.

The music was composed and directed by one who is sure to take his place among the greatest maestros in Italy. Ladies and gentlemen, I give you—

Anna Maria slumps a little. Her teacher's name stares back at her from the page. What would she have given to see her own! But there is time, she tells herself. It is coming.

The *gazzetta* continues its journey around the girls, passed between their excited chatter, gasps, and bursts of exultation.

"It was a remarkable effort," her teacher is saying. "I have been informed of a large donation to the music program from the governors. Our music worked. Our performance worked."

He looks at Anna Maria. She stares back at him.

It worked. It worked!

Her name is called at the end of class. She stays behind, shuts the door. There's a muffled silence, the *fortissimo* of the corridor diminished by the lock clicking shut.

"What we achieved this week was miraculous," he says, his pale gray eyes wide and excited, his hands clutching hers.

She stares up at him, the praise bubbling through her. The feel of his smooth skin makes her heart beat quicker.

He is saying, "I want us to do more. Much, much more. Just the two of us. It will mean gold for the Pietà, more concerts, more performance opportunities. It could be—"

"Yes," she says. "Yes."

He is smiling now. He squeezes her hands tighter. But then his face falls into a frown.

"You won't be able to tell the rest of the *figlie*. It will need to be our secret if this is to carry on." He lowers his voice. "There is a feeling, among some of the governors, that you should be focusing on your performances only, that—"

"That we should not be allowed to compose, I know."

He nods. "I disagree. I can see you have a skill, that there is something to be honed."

There is nothing for her to consider. She is the one who has been selected above all others. He is giving her an opportunity to develop her composition skills. An opportunity to be remembered forever.

She nods, serious now. She will keep this secret. Their secret.

———

Her mind is giddy with praise. She wanders the corridor, vaguely thinking she will head to the refectory, to her first proper meal in . . . she cannot remember how long. But first she must return her violin to her room. Tuck it in, make sure it is safe.

She rounds the corner. Stops abruptly. Sister Clara is standing outside her door with a smile on her face that shows off her large front teeth.

"Take a look and see, won't you?" she says, pushing back the door, answering the question on Anna Maria's face.

Anna Maria blinks, wonders for a moment if she's in the right place. There is an ornate handheld mirror and brush on her desk, pearl edges rippling with silver, blue, and purple. Scattered around it are colorful boxes tied with ribbons, flowers in a tall porcelain vase.

"What is all this?" she says, bewildered.

"Gifts, Anna Maria. From the concert attendees."

"But . . ." She is searching for the words, trying to understand. "They barely even saw me."

"They did not need to see you," Sister Clara says. "You are in the *figlie di coro* now. They could hear you."

Anna Maria walks toward the desk, takes the box closest to her. It feels small and weighty in her hand, like a perfect little rock. The ribbon it is wrapped in must be worth more than all of her clothes combined. She strokes it gently, soft against her thumb.

"Oh," Sister Clara says, turning back before she leaves. "And your first payment has been deposited into the official Pietà bank." She clicks the door shut.

Anna Maria slumps, speechless, onto the bed, the box still cupped in her hands. Her own money. Her own possessions. She places the box down, picks up the pearl mirror and sees her reflection. She doesn't notice how her features are becoming more intense and defined, her eyes bigger and darker. She sees only the girl on the ceiling of the ballroom. Staring down at her, hungry.

Forward, she tells herself. More.

15

April. Two pigeons on the Pietà windowsill coo, fluffing feathers until they are no longer birds but plump orbs with beaks. One twists and fidgets, the sun beating down on its body, finding that it is difficult to tuck its wings in on the ledge. It peers through the glass as it adjusts itself, round and round, each time spying a man with a shock of red hair and a teenage girl with long brown curls, hunched over a table inside.

Months have passed this way. After *figlie* practice, the two of them hard at work. Sometimes they can go through three candles right down to the stub, sunset swept beneath the dark cloak of night. When they hear footsteps in the corridor they have to stop, pretend Anna Maria is the one playing, and that he is the one composing. Sometimes Sister Clara comes to get her, says it's time to stop, says she needs to rest.

But they cannot stop. Not now. Not when what they are creating is so miraculous, so remarkable.

Sometimes an idea jumps from him to her without them even having to exchange words. She drinks in his notes, he drinks in her ideas, they dive down and drown in them, not even realizing the time. Her ribs are starting to show from the meals she keeps missing, but food is secondary, unimportant. They are inventing music that feels truly different and new. And Anna Maria is here at the heart of it. A collaborator. An equal. This, plus her performance schedule ramping up, and nothing can stop her now. *Maestro* beckons her. It calls out in her sleep. From there she is just inches from being an official composer. Her name will be remembered forever.

A blot of ink drips from her nib onto the parchment. She rubs her eyes. Pauses for a second on this thought.

She hasn't been able to work on her own compositions recently. There has been barely a moment to spare, what with practice and performances and helping him with his compositions. But he is so happy with her, so impressed. She needs to get through this phase and then she can get back to her work, her ideas, to developing her own voice in secret.

She stands, stretching now. Moves toward the window. She glimpses her reflection, icy and transparent. At fifteen, her face has grown longer and slimmer. Her eyebrows are thick and arched. She shifts focus, looking through herself to the world beyond.

A boat is on the horizon, white sails faded and ripped. A song floats toward her. Anna Maria can hear from the music that the sailors are Dalmatians. It is happy, upbeat. A folk tune she recognizes. They must be crossing back into Venice from the sea beyond.

She watches for some moments, imagining herself standing on that deck with the breeze on her cheeks, sailing over the horizon.

Now the boat is in the lagoon and she can see the men. Tanned, muscular arms pulling the oars to the rhythm, surrounded by stacks of timber, bags of salt piled high. The top crystals float away, casting a white dust across the sky.

She leans against the windowsill for a moment, head on her hands, listening to the melody drift toward her. Two strong beats followed by a weaker one. Bar, bar, bat. Bar, bar, bat.

She turns back to her manuscript, matching their rhythm to her notes, scribbling so fast her hand starts to cramp. He has not noticed, too engrossed in the section he is writing.

"My Anna," he says, cupping her cheek as she slides the manuscript across the table for him to review.

"Anna Maria," she corrects him.

But he is reading, he is nodding. He is skipping through the pages, his eyes rushing from note to note. He likes it. No, more than that. He loves it.

Maestro, the crowd cries. *Maestro.*

Anna Maria is allowed to leave morning prayer early the next day. She smiles, thinking of how her teacher favors her, how he extracts her from all other menial distractions. She is crossing the courtyard from the chapel, heading up to the music rooms to meet him, when a strange noise makes her stop.

She stares at the thick stone wall which backs onto the alleyway running down the side of the Pietà. There is nothing remarkable about it; nothing but a small hole in a shadowed nook, just large enough to fit a baby.

She approaches the hole, following the snuffle and squeak. Perhaps a bird has fallen from its nest.

There is a smell in the air as she gets closer, melding with the shadows. It is sour. Bad milk. Rust.

She wrinkles her nose, her eyes adjusting from the brightness of the open courtyard to the dim light of this narrow space. And then she sucks in her breath.

There is a creature in the hole. Human in shape, but so small that it cannot possibly be. It is naked and—she steps back—diseased. Flecked with patches of something dark. But she blinks, looks closer, sees that these are bits of dried blood, and something white like a yolk. She has never seen such a thing. So helpless, so small.

The baby is wriggling, its back scratching against the debris in the hole. And then there is a movement on the other side. A breath. Anna Maria looks up, her eyes meeting another pair, small and dark. And then a rush of fabric moving, the sound of footsteps running away.

Anna Maria is numb, her breath shallow. She reaches forward and slides the child out. Its face is soft, round. An idea not yet taken shape.

She holds it out in front of her like a shoe on a cushion. Walks quickly, frightened, to the nursery, where a sister takes it from her, tutting.

She must wash her hands, she thinks. She must go to her violin.

She walks back into the main building, her playing card floating into her mind.

The tears are warm as they roll down her cheeks.

June. She stands alone in a narrow stone corridor of one of Venice's greatest churches, the Basilica Santa Maria Gloriosa dei Frari, or "the Frari" for short. Her violin is in her left hand, her bow in her right. It is tapping the rutted wall, moved by her shaking hand. Each hit matches the beat of her heart.

Tonight she, Chiara, Sanza, and a *figlie* cellist called Rosanna will perform to over three hundred paying attendees. To be selected by him not only to compose but to perform in such a small group was a sure sign of her skill. But with moments to go until the concert begins her stomach is tightly knotted. She knows the music is good, that the rehearsals have gone smoothly and the pieces are as exciting as they had hoped. But still she feels the nerves, the pressure. So she had to sneak away, just for a moment. Find a quiet space to clear her mind before going onstage.

She takes a few deep breaths, focuses on what they will play this evening. They are performing the latest works she and her teacher have composed, and a solo each. The first piece is a concerto in D minor, written for three violins and one cello. They have followed a fast, slow, fast formula for the composition. The aim is to grip the audience from the start, then lure them into a sense of peace and calm, before electrifying their souls with the intensity of the music toward the end.

Afterward, for her solo, she will play *The Devil's Trill*.

Notes start to bloom, a landscape of purples and pinks that flows through her mind, making her breath slow, calm.

They will love us, she thinks, squeezing her violin neck a little tighter. They will.

She repeats these words until the quiver settles in her hands, until her heart returns to a gentle thud.

She turns, raises her arm to push the door open, when two women come crashing through it. She is shoved back against the wall, the pair of them laughing so hard one of the women has to peel off her silk glove and wipe her eyes. They haven't noticed Anna Maria, pushed back into the shadows. She opens her mouth to speak her mind but—

"When did he become so desperate?" the one with the peacock feathers adorning her hair is saying.

"Exactly," the one with the glove says, dabbing at her face. The tears have left a white line running through the rouge on her cheeks. "He can't make a large sum at the Pietà, why is he covered from head to toe in gold lace? And that ridiculous collar! He bears a frightening resemblance to my dog."

Her companion shrieks with laughter again. Anna Maria slinks back, listening.

"Apparently he has always been like that. I know someone who was ordained with him. Sniveling little creature, always following others around."

"Pathetic," the woman says, tugging her silk glove back on. It stretches almost to the shoulder. "And did you see the governor? Apparently his wife has no idea about his little affair . . ." Their conversation fades as they disappear down the corridor.

Anna Maria is shaking. How dare they talk about him like that? He is not desperate. He is remarkable, he is a *maestro*. She has a mind to go after them, but the door is opened once again.

In the archway now stands a woman, about a foot taller than Anna Maria. She is wearing an astonishing black gown covered in leaf-shaped gems. A smell, musky and expensive, threads around her. One hand is at her side, the other poised elbow to waist, hand relaxed as if about to sprinkle confetti on the ground. Her eyes widen as she takes Anna Maria in, her lips bending into a smile which points down on one side.

"Ah. The child prodigy," she says.

Anna Maria glowers at Elisabetta Marcini.

"Anna Maria," Elisabetta whispers now, coming closer, so close that Anna Maria feels the warmth of her breath on her face. "An angel sent from heaven itself, they say."

Anna Maria clutches her violin more tightly, feels the strings pressing into her palm.

"I'm no angel," she says, tilting her chin up. "I work hard, and I love music, that's all."

"Is it that simple?"

"It is," Anna Maria says.

"Well, you are certainly making a name for yourself."

Anna Maria breathes out quickly. And I made it without your help, in spite of your interference with my lessons, she wants to say.

Elisabetta sighs. Seems to have become bored. "Anyway, did Viviana and Francesca come past?"

Anna Maria points, disapprovingly, with her bow. "They went that way."

"Too kind." Elisabetta sweeps her dress behind her as she turns.

Anna Maria should let her go, but she cannot stop herself. She calls out, "Is it the same for the rich girls?"

Elisabetta slows, stops, looks back at her. Anna Maria grips her bow tighter.

"Those rich girls you fund. Do they work hard? Do they love music so?"

Elisabetta holds Anna Maria's gaze, seems to be deciding if she will speak. But then her name is called. She does not look back as she disappears down the corridor after the other women.

And now the door is opening again and—

"What is it?" Anna Maria snaps.

Chiara stands in the doorway.

"I'm . . . sorry?" she says uncertainly.

"Oh," Anna Maria says, "no, I'm—"

"It's only that we're due onstage any moment now."

"Right, yes." Anna Maria straightens her black cotton smock. "I'm coming."

"Very good," Chiara says, smiling gently before she adds, "Did I see Elisabetta Marcini coming through here?"

The distaste is thick in Anna Maria's voice. "She was looking for her friends. And calling me a child prodigy."

Chiara frowns. "Surely that's a good thing?"

"It was the way she said it." Anna Maria looks up at Chiara, but there is only confusion on her face. "Never mind. I'll follow you out."

"No, it's just . . ." Chiara moves closer, drops her voice. "These people have a lot of gold, Anna Maria. They are the ones who book us for the concerts, who make donations to the Pietà, who send the gifts. Having their support can change everything. We need them to love us. We have to play the game."

Anna Maria's nostrils flare. She wants nothing more than to tell Elisabetta Marcini exactly what she thinks of her. To run after her and spit on her perfectly silken shoes.

And yet she knows Chiara is right. She cannot make the elites her enemies, not if she wants to be *maestro*. She must charm them. They must love her.

She nods, just once, wondering if Chiara might be someone she can trust. Chiara smiles back, and Anna Maria feels a rush of energy.

She raises her gaze as they step out into the heart of the church. Three hundred seats stretch back in long, curving lines, and every one of them is filled. The audience moves more as a swarm than as a set of individuals. They waft and sway together, anticipating the start.

She, Chiara, Sanza, and Rosanna take their seats in the chairs that have been laid out in front of the choir stalls, facing the crowd. Behind them, the walls are lined with carved wood. Anna Maria is on the left, beneath a depiction of Christ on the cross. He is tinged with green, more corpse than human, a thin sheet hanging at his waist.

The thud of a door, hurried footsteps. Elisabetta Marcini and her two friends emerge from a side door and take their seats.

Anna Maria scans the crowd, just as always. She likes to breathe them in. She smiles widely, tries to meet as many eyes as possible. Play the game, she thinks. In the dim candlelight of the church this evening their faces look warped and eerie. She can pick out the features closest to her: a large nose on the man in the middle at the front, the wide smile of a woman toward the end, her teeth glinting against her dark curls. Behind her there is a gentleman in a red cloak, lit by the glow of a lamp.

"Who is he, second row on the right?" she says, leaning over to Chiara.

Chiara flicks a look at him as she begins to tune her instrument. "Tartini," she says. Ever the professional, not another word uttered.

Anna Maria's stomach jolts. Tartini the composer. Tartini, who wrote *The Devil's Trill*, is sitting here, in the audience, come to listen to her play. The nerves flutter up again, louder than before. But she does not, will not show them.

She connects her instrument to her body, begins to tune. The warm notes flow through her, releasing calmer, better thoughts.

Give him something to remember, she silently tells her instrument.

Their teacher steps out to the applause of the crowd. He is bedecked in gold velvet. His hand moves to his large, tight collar, tugging it away from his neck. Anna Maria doesn't care what those women say. He looks magnificent. He looks like a king.

He raises his arms to the four of them. They lift their instruments. Sound begins to reverberate around the cavernous space of the church, Sanza leading them in with a lively melody. Anna Maria imagined running through the streets of Venice when she and her teacher composed this, of sprinting behind blues and greens, reds and oranges, blasting between shops, through windows, and out of doors. Her heart pumps, fingers moving rapidly across the strings, not thinking, just focusing on the landscape of the music she has helped to build, of the energy she wishes to convey.

The four performers exchange looks every now and then.

172

An invisible conversation, of keeping the time and shape of the music. Though she wants nothing more than to be playing the lead part, the part that she helped to write, she does not think of it now. She simply leans forward, into the colors of the music they are spinning, until she is somewhere else entirely.

She opens her eyes when the piece is over and is, momentarily, surprised. She had almost forgotten about the church, the audience. But now her teacher beckons her and she is standing, and she is raising her instrument again, playing her solo, playing for Tartini. She closes her eyes and she is dancing with the devil himself. When she paints the final notes she is sweating, a few of the hairs on her bow loose from the effort. She scans the crowd, savors the vibrations of the applause, and then her eyes meet Tartini's.

He stands. He is looking at her. He is raising his arms higher, pointing them toward her, continuing to clap.

Her breath stops. The fine hairs on the back of her neck shiver. The famous Tartini is standing for her!

Instantly she looks to her teacher. He turns, bows to the crowd. Then he spots Tartini, notes that his praise is directed to Anna Maria. And it is not until he acknowledges this, until her teacher turns back and nods at her, that she feels the light shine through.

Three sharp knocks on her door. Anna Maria snaps her manuscript book shut.

"Just a moment," she says, tugging up her mattress and shoving the book into the space beneath. The door is already creaking open when—

"Yes?" Anna Maria says, trying to look innocent.

She had been reviewing a new idea of his, a sprightly tune complemented by cellos and flutes but which feels too repetitive at present.

Sister Madalena stoops into the tiny room, taking up most of the space with her huge frame. By the look on her face, she has just taken a sip of something sour. Perhaps the milk today is off.

She looks around the room, notes the floral vase on the desk, the pearl earrings and matching necklace in the open box on the floor. The latest gifts from admirers. She tuts, then says, "You have a visitor." She slips her swollen hands into her robe pocket, extracts a *gazzetta*. "And you are mentioned in this. Sister Clara asked that I bring it to your attention."

Anna Maria reaches forward for it, but as it touches her fingers Sister Madalena snatches it back. "I disagreed with her." Her eyes glance at the gifts again. "All of this attention is not good for a young woman. You will get ideas above your station."

Anna Maria's hand is still held out straight, because there is a knack to Sister Madalena. If you wait silently you usually get what you want.

"There is no room for pride, understand? Even members of the *figlie* get the whip when they misbehave."

Anna Maria nods sincerely. Sister Madalena grunts, drops the *gazzetta* on the bed, and stomps out of her room.

She reads that a record number of tourists visited the Republic on their Grand Tour this month, and that there is a disagreement over a new theater which is to open in the city. It will, the *gazzetta* suggests, only encourage more sinful behavior. Below is the latest review, which names her personally. It says that while the four selected *figlie* members put on a fine performance, it was her, and her alone, who stood out.

Pay attention, the review finishes, *for she is sure to be a star of Venice before long.*

Anna Maria rolls over on her bed, pressing the parchment to her chest as if to subsume it into her very skin. He has to let her go for first violin now. He has to.

She breathes the glory. In, out, in . . . Then she remembers. A visitor. She jumps up and, running now, heads for the entrance to the Pietà.

The sunlight from the street casts a line across the stone floor of the hallway. When she sees who is standing in it, she stops abruptly.

He is wearing a long red cloak, his face set with a hooked

174

nose, deep shadows under the eyes. One hand is on a sleek black cane, which he taps against the floor as he says, "Anna Maria. It is a pleasure to meet you."

Giuseppe Tartini is offering her his hand.

"You are my visitor?" she says, moving slowly toward him, taking his hand like it is a dove. Delicate, fragile.

He chuckles, nods, his laugh far kinder than his appearance. "I have come to congratulate you. I was enraptured by your performance last night. I felt compelled to visit, to tell you in person."

The world is brighter, hotter than seconds ago.

Smile, Anna Maria, smile wider.

"I admire you . . . I mean—your music," she stumbles, cursing herself for not being more composed. "I've been playing it for some time now."

He nods like this conversation is normal. Like her being here, speaking to Tartini, *the* Tartini, is the most natural thing in the world.

"You have a gift, my child. A oneness with the music. It is a delight to behold."

She drinks in these delicious words. Then she realizes she is still gripping his hand and blushes. He laughs as she drops it too fast.

"I won't keep you long. But I wanted to give you a small gift, a gesture of my respect for your performance last night."

Hanging over his forearm is something black, made of velvet. He holds it up and she takes it. The fabric tumbles down from her hands and sways. It is a cloak, with a tall collar edged in golden thread. At the center of the clasp there is a single stone. Though she has never owned one, she is sure from the colors it casts that it is a diamond.

Surely she can't accept something so expensive from someone she has only just met. Even though part of her does know him. Knows his music. Knows his language. Knows his mind.

He must see that she is uncertain, because he closes her palms around it. Says, "My dear, you played my piece better than the devil himself. Take it, please. I hope it brings you luck in future performances."

Heavy and soft, the cloak sways behind her as she walks back to her room. She touches the collar, the intricate embroidery. Her fingers move toward the diamond at her throat, and then she touches the wall, feeling the cool stone beneath her fingertips. Earthing her to reality. Reminding herself that this is real, that she is wearing a gift given by one of the world's most famous violinists, because she impressed him. Because she is Anna Maria della Pietà.

She takes the spiral staircase slowly, appreciating every twist, every detail of the walls and the railing.

And then she hears the scream.

She gasps, runs toward it. Reaches the third-floor corridor, her breath sharp. Who is hurt? What is happening? She turns the corner as one of the music room doors flings open.

Out of it flies a violin. It smashes into the wall, shards of wood exploding across the floor. Anna Maria flinches as the neck snaps like one of Cook's rabbits. A wave of music flutters out behind the instrument. Now the floor is a murder scene of notes and strings and she cannot bear to look. But she is edging closer, and she is peeking into the room, and . . .

Prudenza is on her knees, the scar on her cheek glistening with her tears, her teacher's hand in hers.

"Please! I'll do anything, anything. I simply need some help. I need—"

"Silence. Have some dignity," he says, shaking her hand away. "Your progress is mediocre at best. Would you drag the others down with you? Is that really what you want?"

Prudenza's answer is mumbled—Anna Maria cannot hear it. Next thing she knows he is marching toward the door, toward the exact spot where Anna Maria is standing. Blood roars in her ears. She has to leap into the next room, crouch by the doorway.

She is caught. Surely she is caught.

But she hears the clip of his shoes dissipating, the noise of

Prudenza following him into the corridor, crumpling to the stone floor. Anna Maria edges back to see what is happening. Does not realize that she is holding her breath.

"Please, Signore! You know what happens to girls who leave the *figlie*!" Prudenza screams.

She stands, following him as he turns the corner. But Anna Maria sees nothing more. She is running. Away from this noise. She will not go near it, will not let it infect her.

When she gets back to her room she slams the door shut. Lurches across the bed, making the vase shiver on the desk, and pulls the covers back.

She tugs her violin case close to her, wraps both arms tight around it. She is, she tells herself, still his favorite.

September. When practice finishes, his voice glides over the noise of the rest of the *figlie* placing instruments into cases, shuffling round chairs, talking about what might be for supper.

"Sanza, Chiara, Anna Maria, you will stay behind."

The three violinists from the Frari quartet in June. They look at each other quizzically. Perhaps there is a new concert they must prepare for. They shuffle toward him in a line.

The door closes, submerging them in silence. He is looking out the window. Hands behind his back, body rigid.

"The role of first violinist within the *figlie di coro* is one of the most coveted positions in the entire city," he begins. Anna Maria's eyes flick to Sanza. "After the conductor, it is the most significant role in the orchestra. It carries great responsibility. One must master complex solos, lead the tuning of the rest of the orchestra, and guide the tone and execution of the music for the entire violin section." Sanza stands a little taller, proud. "Needless to say," he continues, "it is vital the role is occupied by the best of the best. Today we will see who that is."

"Signore?" Sanza says quickly, her skin fading to gray.

He does not turn. "On-the-spot auditions are a fact of life for professional musicians. The person who deserves the position of first violinist will win."

"Wait just a moment." Sanza takes a step forward, then another.

Finally he looks at her. "If you still deserve the position, then there should not be a problem," he says. "Surely you would not want the role if you were not the strongest candidate for it?"

Sanza lowers her eyes, trying to hold back tears.

He looks to the group. "Gather your instruments."

Anna Maria's heart has been slamming against her chest ever since he said the words "first violinist." This is it. Her chance. First violinist will be hers.

Sanza is following him now, pacing rapidly. "Anna Maria is only fifteen, she shouldn't be allowed to compete."

Anna Maria glares at her, clutches her bow like a dagger.

"Anna Maria is one of the finest violinists in the whole orchestra, as you well know. Her age is irrelevant. She will compete."

Anna Maria marches forward. "I'm ready," she says, holding the curved wood up to her neck, widening her stance, raising her bow.

He takes a seat on the other side of the desk, knees pressed together. "One slow piece, something that shows your understanding of musicality and style, and one to demonstrate technique, speed, and virtuosity. Go."

Pressure shoots through her. She decides to play *The Devil's Trill* again. It's the one she knows best at such short notice. She imagines the devil, the colors, the intensity of character, and she begins. She is about two minutes in when he holds up a hand. But she does not see it, she is in her world, the colors shattering into a million fragments all around her.

"Anna," he says gently, "stop."

His words snap her back to the room. It's Anna Maria, she thinks, but stops herself short of correcting him.

"And now your second piece."

Dare she? There is something she was working on before their schedule ramped up, an original piece of hers. It is slow, alluring to begin with, but by the end it speeds up, as vibrant and alive as her mind. Without another second to decide, she plays.

Shades, bright and dark, rich and pale, shimmering in the sunlight, tumble toward her.

When she finishes his face is blank. She falls back in line.

Chiara goes next. She starts with a segment from their concert last month, which she plays with her usual elegance and grace. Anna Maria is transported by the notes, rapid and then serene, gliding through the room. They're easily as good as one another. The thought makes her stomach clench.

Chiara now moves on to her second piece, a concerto by Corelli. But her sheet music falls off the stand midperformance and though she bends to pick it back up, their teacher has stopped her.

Anna Maria feels a thrill shoot through her.

That leaves Sanza, her cheeks washed of all color. She steps forward begrudgingly, raises her bow, starts to play. But within moments his hand is up, asking for the next one. She begins a piece by Lotti but soon she is crying, tears dripping onto her instrument, and his hand is in the air again.

"Please, Signore," she is saying. "Please."

"Enough," he says. He stands, looking at them all. "Anna Maria, the role is yours."

Sanza rushes out of the room, her sobs echoing down the corridor. Chiara packs up her things, says, "Thank you, Signore," and leaves quietly, not catching Anna Maria's eye.

And Anna Maria is left, still in her wide stance, clutching her instrument and bow in her right hand, as the feeling floods her veins.

Power. Thick, delicious power.

He turns to her. Comes so close she can feel his warmth.

"You are the finest violinist we have, Anna Maria. Rules be damned, it is high time we let you shine."

And how I will shine, she thinks. Just wait and see how I will shine.

She is packing up, walking to the door, when he says, "That final piece you played was miraculous, by the way. Who is the composer?"

"It was in the pile of donations, anonymous," she lies.

It is not time to share that. Not yet.

"We should study it for inspiration, see what we might draw for a future concert."

Yes, she thinks. We should.

16

She feels every pair of eyes on her when she walks into practice the next day. The air, though summer is only just ending, is ice. Anna Maria has a strange sensation, like the walls are moving toward her, like the floor rises at her feet.

She tenses, focuses, will not let the feeling take hold. She walks toward the far left of the front row, where Sanza sits, arms crossed and furious.

"You're in my seat," Anna Maria says, staring her down.

Sanza growls, stands up. She spends far too long moving her music, her stand, arranging her instrument. Eventually she takes a seat in her new position. A one-place demotion.

Anna Maria looks straight ahead as she takes her throne. It is the same chair as the others, four simple wooden legs, a leather-covered seat with a few cracks in it. But not to Anna Maria. To her, this chair could be covered in gold, adorned with velvet and diamonds and beads.

She is first violinist! She is first violinist!

The dreamy glow stays with her right through class. He hands out her first official solos and they run a few pieces from the collection they are building. The glow is still shimmering around her when she walks toward her room after rehearsal.

Finally, for the first time in months, she has a little time to herself. She will close her door, work on her own compositions. She's been having an idea about spring. She can't quite place it, but she feels there is something there, in the most vibrant season of the year.

Then, a tap on her shoulder.

Anna Maria stiffens, seeing that it is Chiara. She holds a violin case in one hand, a leather manuscript book tucked beneath her other arm. But she is smiling.

"Congratulations, Anna Maria."

Anna Maria frowns. She looks over Chiara's shoulder to check if there are other girls waiting for the punch line, giggling in the background.

"And don't concern yourself with Sanza," Chiara continues. "She will mellow. Being in the *figlie* is not really about competition, it's about learning from one another. It's like a harmony—it cannot be created alone."

Anna Maria does not lift the frown. Not yet.

"The Frari concert was special," Chiara is saying. "Tartini stood! And your audition. Well, bravo. There is a lot I can learn from you." She places her hand on Anna Maria's forearm. There is something calming about it. "I am not your enemy, Anna Maria, I promise."

Anna Maria stares at her for a moment longer. Chiara's expression is sincere. Anna Maria feels something inside her shift, a weight lifting. She can't help but believe her.

"I appreciate that," Anna Maria says stiffly.

Chiara nods. "Until practice tomorrow, then?"

"Until then."

When she is gone Anna Maria throws her head back. Her arms reach to the sky in silent exultation. She is running, skipping back to her room. The blues and yellows and golds of a piece start to tumble out, swirling around her when—

"Anna Maria! There you are."

He is edging through the crowded corridor, between the girls rushing to the refectory, his red hair in perfect ringlets. Arriving in front of her, he takes her arm, guides her to the side. His touch is cool, electric.

He looks over her shoulder, to where Chiara is disappearing from view. Then he pauses, considering what he's going to say.

"What is it?" Anna Maria presses gently.

"I . . . I would be wary of growing too close to the other *figlie* girls if I were you."

Anna Maria shifts. "What do you mean?"

"People think greatness simply happens to you. It does not. You have to work at it: you have to work so very hard for it." She is nodding fast, not blinking. "Do you think I have time for friends with a job as competitive as this?" He laughs at the idea. "What we are doing, what we are achieving, it is too big to be squandered. You cannot trust other people. Not when you have talent such as yours."

Anna Maria smiles. He is kind to look out for her, and the praise feels as luscious as ever. She's distracted though, the colors still surging around her.

"Anyway." He smiles a little awkwardly. "That is not why I desired to speak with you. I've had word of another concert, two months from now. A small party—the two of us will perform. It will give you a little time to become accustomed to your new position in the orchestra, and then this event will be the moment to announce you as our new first violinist."

"That's wonderful." She beams. But the colors are clashing and curling, starting to escape now. She needs to run; she needs to catch them. If she's fast she can just about—

"Are you coming?" he says. He is already some way down the corridor, waiting for her, looking back. "We will need to create some new material."

"Right, yes," she says.

She follows him, looking over her shoulder as the colors round the corner and drift away.

The following day after practice, some of the *figlie* are clustered in the corner, laughing, whispering among themselves.

Anna Maria hears her name called, looks up to see Chiara among the group, smiling, beckoning her over.

For a second, a crooked smile and deep hazel eyes swim into her mind, and a memory, of cawing like a bird on a rooftop.

Her heart lifts. The corner of her mouth creases up. She takes a step forward to greet her, to join them. And then she stops. Looks at Chiara, at the girls around her now.

No, she thinks as she closes her case, as she leaves, giving Chiara a polite nod. Not when I have talent such as this.

There is a commotion in the entrance hall the following week. Several of the sisters are clustered by the doorway, receiving something from a man with a cart.

"Bring a table," Sister Clara is calling, clutching one handle, Sister Madalena the other. "Out of the way now," she says to some of the younger girls, who are crowding by her side.

Anna Maria cannot see what it is, only that there are glimpses of something vivid in color. It makes her stop, hearing a note. It makes her change path, move closer.

The item is placed on the table facing the doorway, displayed for all to see. The girls are giddy, gleeful. "What are they?" "Who sent them?"

Sister Madalena waves them away. "Move, get back. You will knock the whole lot to the floor."

"They have been sent by the grand duke of Tuscany," Sister Clara answers. "The famed flowers of Florence. Dug from the soil and brought here, five days on horseback and boat."

Gian Gastone de' Medici. Anna Maria had heard that he was visiting, that he met some of the younger girls last week. Rumor is that he is a kind man, abolishing taxes for the poor in his territory, even ending public executions.

"They have been delivered here at great expense," Sister Clara says, puffing her chest out like a hen.

It takes Anna Maria some moments to find a gap in the crowd.

The flowers are like nothing she has seen. Upside-down chandeliers with five petals per stem, each one patterned and flecked like an eye. The smell is earthy, green, a hint of something spiced and soft beneath. But it is the color of them that makes her move closer, reach out her palm. A blue-purple so vivid it could be blown from molten glass. And a sound is coming from them, a single mellow note, smooth as cream. She stretches to glance the petal with her fingertips, to feel it move through her, when there are noises behind.

A gap has formed around Elisabetta Marcini. She is standing, staring at the flowers. She is staring like she has seen a ghost.

"What are these doing here?" she says, her voice trembling.

"A gift, Signora, the grand duke of Tuscany has sent—"

"Get them out of here," Elisabetta says before Sister Clara can finish.

"But, Signora, they are just arrived. They've come all the way from—"

Elisabetta looks at Sister Clara like she may snap her. "You question me? Do I not pay enough for this program, for this place?"

Sister Clara lowers her gaze, curtsies silently.

"I will be back in an hour," Elisabetta says, turning, leaving through the front doors. "They will be gone when I return."

Anna Maria is digging her nails into her palms. How can this woman be so cruel? Is it not enough that she cuts their classes, uses the music program for her own spoiled pets? Now she must take their gifts from them too? Anna Maria would follow. She would like to say, No, we will not move them. You can leave and never return.

But Anna Maria is not allowed out of the building alone. And so she runs, up the spiral stairs, watches Elisabetta from the window at the end of the first-floor hallway, her breath seething out of her.

Elisabetta is striding down the promenade, her silk gown skimming the pavement, pedestrians rippling in her wake. But now she has stopped, and she is turning, looking back.

Anna Maria has to press her face to the glass to be certain of what she is seeing.

Elisabetta is bent forward, a hand on her hip, her body shuddering. There are tears streaming down her face.

Anna Maria takes a step back. She watches a moment more,

until a dark feeling spreads through her. She turns, into the cold, small corridor, as the anger evaporates from her.

November. Flakes of snow drift from the milky sky, flurrying at the door of Caffè Florian, a coffee shop in the Piazza San Marco. Recently opened, it caters to the elites of the city, serving them hot drinks and delicate bites on silver trays. But it has been closed this evening, for a private event with wine and cake, to celebrate the birthday of a man called Giacomo Casanova.

Though it is but five minutes' walk from the Pietà, it is another world entirely.

Anna Maria is in the side room, tuning her instrument, listening to the polite chatter of the guests arriving into the main space with its red velvet benches, marble tables, and gold-framed paintings of Venice's most famous men.

She is wearing her black velvet cloak that, like a carnival mask, helps her to become someone else. The fabric, the diamond, they make her look like she belongs here among the city's social royalty. But her eyes move to the cabinet, to the perfectly round tarts adorned with cherries and the layered cakes with the glossed icing. Food that practically makes her drool. Food she has never tasted, never even seen.

Outside, people rush by, long cloaks casting ripples in the white dust, fabrics clutched tight to their bodies. Inside, the guests clink and sip from Murano glass flutes.

"Ready?" Her teacher pokes his head round the door. He spots his reflection in a large mirror in the hallway and stops, brushing a few flecks from his satin coat, arranging his red curls, before leading her into the room of guests.

They will play their Concerto for Two Violins in A minor, a piece they have been working on in the past month or so. It is split into three parts. The first section, the *allegro*, shows all the dash and verve their music is becoming famous for. It is a balance, as Anna Maria sees it, between beauty and virtuosity. The second, the *larghetto*, is slower, giving her and her teacher the freedom to spin their own variations, and then the finale offers a tumble of notes to speed things up again and, hopefully, leave the audience craving more.

It is becoming easier and easier to compose pieces like this with him now that she understands his style so well. This is just the latest in a string of new works they've made together. Playing them has become simpler too. She no longer needs to practice for hours each day just to master the technique. She can see the sheet of music once and immediately it will sound good when she draws bow to string. She will spend perhaps two weeks per composition mastering it before she is, like tonight, ready to perform.

Anna Maria bows politely to the room. About fifteen men and women have gathered, spun in lace and silks, adorned with feathers and beads.

She doesn't think much of their host, who has already drunk too much and whose hand is riding up the thigh of the woman next to him, who slaps it away.

"But it's my birthday," he moans, childlike, making some of his male friends laugh.

They say Casanova is an adventurer and author who has explored much of Europe. It sounds like the job of someone with grace and manners. That is not this man. He doesn't smile, he smirks.

It is a dramatic start, both of them seizing the breath of the attendees with the bold melody. Anna Maria is smiling, looking into her teacher's eyes as the colors explode, as they weave a tale through music. The molten sound of her instrument seems to pour from her own skin.

This, her first performance since becoming first violinist, is everything she had hoped for. The guests are charmed by the whirl of energy, a building theme that makes every one of them sit up in their chair.

She loves the way their styles complement each other when they play. Anna Maria is malleable. Her body moves with the music, swaying as it chases the hues and the shades. Her teacher, on the other hand, is more intense. Furious even: his legs snapped together, his whole being rigid as the instrument sings. It makes for great drama, this combination. Hot and cold. Earth and air. Day and night. Opposites, yes, but you could never have one without the other.

Casanova jumps up when they are finished, his white curls tumbling across his shoulders.

"Bravo, bravo!" he says, slinging an arm around her teacher's neck, making his knees buckle. Casanova towers above him, a bull to a calf. "But a word of advice, dear friend. You could try looking a little less . . . bound next time. One might think you in need of prunes to ease the obstruction."

The room explodes into laughter, her teacher's face flushing puce.

A rapid thud in Anna Maria's chest. She has stepped forward. How dare he speak to a *maestro* like this?

But Casanova slaps her teacher's back too hard, sending him into a fit of coughs, saying, "I speak in jest! In jest, of course."

The laughter continues. Anna Maria moves toward her teacher slowly, carefully. His breath is labored, but he does not look angry or tense. He is simply struggling. She watches him a moment more before placing a hand on his back.

"I'm . . . fine." He staggers between wheezes. "Gather our belongings."

Casanova is getting louder, more raucous still, feeding off the energy of his friends. "The girl, however, now, she is quite something. Easily better than you." He chuckles.

Anna Maria feels the blood drain from her face. Her teacher is remarkable, a genius. Why would Casanova say it? Why would he pit them against one another?

She does not hear the mumbled response: she has bowed her head, rushed from the room. Her teacher must have tried to make light of it though, because Casanova's booming voice drifts toward her, saying, "That's the spirit. Here." She hears the jingle of a sack of coins. "Thank you for your time."

Anna Maria places the violins into their cases. She will pretend she didn't hear the end of the conversation. There is no need to discuss it. Not now, not ever.

But when she reaches the exit her teacher is gone. She has to wait alone in the side room holding both their instruments, until Sister Clara comes for her, with worry moving cold through her veins.

The next day he does not come to rehearsal or private practice. The *figlie* are told they must wait for his return, are instead put to work. Anna Maria protests, but still she is made to stock the fireplaces with wood.

She builds the fires silently, jaw tight, thoughts churning like milk in a pail.

She must see him. She must do something. If she has made him angry, if she cannot fix this, she will be ousted. The fear lumps in her throat, in the pit of her stomach, heavy as the basket she grunts to lift.

She stands, lower back aching, and reaches the staircase. She lugs the wicker basket up another floor, ready to hurl the whole thing over the banister, to yell into the air.

Anna Maria can feel that he is back. His energy, tense, brilliant, moves through the corridors, catches her like a net, makes her stop. Now she sees him, walking through the busy entrance hall as she is coming back in from the chapel.

She calls his name, calls it louder now. She will speak to him, put this right, assure him that she is no threat. But he does not turn back. She follows him up the spiral staircase, quickly, urgently, her shadow dark against the cold stone wall.

A girl from outside the Pietà is waiting by the music rooms. Lace gloves, a bonnet. Another project of Elisabetta Marcini's, no doubt.

He sees her now, standing on the threshold.

"Close the door, Anna Maria," he says as the roar of water builds in her ears. "I have a paying lesson."

———

In the evenings, when he leaves for the day, he stows his manu-script book in the cupboard. Anna Maria sneaks in, checks what he is working on without her. There is little development, just a few bars that jar against one another most days.

An opportunity.

And so each night she takes out a clean parchment and, care-ful as anything, makes a copy. But in her copy there are new notes—notes that flow and meld like clouds skipping across the sky. She smiles, tucks these fixed versions back into his book.

She will solve this void between them, delicately, with devotion.

She takes his old parchment, his simple, broken ideas, and dis-penses of them in the fire. The winter passes this way.

March. Still he is cool, distant, withdrawn in their lessons. He barely looks at her, barely offers advice or encouragement. There have been fewer concerts over the winter, less demand for new work. He tends to reuse their old compositions. Anna Maria misses the collaborations, misses the late nights riffing together so.

Her bow is laid across her legs, which judder up and down as she waits.

She just has to keep her head down, she tells herself. To keep working hard, to believe. He will come back to her when he is ready. He has always had a place in his world for her.

Spring unfurls like a ribbon through the room; a warm, soft breeze.

Today is the last rehearsal until next week because auditions for the *figlie* will be held all day tomorrow. And though she has been a member for two years now, though she is first violin, she feels a tightness in her stomach. She looks around the music room to seven empty chairs. Three violinists, one cellist, two oboists, and a flautist. Dropped. Destined for a life of marriage or lacework, child-rearing or laundry.

And what of their own wants? Anna Maria wonders as he walks into class and, not looking at her, begins.

There is a queue outside the music room when she arrives today.

Anna Maria approaches, her velvet cloak swaying gently at her feet.

"What's happening?" she asks Chiara, who is standing in front of her, her manuscript book open in her arms, studying a piece of music.

"He's announcing who's been accepted to the girls who auditioned," she says.

Anna Maria's stomach lurches. She brings a hand to the collar, touches the diamond at her throat. She reminds herself how she got it. She tells herself she belongs.

"I thought they placed a note out to announce the new members?" Anna Maria says, motioning back to the music room.

Chiara shakes her head. "That was before. This is his way."

They watch as several girls pour out of the music room. Some of them look like they may vomit, some of them are crying. Anna Maria has to look away. She follows Chiara into the room.

There are seven new members scattered around. But Anna Maria sees only one. Her eyes move immediately to the young woman in the middle, with the dark blond curls and one piercing blue eye. Paulina is grinning back at her, her eyebrows raised in shock and delight, her oboe in her hand.

"I didn't even know you were auditioning," Anna Maria says, her voice high, excited as they leave class.

"I wasn't certain that I should, but he encouraged me to!" Two pink dots of pride flash on Paulina's cheeks.

Anna Maria feels a pang of jealousy but she forces it away. She was the youngest ever member, no one can take that from her. And Anna Maria's schedule has separated her and Paulina for so long, just when their friendship was starting to heal. Now, finally, they can be together again.

"I keep thinking of Agata, how she could have been audition-ing too," Paulina is saying. But Anna Maria stops, heat flushing her body. She can't hear that name. Can't think of that. Of her. "She would surely have made the *figlie*—"

"Have you met Chiara?" Anna Maria says quickly, beckoning her over. "Chiara, this is Paulina, one of our new oboists."

Chiara gives Paulina a warm smile as she approaches. "Hello, congratulations." They shake hands. "I'm headed to supper with some of the others. Would you like to join us?"

Paulina smiles, nods, turns to Anna Maria. "Are you coming?"

But Anna Maria is looking back, and he is leaning out of the music room, he is beckoning her toward him.

"You two go ahead," Anna Maria says, feeling her chest tighten.

Anna Maria slows as she reaches him. It is the first time he has looked at her properly in months.

"Come in, close the door," he says. He moves toward the empty fireplace, one arm resting on the mantel, and she follows until she is facing him. She is surprised to feel his hand come to rest on her cheek.

"You did well today," he says.

She stares into his pale gray eyes, lets the praise filter through her. She has missed these moments. She has missed him so much.

More, her mind begs.

"The summer season is coming. We will need new compo-sitions." His eyes flick away, then back to hers. "I have been working on some ideas, many promising leads. I wondered if you would like to help with them again?"

Something glints inside as she thinks of the copies she has been leaving him. He likes them, they have helped him.

She must say the right thing now, show him that this atten-tion is appreciated, that she honors his greatness above all else. Smiling, she places her hand over his palm. "I'd love to. Yes."

"You cannot tell anyone, you understand, it must be—"

"*Maestro*," she says, her head bowed, "it is our secret."

—

April. Tonight, like every night, she crashes through the surface into the depths of her dreams, violin tucked beneath her arm. The water curls around her, fading from greenish blue to a deep, sinister scarlet. An ache moves through her body as the colors start to change. It travels from the outermost edges of her fingers and toes to the center of her, until it is thrumming in the depths of her stomach. She clutches it, looks down to check how she is wounded. And then she notices her violin beneath her arm, a thin trail of red liquid pouring from one of the f-shaped holes at the front. Her hand rushes to the opening. To cover it. To stem the bleed. She kicks up and erupts into the night by the sheer will of this thought.

I will save you. I will save you.

She is heaving for breath; she is clutching her instrument. Beneath her the bedclothes feel damp and sticky. The moonlight filters through the window, illuminating her blankets. She sits up, pulls them back to see the stains the other girls have been getting once a month for years now.

It is not the violin that is bleeding. It is her.

She groans, but at sixteen her womanhood is no longer deniable. Her shape has grown curves, her limbs more slender and strong. Her hair is thicker, sleeker than the froth of curls she would wrangle as a child.

There's a tap at her door. She gasps, shrinks back against the bedframe. She cannot be found, not like this.

It creaks open. And into the gap, a slim face. The only face Anna Maria would ever want to see at a moment like this.

Paulina whispers her name in the dark, then says, "I thought I heard something from my room. It sounded like an animal being trampled."

There is a pause, and then, "It happened." Anna Maria's voice is small.

"Oh," Paulina says. For a horrifying moment she is gone again, and Anna Maria wonders if she will be left like this. But now she is back, and she is holding something in her arms. She hands Anna Maria a wad of cotton rags, folded neatly. "Here, place it between your legs."

Paulina strips away the bloodied sheet, then sits on the bed next to her. She raises her hand. Anna Maria flinches.

"Shh," Paulina chides. She starts to stroke Anna Maria's hair.

Anna Maria feels a knot in her stomach releasing in the gentle silence. Outside, the moon rises higher, bathing Venice in a silver glow.

Then she whispers into the darkness, "Does this mean they can marry me out of the *figlie*?"

"A girl as talented as you? I shouldn't think it likely." Paulina guides her shoulders back, until Anna Maria is flat against the mattress. "Quiet now, sleep."

And despite the fear, despite the tension, Anna Maria's eyelids flutter closed.

TRE

17

Some six miles from Venice, cushioned between the silty shores of the mainland and the thick wall of the peninsula, lies the island of Burano. It is a simple place. Quiet, unvisited. Damp-stained shutters creak in the breeze, a moat of corn and weeds grows at its edge.

Here in the mud-clad backwaters of a narrow canal, a small body floats, silently, downward. The girl is just weeks old, wrapped tightly in a pale shawl which begins to unfurl in the depths. Gently, softly, like breath.

There is no spectacle, no commotion; no person turns back to save her. She simply drifts into syrupy dark, a thick muck, her final resting place.

Her tiny body reaches the riverbed. The sediment does not ripple.

A spring breeze dances in the air above, nudging a ripped piece of parchment which is floating on the surface. Its scribbled message is now just a smudge of ink caught in the sun's glare. No one will ever know what it said. No one will ever remember. There is no hole in any wall here.

The note skips and twists in the wind, until it becomes entangled with a scum of bubbles and dirt, swept onto the dusty earth at the canal's edge, and trampled under the boot of a young woman hurrying north along the banks of the water. A snow of blossom flurries in the air around her, dancing, chasing her as she runs. She does not see the girl drifting deeper, deeper in the canal.

The woman's breath heaves as she approaches the door. She is skinny-legged, barely eighteen, employed at the laceworks for two years now.

A sister stands at the threshold of the large brick building holding out an expectant hand.

"Do you think that you are special?" she is saying. "That there are not a hundred more like you that I can hire?"

The woman hangs her head in shame, mumbles her apology for being late. She hands over a coin, her payment for the privilege of working here, and is dragged into the building by the shoulder. It is the last daylight she will see today.

Inside, hundreds of women sit in rows, hunched forward over individual wooden desks, divided into factions. Sketchers and cutters and stitchers and joiners, pinners and those who prepare the final works for sale. They do not look up as the woman pulls on her cross-backed apron. Silence is ordered here.

The woman takes up her needle and thread and begins.

Tug, tug, twist. Tug, tug, twist.

She is a stitcher, forming the first white loops on the net, the edge of one of four hundred roses she'll craft today.

Tug, tug, twist. Tug, tug, twist.

An hour goes by, and her hips begin to ache, her bottom numb against the hard wooden seat.

Tug, tug, twist. Tug, tug, twist.

Another hour and she clicks her neck, rolls back her shoulders, hushes her bladder that is prickling to be relieved. They get one break a day, she needs to be strategic.

Tug, tug, twist. Tug, tug, twist.

Nine hours later and she is wiping her strained eyes, blinking against the amber candlelight. She needs the money, with a husband lost at sea and an ailing elderly mother. She reminds herself of this. Her eyes will never grow accustomed to the darkness.

Tug, tug, twist. Tug, tug, twist.

A bell tolls and she looks up, breathes a sigh of relief. She holds in her hand a bouquet of roses stitched with threads of pure gold, almost realistic enough to sniff. They are pinned and joined until they form a Burano lace shawl, one of the most coveted items available in the Republic. The lace is delicate as a butterfly's wing, as if threaded with air itself.

She stretches up to see it, now at the far end of the room. She would like to lift it to her shoulders, dance about in it for a moment, imagine herself as the woman who wears, not makes, this garment. But that instant it is snatched from her view.

Tomorrow she will return, stitch the very same again. And the next day, and the next. Years will pass, until the promise of the tug, tug, twist will drive her toward her late husband's small, cracked boat. She will sail out, toward deep water, a storm from which she will not return. Her last moments, as she howls like the wind itself, as lightning splits the sky, will feel, to her, like freedom.

Now, though, the rattle of a wonky wheel turning on the dirt path outside cuts the silence. The shawl is folded into fresh linen, packed carefully into a wooden box, and lifted onto the cart waiting outside. The woman's name, her work, will never be recorded.

The man tugging the cart is yelling now, telling the sisters to hurry, to pass it over, that he needs to make the last shipment back to Venice and that now he will have to run. It will hurt, knees weak as his are, but if they hurry, if they are quick, he can just about make it.

He is sweating, dragging the heavy wooden wagon, the wonky wheel making his job twice as hard. More than once he has to lurch, to stop the whole thing from tumbling over, to save these precious shawls from sinking into the dirty, festering canal.

"One more to come," he calls out at the docks, passing women repairing nets, great piles of them like hair from the ocean.

He hurries toward the cog, rocking gently on the water. A

bead of sweat flicks from his dampened brow, lands on the box of shawls.

It is with a huff that the captain holds down the gangplank, that he waits a moment longer than planned.

On the horizon, Venice is a flat, silent land, the islands like discarded clothes floating on the skin of the sea. But as they draw closer, it changes shape. It is lifted into mountains of sound.

The canals the strings, the islands the body, vibrating and melding, clanging and whistling. A giant instrument of a place. The sounds lift off from the Republic, float toward the ship, inbound with its cargo.

The pluck of a tooth being pulled from a mouth, the squeak of a marmot laced with a chain. The slug of a drain being drenched of its muck, the cheer of the crowd by the tall shadow box. The clink of coins: one *soldo* a look, the whispers of tellers spewing fortune and luck. The rustle of seeds drifting out of wood baskets, the screams from the inmates in the bowels of the palace. The shriek of a blade being sharpened against stone, the click of a lock as a man stumbles home.

The captain follows the sound, higher, higher, until the spring breeze catches in the sails above his head. They become billowing silk, the finest ball gown he's ever seen. His sailors huff, muscles flexing against oars. He chuckles to himself. They will be there in record time.

A gaggle of boys, lanky, scruffy, loiter at the harbor in the Bacino di San Marco, awaiting a job.

"I need only three," the captain calls, and he points out his choices. He can tell the trustworthy ones: it's all in the eyes.

The tablecloths are to go to the Marcini villa, the gloves to the Mocenigos. The cuffs and handkerchiefs make their way to the Rialto market. The final box, complete with the shawl, he will deliver himself.

The breeze follows the captain, an element with its own personality, ruffling the feathers of clucking chickens, blowing blossom across the pavement, cajoling scents high into the air. Carrying the box before him, the captain breathes in the smell of oranges, lemons, tomatoes from the market nearby. But now he turns a corner, toward the butchers, the slaughterhouse. He grimaces as the smell of vegetables melds with that of iron, of flesh. He shifts the box under one arm, tries to cover his nose, but there is a squeal, a snort, and he presses himself against the wall just in time to let the pig tear past him. It is a soft creature, wide-eyed, pink as a baby's skin. Its ears are flicking in fear. It is pursued by a black dog which is snapping at its tail.

The pig is young, clever, intent on living. But it is surprised by the captain with the box leaping out of the way, by the butcher who emerges the same second from his left. Straight on, the pig runs, straight through the slaughterhouse gates. There is a clatter as the wooden door shuts behind it, and now a banging, a squealing, as it is forced into a pen.

Inside an orphan, but this one a boy. No violin, no oboe, no music for him. At ten years old he must bottle blood and render fat, clean the carcasses and supply the butchers. He leaps out of the way as the pig comes tearing in, drops the glass bottle he was holding, crying out as a shard slices his thumb. He shuffles into the corner, holding it to his mouth to stem the bleed.

The pig, the boy knows, did not eat its slops this morning before it ran, before the commotion, before being chased in the streets by a dog. He knows because he is attentive to it, because he worries for it, because he has grown to care for it so.

It is for this reason that he looks away. That tears spring to his eyes as the pig is forced down, as the knife is drawn, as the neck is sliced.

When the butcher shouts at him to stop crying, to hurry up, he does not pause, does not waver. He knows the pain of the belt too well. Feels it already, the sting of it across his hands. He bolts toward the creature, bottles the blood that drips. He snatches his tears away with the grubby back of his sleeve.

The captain huffs, tuts, wipes the mud that has spattered his coat in the commotion with the pig. He sets off again, past the perfume shop where the orphan boy will deliver the fat later, past the master perfumer who will churn it with freshly cut jasmine, plucked at dawn for the finest scent. The essence—of pig, of flower—will marinate for a day, then be distilled into fragrance. The captain passes the woman who will buy it, walking her small dog. She will pour it into a jeweled pomander, dab it onto her wrist, waft it about so that others will comment. She will use it for a week before she tells her maid to pour it into the street.

The breeze blows east now, tracking the captain's steps. It catches a ribbon, fluttering, snagged against the spiked iron bars of a window he passes. The breeze sends it into the sky, high above the captain's head, dancing among the scents of fat and jasmine, of orange and tomato, of iron and flesh and death. It is red, silk. It toys with the smells and the breeze, chasing the captain through the labyrinth and onto the promenade. He reaches his stop. The Ospedale della Pietà, overlooking the lagoon. He knocks, waits, hands over the box. He gives a specific name.

In the sky above, the ribbon meets a note. A sultry, velvety blue, drifting out from a barred window. It spirals with the ribbon until the spring breeze softens. The ribbon falls from the air into the path of a small child. She might be four or five years old, elegantly dressed in a satin cap and lace-lined smock.

The girl stops, bending down, delighted to collect her gift from the sky. But as she straightens up, breath labored from her game of skipping and chase, it is the velvety notes that catch her attention.

The girl moves closer, clinging to the bars she stands before, her eyes following the sound. The wistful melancholy of a violin drifts out of a window from one of the upper floors of the Pietà. A figure can be seen pacing back and forth. She is slim with long dark hair, known throughout the Republic to be but seventeen years old. And though she is human what she is playing is not. This is something else, from a dream or a memory or a distant land.

The child's fingers grip the iron gate more fiercely, her knuckles whitening with the effort. The sound makes her want to leap into the land of the ribbon: leap right up into the sky.

A hand on her shoulder and the child's mother is with her now, staring up, following the notes to their source. "What have you found, little one?" she asks. But the violin, not the child, provides the answer.

They stand there, frozen by the sound. It is like the mother is hearing her hopes and her dreams. This young woman, this angel in the window, is delivering a story. Her story. She sees her life stretch out before her. She sees the memories she will make, the choices she will face. She grips her daughter's shoulder tighter, listening to her desire to watch her flourish and grow. Her eyes are filling with tears now, just to be here, just to hear this. The music develops, it swells and grows, and she sees her own death. Sometime in the distance, peaceful and calm and kind.

When the music finally stops, the mother emerges from this trance to realize she and her daughter are surrounded by others. Some are lace-gloved, satin-cloaked. There is a captain from a boat. Others are in scruffy rags, blood-spattered aprons. Citizens of Venice, drawn to this building, to this window, by this young woman. Their souls have been spoken to; their stories brought to life.

"Who is she?" one of them whispers, edging closer to the bars.

And another, from somewhere behind them, answers, "Her name is Anna Maria della Pietà."

18

The note said he would be away for a week. To Rome, for business.

Prepare the showstopper from your figlie *audition* was scribbled in his frantic scrawl and delivered on a torn piece of parchment one night. So Anna Maria has spent this time practicing without him. She plays in her room, there being no real need to go to the music rooms if he's not there. Both the *figlie* rehearsals and the private tuition are less frequent because he is in such demand. She glides back and forth, running the same few bars again. Habit means she still stretches backward at the spot where he taught her, where her hand used to contort into a claw. But now her fingers are long and slim. She can reach every note with ease.

She is smiling, realizing that this piece no longer requires the concentration it once did. Something has changed in her this last year. All she has to do is let her instrument and body lead the way and her mind relaxes completely. It's the same with the *figlie*: they are playing at such a high standard now and performing so often that they do not need to rehearse for each event specifically.

A shriek, and then another, sails up from the courtyard below. Sounds of the younger girls inventing games of chase and tag. Anna Maria's fingers move faster, faster across the strings.

With this time away from her usual schedule with him she has been able to play and compose freely. She has discovered new quirks in the music she has known for so long, begun to reacquaint herself with the shreds of ideas she is often too busy to pursue. She wakes each morning at the first light of dawn, the promise of her creativity launching her from the bed.

She finishes, sweat on her brow, and places her violin in the open case on her bed. A fine silver chain around her neck falls forward as she leans down. She straightens, stroking this gift from a stranger, wondering how much money must be in her account by now. She imagines great mountains of gold, light shimmering off their peaks.

A soft breeze flutters through the window. The half playing card that lies on her side table wafts onto the floor. She spent last night clutching it, inspecting it again. A key to some unknown door. Then frowning, whispering, "No, please," as the water of her nightmares started to pool around her feet before she was dragged beneath the surface.

She bends and plucks it up from the gap between the wooden planks. Tucks it into the pocket of her cloak which is hung across the back of her chair.

She turns to see her door creaking open.

"Only us," Paulina says, poking her head inside. She looks a little paler than usual. She is holding a wooden box. "This has been sent for you, Sister Clara asked that I bring it up."

Chiara ducks in next to her, closing the door carefully behind her.

This has become a regular occurrence—the two of them checking in on her each day. Perhaps to ask a question about the upcoming concert, or to gather some advice on a section of a new piece they are trying to master.

"Thank you," Anna Maria says, lifting the lid, seeing a delicately crafted shawl, decorated with roses, woven with gold. "Could you place it over there, with the others?" She points to the corner of the room, where several boxes are stacked one on top of the other. Each of them bearing a crest. A product of Burano.

Paulina places it down.

"What were you playing before the *Trill*?" Chiara asks. "It was beautiful." Her eyes move to the pile of manuscripts on

Anna Maria's desk, the mess of notes and pages strewn across the floor between the velvet jewelry boxes, lace-lined handkerchiefs, a turquoise jug made of Murano glass. Other items that she has been gifted of late.

Anna Maria's stomach twists. She begins shuffling the parchments together quickly. How can she have been so careless? She has managed to hide them without discovery for years. But today she has been distracted, caught up in the music. She hadn't realized they were left out, plain as day for anyone to see.

Paulina crosses her legs on the bed, starts smoothing out the creases on Anna Maria's pillow. She looks up, expectantly, for an answer. There is an awkward pause, Anna Maria still shuffling, trying to think what to say.

She looks at the wad of manuscripts in her hands. Thinks of what her teacher once told her. That she cannot trust the others, not with a talent such as hers.

But then she looks back at Paulina, one eye wrinkled and shut, the other bright and dazzling in the sunlight. This is her oldest friend. And she is finally back in her life. Chiara has always been good to her. What is the point of composing if she can't share it with them both?

"Can you keep a secret?" Anna Maria says.

"Yes." Chiara edges closer.

Paulina looks her most excellent when she hears the word "secret." Her smile lights up like a lamp in the shadows. "Always," she says.

"My Anna," he says when he arrives back on Monday.

She cannot remember the last time she corrected him on her name. More than a year has passed, but the cool reception she received for the Caffè Florian concert haunts her still. She cannot risk it again. She needs him on her side. Besides, it is just a word, just a name. It doesn't matter anymore.

Though he is eighteen years her senior, time seems to have warped and then snapped. They are no longer simply student and teacher but friends, equals. She plucks a stray feather from his jacket, takes his violin case from him and sets it down. "Why don't you take a seat? You sound a little breathless."

He nods gratefully as she pulls a chair up beside the instrument cabinet, allows her to move around him, taking his coat and bag, making him more comfortable.

"Shall we begin with the showstopper?" she suggests. It is two days until the next concert, which will take place at the Barbarigo Palace. She is keen to show him the speed with which she can now play the piece.

He sits up, excited and intense. Doesn't seem to hear her. Rome was energetic, alive, he says. "I was inspired, Anna, inspired more than I have been in months in Venice. I created an entire piece by myself while there—that is, a piece just for you."

He is leaning down, tugging out some parchments from his bag.

"Thank you," she says, surprised, taking the music. The paper crackles in her hand as the sound pours from the sheets.

The start is cheerful and mellow and simple. Her lips tighten, looking at these introductory bars.

"Play," he is saying.

She places the music on the stand closest to him, collects her violin, and begins weaving this easy tale, trying not to let her expression give away her displeasure.

He is nodding as the notes come.

But then the music becomes stronger, more dramatic. She has to focus, lean closer, her hands working harder with her instrument. Here is that intensity she first noticed in him, that she identifies so strongly in herself. A heat rises as she plays and the colors, finally, start to emerge before her eyes.

"A little lighter there," he says, eyes closed as he listens. "Let that note really sing . . . that is it, like that."

The piece in its entirety is complex. It is multifaceted. It is her.

"What do you think?" he says, eyes wide as she finishes.

She looks at him. "I love it. Truly. Thank you."

He stands, moves closer, takes her face in his hands. His palms are cool against her skin.

"What did I do to deserve this angel?" he asks, his voice filled with awe.

"I'm not an angel . . ." she begins.

"It's like you have lived a life already. How is that? How can you be so expressive, so wise in your playing, when you are still so young?"

She cannot explain it. It's just something she feels. It's something she's felt since she first picked up the violin at eight years old.

"It is like I had been painting the same picture, over and over again, and I didn't even know I was doing it. A flower, simple and beautiful, but just a flower. And then you came along. This wild little creature, you showed me that beneath the flower there were leaves, around it there were trees and mountains, rivers and birds. You showed me the sky, Anna. You showed me God Himself."

He is so close she can feel his heat. She is still here, still his favorite when so many girls have lost his trust, his respect.

Keep going, don't stop, her mind begs. But he sighs, pulls back, starts to pack his things.

She stands frozen for a moment, the loss of his touch pooling inside. But as he closes his violin case she finds that she feels proud. He hasn't even checked the showstopper before the Sunday performance, such is his trust in her ability now. And a thought follows now—if they are sharing individual compositions perhaps this could be her chance. After all these years, and with this bond they have built, perhaps now is the moment.

"Actually," she says, "I have something to show you too."

From her violin case she plucks the piece she has been working on this week. It is hidden, tucked beneath an edge of fabric which is coming away. She unfurls it, straightens up holding it in her hand, and then stares around the room.

But he is already gone.

Venetians pay a premium to live on the Grand Canal because of the smell. In the maze of streets and canals in the city the stench wafts, warm and putrid most of the year. But here on this wide snake of water, the air is fresher, cleaner. The sweet perfume of spring flowers from the palace gardens and salt from the ocean float on the breeze, through the open windows of the palace Anna Maria now stands in, overlooking the gondoliers sailing by. She cannot imagine how much it must have cost the Barbarigo family to buy a property like this, the entire exterior set with mosaics of Murano glass in green, blue, and gold.

It is Saturday, and she stands at the end of a narrow corridor next to a tall window with lead squares. She is running the final notes of the showstopper in her mind, about to step out into the ballroom to greet her adoring crowd, when Paulina appears at her side.

"I need a moment."

"Now?" Anna Maria says, looking quickly to her friend, then out to the audience through the archway, then back.

Paulina is biting her lip, her cheeks pink with worry.

"Fine," Anna Maria says, "but quickly."

They squeeze past the other members of the *figlie* and slip into a room on the left filled with gold-framed portraits. The fabric-lined walls muffle the sound of their voices. "Don't worry," Anna Maria begins, placing a hand on Paulina's shoulder. "It's normal, nerves pester me before the performances too, but the crowd—"

"It's not that," Paulina says.

"They loved me even more than I expected and—"

Paulina grabs her by the forearms. "Anna Maria, you're not listening to me. I am not nervous about the concert tonight."

"What is it then?"

"It's my menses," Paulina whispers. "They didn't come this month."

Her hands drop to her lower stomach, cradling it. Anna Maria looks at them. It is like the air has been sucked from the room.

"Oh." Anna Maria's voice is more high-pitched than she means it to be. "Well . . . I think that can happen, I think that sometimes—"

But Paulina is shaking her head. Her voice is quiet, small. Her head hangs as she adds, "They didn't come last month either."

Anna Maria holds Paulina's stare. Her friend gives a nod, a small movement that shatters everything.

"Don't cry," Anna Maria whispers as tears roll down Paulina's cheeks.

She lifts her hand, wipes them dry. Feels the sensation she has felt all her life: that Paulina is her sister, a part of her, that without her she is incomplete.

And suddenly she can feel something lingering in the room with them. It is a shadow, a presence, deep and sinister as a blackened canal. Watching, waiting to rip them apart once again. She is thrown back to the *infermeria*, to clutching a lifeless hand, to whispering another friend's name. Three notes follow. Scarlet, bronze, honey brown. A shiver moves through her. She urges the thought back into the darkness.

"We'll find a way, we'll fix this," Anna Maria says.

"But how?" Paulina whispers.

The clink of a bell calls them to the stage. They are ripped apart from this moment. Three hundred sets of eyes watch them. Three hundred sets of eyes demand brilliance.

Smile, Anna Maria. Smile.

She takes her seat in the soloist position at the front of the small wooden stage, the rest of the *figlie* forming a semicircle behind her. Her heart is pounding. Paulina is . . . She can't even think it. She will be put in Correction. She will get the whip. Worse than all that, she will be dropped from the *figlie* forever.

Anna Maria can't lose her. Not now. Not again. But the audience is watching and she must give them what they want. She must focus.

He is in front of her.

Ready? his look asks.

She takes a sharp breath, nods. He lifts his arms. The orchestra swells, the colors start to shudder through Anna Maria and around the room. Her violin bumps along one string, and then she stops, feeling her stomach twist. Because suddenly she realizes something is very wrong.

What is happening? What is this music? Her eyes snap to him, horrified. He is playing Corelli. It is not the showstopper from her audition. It is not *The Devil's Trill*. It is not the piece she has learned.

What is it? he is asking her. *Start playing.*

But she shakes her head. *This is the wrong one. This is the wrong one.*

Their silent conversation, one of widened eyes and subtle movements, lasts only seconds. He keeps conducting, driving the *figlie* toward Anna Maria's entrance. A part that she has played only once, at a concert two years earlier.

This cannot be happening. Not now. Not with Paulina's news. And on top of this there is a flicker of a thought. Tiny, almost imperceptible, in the back of her mind.

Did he do this on purpose? Is he punishing me still?

As with all her concerts, she does not have the music. She could rush back, try to see over Chiara's shoulder. She could stand. She could run away. But there is no time. There is no time at all. The *figlie* are repeating the first bars, they are waiting for their first violinist.

The whole world seems to narrow to a tip, until it is just him that is in focus.

He nods at her. *You know it. You must do it. Now, Anna Maria, now.*

By now the audience can see what is happening. The welling in Anna Maria's eyes, the way her hand has started to tremble.

She does the only thing she can think to do. She closes her eyes. Takes a deep breath, pushes the world away from her. She lets the notes engulf her, lets them pour down her throat until it is them that she is breathing. And with this action she transforms. She moves to a different time, where things as explainable as notes and words do not exist. It is like touching a painting and finding that your hand slips into it, that you can step through the frame, explore the color and texture of its world from the interior. She is no longer outside, no longer looking in.

She does not dare to look when they finish. She plucks open one eye at a time, feels the moment swell and warble. She blinks. The audience are on their feet. There are feathers and jewels tumbling onto the stage and people are crying. They have journeyed with her. She has given them a miracle.

There is a crowd of at least fifty people at the palazzo gate when they try to leave. Locals, tourists, who have heard her music flowing through the open windows and been drawn toward it, gulls to a fish market.

"Anna Maria, Anna Maria," they chant, the stench of their bodies pungent in the heat.

They reach out, try to touch her. She can hardly hear from the roar of voices, hardly breathe for the crush of bodies closing in. Someone grabs her cloak, tugs her back. She chokes on the clasp; Chiara has to smack the hand away. Anna Maria grabs for Paulina and pulls her through the throngs of people grasping, calling her name, until Sister Madalena bats them back, and she and the other sisters form a protective shield, escorting them back behind the gates of the Pietà.

"They are deranged!" Anna Maria says, huffing for breath, staring back at them. Some of the locals are rattling the bars.

"They're just excited. They think you are a gift from God Himself," Chiara says.

Anna Maria groans, leads the way back to her room through the cool, dark corridors. Inside, one corner of her desk is piled high with ribboned boxes. A bouquet of flowers stands, dry and gathering dust, in the vase.

She shuts the door and turns to Paulina, who has pushed aside a pile of silk wraps to make a space on her bed and is saying, ". . . incredible, Anna Maria, how did you know what to play? I felt like I was watching—"

"Who did this to you?" Anna Maria says, pointing to her stomach.

"Don't be fierce," Paulina says. "It won't help."

"Who did what?" Chiara looks concerned.

"Tell me who did this. We can tell the sisters, make a complaint." Anna Maria's palms are clenched into fists. The rage is moving through her body in bursts. "Whoever he is, he will not escape this."

"No, please. I don't want any trouble."

"You don't want any trouble!" Anna Maria repeats, high-pitched, strained. She could laugh if it wasn't so sick, if she wasn't so terrified.

The pair lock stares for a moment.

"Speak his name," Anna Maria demands. "Why protect him?"

Paulina's chest is rapidly rising and falling, her cheeks bright, flushed.

"Paulina?" Chiara says, edging closer, placing an arm around her. "What's happened to you?"

"A baby," Paulina says. Tears roll down her cheeks.

Anna Maria growls. She is pacing, her voice growing louder. "How can you be so foolish! This will be the end of you, the end of everything. When they find out you'll be dropped. God knows what they'll do with you."

"Anna Maria," Chiara chides. "Perhaps that isn't—"

"Do you think I don't know that?" Paulina retorts, like she has been stung. "I know that. But this is my situation. This is the way of things."

Anna Maria is hardly listening. "Perhaps we can do away with it somehow. There must be ways. Poison or some kind of instrument or—"

But Paulina is standing now, she is staring at Anna Maria. "'Do away with it,' like the world wanted rid of us?"

Anna Maria stops.

"I won't do such a thing."

Anna Maria opens her mouth to respond, but her stomach lurches, tumbles. For a moment she is deep in the canal, gasping for breath.

She slumps down onto the bed next to Chiara. Paulina joins

them. They watch as the evening sun fades to dusk. They let time spool out around them in the silence of this new reality.

Anna Maria wakes with a gasp.

At her feet, Paulina and Chiara have drifted off, the three of them curled on her bed like they are children still. Anna Maria stands, lights a candle, still early enough to be dark. She places it in the holder on the bedside table.

There is a second, as Anna Maria rocks Paulina and Chiara gently awake, when Paulina smiles. In the calm of sleep Anna Maria can tell she has forgotten. But now Paulina sits up, places a hand to her head, rubs it back and forth across her brow.

Chiara rearranges her dress. She is the first to speak. "Perhaps you don't need to," she says quietly, as if their conversation never stopped.

"Hmm?" Paulina says.

". . . do away with it," she adds, turning to Paulina. "We could hide it."

"Hide it?" Paulina says. "How can we manage that?"

"We live in an orphanage. Baby girls get sent through the wall every day. Hiding could work if we are shrewd."

"What about my bleeds?"

"We can fake them so the sisters won't know," Chiara says. "I've heard stories of girls doing it here before. And we'll find you looser smocks so the bump doesn't show."

Something flickers in Anna Maria's chest. Chiara. Brilliant Chiara has found a way to save her friend. She is nodding, hears herself saying, "You're so small anyway. When it's time we'll find somewhere quiet and deliver her ourselves. Sneak out in the dead of night and post her through the wall. No one ever needs to know she's yours."

Chiara says, "I think it's the only way to ensure you're not dropped from the *figlie*."

Paulina pauses for a moment, considering this idea. Then she looks at Anna Maria, suddenly a little brighter. "Her?" she asks.

"Yes, her. I have a feeling. It's going to be a girl."

19

A *gazzetta* arrives the next morning. It is a single sheet of parchment, printed from a handwritten note. Beneath the news that a new painting by Canaletto, entitled *A Regatta on the Grand Canal*, has been bid upon by Russia's Catherine I, Rousseau writes:

Last night at the Palazzo Barbarigo, Venice was handed a surprise. First violinist of the figlie di coro, *Anna Maria della Pietà, was well prepared to play Tartini's* Devil's Trill. *A diverting beauty with rich dark curls, you can imagine her surprise, then, when her conductor began playing Corelli's Concerto in D Major! The audience watched the horror unfold on her face as she realized what had happened. The confusion, the tremble. She was ready, but with the wrong piece. So what did she do? She closed her eyes, she trawled her musical memory, and she played Corelli. It was, most certainly, a gift from the Lord Himself. Each of us was left with one certainty above all others. Anna Maria has not her like, in this world or the next. There is nothing that can frighten her. She is the most talented female violinist Venice is yet to produce.*

Female violinist. Anna Maria rereads the last line several times, then thuds down on her bed. So strange, she thinks, that Rousseau singled out her sex. If she is the most talented let her be the most talented. Then her teacher swims into her mind and her stomach drops an inch or two, wondering what he will make of this review. It could threaten their relationship like the night at Caffè Florian. She cannot have that, not when she is so close to achieving everything she's ever dreamed of. *Maestro* must come next, and then she can publish.

But there is only one place at the top. Only one person can be the greatest. She brings her fingers to her temples, massaging the headache that is emerging there. Is this how it will be each time they perform now? Him versus her?

She scrunches up the parchment, tosses it under the bed. It is trouble, and she does not need any more trouble.

One month later, Chiara has stopped Anna Maria in the hallway between the *figlie* bedrooms, her smock bulging, her arms cradling a small bundle. She gives Anna Maria a look with her large dark eyes, one that suggests she should follow. The pair of them creak back the door into Paulina's room. Her oboe rests on the desk, quietly awaiting its next chance to sing. There is a smaller window than in Anna Maria's room, the panes cracked open to let in the afternoon breeze.

Paulina is sitting on the bed, one arm supporting her lower back, her dress pulled up to investigate her stomach. It has grown rounder, the skin more stretched and tight since their conversation that fateful night. It looks like one of the Republic's cathedrals, the navel jutting out like the peak of the roof.

"Put that back," Anna Maria says, hurrying forward and tugging down the material so the cotton sags around Paulina's tiny frame. This is the latest smock, stolen yesterday from Sister Clara's cupboard. It will last a month or so, and then she or Chiara will need to take another without being caught.

"So strange, I felt her move today," Paulina says, still staring down at her waist.

"Don't think about that. Just focus on keeping her hidden," Anna Maria says.

She helps her up, and then Chiara pulls out the bloodied cotton wad she had been hiding and tucks it beneath the covers, dabbing the sheets for good measure. Every evening, the sisters check their beds to make sure the red stains come at least once a month. Anna Maria and Chiara have been taking it in turns, rushing to Paulina's room and depositing their own soiled rags when their bleeds come, before the sisters have reached her. It's working so far, but Anna Maria can't help checking over her shoulder, her ears more attuned to every tiny sound, awaiting the crack of Sister Madalena's knuckles, the tap of Sister Clara's feet coming down the corridor.

"There," Chiara says, tugging the sheets back into position.

The church bells start to toll, a deep shade of purple rolling in through the window.

"I have to go," Anna Maria says, as it drifts and swells around her.

That night, Anna Maria sits next to her teacher sailing up to the gates of Ca' Rezzonico, a stone-pillared palace where they will perform tonight.

The world spins faster than it used to. Often Anna Maria has three or more performances a week, plus composition work for him, plus individual and *figlie* practice. This week alone she's played with Chiara and Sanza at the Pietà Sunday concert, performed for the king of Denmark, who is visiting Venice on business, and represented the *figlie* at a fundraiser for laceworkers who are in need of renovations to their factory. A twinge in her forearm is starting to pester her when she plays for an hour or more. But she does not stop, does not complain. With the new girls in the *figlie* she can't have anyone challenging her for first violinist. She's so close to *maestro* now.

The summer heat drapes itself around them. Her smock is damp under her arms and clinging to her skin. Her teacher sits with his hands resting on his violin case, knees pressed together, humming a tune. It is something new they have been working on, to release at an upcoming gala concert for the empress of Russia, who will visit the Republic soon. Anna Maria told him her idea about spring, and it has turned into a story of the seasons.

Music, she has discovered, can be molded like clay. With the right instrument and the right rhythm and tone they have been able to give character to the seasons themselves. They have discovered the delight of spring with a bouncy collection of notes, the soft breeze of summer with their sultry time signature, and the light and dark of autumn with variations in volume from the ensemble. The force and drama of winter is built through *tremolos*, a wavering effect created by the rapid reiteration of notes.

It is perhaps their finest work to date. He says it is everything he has been hoping for, that it could define an entire generation. She's even been wondering about asking for a credit. Chiara and Paulina have encouraged her, and it would help with publishing her personal compositions once she's named *maestro*.

Anna Maria pushes the thought out of her mind. Focuses instead on the sounds of their gondolier calling out, advising an approaching boat to wait while they round the corner, so the two vessels do not collide. They sail by one another in silence, water lapping at the edges of the boat, until they reach the entrance to the palace.

A doorman in a tricorn hat and gold-buttoned coat extends his gloved hand, offering to take her violin first. But Anna Maria will not part with it. Instead she gives him her own hand, clutches her case more tightly in the other. She steps onto land, careful not to let her feet touch the water.

"Five!" she says as they are leaving. The air bulges, heavy like it is ready to snap.

"You should be grateful to be so popular. I've heard whispers, Anna Maria, whispers of *maestro*."

Five concerts next week alone. It will stop her from composing anything of her own. She'll barely have time to work with him on their joint pieces. She'll have to lean on Chiara even more to help with Paulina's condition. And her arm is throbbing after that performance. The practice it will take for these concerts will make it scorch. But *maestro* is whispering, he says. It could be soon. It could be sooner even than eighteen.

"You're right," she says, "I'll do it."

They come to a halt by a short wooden jetty in front of the palace. But their gondola, which should be tied to the post, is nowhere to be seen. The sky rumbles and begins to sputter in relief, tiny droplets denting the surface of the canal, making it churn and spark.

"Quick!" Her teacher throws a hand above his head and rushes toward the cover of the entranceway. Anna Maria sprints to follow and they shelter in a shadowed arch. Chatter from the gathering upstairs filters down toward them.

Her teacher is panting, tugging out his handkerchief, anticipating the coughing fit that will surely follow. But when it does not come he starts to laugh. His red hair glistens with tiny beads of water, a spider's web in the mist.

She is laughing now too, shaking her arms of the droplets that have landed, until he lifts a hand, strokes her cheek. It is cool as always, the movement gentle. She breathes in, something flickering inside.

His hand moves to her chin, raises it until their eyes meet. He looks proud. She smiles. She should thank him for all he has done for her, for how he is helping her.

But before she can speak, a chill crawls under her skin.

His finger is tracing the thin, smooth lid of her eye. She flinches, her back hitting the edge of the arch. But he reaches closer, his other hand gripping her arm, holding her in place. His look is different now. Starved. A vulture circling its prey.

His finger finds the corner of her eye. It is a place that is intimate, raw. A place where she has never been touched.

Her heart speeds, something inside her breathes, *No.* She stiffens, shifts, but still he touches her. Still she is held.

The sky screams, the rain shattering the surface of the water.

A beat, and then—

"Sleep," he says, smiling awkwardly, pulling back.

There is a pale, crusted dot on his middle finger that was once hers. He lingers, his gray eyes searching her face.

There is something hot rising up her neck. She is, she suspects, supposed to laugh. She lets out a stifled sound.

Suddenly it is like the water has been sucked back into the sky. The rain stops. Anna Maria places a hand on the wall. Steadies herself.

Beyond the archway something shifts. Her teacher has not seen it. A figure turns, hood up, cloak swaying as they walk quickly away. *Stop, don't leave me*, she wants to say.

Their gondola, slick and black as tar, slides into sight. The air stings cold.

"You should get some rest," he says, wiping this part of her on his satin coat.

Anna Maria stutters her words. "You're . . . you're not coming?"

"I think I will walk."

And as she steps onto the boat, as she refuses to look into the water, there is a feeling inside that she cannot voice, that she is not even sure she can play.

That night she stands at the end of her bed. Paralyzed, momentarily, by what the darkness will hold. She pictures the rain hammering the surface of the canal. Feels his fingers on her and shivers. But then she shakes her head, forces the thought into the darkness to remain hidden.

He was simply helping her. Just as he has always helped her. Just as he will always help her.

When her head hits the bed, she is sucked like a pebble to the depths.

The lagoon looks like it is alive the next morning. It ripples from slate gray to bark to the silver of a coin. Anna Maria watches it. Terrified. Transfixed.

A few other members of the *figlie* have started arriving for rehearsal, setting up. Anna Maria turns as Chiara walks in. A knowing look passes between them.

She moves to greet Chiara properly, but then the floor thuds, someone large moving toward their room at pace. And before she has arrived, before she can speak, the dread has risen up in Anna Maria's bones.

Sister Madalena stomps into the room, her chest heaving. Her coif has been knocked back in her haste, a line of dark gray hair revealed. She has the energy of a bull huffing through its nostrils.

"Is it you?" she roars, lunging toward the cellist Rosanna, who gasps and is caught, as her skirt is pulled high above her waist.

She is struggling to push the fabric back down. "What do you . . . what are you talking about?"

Another girl calls out, "What's happening?"

Sister Madalena pulls the skirt back down, lunges for the next nearest girl now. There is some pushing, squirming between the group, to move back, to get away. Anna Maria is the one to be caught. She feels the cold rush of air across her stomach, Sister Madalena's large calloused hand press her center. Sister Madalena growls as she pulls back.

"Some girls were whispering in the refectory this morning. They spoke of a Pietà student with a baby in her stomach." She looks to Chiara standing by the door, a hand on the back of a chair. "Who is it?"

Chiara's eyes flick to Anna Maria, then she lowers her gaze. "I do not know, Sister."

"You," Sister Madalena says, turning, bearing down on Anna Maria again. Her hand closes over a clump of her hair, jerking it sharply. "Who is it? Who has the child?"

Anna Maria does not speak, just tries to shake her head, her heart slamming against her chest.

"Sister Madalena, if I may." Chiara has stepped closer, speaking softly. "I am certain it was just a story; you know how a rumor can excite the crowd. And besides, it cannot be a member of the *figlie*, we are all far too busy, too focused on our work."

Sister Madalena stares Chiara down, Anna Maria's hair still twisted in her fist. But she makes a noise, like she is satisfied with this response, and Anna Maria is released.

At the door, Sister Madalena turns back, eyes them both before she leaves. "Whoever it is, I will find her."

It is everything Anna Maria can do not to tilt her head back and scream.

Anna Maria stands in her room later that afternoon with Sister Clara, sweat gathering between her thighs. The heat outside is visible, it makes the stagnant air warble and shiver.

Sister Clara has taken to pruning Anna Maria's hair, powdering her face, while she practices before each concert. Her curls are piled so high on her head they make her neck ache. Many patrons send clothing for them for concerts, to make them look less like orphans. To make them fit in.

"This is ridiculous. I can barely move," Anna Maria says, lifting her arm to demonstrate how she is bound by the long sleeves of a tight satin gown. It moves only two inches from her waist. "How am I supposed to play?"

"Signore Dandolo sent it specially. You know he has asked that you wear it this evening."

"But I can't *breathe*," she says, feeling the pressure on her chest. "Let me wear my black smock and cloak."

Anna Maria leans across to where the cloak is hung over a candle mount on the wall, but Sister Clara slaps her hand away.

"The cloak is too masculine. Signore Conti has one practically identical, for goodness' sake. We need to show you off, you're a real beauty these days."

Anna Maria tries to contort her body closer to her violin. She doesn't have any more time to talk about clothing.

"There, you see, you can play," Sister Clara says. She moves closer with a little pot of rouge. Dabs at it, bloodred fingers reaching for Anna Maria's cheeks.

But Anna Maria growls, and with it one of the whalebone ribs in the bodice cracks, the angle too deep for the delicate structure. And she is tugging at the fabric, pulling the ribbons loose, and stepping away from the mound of satin, before Sister Clara can stop her.

All Anna Maria can do is focus. On her notes, on her world of colors. Her arm twinges as she plays, but she can't stop. Won't stop. The pain starts to flow toward her shoulder, and from there to the center of her chest.

When she enters rehearsal the following morning he is standing at the front of the room waiting for them all. There is a new manuscript on the stands. Anna Maria frowns. It's not one she recognizes. At a glance, the page is in his handwriting and covered in black, the notes tightly packed, racing up and down in sharp angles. The piece will be intense and fast. Normally he asks her opinion, normally they work on things like this together.

"Hurry up, take your seats, instruments out," he says, pacing back and forth now. There is an energy about him. She brings her violin to her throat.

He lifts his arms and they begin to play. They are hurtling through the piece when he turns to her. "*Presto*, Anna Maria."

Her stomach clenches. She blinks, focuses harder, forces her fingers to move quicker.

"I said *presto*, can you not read music? It says it at the top of bar one."

Her eyes flick to him, then back to the music. She is playing it *presto*. She is playing it faster than *presto*.

He starts to clap his hands, suggesting a quicker, even more aggressive pace. Her tendons are flaring now.

"Are you understanding me?" he says. "Faster, faster. Play it faster!"

The muscles in her lower arm start to scream. But she pushes further, for more, until the very last note. Until hand aching, heart pacing, she brings her instrument back down. Looks into his eyes. Sees him shaking his head slowly. Sees the eyes of the *figlie* burrowing into her, scavengers ready to feast.

She waits as the class filters out.

"I don't understand," she says now they are gone. "I was playing it as you asked."

He is sitting at the desk, his eyes fixed on the manuscript in front of him. She watches his chest move up and down.

"Chiara came to see me this morning," he says finally, "with a composition of her own. She asked if she might be considered to join our little team."

The fear rushes through her like a wave. How could Chiara do it? Anna Maria shared with her and Paulina in secret, a gesture of trust. She has gone and used it to her own advantage.

"You told her," he says, looking up now.

Shame bulges. "I didn't, I don't—"

His gaze flicks back to the desk. "I don't want to hear it."

"Please," Anna Maria begs, "I can explain."

His voice is louder, red rising in his cheeks. "I said I don't want to hear it! Just get out. Get out of my sight."

She can think of nothing more to say. The thud starts in her wrist, pulses through her body until her heart is a drum.

Chiara della Pietà has ruined everything. Chiara della Pietà will burn.

20

A handful of girls from the *figlie* are standing in a circle at the end of the second-floor corridor waiting for the arithmetic teacher, Signore Perotti, to arrive.

Of course Chiara is laughing. Of course she is stroking her sleek hair as the other girls crowd around her, smiling, listening.

The words fly from Anna Maria's mouth before she even reaches her. Words she's only ever heard other girls use, words she barely knows the meaning of.

Chiara staggers back, wounded by them. "What?" she breathes, her eyes wide. "Anna Maria, what are you—?"

"You told him!" Anna Maria is closing in on her now.

A flash of acknowledgment across Chiara's face. "Not here," she says, dropping her voice.

"Is everything all right?" one of the girls says.

"It's fine, give me a moment."

Anna Maria storms back down the corridor with Chiara in her wake, down the spiral steps, and out into the courtyard by the hackberry tree. Its leaves are glossy in the blazing sun, the branches spattered with small dark red berries.

"Anna Maria, I can explain . . ." Chiara says, stopping with her hand resting on the cork-like trunk.

Anna Maria whips around. "It was a secret, I told you it was a secret."

"I'm so sorry if I got you into trouble, I just thought . . ." She runs her hand through her hair. "Look, I've been in the *figlie* for years, Anna Maria. And I'm grateful, believe me. But he never selects me for the special opportunities. I wanted to try something new, something different. I thought that with your busy performance schedule and the composition demands on you both you might require more help. I thought we could work together. I've been developing some pieces for months."

"If you wanted to work together, you should have said," Anna Maria says, then adds, "and you've been working on pieces for *months*? Why didn't you tell me?"

"It's just, I didn't know if—"

"You didn't know if what?"

"You're so ambitious!" Chiara's hands fly up in the air. "You're on this mission to *maestro* and sometimes it feels like anyone who gets in your way be damned."

Anna Maria feels her body tense. "We're all pitted against one another every day. If we can't be great musicians, what else is there?"

"I just . . . I wasn't sure you'd let me speak to him about it."

"Why wouldn't I? What have I ever done to make you think I wouldn't? I've been nothing but a friend to you."

"I don't know, I . . ." Chiara pauses, looking pained, uncomfortable. "I got the feeling you would choose what was best for your career."

The truth of this stings, somewhere in the depths of Anna Maria's chest. Three notes rise up, flow toward her. Scarlet, bronze, honey brown. She is shaking her head, she is staring at Chiara as if she hardly knows her.

"Chiara, Anna Maria? What is this about—?" Paulina is hurrying as fast as she can across the courtyard, restricted by the weight of her bump.

"We're leaving. We can't trust her." Anna Maria takes Paulina's arm, starts dragging her, perplexed, back in the other direction.

"But, Anna Maria, we need her help, what about the baby, what about—?"

"Anna Maria, please!" Chiara calls.

Anna Maria turns so fast Chiara flinches. "Leave us alone," she shouts. "Don't come near us, don't come near me."

When she tries the music room door the next day it is locked. She is due to have her private lesson. It is straight after noon prayers every weekday. She rattles the handle, peers through the mottled-glass window, and feels a shiver pass through her. She can see a shadow pacing slowly back and forth.

Perhaps he hasn't realized she is here. She knocks on the door, whispers his name. But there is no response, no movement. She releases her grip, wanders slowly back down the corridor.

So she is being frozen out again. This is how it begins. And from here, being dropped no doubt. She feels dizzy, terrified. She needs to get back to her room, but she does not know which way to turn, which route is safe. She's never felt like she is drowning while awake, that's always been reserved for her dreams. But not now. Not anymore.

When she arrives there is a note on the desk written in his scrawl. A trunk lies open and empty on her bed.

Cardinal Giovanni Barbarigo requests your presence at his countryside villa. You leave this afternoon.

Paulina is in her doorway before Anna Maria can turn and run for her.

"I'm being summoned to the countryside. I don't know how long I'll be gone."

Not summoned. Banished.

"I can manage," Paulina says, a hand on hers. "Honestly. The baby isn't due for months and the smocks you stole for me are huge. I have the hang of it. Go, or you'll be in even more trouble than you are now."

Anna Maria can see from the way the pink is rising in her cheeks that her friend does not mean this. But they have no choice. She packs her things.

Anna Maria had dreamed of leaving Venice one day. Of venturing out to freedom, to inspiration. But Villa Barbarigo is not that. This huge complex, with its gardens and fountains, countless balconies and turrets, feels just as stifling as Correction.

She kicks at the perfectly pruned hedges as she walks down the graveled path leading away from the villa. There is the hum of monks worshipping in the distance, the heat of the sun beating down on her neck.

The voice behind her is smooth, that of someone sucking a sweet.

"When my uncle envisaged this refuge," Cardinal Barbarigo says, placing a hand on her shoulder, "he did not, I think, intend for it to be grazed by angry boots."

"Sorry," Anna Maria mumbles.

He pats her gently, moves away, through the gardens toward the pavilion.

The cardinal is not so bad. He spends all of his time praying. She is free during the daytime to wander the grounds, to explore the network of gardens. She could—she should—be practicing, composing, but she can see little point now.

Her evenings are spent at the far end of the salon, a long room with stone walls and ornate maroon rugs, performing their compositions while the cardinal's eyes drift shut and his staff fuss around him. His snores distract her from the colors, the notes.

She takes the curving stone bridge now, crossing the moat that leads from the main garden to Rabbit Island. The same route she has taken every afternoon this week. It's true what Sister Clara said when they were little. The islands really do exist.

She crosses her legs, sitting on the perfect carpet of grass, smiling as the fluffy little creatures hop across her lap. Until the smile fades. Until she remembers that their days are numbered. That a sharp knife and a chopping board await them all.

The thought comes with color. A bolt of red. She looks up, sees it hover above, calling her from the sky.

No. There is no point in composing anymore.

But then she thinks of Paulina, of the swelling stomach that she did not want. And with it comes a yellow. It rises up, joins the red. They begin to turn in the air.

And she thinks of herself now. Sitting on this island, a prodigy with nothing to show for her career, here only to provide entertainment for one very tired old man. It sends a pulse of heat through her veins. And that brings more shades, rising up from the moat, swirling in the sky. They call to her, spell out a melody, demand her to tug them from the air to a manuscript.

In an instant she is standing. She is running for her parchment, sending gravel bouncing into the air before any more thoughts can stop her.

At night she lies in the huge four-poster bed in her room, staring at her half playing card as a deep, feral dread floods her body. She tumbles into the water, the light fades to black. She spins and kicks and grabs but cannot see. She feels strings, sturdy beneath her fingers, and the slick shape of her instrument. She grabs hold of it, tries to pull herself up by its neck. But she is taken by the current. And every night she drifts further, further. She floats; she fades away.

Monday, midmorning. A crowd of thousands swells on the promenade, clapping and cheering, awaiting the doge. Today he will sail the lagoon and toss his golden ring into the water, signal the dominion of the Republic over the seas.

It has been only two weeks since she left, but it feels like everything has changed. Anna Maria stands at the bottom of the spiral stone staircase in the Pietà, the sound of the *figlie* floating toward her among the stomping of the crowd.

Why is the orchestra practicing at this time? And why without her? Her head thuds, overwhelmed by melding noises. She starts to run up the steps, her violin swinging by her side. She flings around the doorframe and into the music room. The sound stops abruptly. Paulina looks up at her, Chiara opens her mouth, other girls shift awkwardly.

"Ah, Anna Maria!" He lowers his violin, he is smiling, looking directly at her. Outside, the crowd screams. "I'm glad to see you are back. I trust your time in the countryside was pleasant?"

Anna Maria cannot understand it. She shoots a look at Paulina, who nods almost imperceptibly. Anna Maria tilts her head up slightly.

"It was . . . fine, thank you," she says.

He nods. "Very good, take your seat." He points to it with his bow.

So she is still first violinist, for now at least. She strides across the room, takes her instrument out of her case, clutches it close on her lap. Strokes the smooth wood with her thumb, hysteria rising on the promenade. The crowd has begun to applaud in unison.

Clap. Clap. Clap.

As he begins to talk again, about the piece they are currently practicing, she glances around the room.

"Are you all right?" Paulina mouths.

Anna Maria nods. And then her eyes slide down the row to someone new. A few seats from her there is a little girl. Little, in that she is slight of frame, but also little. Childlike. Anna Maria surveys her rapidly. She has a mess of black hair, olive green eyes. She can be only thirteen at most. Is she, could she be, younger than Anna Maria when she got into the *figlie*? What is she doing here?

They lift their instruments to play on his command, but Anna Maria is only half concentrating. Her ears push away the clapping of the crowd, the thud in her brain. They tune into the sound coming from the girl's violin. Luscious, sultry. A deep, vibrant red. It makes Anna Maria shiver. It sounds so good she wants to reach across and eat both violin and girl whole. Swallow them down in one delicious bite. Anna Maria doesn't even notice that the girl has stopped playing, that now she is simply staring at her.

"Is there something wrong?" he says, standing by Anna Maria's side, his smile curving.

Outside, a thick hair of seaweed slaps at the banks. The crowd begins to stamp, to howl. The doge is on the water. The doge is sailing past.

"No." Anna Maria snaps back to the room, stares straight ahead. There is a crushing feeling, of water filling her lungs. "Nothing's wrong. Nothing at all."

The ring glints, arching in the air. It sinks into the deep.

"Anna," he says brightly as she is leaving the room at the end of class. The frenzy of the crowd has dissipated at last. She turns back, moves toward him. "I've missed you."

It takes her a moment to hear him. Why is she not being dropped? Why is he not furious with her still?

"Listen, about Chiara . . ." Anna Maria begins.

His face changes, the smile fading. But he says, "It is in the past. It is forgotten."

"I didn't mean to upset you—"

"It is forgotten!" His voice is higher now. He moves, animated, toward the desk. "Now, we must return to our schedule. Your little excursion to the country has left us quite behind. You will meet me back here after supper."

"Are you sure?" she says. There is something odd about his demeanor. She would rather discuss how he feels so that they can move beyond it.

But he is scrawling notes on parchment again. "Hmm?" he says, not looking up.

She can feel her own work, bulging in her case by her side, begging for life, for breath. She is so close. She is so very close.

"See you then," she says, turning again to leave.

"Are you ever going to forgive her?" Paulina sighs.

It is August. A lazy heat lifts off the promenade and flows through the windows of Old Procuratory, a decadent apartment building framed by tall pillars on the Piazza San Marco.

Anna Maria is ripped from the colorful landscape of the music she is running in her mind back into the room. They have been asked to wait in one of the galleries, a cavernous space with paintings of men framed in gold on the walls. Her eyes snap open. "Forgive who?"

Paulina motions toward Chiara. She is standing at the other end of the gallery surrounded by fellow members of the *figlie*, quietly tuning her violin. Just the sight of her makes Anna Maria's stomach turn.

"No," Anna Maria says. Then she looks at her friend. "How are you feeling today?"

Paulina's hand rushes, instinctively, to her stomach. "I'm fine. Tired, aching. I felt her wriggling earlier."

Anna Maria pulls Paulina's hand away from her stomach, tugs her robes around her so they're looser. The bump is mercifully small, just like Paulina's frame, but Sister Madalena is still on the prowl. They have to be careful.

Paulina begins again. "She didn't mean to get you in trouble—"

"Enough," Anna Maria snaps.

She can't think about Chiara. Not now. Tonight they will play to the empress of Russia. The whispers are that it will be the finest celebration of the entire year. The audience needs her to be ready. They need her to give them everything.

The *figlie* will debut a piece Anna Maria and her teacher have been working on for more than a year. A story of delight and celebration, nostalgia and fury. A story woven late into the evening, night after night. A story of the seasons.

Paulina follows Anna Maria out of the gallery and up a narrow winding staircase. Anna Maria hears her diamond earrings clinking against one another, the latest gift from an unknown sender. Her hair is swept up into an elegant twist, parted at the front with curls framing her face. The rest of the *figlie* fall in behind them. They emerge onto a steeply tiered stage overlooking the ballroom. Anna Maria and the violins take up the first row, Paulina and the wind players are in the second, and the singers are high up above them at the top. He is standing in the pulpit at the front of the stage, his back to them, looking out over the ballroom, dressed in a white coat with silver embroidery and a large lace collar.

Anna Maria takes her seat in the middle as the rest of the *figlie* fold out around her, ink in water, and begin to tune. The warm tones of forty instruments communicating spread through the room.

Catherine I of Russia is magnificent, seated on a carved throne against the wall facing the *figlie*, bedecked with pearls.

Her brown curls are split so half tumble down to her waist, while the rest are piled high on her head.

He nods to her from the pulpit, and the empress, without smiling, raises a hand to acknowledge him. The audience fans out around her, dancing, talking. They look like birds of paradise, embellished in satins and silks in bright flourishing colors.

Now he turns toward the *figlie*, the tails of his silk coat whipping round with the speed. His arms are raised, he looks to Anna Maria, and they begin.

A polite murmur spills around the room as the yellows and greens begin to flow. The start is sprightly, as energetic as spring itself. The *figlie* fall back and Anna Maria begins to weave a trill of leaves. She watches the empress start to smile, letting the feeling flow through her.

They love me.

She closes her eyes, blocking the audience from view. But when she plays, Anna Maria is surprised she does not see the story she dreamed up. She is not watching leaves ripple through the air, nor the buds of summer basking in the heat. Now the notes are tumbling and the colors are whirling and a collection of memories starts to race before her. She sees Paulina's stretched stomach. The way she cowers, clutching it when the child kicks. She sees Chiara, her betrayal melding with a churn of violet and puce from the music. And she sees herself, standing outside a room, watching a shadow pace as her hand shakes, gripping the handle. With this thought something inside her is shattered, broken out of this place. The light crackles and sparkles as she rises, dancing with her rage. She looks down, sees the audience swirling beneath. And Catherine watching her from her throne.

She soars higher, higher, until she places a hand on the roof, watches it crumble at her touch. She tugs it back with one hand, tearing at the wood and brick until a crystal sky appears above her. She breathes in the cool air, sucks the colors into her lungs, lets them pour back out. And then she crawls through, takes off. Upward, onward, with such clarity it calms her very bones.

Until it is done, and it is over, and she is drawing her bow across the strings. She snaps back to reality as the last note fades to silence, blinking, staring out at her audience from her tiered stage.

"*Maestro!*" someone in the crowd cries.

It is a man. A man in a red velvet cloak. Could it be? Is Tartini himself calling these words?

"*Maestro!*" he says again, his hands raised just for her.

Another is standing now. Then another, and another. Soon the whole crowd is on their feet as they cheer for her. *Maestro, maestro, maestro.*

She rises, legs trembling, for the crowd. Her heart thuds, louder, faster. It is her moment. Her podium. Her dream.

The candlelight shimmers off the chandelier, blinding her, swaying around the room. The pride swells, glowing and endless and volcanic. But with it comes heat, too much, too fast. She raises her hand to her eyes, tries to block out the glare. But now her mind spins, reality blending before her. Her body starts to tremble, the blood drains from her face. She blinks. A long, slow movement, and when she opens her eyes again, she gasps.

There are no longer people in the audience but masks. Hundreds of them. They are white with black holes for eyes. They move, lips curling, laughing grotesquely, edging closer to her. Anna Maria is stepping back, she is tripping on her chair, her hand is stretched out, she is saying, *No.*

As she says it the masks part, creating an empty space, an aisle between pews. And from the back of it something is moving. A new mask emerges, one which stands out among a blur of dark eyes and howling faces because it is split in half, drawn across the diagonal. Because it is a perfect match for the one she has kept by her side all these years.

It tilts, looking at her. Anna Maria stares at it, heart pounding in her chest. Her lungs begin to fill. She is gasping for breath. Someone in the audience screams. And finally the world turns dark.

21

The sun beats into her room, casting a square of light across her wall. Already it is stiflingly hot. It can only just be dawn.

She rolls onto her back, staring up at the ceiling. The wooden beams are rutted and cracked, thin lines running the length of the dark wood, then curling into tight knots.

What happened last night? She remembers waking as she was being carried out of the palace by the sisters. How she tried to sit up, how Sister Clara pushed her back down. Everyone saw her faint, saw her escorted out.

She shudders now, remembering how the audience warped into jeering masks before her eyes. They were so real, so frightening. And that one. That one just like . . . She reaches across to her bedside table, slides the half playing card into her palm, and then lies back down, holding it above her. It was the way she felt when she saw it. The water filling her lungs, the pressure and weight of it.

She breathes, staring at it. Am I losing my mind?

She drops the card on her lap like it is a hot coal. Shoves it off and onto the floor.

But then her mind ventures back. To the crowd, to the candlelight, to the cheers and the cries. *Maestro.*

The door creaks open and Paulina is there, lit by the sun. She takes a seat at the end of the bed, a *gazzetta* clutched in her hand. The pair of them rest in silence for a few moments, until—

"Remember when we were little, and we thought you'd receive a certificate?"

Suddenly she is eight, and Agata is clapping in the corner, and Paulina is leaping with excitement at the end of their dormitory bed.

"It's all in here, Anna Maria," Paulina says, lifting the *gazzetta* higher. "They say there is no one comparable." The pride glows on her skin. "You did it, just like you always said you would."

Anna Maria's eyebrows are raised. Her body can hardly believe it. She always knew she could, always knew she would. And yet it was just a dream for so long. Just childish wants. She tugs her violin toward her, strokes the wood beneath her thumb, and she is shaking her head, the realization finally setting in. "I know," she says quietly. "I know."

There is no more time to be wasted. No more hiding in the shadows. Now she will make her enduring mark on the world, release her compositions, show everyone the true depths of her potential.

She marches into private practice with him with the manuscript in her hands. She has selected a piece that she originally wrote some years ago but which she has been tinkering with ever since. It starts slowly, mysteriously, drawing the listener into an enchanting world, but then it speeds up—it challenges them to understand. She has studied every composer in Venice and she is certain nothing like this exists. This is something new, something revolutionary.

"Good afternoon, *maestro*," he says, smiling. "Have you recovered from your episode last night? It is not every evening one becomes a master in the eyes of the crowd."

She hates that she fainted. Hates that it is this he chooses to mention. She should have been more professional, should have managed the situation. But she does not respond. She will move swiftly past it.

"There is something I'd like to show you." She tugs the parchment from her bag and hands it to him with an outstretched arm.

He frowns, curious. She can see through the paper to her

notes. It takes everything in her not to lift off and join them, curling around the room.

He is at the end of the first page when he stops, looks up. "You wrote this?" he says.

"I've been developing it whenever I have a little spare time."

She won't tell him about the forty or so other pieces she's been working on at the break of dawn and in the depths of night. Without sleep, often without food, for years. Honing and perfecting. Listening and learning. Let him take this piece in. Let her hear what he has to say about this one first.

He moves to page two, page three.

"My God," he breathes, his eyes shifting left to right.

"You like it?" she says.

"It is . . . it is quite unexpected. Different, fresh, I suppose."

She feels a smile growing. "I was hoping to perform it. Now that I'm a *maestro*. Perhaps at the Sunday concert at the Pietà next week."

It is a special occasion, as they both well know. A charitable event to which fifty members of Venice's society have been invited, encouraged to donate to the Pietà's music program. The ticket price is the highest it has ever been, Anna Maria's name being the draw.

There is a pause. He places her manuscript on the desk, his palm pinning it down. "Are you certain this is the piece you want to show?"

Her gaze flickers.

"A master knows when it is ready, do you remember?"

Her mind is tugged back to the kitchen, to a puff of flour in the air, sprinkling down on his hair all those years ago. Is she certain? Does she know?

She stiffens. Yes, she tells herself. You are a *maestro*.

She nods.

"Well then," he is saying, "of course, if you are certain. We will work on this today. It is a good idea, Anna . . ." He stumbles, then adds, "Well, I should say, *maestro*. It is a very good idea."

"Thank you," she says, feeling a smile split her face.

237

It is Sunday, and Anna Maria is sitting on the stage in the cool
Pietà chapel.

"Ready?" he says, by her side now.

His voice jolts her from the thought of her last nightmare.
There had been a scream, the noise of a desperate child, and her
playing card, hovering, haunting her from the depths. She has to
grip her violin a little tighter, remember where she is.

She likes performing here, she reminds herself quickly. The
Pietà is her home, this chapel the first place she ever performed.
And today is special. Today is her first opportunity to show the
world her worth, not only as a performer but as a composer. She
should be excited. She *is* excited. She shakes her head, sits up
straighter.

"Always," she says, forcing her focus straight ahead. On the
crowd. On her music.

The pair of them lift their instruments. Their eyes connect,
her pulse starts to thump in time, and she nods, pulling her bow
across the strings as they launch into the lively introduction. She
has named it *La Stravaganza* after the colors that burst and pour
from the manuscript. The music is energetic, eccentric, a feast
to behold.

He stands rigid, in fierce concentration as she starts to smile,
her body bending and curling to shades of apple green and
cherry, periwinkle and plum. Her wrist is supple, her body
strong, the finer muscles of her shoulder and arm flexing to the
challenge of the sound she has created.

The notes crackle like fat in a pan, the music so vibrant, so
alive that the crowd starts to move. Not as individual members but as one organism with a hundred arms, a hundred legs.
Chests rising and falling in unison, feet tapping as the colors spin
around them. Anna Maria has been playful in her composition,
layering new textures, exploring melodies she has never tested
with him. The notes shift and swirl. Ice blue, seafoam, billowing
like a sail in the wind, spreading and mixing in the air. And soon

her skin could be bubbling, hot lava for all she cares. There is nothing else but this.

The last note rings victorious as a tolling bell. The crowd beams, clapping furiously. Her heart raps. They love it. Her music. They love it!

Her face breaks into a smile, the warmth of this reaction washing over her. And then she sees something out of the corner of her eye that makes her go cold.

He is standing. The world slows as she watches him, the frantic claps of the audience blurring into a messy, slow-motion whap, whap, whap. Her head tilts, watching the fabric of his cuff tremble as he takes a bow, as he waves. She blinks, face set in a smile she no longer feels, waiting for him to sit down and instead tell her to rise. Anna Maria the master. Anna Maria the creator. But now he is lowering himself, and he is picking up his music, and they are moving on to the next piece, by Lotti. They are moving away from her work.

She feels her bow clatter to the floor.

He shoots her a look. Reaches down, hands it back to her.

What is wrong? his expression asks.

Her eyes move slowly back to the music. The next piece.

A cough from the crowd and her attention snaps to them. Waiting. Blinking. She tries to concentrate. But the blood churns in her veins. The first note she plays screeches out of her instrument. The audience visibly flinches. The next is jagged, cold. She shakes her head, tries to soften her hand. But the bow moves across the strings like a saw to wood. Her instrument buckles, a bolt of pain splits down her arm.

He took the credit. Took it for himself.

The audience is frowning. There is a groan of dissatisfaction, then a tut. Some people get up. Now a few more join them, heading for the chapel doors. Her bow screeches across the strings. Her tendons scream for her to stop. And the sound is bitter, deadly, acidic.

———

She has stowed her violin and is storming back into the chapel when she spots him. Tartini has his back to her, engaged in an animated conversation with three other men. Her heart slams against her chest. If her teacher will not do it then she will tell them herself. That the first piece was her creation, that now she is looking for a publisher. She redirects toward him and taps him on the shoulder.

His face breaks into a smile. "Anna Maria!" he says. "I was just greeting some of my colleagues. Of course you know Corelli, and have you met Vandini and Lotti?"

She has walked into a circle of the world's most celebrated composers. Breath fills her, her lips part to speak. But the words do not come. Instead, a tap, tap, tap. Her hand is shaking by her side.

The men blink. A few eyes shift from one to the other.

Her insides swell and blur like the colors of a piece. Is she certain of what has happened? Perhaps she has somehow mis-interpreted things. Maybe her teacher has some bigger plan to reveal that she is the composer. He is probably at this moment discussing further commissions, opportunities for her.

Tartini frowns. "Anna Maria? Is everything all right?"

She strengthens her stance. If her teacher had wanted to credit her he could simply have done so. But he stood. He stood, and he left her sitting silently behind.

"Gentlemen," she begins, her voice strong. "I hope you enjoyed tonight's performance. It is for this reason that I have come to speak with you all. For the past five years I have been working on—"

"What happened?"

Her teacher arrives by her side, his voice sharp. He takes in the circle of composers, listening to her with interest.

"Excuse us," he says, an awkward smile on his lips. He takes her by the arm, his fingertips pressing into her flesh, guiding her away. And the composers are laughing, and the circle is clos-ing, and Anna Maria is on the outside of it, in the corner of the chapel now, with him.

Her teacher's cheeks are pinched with stress. "Did you know Governor Rossi was here today watching? You know he's one of the main patrons for the Pietà's music program. You're lucky he likes me, I had to talk him down from pulling his entire donation for next year."

One hand rubs her temple. She is trying to process, trying to think. But the words come fast because they must get out, they must be spoken.

"You took it," she says, her eyes meeting his.

He blinks. "What are you saying?"

"You stood up and bowed at the end of my piece. You didn't acknowledge me at all."

He frowns, shifts a little. His voice, when he speaks, is higher than normal. "I simply addressed the crowd as I always do." He is chuckling, his hand moving toward her. "Anna, dear, don't be so dramatic! It doesn't suit your beautiful face."

"It's Anna Maria!" she says, slapping his hand away, her cheeks flooding red.

He looks to his palm, then to her for a moment. She feels the air between them freeze. "Do you not trust me? Is that what this is? Have I not been good to you all these years?"

"You have, but—"

His name is called. His eyes move across the crowd. "I have funders to speak to. I have to handle your mess."

He is away before she can say another word, swallowed up by a crowd of feathers and gowns. She turns to follow him. To finish this. But Paulina is behind her now, and her face is ashen, and her hand is on her stomach.

"We need to go," she says.

"It can't be, it's too soon. Far too soon."

Anna Maria is in Paulina's room, kneeling next to her friend. Paulina is flung forward, her palms and knees on the floor. She is panting for breath. The panting gets faster, until her scream reverberates around the room.

Anna Maria looks to the window, terror flooding her body.

It is almost dark. Supper will be finishing. Soon there will be girls filling these corridors, heading to the dormitories, to bed. They will be caught.

"Shh, there, there," she says, taking her friend's hand in hers. But the scream comes again, rapid and animal, and Paulina squeezes so hard Anna Maria shrieks too, feeling her bones crushed together.

The door opens. Chiara is standing in the frame, carrying armfuls of cotton, a small bucket of water.

"Get out, get away from us," Anna Maria says, but Chiara comes in.

"I'm not leaving, not when she's like this."

Anna Maria wants to argue, but Paulina screams out and the pain in her hand is immense once again.

"Let . . . her stay, Anna Maria." Paulina breathes in between the cramping, fine beads of sweat gathering on her forehead. "I need . . . you both . . . here." The final word is a screech, so loud it echoes right into the hall.

Chiara tries to stuff some of the cotton rags into Paulina's mouth, but she is squirming and she is yelling and Chiara cannot get them in.

"Paulina, hush!" Anna Maria rushes to the door and pushes it closed. "You have to stop, you have to be quiet."

Paulina is huffing, and she cries out again, this one even louder than the last. She looks so small, so young, her body not ready for this pain. Anna Maria feels her hands begin to shake, a damp sweat on her neck. She thought she could help; thought they could hide this. But she is just a child, just a stupid child who has no idea what she is doing.

Paulina screams again. The noise clangs through Anna Maria like a warning bell, like an alarm. They are going to be found out. She is going to lose everything. Just as she finally has it. *Maestro.* Her chance to be published. Her chance to be remembered. A sudden feeling of sickness, and pain in her stomach like a tear. She is standing before she knows it, her hand plucked from the clutch of her friend.

Paulina's head snaps up toward her. "Don't you dare," she growls as Anna Maria takes a step back. As her eyes flick toward the door.

The words escape her. "I can't do it. I can't be here. I'll be dropped, Paulina, they'll find us, they'll—"

"Anna Maria, don't go. Please help us," Chiara says, desperate.

Her words are broken by Paulina's scream again. By the sound of something ripping. Blood trickles across the floor.

And Anna Maria is turning away from it, from them both. Through the doorway, into the hall, sprinting as fast as her legs will take her, tears shattering her view.

"Go then," Paulina screams as the pulse comes again. Tears stream down her blotched face. "Just fucking go!"

QUATTRO

22

Hundreds of gulls storm in the sky, squawking above the heads of cowering Venetians. Below them the lagoon is ash gray and churning with fish the boats have kicked up. The birds swirl and screech, an angry whirlwind, splintering the waves as their bodies pierce the surface.

Inside her room Anna Maria shivers. Her sheets drip, damp from the sweat. A screaming rattles her brain.

Stop. Just make it stop, her mind begs as she twists back and forth.

But she is sucked down deeper, and the screams get louder, and she is trembling, sitting up, her face wet with tears when dawn eventually breaks. She opens her eyes to reality hanging above her like a heavy mesh. She drags her violin closer, clutches it to her chest.

It is the first time she has ever felt this. A dull, heavy ache in the depths of her body to be loved. Not by an audience, not by a crowd who want to feast on her talent, but to have her hair gently stroked, to be told everything will be all right. To be told she is not a bad person. That she did what she had to do to protect everything she has built. Perhaps even to be told that she doesn't have to play today. That she can rest here. Sleep without being woken, without drowning in her dreams.

But there is no one here to soothe her. No one here but her.

She slides the note from her bedside table, feels the soft paper beneath her fingertips.

Know that you were loved.

Where is the person who wrote this? Why couldn't she love her, keep her, protect her? Why must Anna Maria always end up alone?

She knows the answer, of course. Because she doesn't deserve that kind of love. Not after what she has done.

She left her. Left her best friend screaming and bleeding on the floor. Just like she always does. Just like she did when she was younger. To the only other person who has ever loved her. To Agata.

A wave of nausea moves through her. She flings back her covers, runs for the basket in the corner. But she has not eaten in more than a day, and all her body can wrench up is a lime-green bile. She heaves and chokes but nothing more comes. Eventually, she staggers back to her bed.

She left her. She left her. The thoughts start to crawl up her body like spiders, pushing her beneath the surface, into the depths. She has to stand, literally shake them off. She will not go under. She cannot go under. She still has so much to do.

And then he floats into her mind. And with him comes rage.

All of this began when he came into her life. Not being there for Agata, losing Paulina twice. The realization is quick, sharp, and clear. It powers her.

Her mind now holds one thought and one thought only. She will confront him with her music.

She stands, flips up the mattress. And then she stops dead.

Her manuscript book—bursting with her ideas, thick with sheets of paper sticking out at awkward angles, with the musical stories of her passions and her memories and years of her life—is gone.

"Wait, stop," Chiara calls from behind.

Anna Maria's pulse beats at her temples, a throb, throb, throb. The air is humid, close, like it is closing in on her. Still she presses forward. She will not look back.

"Anna Maria, wait!" Chiara calls, sprinting closer.

"Just leave me alone!"

Chiara slams to a halt. "They found us yesterday. They've taken Paulina."

Anna Maria begins to run.

"I don't know what became of the baby. Help me, please, Anna Maria!"

Tiny pieces of brickwork shudder onto the floor as she storms down the corridor and into the large music room. He is standing at the front of a class. They might be twelve, thirteen years old. The girl from the orchestra is there. The one Anna Maria noticed the other day, with the short dark hair and the edible notes.

His eyes flick to the fireplace and then to her when she enters. Odd, she thinks, that it is burning on a day as warm as this.

"What a surprise. Class, we have a *maestro* in our presence."

His face, his speech. They temporarily paralyze her. The class smiles, innocent and excitable, clapping politely. He is saying, ". . . and recently she performed a beautiful rendition of Corelli's Fifth. The crowd were on their feet applauding—"

"Don't do that." She will bite his words. Chew on his thoughts, then spit them back out at him.

"Don't do what?" he says, confused.

"Don't pat me on the head and tell me what a clever little angel I am. Do not mock me. You've been taking my ideas and passing them off as your own since I was thirteen years old."

His face flickers. "Anna Maria? What are you talking about?"

"We are doing this now, whether these girls are here or not."

He sighs. "Very well, then, everyone out."

The girls exchange looks, but they scamper away obediently. When the last one dashes into the corridor he turns back to Anna Maria, stands quite still.

"Whatever you are planning to say next, I'd advise you to remember to whom you are talking."

"Do you know I really thought that once I was old enough, you would credit me? I thought I held your respect." Her laugh is harsh. "I've been a fool."

"I do respect you," he says simply.

She is pacing now. "We've created something extraordinary. Our music is like nothing else that exists. It's special. It will be remembered. We could both be remembered for it. But you won't allow it."

"Well, this is my music, my writing style, Anna Maria."

She stops, blinks. How can he not see?

"I honed you in my image, gave you opportunities the likes of which most would never dream of." He assesses her for a moment. "I created you."

Her hands shake, nails digging into her palms.

"You are, after all, a girl, a woman. What did you think? That you were going to take a place in history as one of the greatest composers of all time? To have your work published in your own right?"

"That is exactly what is going to happen," she says, heat flushing up her neck. "I am a *maestro*, I am the best that there is."

"Dear girl, one critic, one crowd's opinion cannot change this. It takes years of acclaim to cement your position in our Republic, and besides," he moves to the desk, stabs at the papers strewn across it, "look at these. What do you see?"

She steps closer, hears the notes rising from them, the colors blurring beneath her anger.

"Men!" he is saying, tapping the paper faster, harder now. "These are all men's names—"

"And they are probably women's ideas, squashed by the conceit of those like you," Anna Maria says. "You have made us just clever enough to understand all that has been taken, all we cannot do. Why teach us how to use our minds just to bar us from their riches? How can you be so cruel?"

He stands, slapped. He is looking at her like something inside him is breaking. "You are a child. You know nothing of the world."

She cannot stop. She will not stop. "You can't face the fact that I'm better than you. I am a better performer, and a better composer too. Speaking of which . . ." She marches closer, so that she is only feet away. "Where are they? Where are my pieces?"

He watches her. But he does not answer. Instead, his eyes flick back to the fireplace.

There is a beat, a second. Her eyes widen. The flames, in that instant, are mesmerizing. And then a sound escapes her, as if something large and heavy has just swung into her stomach.

She was right. It should not be burning. Not on a day as hot as this.

Her breath slows. She cannot move. It is like he is gripping her wrists, holding her back.

A thousand minuscule choices lead up to a finished piece of music. To go up or down, to stay or move on. To reach higher, faster. To snap. To surprise here but mellow there. To build. To build and build and build and build and . . . breathe. Let it linger, hold for a moment. And then that final note, the end. The inevitable, crushing silence.

Choices. On their own, insignificant, but pieced together over years with care, with attention, it is possible to create something remarkable.

Her heart, she is certain, has stopped. She is dust, falling from the sky, rock crumbling beneath her feet.

It is not just a book. It is fabric splashed with countless flecks of color she never knew she'd paint. It is darkness, the unexpected, something bold and astonishing and new. It is the opportunity to interpret, again and again. It is work that will speak to every soul, every year, for eternity. This is the beauty of her mind on paper. This is proof of everything she is capable of.

There is a break now, the grip released. She skids across the floor, plunges her hands right into the flames. And from it she pulls two palmfuls of gray, curling ash.

Anna Maria della Pietà had notes before she had words, and those notes always had colors. She kneels here, watching those colors fade. They drift away from her, along with smoke from the fire, until everything is as lifeless as the embers in this grate. Until there is darkness. Until there is nothing.

The words must be dredged up, loosened from the deep.

"I wish you had never come here. I wish I had never met you," she says.

His voice behind her, so close she can feel his breath on her neck. "You should have drowned in the canal like the others."

The second he whispers it she feels it. Her body screaming for air.

"What are you talking about?" she breathes as her lungs start to fill.

"Have I touched upon a nerve?" he says coldly. "That's what happens to you girls, the babies. Left face down and lifeless. Last year alone they fished out two hundred. Two hundred versions of you."

Her hands rush to her throat. And then she is running.

"Now I want you to clap your hands together like this," Signore Conti is saying, his blond curls bobbing up and down as his hands pat together. Anna Maria looks at Paulina on her left, Agata on her right. They are giggling. They are always giggling in his class. They weave their arms together and they start to clap, so it's unclear which arm belongs to which body. The sun streams through the window, illuminating their youth-filled faces.

"And now I want you to stomp, like this." He demonstrates, his feet lifting one by one about a foot off the floor and then hitting the wood, throwing shadows across the gloss. "But don't stop clapping! We are stomping, and we are clapping, and we are following what is called *the beat*."

Now they weave their legs between one another and start stomping. So loudly the floor starts to quiver. It's so silly, so funny, Anna Maria thinks she might wet herself. Agata is gripping Anna Maria's arm to her side, Paulina's hair is grazing Anna Maria's shoulder. They are a blend of limbs keeping time.

It is the happiest thing Anna Maria can remember. The happiest she has ever felt in her life. A memory, from more than twelve years ago.

Her run slows to a walk, now that she is away from the music rooms. Away from the fire. Away from him.

Now she hears the music. Those first notes that she heard him play. The way they soared through the air, drew her closer. They had to be hers. She had to know that sound, that instrument, as her own.

Now it is the first time she stuck her tongue between her teeth and put note to paper. The color of it, her eyes widening at the potential.

Her arm twinges, and she looks at her finger, now covered in ash. It is still oddly dented from where the door hit it before her audition. She tastes the medicine, the acid sour of the coffee. Coffee Paulina brought her, when she was in trouble, to help.

Now she is walking into class, and she is looking up, and seeing Paulina grin back at her. Her friend, in the *figlie*.

And now she is in the *infermeria*, and she is clutching a small, frozen, lifeless hand, and she is saying, "Come back."

And she is walking away, and her friend is bleeding and screaming on the floor, and she is not stopping, not turning back to help her.

Her hand comes to rest on her bedroom door, blood thudding through her body.

Everything makes sense to her now. The drowning dreams, the fear of the water. What must it have been like to hold her down? To watch her struggle beneath the depths, to hear her scream as she plunged beneath the surface?

Who would do such a thing?

There is only one explanation. One that makes her clench the handle tighter, until the cool metal is shaking in her hand.

She was born of a monster. And of a monster comes a monster. That is why Anna Maria is so cruel. That is why she is the way she is.

She slams open her door, looks around her room. It is packed, floor to ceiling, with things. Lace shawls and cotton ties, floral vases and gilded mirrors, pocket combs and pearl earrings. The sight makes her recoil. What is all this? What is it for, what does it mean? They do not know her, the givers of these gifts. All they know is her performance. All they know is the way she can transform a tune, make her audience dive in and drown beneath the waves of a piece. And for this they adore her. For this they shower her with praise.

She laughs, a hollow sound. Not one thing in this entire room belongs to her. Every item a donation. Her creativity, her dreams, have been bought up with pretty frills. She is a note, tumbling, unraveling in the air.

She has the earnings in the bank at least. But now her hands are running through her hair and her heart is beating a little faster. She has no idea how much she's earned. Which bank the gold is in or where. She's never seen this money. Never even thought to ask. Her stomach clenches. Do her savings even exist?

She is shaking her head. Everything is clearer now.

She owns nothing. She has nothing. She is nothing.

The mirror goes first. Tiny shards of glass scream across the room as she smashes it against the desk. The pearl casing shatters into pink fragments, cast across the floor. And now she is taking the flowers from the vase and smashing them against the wall. Purple petals explode into the air. Earrings and necklaces go flying. She is ripping up her pillowcase, she is hurling the chair at the bed. And there is the note. That message from the woman who did this, who left her. She snatches it from the bedside table. Rips it from corner to corner until the dust falls to the floor. "Know that" on the chair, "loved" on the ground. No longer a message. Just meaningless words, scattered and alone.

She staggers back, heaves in her breath. Only one item in the entire room remains intact. Her case, and inside it her violin and bow. She scoops it into her arms, tucks it beneath her velvet cloak, and then she turns. With one last look back, she vows to leave this place of lies, this place of monsters, forever.

23

The world ebbs and flows out here. The air is thick and hot and heavy, the light too bright, too dazzling. Anna Maria has to raise her hand, shield her eyes. She seems to spin down the alleyway, her brain dizzy, caught in the city's energy.

The doors to the Santa Maria Formosa on the *campo* crash open and a throng of people pour out, fish bursting from the tight twists of the canal into the wide-open lagoon. Many of the faces among them are masked. Warped, eyeless, they jeer at her, laughing mercilessly.

"Watch yourself." "Hey," the crowd chides, pushing Anna Maria back as she is wrung between them like a cloth to a press. They jostle her forward, twisting and gasping, unable to stop her movement. A bird screeches above, its underbelly glaring golden in the sun. Let her take off and join it, her mind begs. Let her soar away from this place forever, wings beating against the sky.

She is shoved forward, into the woman next to her, whose laugh becomes a cackle shaking inside Anna Maria's brain. And now she is staggering back, further and further, pushed to the edge of the square, until the waters of the canal lick greedily at her feet. Her foot slips on wet stone and she lets out a gasp, teetering on the edge, her body rocking, unsteady, inches from its depths. She shoots her hand out, grabs for the first thing it makes contact with. The coattails of a tall man in front of her. He catches her elbow. Her body sways and then stabilizes, two feet on solid ground once again. The milky waters recede in mock innocence. She won't look back at them. Won't meet the eyes that she can feel peering up at her from the jade depths.

The man is looking at her, a wrinkle in his tall forehead. A look of recognition, like he knows this face from somewhere, with the green eyes and the dark beauty. His head tilts, his mouth opens to say, *You, it's you,* but she has wrenched her elbow from his grip, slipped around the edge of the crowd, and she is running, exploding into the light of the promenade.

She checks over her shoulder, panting for breath, and slows to a brisk walk. She cannot be out in the open, wandering the streets like this. She will be spotted by some other aristocrat, mobbed by the crowds.

She spots a kiosk some twenty steps ahead, ducks toward it seeking a solution. The owner has one hand on a bulging hip. He is haggling with a woman over the price of a hat. The volume rises as she nears.

"There's no way it's worth that," the woman is saying, pointing with her cane. "What about the red one, with the feathers?"

The owner plucks a hooked stick from the stall, reaches up high to snare the hat from the top rung.

Quickly, quietly, Anna Maria lifts the nearest mask from the rack in front of her. A sleek black band that covers only the eyes.

"This one is twice the price," he is saying, but he never sees what happens next. Doesn't notice Anna Maria slip his mask onto her face, tying the ribbons over her dark curls. Doesn't see her disappear once more into the shadows of the labyrinth.

The streets are so narrow she has to breathe in to squeeze through the throngs of locals with their shopping bags and fruits, their vegetables and spices. She paces quickly, not knowing her destination. A dull thud of realization as she rounds one corner, then another, wondering if she is moving in circles. She has no knowledge of this city. She has seen Venice only through the windows of the Pietà, from her rooftop hideout, or as a passenger, guided through it by others en route to concerts. She has stood in the finest palaces in the city, and yet she has no idea of the land in which she lives.

Her heart keeps pace with her step, a sharp thud against her ribs. She cannot go back, but where now, where next?

She walks for so long her feet start to ache. Turning this way and that, guided only by the stench of the water mixing with puffs of cinnamon and clove. Time and again she finds herself face-to-face with the jade canal, no way to turn but backward.

She slows and stands for a moment, catching her breath in front of a shopwindow. Reels of thick, colorful paper are displayed in it. She eyes them, searching for what, she cannot think. In the back of her mind a question hums gently, a question that makes her stomach churn.

Could they be there? Hidden beneath the stack? But no, she tells herself, she knows they cannot.

She looks down at her hand, half expecting to see it there. Her book with her life's work in it. She can feel its weight and thickness, the way the sheets of parchment tickle her skin. The blobs of ink running down the margins. How can her palm be empty? How?

She turns, rests her back against the window, her eyes searching the people passing her now. Are they hiding her music beneath the folds of their cloaks? Have they tucked them into the shadows between their skin and their shirts?

She knows it is gone. But she cannot stop looking, her mind cannot stop searching. They cannot be turned to ash, a pile of dust lying at the bottom of a metal grate. They cannot.

She'll need money, a place to stay for the night, at least. Her hand rushes to her neck, and relief floods her veins. She is still wearing a necklace, a gift from some faceless admirer. One of the few things she didn't destroy in her rage. She emerges into a square, stops a woman hobbling along with a rug beneath her arm, asks for directions to a pawnbroker.

"You'll have to go to the Jews," she's told, and does her best to memorize the woman's rapid directions. She walks for twenty minutes or so and, after a few wrong turns, finds herself at a large iron bridge with a locked gate. An elderly man is standing at it wearing a red skullcap, a large key hung from his neck with string. She tells him her business and, wordlessly, he creaks open the metal.

The smells are different on the other side: fresh bread, sweet onion, and frying fish. The ghetto is separated by tall walls from the rest of the city across the bridge. She slips into the hum of activity, wondering why the Republic has gone to such trouble to divide its people. Passes the hodgepodge of informal shacks and shops squashed together. It is not a Venice she has known.

The sign above the door flaps in the breeze. It's blue and white, just like the woman said it would be, the name written in both Venetian and Hebrew.

She enters to the clang of a bell, nods to the portly man behind the wooden counter, dark hair spraying out from beneath his three-peaked hat. It's a busy shop; she stands in line tapping her foot in time with her heart, waiting behind three other customers. And then it is her turn.

"How much for this?" she says, unclasping the chain around her neck and sliding it across to him. He picks the necklace up, running it through his long slim fingers.

"A nice piece," he says, surveying it with a small glass instrument. Several beats, then he makes his offer.

"It's worth triple that," she says quickly, one hand on the counter, the other clutching her violin to her side. In truth she has no idea how much it's worth. The thought makes her sick. She has no idea how much anything is worth.

"That's the best I can do. It would be more if you sell me whatever you've got in that case." He peers down to the violin in her hand.

She feels it butt against her leg as she clutches the handle tighter. What price could she possibly place on this? On the only thing in the world that makes her certain, still, that she is actually alive.

He is waiting, watching the thoughts flit through her mind.

Eventually he leans closer and says, "You can take my offer for the necklace, or you can be on your way."

She stuffs the coins into her violin case, and she is back on the street.

She can't keep walking like this. She needs to find a place to stay. But she's been out for so long, twisted and turned through the maze of people and streets and canals in every imaginable direction. She doesn't recognize this area, it can't be close to anywhere she's ever performed before. She slows at a splintered wooden door. Curling writing over the arch reads "*Osteria Manzoni.*"

"No *cortigna lume* allowed," comes a voice from a small room to the right of the entrance. A small man, at least a foot shorter than Anna Maria with a long, crooked nose, pokes his head around the frame. He eyes her suspiciously.

She lets out a noise, one of surprise, distaste. "I'm no street-walker," she says, jutting her chin up. She wants to tell him to whom he is speaking. But he is walking away, down the narrow hallway, carrying a basket filled with laundry. She has to chase him to catch up.

"Doesn't matter," he is saying, hoisting the basket higher in his arms. "No females allowed."

"Well, where can I go, on my own?" she says.

"Brothel," he responds, turning down another corridor and extracting a large bronze key from the loop on his belt.

"Brothel?" She coughs the word. "Did you not hear me before?"

He turns sharply toward her. "I can't help you, understand? Nowhere in the city is going to take a young woman alone."

She is unbuckling her violin case, digging out the coins.

"Not even a young woman with a palmful of these?" she says.

He pauses, looks her up and down again. "Come," he says begrudgingly.

The room is about twice the size of her one at the Pietà and smells musty, of dust and boiled vegetables. It is where imaginations come to die, she thinks, looking around at the moth-eaten curtains, the sure-to-be-flea-ridden bed.

The door slams behind her, but she turns and opens it instantly, craning her neck into the corridor, addressing his hunched back as he hobbles away. "I'll need a bucket, water, and some soap." Her stomach growls. "And something to eat."

"No food here. You'll find the vendors on the street," he grumbles without looking back.

She shrinks back into the room. She doesn't want to go out there into the heady crowds.

She drags a broken wicker chair across the room, positions it so the back is under the handle. Surveys the peeling walls, the view down to the canal below. The calls from the street are loud. Drunken jeers and rowdy catcalls.

It's just for the night, she reminds herself. And then where? Perhaps to Paris—she's heard they are music lovers there. She might find a job, performing in some theater or church. Or Rome? But, alone, would they allow it? There is so much she doesn't understand. She could tell you the exact position of fingers on string to bring out the richest tones. Could paint a whole book of notes that cast the brightest colors, and those that summon the darkest shades of the night. But she does not know this world and its rules. She knows nothing of being a woman at all.

She tugs closed the shutters, chides these thoughts for now. She will retreat to the darkness, to the bed, and formulate a plan in the morning. But there is a knock at her door. She moves the chair barrier. A small pail of water with a used bar of soap resting on the edge greets her, the fat cracked but still pungent. On the floor next to it is a thin cotton towel. The bath she requested. She places the pail on the side table in her room, shrugs off her cloak and smock. The stench of the low canal and the stench of her body have curled into one after her day of running, of being tossed through the crowds. This, at least, is something she can do. Let her start here.

The sight of her naked body surprises her when it is revealed. Once plump flesh now a tight band of skin across collarbones.

Ribs jutting up against her sides. When did this happen? she wonders, as she washes the dirt and decay from her skin.

The last spears of daylight shoot through the shutters, one creaking on its hinge. Her stomach growls again. There is a chipped bottle on the side table next to the pail, a stumpy glass to accompany it. She takes a swig of watery wine, then another, but it does nothing to stem the hunger. Her mind rushes to the meals for the *figlie*. Roasted pike with crispy skin, nestled among a bed of rosemary and garlic. The fruits, fresh as spring flowers, with juice so sweet she would lap it up as it rolled down her chin.

She sighs.

She must leave, find something to eat. Her eyes flick to the pile of change on the side table. It's the first time in her life she's ever had to think about where her next meal might come from. She is unsure how many meals she might be able to pay for before the gold from the necklace runs out. And how she might protect herself. There is a pang of something other than hunger in her stomach. It whispers from the darkness, *Have you done the right thing?*

Her violin lies at the foot of her bed. She can't take it—it wouldn't be safe. But she doesn't want to be parted from it. Not here, not now. She takes a deep breath, stares at it awhile longer. But she cannot wait. She cannot go a moment longer without food. She tucks her violin carefully beneath the folds of her bedsheets, slides the door key into her cloak as the lock clicks shut.

The street has a nervous energy. The crowd down here is enlivened, powered by something more than fish and wine alone. Women and men slow as they pass her, eyes boring right through her body. She has to remind herself she is in the mask. They do not know her. They cannot know her.

The smell, not a pleasant one but of food nonetheless, draws her down the narrow alley that leads from the inn and toward the little curving stone bridge at the end of it. On the other side of the canal a vendor with a small wooden stall is boiling something over a fire in a large metal pot.

"One, please," she says, instantly cursing Sister Clara's teachings for making her so polite. She stiffens her posture, tries to make her body seem bigger, stronger, in case this merchant thinks she is easily swindled by virtue of her good manners.

She is handed a bowl of mushy vegetables in a watery broth, a few white flecks of fish visible within it, and a hunk of stale bread. It is all brown, like the food she used to eat before she became the youngest ever member of the *figlie di coro*. But nothing can stop her hunger. The merchant is holding out a little bowl filled with salt crystals, but she is already cramming the bread into her mouth, she is slurping at the soup, she is licking the sauce off her fingers. And the ravenous creature inside growls for another portion, and then another, and she feasts, not stopping for air, not bothering to breathe.

The city has fallen quieter with the darkness. She wanders back toward her inn, windows of the taverns glowing like coals in the fire. The quiet calms her, the full stomach lifting her mood an octave or more. She sits a moment on the stone wall at the edge of the water, breathing in the cool evening air. Maybe she can do this. Live a half-life, away from the Pietà, in disguise. Maybe she can journey beyond the city's limits, discover what else is out there besides an endless swath of sea. She places her hand on the stone, connecting herself to the ground beneath her. Breathing through these thoughts.

Then, a sound.

Her head twists in its direction, her mind filled suddenly with colors as notes join the drums. The music speaks to her, weaves a story of her own. It is sad and it is terrifying and beautiful and joyous. How can a life be full of so many things, sometimes all at the same time? She stands, she is following it, unable to resist.

She strides faster now as the music starts to move, twists to the right, then the left. Soon the crowd is growing, guided by *codegas*, men carrying large glass lanterns which swing by their sides, and she is among them, moving from the narrow streets across the Rialto Bridge and into a huge square. There is so much activity her eyes can barely take it in. Tall towers of acrobats, limbs shaking under the weight of one another, and bears growling in cages, clawing at the metal. Dancers dash like silk peacocks, colorful through the crowd, and a trainer instructs his marmot, the tiny creature standing for claps and cheers. *Zaletti! Zaletti!* a man passing cries, a flat basket of yellow biscuits in his arms. She curves through the throng, breathing in the sugary smell of roasting nuts, the square around her glowing with hundreds of oil lamps, more candles than she can count. To her right, the crowd gasps. A boy is arching back, fire bursting from his mouth. But she does not stop following the river of the tune. With her back to the wall of the square, she edges closer, closer, until she spots the source. A trio of violins, played by three men in black caps and white masks. The piece speeds up as she nears, growing in energy and ambition. The performers are moving through the crowd, guiding a band of locals who dance to the music they are making. She finds herself among them, the colors swirling between her limbs.

She shouldn't follow. She should get back. But her body has other plans. She starts to sway, her form and the colors blending into one, until she is away from the square, and she and the locals are following the violinists into a building together, and they are moving through a door from this world into the next.

24

She has entered the underland: a sprawling dark cavern. She winds past round tables with men in three-peaked caps, women with rouged cheeks sitting on their laps. One woman is whispering in a man's ear, another's back is arched. She is laughing manically. Anna Maria moves quickly past them, following the musicians, smelling the bite of alcohol in the air. The space opens out, the sounds of laughter and drinking, music and entertainment, thrumming around her. Her eyes track a staircase which leads up to a mezzanine, and she makes a small noise. One man is bent back over the banister and another man is holding his waist, kissing him passionately. In the nook beneath this, there are large velvet cushions, and sprawled across them are men and women in their underclothes. Anna Maria turns. She should leave. But a masked woman approaches her, smooth lips visible beneath the curls of green and gold on her mask.

"Sip," she says, "and forget."

She holds out a tall flute, the liquid inside it as dark as ink. Anna Maria knows she should get out of this place of sin, of decay. But to where? For what? She has nowhere to go, no friend or family who will care if she returns. There is no one waiting for her now.

The woman smiles again, lifts the flute a little closer.

Anna Maria closes her eyes. Let her forget this world, this place. Let it dissolve forever for all she cares. The flute reaches her lips.

The first sip dulls the pain of her stolen life's work. It's less of a sharp stabbing in her gut now, more of a muted ache. The second burns her tongue, and with it the memory of losing Paulina. The third singes the fear she holds, the recognition of what she has lost. And so she doesn't stop, just lets the liquid slide through her, lets it obliterate the suffering. She stares at the empty bottom of the glass as the final dregs drip down her throat.

The shutters of this world open and close sporadically, not of her own volition. Her body feels heavy against the cushions, but the world is light, free. Music floods through her veins like some delicious poison. Her mouth is opened, purple grapes laced with something sharp slipped between her lips. There are bodies touching her, a sensation she now realizes she craves. It is like tasting sugar for the first time: vivid, addictive. She drinks in the feeling of skin against hers, and then the darkness comes again.

When her eyes open her mind shines a little clearer. There is a table in the corner, young men gathered around it, cheering and scowling, playing games of chance. She hears snatches of their conversation, words in French, German, and English. A noise and she looks to her right, where there is a child next to her, a baby not yet walking. Its huge eyes blink slowly, taking in Anna Maria's face. And now she sees her own body, her head tilting as she tries to understand it. There is a woman next to her, her leg pulled high across Anna Maria's waist. Anna Maria twitches, trying to extract her limbs from those that do not belong.

"Hush now," the woman says, rousing from her slumber and placing a hand on Anna Maria's forehead. Her eyes are so big, so dark, she could tumble into them. The woman's palm feels warm, soft. Anna Maria relaxes against it as the woman lifts the glass again and says, "Take another sip."

Anna Maria does not know how long this lasts, this darkness, this pleasure. Knows only that she does not care, that she can think of nothing but this music, can submit to nothing but the luscious poison inside.

The throb in her brain rouses her. With great effort, she pulls herself into a seated position. Takes a moment to understand what she is seeing. The pile of groaning bodies, of the large heavy man snoring at her feet. She stumbles up, her brain a shriveled nut clanging against the sides of her head. Her vision blurry, she staggers from darkness to . . . light. How can it be dawn? How can it be day already?

She takes a few unsteady paces away from the tavern door and then turns into the alley running along its side. She is about halfway down when she has to stop. Her body pulses, her back pressed up against the wall. She hurls forward, throws up the remnants of that godforsaken drink. And then the air is heavy with the perfume lick of musk.

"And what is a nice Pietà girl like you doing all the way out here?"

Her hands rush to her face, but there is no mask anymore. She must have lost it in that den. She bows her head, turns away. Tries to hurry in the other direction. But the footsteps are catching up with her. A hand on her shoulder; she is turned around.

Elisabetta Marcini is staring down at her. The fine wrinkles around her eyes have turned into deep lines, and she wears a dark wig. She is dressed plainly today. No decadent gown, no leaf-shaped gems. She wears a simple cotton dress, a black shawl about her shoulders, a basket filled with bread rolls in her arms. Anna Maria's heart sinks. There is perhaps no one, apart from her teacher, she would rather see less.

"What is wrong with your eyes?" Elisabetta says, peering into Anna Maria's pupils. She stands with one hip jutted to the right. She is flanked by two maids, white aprons across their shifts, hair covered with cotton caps.

"Nothing. Leave me alone." Anna Maria shrugs Elisabetta's hand away. But the vomit is coming up again now, and she is hunched over, retching once more.

Elisabetta turns to the women behind her, hands one the basket she is carrying. "Continue handing these out. I'll stay here," she says.

The maids nod and begin down the alley as Elisabetta

turns back to Anna Maria. Anna Maria straightens up, wipes the bile from her mouth on her sleeve, the sting of vomit in her throat.

"We should leave." Elisabetta's voice is matter-of-fact but hurried. "There's a brawl the other side of the Rialto Bridge. It's not safe out here. The men get silly at this hour." She looks over her shoulder, then adds, "Sillier than usual, that is."

But Anna Maria is shaking her head, her body shivering from the poison in her veins.

"We don't have to go back to the Pietà, I have an apartment at the palace on the other side of the Grand Canal. It is private enough. We won't be bothered. Come."

Anna Maria grimaces, but she has little alternative.

"My violin." She coughs between the words, feels her insides contract. "I need to collect it first."

Elisabetta nods. "Lead the way."

Anna Maria shakes the handle a second time, but the lock won't turn. She bangs on the wood, yells at it, "Hey! Let me in, let me in!" Her violin is in there. How could she have left it? How could she have been so stupid?

Feet shuffling behind the door, and it flings back to reveal a tall man with a tuft of silver hair sticking up at odd angles.

"What in God's name . . . What time is it, what do you want?"

"This is my room."

"Not since Saturday, I rented it for the week."

Saturday? Anna Maria recoils. Elisabetta has to grab her arm, steady her. She was in the tavern for three days and three nights.

"It can't be, I . . ." Her brain is spinning, she can't get out the words. "I left my violin in here."

"Don't know anything about that," he says. There's a rush of air as the door slams in her face.

And now she is running, back down the corridor, over the stained rug, her fists are pummeling the little door to the right of the entrance.

"What have you done with it? Give me my violin!" she shouts as the lock clicks open.

The owner crosses his arms, his face unimpressed. "You paid me for one night and then left your belongings for free. I took the violin as payment."

"What have you done with it?" she says again. "If you have hurt it, I swear to you—"

Elisabetta steps between them, tall, elegant. Gently, she guides Anna Maria back. Her voice is soft when she speaks. Soon the man is laughing, and he is tugging Anna Maria's violin case off a shelf behind him, and Elisabetta is handing him some coins and taking his palms in hers.

"Thank you," Anna Maria mumbles, snatching the case into her arms.

Anna Maria watches, eyes narrowed, as Elisabetta thanks him, as she asks after his business and his family. She plots her next move. Elisabetta and her rich girls interfered with her education. Elisabetta dislikes her. Elisabetta may have got her violin back, but she is not a woman Anna Maria can trust.

Anna Maria makes her decision. She will get away from her. She will go. Now.

She is back on the street, heading down a narrow path next to a canal, passing window boxes full of rosemary which are scenting her way when—

"And so she ran," Elisabetta says, a few steps behind her. Anna Maria groans, turns around. Elisabetta sighs. "If you turn right at the end, over the canal, and keep going straight on, you come to the lagoon. From there you can find your way through the city. My home is across the Rialto Bridge, on the waterfront behind the market. It is the one with the carved double doors, should you ever consider stopping by."

"I don't want your help," Anna Maria says.

"Of course." Elisabetta nods. "So be it."

A merchant carrying a basket of fish approaches, the smell

of salt and sea weaving between them as he passes. Anna Maria moves to leave, but Elisabetta speaks again.

"I ask only that you remember this: I have lived in the Republic more than fifty years. I have known a lot of Anna Marias in that time, and I have watched this place destroy people like you. There is no shame in seeking help when it is needed."

The night is dark, cold, the sky beginning to spit. Anna Maria sits with her back pressed against a crumbling brick wall, an arched bridge in front of her, the canal snapping angrily at the banks. She has placed her violin behind her so no one can see it, try to take it. Her muscles are tensed, ready to fight.

An old beggar woman approaches, her head down, a black cloth tied around her hair. Her back is so hunched it is almost parallel to the ground. She holds a small cane, dragging it along the ground with a slow scrape, tap, scrape, tap. Anna Maria feels her pulse quicken.

The woman reaches Anna Maria's side. The smell of rain-spattered dirt in the air. Anna Maria draws in her breath. But now the woman is reaching into her cloak, and she is taking out a coin, and she is flicking it into Anna Maria's lap.

Anna Maria stands in surprise, watches her go. A beggar woman is offering Anna Maria her own money. Is this what she has become?

And then a rush of feet, so fast she has no time to react.

The man knocks her back, stealing her breath as she is hurled against the wall. She flings her hands up for protection, but another man is barreling toward him, and they are sprawled on the cobbles, the rain pouring down on them, a mess of punches and sighs and groans. She freezes, terrified that if she moves they will notice, turn their weapons on her. There is a squelch, a grunt. One man is running away, the sound of footsteps splashing in the puddles, and the other is staggering up from the ground, clutching a bloodstained patch above his hip, shuffling back the way he came.

Anna Maria does not stop to think. She grabs her case. She sprints with everything she has. She heads for the Rialto Bridge.

She is wide-eyed, checking over each shoulder, panting as she knocks. Her cloak and hair are soaked through from the rain. There is blood on her dark smock, sprayed by the fighting men, and the hem is muddy and wet.

So when the servant answers, when she sees the young woman who stands before her, she tells her to get back, to go, there is nothing for her here. It is Elisabetta, standing in the hallway behind her now, who says gently, "Take her to the room."

Days pass beneath the folds of silken bedding. Anna Maria tries not to wake. Opens her eyes only sporadically to sip the broth that has been left at her bedside table. The thoughts that churn in the shadows make her tug the blankets higher, dig herself deeper into the silence.

She is a mess, an object of pity for the elites. She has been so foolish, so careless. She groans, turns over, buries her face into the mattress. There is no further for her to fall.

But now Elisabetta is here, standing at the end of the bed while Anna Maria shields her eyes from the light of freshly opened shutters. Elisabetta leaves a steaming copper pot of water, an embroidered cotton towel, and a pearl-handled hairbrush on the dressing table by the window. A robe made from crisp linen lies next to them. Anna Maria's smock has been washed and dried.

She turns back now, placing a hand on Anna Maria's velvet cloak, which has been dried and slung over the chair. She is about to speak, but then she bends down, plucks the half playing card which has tumbled out of the cloak and onto the rug. She holds it up to the light, studying the sharp diagonal cut, the gold dots and curls on the Queen of Hearts' mask.

"That's mine," Anna Maria says quickly.

There is something in Elisabetta's eyes when she looks over. Anna Maria's throat thickens. Elisabetta places the playing card on the dressing table, her hand lingering on it a moment too long.

"Meet me in the parlor downstairs when you are finished," she says as she leaves.

It takes Anna Maria every ounce of her will to extract herself from the bed, but there is something about Elisabetta that makes her get up, do as she says. Her stomach feels like it has been turned inside out. Washing helps, the warm water caressing her limbs, and now she creaks back the door to her room, emerges into the wide, light-filled hallway, starts toward the curving staircase wearing the fresh robe.

The marble floor is cool beneath her feet. One of her hands grazes the fabric-covered walls, the other clutches her violin case. She will not be parted from it. Not ever again.

Opposite her hangs a hand-painted family tree, the first member dating back to 1305. There are portraits running the length of the hall in elaborate gold frames, the subjects wearing lace and pearls. At the end of the corridor is a velvet curtain, fringed with scarlet tassels. The Pietà, by comparison, is a dark, gray prison.

She is almost at the staircase when she stops. A thick walnut door on her right is ajar, a cherub for a handle. A smell pours from it: kind, like a field of wildflowers. She nudges the door, further open.

A small, beautiful room lies before her, the walls lined with peach satin. On the right, a table with slender curving legs. It is glossed, polished, reflective as an eye. On top of it are a lace bonnet and a pair of gloves. Carefully placed, fit for a child's hands. A doll sits upright next to them, feet poking out beneath a tiny velvet gown.

There is a rocking chair in the corner, a cloth embroidered with an "I" across its back. A gilded mirror hangs by a ribbon from the wall. And there is a cot. Wooden, empty but for a white blanket which has been folded and tucked. And yet it is too neat, the lace too straight. It is perfect like it has never been touched.

The creak of floorboards makes Anna Maria jump. Elisabetta

is by her side, looking not at her but into the room. She takes the cherub handle silently, gently. She pulls the door shut.

She does not look at Anna Maria when she says, "You and I are going to talk."

"Sit," she says, motioning to the chair opposite her in the parlor.

Anna Maria plants herself down, places her violin on the floor, the case touching her foot. Elisabetta takes a large chair opposite her, by the fireplace, a fine porcelain cup of coffee in her hands.

The maid moves in, lifting a pot from the table. It is cream and embellished with flowers and leaves, steam curling from the spout. She fills a matching cup, hands it to Anna Maria.

"Thank you, Lucia," Elisabetta says.

The woman curtsies and leaves. Elisabetta turns to Anna Maria. "You are going to tell me what has happened. Every last detail."

"You wouldn't understand."

Elisabetta laughs. Dry and short. "Trust me, girl, when you are as old as I am, you too will have seen it all."

Anna Maria tightens her lips, stares at her a moment before—

"Why are you doing this? Why are you helping me? You don't know me. You don't even like me."

Elisabetta sighs, takes a sip from her cup. "A simple thank-you would suffice."

Anna Maria frowns. "Will you give no reason at all?"

Elisabetta raises an eyebrow. Anna Maria holds her gaze for a moment, the pair of them locked in a match of power, of will.

"Fine," Anna Maria says eventually, because she can stay silent no longer.

And the stories start spilling out of her. The arguments. Chiara's deceit. What her teacher did to Anna Maria. What he took from her.

When she finishes, Elisabetta tilts her head. It's like she's inspecting Anna Maria's face for some deeper secret, some unknown truth.

"And you were surprised that he wouldn't acknowledge you, that he burned your compositions?" she says eventually.

"Yes . . ." Anna Maria says slowly, because it seems so obvious.

There is a short pause. And then Elisabetta is leaning forward, her rib cage quivering with laughter. She places her cup on the table to avoid spilling its contents.

Anna Maria lets out a sound, a mix of surprise and frustration, arms crossing over her stomach.

"Are you quite well?" Elisabetta says now. "Girls who make a mockery of men in this town end up disappeared or dead. Especially a man as insecure as him."

"But it's all true!" she says. "He took my ideas and he said they were his. I have a right to have my music published. I have a right to have my name known by the world."

"And what right is that?" Elisabetta challenges. "What God-given power do you think you have?"

"I'm Anna Maria della Pietà. I'm famous."

Elisabetta is tittering again. Anna Maria would like to lean across and slap the cup from the table, to smash the lavish pot with one stamp of her foot. It is several moments before Elisabetta says, "Your fame means nothing. You are a girl! Heavens, a young woman, even. Did nobody tell you?"

Scowling, Anna Maria stands up. She will leave, find some other place to stay. "Never mind, I knew you wouldn't understand."

"Now wait." Two hands usher her back into the seat. Anna Maria is guided by them begrudgingly. "I'm sorry. I should not have laughed. I . . ." Elisabetta considers her next words. "It's been a long time since I met someone with your determination. I had forgotten what it feels like."

Anna Maria's breath seethes in and out of her.

"I can see that you are angry," Elisabetta says, leaning back, taking another sip from her cup.

"Yes, I'm angry! I'm furious!"

"Then use it," she says simply.

Anna Maria frowns.

"Your anger."

Anna Maria lets out a hollow laugh. "It's easy for you to suggest, with your money, your power." She thinks back, to how simply Elisabetta paid the man holding her violin hostage, how they shook hands, smiling at one another, when she had only been able to scream. "I have nothing. How can I move against him?"

"You may not have money, but you do have power. You have something they cannot help but listen to. You have your music."

Anna Maria sinks back into her chair. The thought holds her in place.

"It's not just about him," Anna Maria says, quieter now. There's a pause. She can hardly bear to speak. "I left someone. I left her."

Elisabetta leans closer.

"My friend. My . . . Paulina." She is choking out the words; tears are dripping on her hands. "She was in childbirth. I was so afraid of being caught. I ran from her to save myself. They took her, she's . . . They got her."

Elisabetta sits up straighter. "Now you listen here. Too many young women end up like her, and no seventeen-year-old would know what to do. You will not let this swallow you up, Anna Maria. You cannot afford to."

Anna Maria cannot hear this. She is shaking her head, saying, "No, you're wrong. I'm a monster. I come from monsters."

"What on earth do you mean by that?"

"She tried to drown me," Anna Maria whispers, barely able to believe it still. Her lungs start to fill, and the world is spinning, and she is heaving for breath. She might just disintegrate, like a raindrop in the canal. One moment a dent on the surface, a spark flying upward. But then it is subsumed, dissolved into the depths. Indistinguishable. Gone.

"Your mother?" Elisabetta asks quietly.

Anna Maria cannot speak. She nods. Just once.

And Elisabetta is standing, and she is taking her by the hand, and she is saying, "You come with me, now."

———

"Where are we going?"

All Anna Maria wants to do is crawl back into her dark room with her violin, to pull the blankets over her head and stay there, an animal in hibernation. Not this. Not sailing down the canals in the bright piercing light. Her eyes track the surface, searching for the baby girls looking up at her, their final horrified expressions, their lifeless faces whispering, *You.*

Elisabetta ignores her, staring ahead as they glide along the waterways, from the wide ripples of the Grand Canal, busy with the shouts of merchants and sellers, into the narrow channels of the labyrinth. They pass shacks, jetties crammed high with fruits and vegetables, the glinting facades of palaces arching up out of the water. The jade waters turn darker here in the depths of the city, gnarly and twisted like old trees.

Elisabetta makes a small signal with her hand and their boatman changes his stroke, turning so they pass under a bridge so low Anna Maria could reach up and touch it. The air becomes thicker, more humid, the sun beating against the stone walls. And then the smell changes, from the expensive waft of jasmine and rose, to urine and alcohol and rot. The water slaps at the sides of the boat, seems to want to suck it down beneath the surface. Anna Maria shuffles away from the edge. The houses do not rise out of the water here, they seem to crumble into it.

They must be near a market, because the noise of people bartering for spices and cloth echoes across the water toward them.

"How much further?" the boatman mutters. His thumb sticks out at an angle, altered by a lifetime of pulling an oar. "You said it was in San Polo, we're here."

Elisabetta tells him to pull up to the closest building. Then she stretches forward, extends an arm, reveals her palm. The gondola rocks gently.

"The card," she says.

Anna Maria tugs it out of her cloak and hands it over.

Elisabetta disembarks, disappearing into buildings for a moment or two and then returning to the boat. For an hour or more they journey like this, but each time Elisabetta comes back she seems to become more resigned. Anna Maria is tired, aching, desperate to turn back.

"Up there, on the right," Elisabetta says, pointing to a three-story house ahead. The plasterwork is peeling, broken shutters clattering against the wall. At the building across from it, two women hang over the balcony, breasts bare, dresses tugged down to their waists. They chatter down, saying things Anna Maria tries not to hear, as the seagulls squawk overhead. She has to close her eyes, look away, until another, larger gondola passes them at some speed, and the women's voices are swallowed, tossed out by the movement of the water. She looks up again to see a tall man step onto the balcony and tug them back behind a heavy curtain with a calloused hand.

"Here," Elisabetta says to the gondolier, who adjusts his oar against the *fórcola*, a walnut claw which helps him steer, and pulls in silently. Then she turns to Anna Maria, holds her gaze with her amber eyes.

"Your Venice is one of palaces and gold. Of music fit for God. Your education was a certainty, your orphanage frequented by kings and queens. But there is another world out there. A city that feasts on sin, on gluttony and lust and greed. At the heart of it all is sex, and the women who are destroyed by it." She leans closer, makes sure her words are clear as the daylight above them. "You do not come from a monster. You come from here." She points up to the building.

Anna Maria feels her anger beating fast against her chest. The boat lurches as she steps out onto the slippery stone steps.

An elderly woman emerges through the tasseled red curtain across the doorway. She has a crooked back, a yellow scarf wrapped around her sagging neck.

"Male or female?" she says, her eyes shifting up and down the canal, not looking at Anna Maria, not catching her confusion.

"I . . . Excuse me?"

"Which do you want? It's more expensive for the fourteen and unders."

Fourteen and under? Anna Maria's stomach clenches.

Elisabetta is by her side. The old woman suddenly bows her head. "Beg your pardon, madam, didn't realize it was you." The pair speak in hushed tones. Anna Maria can hear snatches. The word "orphan," the word "mother." The old woman shifts her eyes to Anna Maria from time to time during the conversation. She nods her head only once, right at the end.

Elisabetta holds out the sliced card. The old woman disappears with it through the curtains. The muffled words "follow me" come from behind them.

Anna Maria reaches forward, tugs the heavy fabric to the side, and leaves behind the light once again.

25

They are waiting in a dark, narrow corridor, sitting on a wooden bench which is propped against the wall, adorned with stained velvet cushions. The ceiling shudders, beads of dust cascading down to the thump, thump, thump of a headboard hitting a wall.

Elisabetta places a hand on Anna Maria's knee. Anna Maria hadn't realized that it is jigging up and down.

Anna Maria takes a breath, focuses on her surroundings. A few pillar candles burn on the side desk near the entrance. There's a large book on top of it. She stands, moves closer. The curling pages are covered with names and prices, even descriptions, scribbled quickly in messy ink. Anastasia is "slim and nimble," Patricia is "pretty and submissive." Anna Maria shakes her head, tries to rid her mind of the image of Patricia. She searches for something else to focus on.

The inkpot lies next to the book, lid off, drying out. The feathers of the quill are ruffled, many are missing. The smell in here is one that she can't quite place. Layers of scent all curl together. There's a heady floral musk, a stale tobacco, the smack of wine, but beneath these something else. Something intimate, human, raw. Something that makes her shift, knocking the quill to the floor.

"This way," the old woman says, emerging from the room on their left. She addresses Elisabetta. "They'll need more cloth rags for their bleeds, water and food soon. Will you be coming back with the donations?"

Elisabetta places a reassuring hand on the old woman's

shoulder. Anna Maria is not sure it's a good idea. Perhaps she shouldn't touch her.

"I shall return with them tomorrow," Elisabetta says.

But now Anna Maria is not focusing on the old woman or Elisabetta. She is looking at the large room they have stepped into.

It's a sort of den, not dissimilar from the one she found herself in the other night. Fabric hangs from the ceiling.

A bald woman sits in front of a cracked mirror, plucking her eyebrows, dabbing rouge onto her cheeks. A wig lies like a skinned creature on the dressing table in front of her. Four other women are asleep, or perhaps passed out, on the floor. The low wave of a moan ripples through the door from the floors above.

"Geltrude knows something," the old woman says, beckoning them toward the corner, where there is another woman Anna Maria hadn't noticed. She is sitting with her legs stretched out, back to the wall, wearing a silk robe, tangled hair plaited on either side of her head. She holds a small piece of fabric, tugs a pink thread through the cotton, embroidering it with flowers.

The old woman ducks down and holds out Anna Maria's half of the playing card. Geltrude doesn't say anything, just places her embroidery down and turns to a large wooden box lying on the floor next to her. The bruises around her wrists are lit by the soft glow of candles. They've been dabbed with a powder too pale for her skin. Some wounds can't be masked.

She creaks the lid back, starts to riffle through with her fingertips.

The box is bulging with items. Buttons sliced in half clatter around at the bottom, and there must be at least fifty squares of fabric, embroidered with birds and trees.

"Why are there so many?" Anna Maria whispers to Elisabetta.

"All the mothers leave them. Tokens, so that they can come back for their babes one day," she says.

Anna Maria feels the anger evaporate from her. Like an ebbing note, quiet and then silent.

The rustling stops. Somewhere, from the depths of the pile, Geltrude pulls a piece of card. Holds it up to the flickering candlelight. Then she holds up Anna Maria's half and, as if they were always destined to be, reunites them. Two pieces of the same soul, connected in the darkness after seventeen years apart.

"Her name was Amara," Geltrude says. Her voice is husky, tired, like it has lived at least one life already.

Elisabetta motions to the cushions and the pair of them join her, legs crossed on the floor.

"Nice girl. Came from a village outside of the city, family of cleaners. Apparently she'd been sent here by her father, delivering a coat to a nobleman. He found her charming, a little too charming for her own good, and made her his mistress. Set her up in an apartment, even got her some lessons. But after a few months he got bored, passed her on to a rich Jew who soon abandoned her too. She tried to go home, but her father didn't want her back, and she had nothing to pay her way. She ended up on the street. Tried to kill herself a few times. Drowning once, I think. Another with a knife."

"Why would she do that?" Anna Maria asks quietly.

"Most of us have at one point or another. What else, when there is no lower to go, no darker that life can get?" Geltrude closes the lid to the box, continues, "She'd left her baby at the Pietà soon before she arrived here. She was a mess, only seventeen years old, struggling for food, dying from thirst." She stops, laughs darkly to herself. "Venice is a land of water and yet we still can't quench the thirst of the poor."

"I broke her," Anna Maria whispers, more to herself than anyone. Her mind shifts from this room to hers at the Pietà. To a note, ripped and scattered like some dreadful confetti across the floor. She can feel every tear she made, as if it was not paper but layers of her own flesh.

"She ended up here after one of the workers found her," Geltrude continues, "passed out outside a tavern behind the Rialto Bridge, I think it was. Took pity on her, nice girl like that. Might have had a future in her still. She brought Amara back here. I was just a child then, watching from the sidelines, picking up a few tips and tricks. She nursed Amara to health, even brought back her beauty. She had these crisp green eyes, just like yours. And this funny way of talking about things. Words had tastes, she said, and colors too."

Anna Maria sits up straighter. "Colors?" she says.

"Used to say that the word 'dance' tasted of citrus. That 'girl' was blue."

Anna Maria's vision blurs. Up until now she hadn't really believed it. That they could be here, in the right place, that this woman, Geltrude, could have known her. But never in her life has she known another like her. A person who could see the world in multicolor. This mother. Her mother. She was real.

"Us girls thought she was funny," Geltrude is saying, "but it was nice, how she saw things. There was some hope in all those reds and greens and blues.

"She started to talk about her daughter, said she'd left her in the Pietà wall. Some of the girls here had gone back for their babies, even managed to raise enough money to keep them. The idea gave her purpose. She got stronger, a little of the light back in her eyes. And her beauty, now that it was back, gave her choices. She got to pick her suitors. It's not like that for all of us, you understand? Most get abused by anyone who'll take 'em. But Amara had her pick. The richest men in Venice. It gave her this confidence, got her off the wine. She managed to save up a nice little lump of money. Had planned to leave us in the summer, go get her girl. Rent a little place of her own."

Geltrude is holding Amara's half of the playing card between her thumb and forefinger, nails chewed to the wick. "She used to keep this in the wall behind the dressing table. I'd seen fabric, buttons, ribbons, and coins before, but never a sliced card like this. I watched her tuck it in some nights. She thought no one knew where she kept it, but I did. I liked to watch her. Patting it down like a little egg. She was nice. Syphilis took her in the end." She sighs. "She must have been twenty-three, twenty-four."

Geltrude takes Anna Maria's chin in her hand now, moves

her face toward the candlelight. "Pox?" she says, inspecting the remnants of scars.

Anna Maria has to remember to breathe. "Yes," she says eventually, "when I was six."

"You got off lightly," Geltrude says, returning to her embroidery. She tugs a few pink strands through the cotton. Then she pauses, looks Anna Maria straight in the eye. "Look, did she mean to have you? No. She was just a girl, didn't have a clue what was happening to her. But you, break her? Far from it, girl. Far from it."

"She was my age when she had me," Anna Maria says, staring down at her lap. Tears drip into her palms as she and Elisabetta glide away from the brothel in the gondola. "I thought she was a monster."

"Not a monster. Just a girl, left with little reason to love anything, least of all herself."

The boat sways gently, cutting through the calm surface, rocked every now and then by a passing boat's wake. They wind through the tight knot of canals and out onto the lagoon, the city diminishing behind them.

"Quite a sight, isn't it?" Elisabetta says.

The boatman works the oar until they are staring back at Venice, buildings jutting from the water like a stone crown.

"This is a city of wealth like no other. We have an eye for art, an ear for music. Anyone with enough vision can make something of themselves. For all its sins, it is the most prosperous and peaceful place on earth. What a thing to be born here."

She looks at Anna Maria now. "Do you see how lucky you are? How much you have that others do not? Yes, you had a mother who couldn't keep you. But instead, you were given opportunities, education, music. It is a gift the likes of which most girls will never know."

Anna Maria doesn't answer. It wasn't easy, she wants to say. There was death and disease, beatings and Correction, the constant threat of failure.

"And the *figlie*," Elisabetta is saying. "To get into the *figlie*, such an honor. Anna Maria, do you understand how special you all are? You alone are remarkable, but together, the *figlie* are a marvel. You are powerful beyond all belief."

"They're not all remarkable," she says darkly. "Chiara was just as bad as him."

"Wouldn't you do everything in your power to save your place there?"

Anna Maria feels a pang in her gut. Hears Paulina screaming at her from the floor.

Elisabetta says, "Music has saved you from so much."

Anna Maria sinks back, shoulders hunched, the wind ruffling her long curls. She is hollowed out, finished off. She cannot bear any more of this. Even hearing about Paulina and the *figlie* and her music feels like she is being cracked apart, smashed like one of her mirrors.

"You said in there that you broke her," Elisabetta says, edging closer. The sunlight highlights her strong jawline, glints off the diamond dangling from her ear. "But what about you? Who broke you?"

"Don't," warns Anna Maria.

There is a weight, like an anchor tugging against the depths of the lagoon. This loss, she realizes, she has carried all her life. It was not her talent, her determination. It was everything she did not have that drove her so.

But Elisabetta is leaning closer, she is speaking faster. "I saw a girl perform on a stage once. She was fire and lightning and storm in a person. I have never seen such energy, such drama and drive. Where is that girl now?"

Anna Maria stares into the water, her lungs beginning to fill.

"Broken. Taken by him. Her life, her music, suffocated in the fire. Throttled without a fight."

"It wasn't without a fight, I tried, I . . ." Anna Maria falls back, can't finish the sentence.

"The Anna Maria I saw onstage wouldn't accept this life. The Anna Maria from before the fame, before the pomp, she would have said no."

The words thrum through Anna Maria's body, her blood pumping a little faster than before.

"What will be your story?" Elisabetta whispers.

Anna Maria glares into the water. She thinks of Paulina. Anna Maria must live with having left her, but who must live with causing the child in the first place? No man will suffer, no penance will be served. And what of Anna Maria's music, her ideas? Who will pay the price for their loss? No one will know. No one will care. Her name will not be remembered. And not because she didn't try, but because it was snatched from her, destroyed by someone weaker than she. And this water, this darkness that has tormented her for so many years—what price will it pay for owning her dreams, for constricting her lungs, for taking her breath night after night?

The blood swells, flooding through her veins, furious and alive.

She will not allow it. Will not let it drown her any longer. She is standing, she is scowling at it, she is raining down on it.

She will decide her own story.

And before the scream, before Elisabetta can lurch forward and yell, "NO," Anna Maria leaps.

She will wrestle this beast. She will bear down on it with all her might. She will show these thrashing waves what she is capable of.

Give me everything, she chides. I am ready, I am ready for you.

But no, what is happening? There is no force, no fight at all. She raises herself up. She is standing, the warm sun drenching her face, the water lapping at her waist.

The lagoon. This body of water, of fear and menace and terror, is but four feet deep. And now Anna Maria is laughing, her head thrown back, beads of water dancing through the air. Is this what she was so afraid of? This plunge pool, this shallow soup?

She crashes back into it, lets her body float up on the surface, the water lapping softly at her skin. And moments before the sun sinks below the horizon, a new fire is lit. One that could ignite even a city set on water.

Elisabetta sits in the large soft chair in the parlor, a fresh cup of coffee in her hand, watching Anna Maria pace in front of the empty marble fireplace.

The sun's glow filters in through the long sash windows, bathing Anna Maria in warmth. She needs to find a way back into the Pietà. She has to go back for Paulina. She has to put this right.

She starts to think about what Elisabetta said. Music is her power. But how to use it? It is just music. Just notes. What help could—

Her fingers dig into her palms.

It is not just music. The music brings in money. And it is her name the crowds flock toward with their coins. Anna Maria makes the Pietà more gold than every other member of the *figlie* combined.

If she wants to be in the *figlie*, the *figlie* will want her back.

Anna Maria's eyes catch on Elisabetta's. She stops pacing, a smile spreading across her face.

Elisabetta raises an eyebrow. "What is it?" she says.

The smile grows wider. She will need Elisabetta's help, need to convince her to put her money toward a new concert, one where Elisabetta selects the players specifically. Herself, Paulina . . . even Chiara too. It might be enough. It could give Paulina a chance.

And then there's the matter of him. He must have no idea what is coming.

"I need another favor," Anna Maria says.

And now Elisabetta's mouth is curving into a smile too, and she is leaning forward, saying, "I'm listening."

The clock on the mantel beats a tick, tick, tick. The sun has risen high in the sky, heat rippling up off the terra-cotta tiles of the palace. Anna Maria walks toward the tall double doors in the front hallway of Elisabetta's apartment, shoes squeaking against polished stone. She stops with her palm resting on the handle, violin case clutched in the other hand, and turns back to Elisabetta.

"Do you think Paulina will forgive me?"

"I don't know," Elisabetta says. "But that doesn't mean you shouldn't try."

26

The campanile bells clang one. Anna Maria and Elisabetta weave through the crowds of tourists and merchants along the promenade. A boy in a brown jacket is handing out *gazzetta*, calling snippets of the news of the day. Two elderly women are hunched over a stall, bartering for a deal on a lace throw. Boats drift across the lagoon; the noise of singing sailors rolls across the water. Anna Maria slows to a halt.

Though only one week has passed, everything has changed. It is like she is seeing the Pietà for the first time. The tall white facade, the barred windows, the painted green shutters. It is an orphanage, but it is also a building with one of the finest footprints in the city. She marches through the open gates, violin in hand, pushing back the wooden front doors.

The buzz and heat of the promenade fade instantly. The stone entrance is cool, silent. The girls are in practice and classes. But now there is the rising patter of feet, and a student skids around the corner from the corridor to the left.

"You," Anna Maria calls as the girl dashes past them. She is small, with arched dark eyebrows, her hair skimming her shoulders.

The girl looks back and, realizing the famous Anna Maria is addressing her, blushes instantly. "I'm going straight back to class, ma'am. I wasn't skipping, I had to relieve myself."

"Don't call me ma'am. And you are not in trouble."

The girl nods.

"Do you know Chiara, one of the violinists in the *figlie*?" Anna Maria says.

"'Course I know her."

"Fetch her for me, please, quickly."

Another nod, and the girl is off.

Anna Maria feels Elisabetta's hand squeeze her shoulder. "I am going to speak with the sisters," Elisabetta says.

Chiara approaches from the corridor, mild surprise on her face. Anna Maria stands alone in the entrance hall waiting for her.

"You came back," Chiara says. She looks calm, mature, her hair swept back and tied with a black ribbon at her neck.

Anna Maria nods. "I wasn't sure I would."

There is a beat. An awkward pause.

Anna Maria lets out a breath. "I'm sorry," she says. "I shouldn't have treated you the way I did, I shouldn't have left you both. You're a good person, a good friend. I didn't understand."

Chiara watches her for a moment. Then a smile spreads across her face. "I'm glad you came. And thank you for saying that."

Shame balloons in Anna Maria's stomach. Chiara is kind. She has always been kind. Why couldn't Anna Maria see it?

"Do you know where Paulina is?" she says now.

Chiara nods darkly. "After they caught her, they took her to the *infermeria* to have the child. It's a little girl, just like you said it would be. There was rumor of them locking her in Correction, but they moved her straight to the nursery. I went to see her yesterday. It's . . . it's not a good situation. I'm not certain if they will keep her there or what will happen next."

Anna Maria is already heading for the other side of the Pietà building, the courtyard and nursery beyond.

"Wait a moment," Chiara calls, catching up with her.

"What else?" Anna Maria says, speeding up now.

"It's . . . well . . . I'm sorry, Anna Maria, I'm not sure she wants to see you."

Anna Maria stops, half her face illuminated by the window,

the other in the darkness of the corridor. "I know. But I have to help if I can. I have to try."

The shrieks and wails of unwanted babies echo out from the building behind the *infermeria*. Sometimes the churn of the canal drowns them out, swallows them up in the water.

The noises become louder as she approaches. Gurgling words, not yet fully formed, but that say, *Me, choose me, love me.*

It is a cavernous space. Instead of beds or cots, the nursery is filled with twelve large metal pens, each of them stuffed with ten screaming children of three years or less. The air smells sickly, of retched-up milk and soiled cotton rags. Anna Maria has no memory of being here as a child. Her first memories come at around three. Paulina and Agata are in all of them. Hiding in the bushes in the courtyard, sneaking biscuits in the kitchen, crafting palaces out of sticks and soil. She remembers the looming presence of the nuns, the sound of smacked bottoms, of whips meeting palms. She does not remember love, not beyond that shared between her and her two friends.

Anna Maria catches the eye of a little girl, probably only one year old, pressed up against the edge of the closest pen. She has huge beady eyes and snot running from her nose; her cheeks are red and hot. Someone should see to her, wipe her face, place a cool flannel on her head. But then there are a hundred or more girls like this, and she spots only three nuns. One is smacking a wailing toddler. Shock crosses the child's face and, instant as a gasp, she stops crying.

A sister is by Anna Maria's side now, a stern frown on her face. "No students allowed in—"

"You know who I am," Anna Maria retorts, braced and ready.

The sister steps back, bows her head. "My apologies, *maestro*," she says.

"I'm here to see Paulina. She had a child, apparently they sent her here."

The sister guides her through the wailing pens of children to a door to the right and back of the nursery. It leads to a small room. Inside there is a metal cot housing eight tiny babies, so small, so wrinkled they're more animal than human. And in the corner—

"Oh," Anna Maria breathes.

Paulina's skin is pinched and gray. Anna Maria is embarrassed to see that her smock has been tugged down to her waist, her naked breasts engorged, sagging under the weight of the liquid inside them. Two pink nipples glare, bleeding and raw. There is a baby asleep in her arms, and Paulina too has drifted off. Her head bobs gently, hanging over the child. Her smock is blood-stained at the skirt and hem. They haven't allowed her to change.

Anna Maria's insides contract. She takes a step back, the door clicking shut behind her.

Paulina wakes suddenly. Shakes her head, surprised to realize she had fallen asleep. She checks the baby in her arms, clutches it tighter. When her gaze lands on Anna Maria, the look is darker than coal.

"Get her out of here," she says to the sister.

"Please, Paulina. We need to talk."

"I would rather die. Truly, I would."

Anna Maria turns to the sister. "Leave us."

The sister sucks her teeth. She'd like to gather a slice of gossip for the other nuns to feast on at supper, no doubt. But she nods, curtsies, leaves.

The baby in Paulina's arms starts to fidget. Paulina shifts her body away from Anna Maria toward the window. Lifts the child up to her nipple, winces as it starts to suck.

Anna Maria speaks quietly. "What happened after—?"

"After you left? Oh, what a fun game. Yes, let's play that." Paulina's nostrils flare. "Firstly I was screaming on the floor. Perhaps you remember that part? Chiara did her best, but Sister Madalena found us. You can imagine her surprise at my little situation! She slapped me in the face when she first saw me. Not that I could feel it. The whole child-coming-out-of-my-snatch thing kept me really distracted."

She sounds like a different person. Someone older, colder, harder.

"Then I had her. On my own, in the darkness of the godforsaken *infermeria*. In the same bed"—she has to catch her breath, stop the tears from falling—"in the same bed as Agata," she says finally. "They dragged us through here soon after the baby arrived. I've been dropped from the *figlie*, naturally. He wouldn't have a whore like me in his ranks."

She puts down the child, but now she is picking up another and wincing again as this new child sucks at her breast.

"What are you—?"

"Did Chiara not tell you?" Paulina smiles, but it is not her smile. It is angry, pained. "All nine of them are my responsibility to feed."

Anna Maria looks again to the metal cot housing the wrinkled babies. She cannot hide her horror.

"Then again," Paulina growls as the baby bites down, "at least you get to play your lovely violin." There is a beat, then another. "How could you do it?" she whispers.

"I'm going to get you out of here. I'm going to fix this."

"Save your energy," Paulina says, turning her back. "You have already helped me so."

Elisabetta stands in the entrance hall watching Anna Maria walk closer, wiping her eyes on her sleeve. She doesn't say anything, just opens her arms. Anna Maria lets them envelop her. She stands there, for how long she does not know, and sobs.

Eventually Elisabetta pulls back, takes her chin in her hand, bends a little lower so she is looking directly at her. "I've spoken to the nuns. The concert will be in one week at my palace. I have requested Paulina and Chiara and all the names you gave me."

Anna Maria pulls back. Nods gratefully. And then she stiffens, rubs her face dry, forces the energy back into her muscles. It is time to get to work.

———

She has always loved this corridor. One thing, she thinks gladly, that hasn't changed at all. She listens to the notes curl out from under the doors to the music rooms, through the gaps between the frame and the wall. Watches as the class filters out, all energy and excitement, dirty stockings and rosin-covered fingertips.

Surprise darts across his face when she enters the classroom. The room has been tidied, the ashes from the grate swept away. It is like nothing has happened here at all.

He looks different too, his red curls slicked back into a neat ponytail. His attire is pared back, the lace ruffles replaced by a sleek white shirt with a tall collar. The picture of a gentleman.

"Back so soon?" he says. "The great Anna Maria couldn't find her way for more than a week outside of the Pietà walls?"

She will not rise to it. She says his name, lowering her gaze to the floor, becoming the girl he wants her to be. "I'm here to apologize. You have been nothing but good to me. You've mentored me, looked out for me, helped me to become the violinist I am today. It's like you said—you made me. And I have been nothing but ungrateful. I'm sorry." She looks up, makes her eyes as big and round as possible. "I am so very sorry."

His eyes narrow, his head tilts like a bird inspecting a worm. Will he eat it? Will he?

A breeze drifts out from the fireplace, whistling like a scream. She glances toward it. She will not look away. Her ideas lay there, remnants now turned to powder and dust. The thought only powers her more.

He takes a breath, then another, and finally he says, "It is in the past."

Her eyes flick back to him. "Thank you. Thank you for being so good, so understanding."

He nods.

She takes a step closer. Eases the conversation forward. "I hear there will be a concert a week from now."

"Another Marcini one," he says, pleased. He shuffles together parchments and manuscripts on his desk, starts screwing the lid onto his ink. "You will play, and a number of others, all selected specifically. It seems you have an admirer there." He looks up for her reaction.

She smiles her widest smile. Blinks, bashful and charming. "Do you have the music? I could start my practice."

He stiffens. "I will be working on that this week, no need to concern yourself. You will have it in plenty of time."

"Of course," she says. "Of course."

They wait in the cupboard across the hall from the largest music room, the silence a calm tune about them. Finally they hear the sound of him opening the door, disappearing down the corridor.

"Are you ready?" Anna Maria says, her knees crossed awkwardly, pulled up to her chest.

"I'm ready," Chiara whispers back.

Anna Maria explodes out of the cupboard, Chiara behind her. She shoves her foot in the gap to stop the door from locking shut.

"You've done this before," Chiara says.

"Once or twice." Anna Maria nods. "He usually keeps some over here, in the cupboard."

They rush toward it.

Chiara brushes up close behind her; Anna Maria creaks the cupboard open. Moments later they are hurrying down the hallway, arms full with parchment, ink, and quills.

There are four girls from the *figlie* waiting in her room when they reach it. Anna Maria steps back in surprise.

"Not to worry, I invited them," Chiara says. "You know Angelica, Camilla, Lorenza, and Rosanna. And there are more coming along tonight too."

She knows them all. But they are not friends. None of the *figlie* tend to speak to her. Or is it her, she wonders now, who doesn't speak to them?

"We've been working on some ideas," says Angelica, a harpsichordist, looking to Anna Maria for her reaction.

Next to her, Camilla, an oboist, nods. "We want to help."

Anna Maria pauses for only a second. "Well then," she says, marching across to her violin. "Let's get started."

The next morning Anna Maria is heading to the refectory down the spiral staircase when her journey is distracted by a set of luscious notes. The sound is so vibrant it glows, the colors moving right through her body. She slips instead into the third-floor corridor, edges closer until she is peering around the corner, watching him with her. The young girl from the *figlie*. So she is receiving private lessons too.

It's so strange, watching this. Like staring at her own past.

He steps closer to the girl now and Anna Maria feels a stab of fear. What will he take from this student? What will he do to her?

He is cupping the girl's cheek in his hand, his face too close to hers. "That was beautiful," he says, "beautiful."

Anna Maria feels heat rising up inside her. It is too much. She is only a child.

"Thank you, *maestro*," the girl says, looking up at him.

It takes every ounce of Anna Maria's energy to turn, walk away.

Not yet, she tells herself.

"Have you seen the way he is with that new girl, the young one in the *figlie*?" Anna Maria asks Chiara, biting down on her segment of orange.

They are in the refectory, the smell of stewed oats and bread in the air, the rumble of girls chatting, of knives hitting chipped china plates. It is the same as it has always been, and yet it feels different. The tables somehow smaller, the scratches and chips in the wood more visible all of a sudden.

"You mean Anna? Yes, I've seen it," Chiara says, shakes her head. "She's only thirteen."

Her name is Anna? How strange a coincidence. She doesn't say this, though. Instead she asks, "Why is he doing this?"

"That's not the half of it. Have you heard he's taking her out of school?"

"To a concert?" Anna Maria says. "He used to do that for me."

"No, not to a concert. He is taking her *out of school*, on tour with him to Vienna. Permanently."

Anna Maria's spoon clatters into her bowl. "He's leaving for good? And he's taking her?"

Chiara nods. "In a few weeks' time, I think. Where are you going?"

Anna Maria stands up so fast the table jolts. But she does not answer Chiara's question, she is running again now.

"You're Anna."

The girl is sitting in the smallest music room by the corner window. She holds a lump of rosin like a precious gem in her hand, rubbing it down the bow. Her short hair is tucked under a white piece of cotton, her *figlie* robes too large for her slight frame.

Anna Maria somehow knew she'd find her here. It's where Anna Maria always used to practice.

"Yes," Anna says, looking up, her hands stopping. "And you are Anna Maria."

"That's right." Anna Maria walks closer, positioning herself next to the music stand, her hand resting on it. "Listen, I wanted to speak with you. I heard you're being taken out of school—"

"Yes," she says proudly. "He wants me on his tour."

Anna Maria clenches her jaw. She won't patronize her, she would have hated that herself.

"I know. It's very flattering. But . . . the truth is, you can't trust him. You don't know what he could do to you."

Anna is frowning, saying, "That's not true. He's a good teacher. Maybe it's you who doesn't know him."

Anna Maria is speaking faster; she's trying to get the words out right. "I do know him. I know him very well. He's a brilliant performer, and a great composer too. But he's also a difficult man. He's cruel, and insecure, and he takes advantage of us and our ideas."

Anna returns to rosining her bow. There is an empty chair next to the music stand. Anna Maria pulls it across, sits down. "Look, none of us have anyone to guide our way, to teach us a good decision from a bad one. But we do have each other." She pushes the bow down gently, so that Anna is forced to meet her eyes once again. "You don't have to go with him. You can stay here in the *figlie*. You can keep up your education."

Though she is but a girl, she looks every bit as confident as Anna Maria did at her age, maybe even more so. "I don't need your help," Anna says, frustrated now. "You don't know me."

"No, I don't. But when I was your age I needed a friend and I didn't have one. So I would like to be a friend to you now. You don't have to leave school, you don't have to live with him. He should know better."

Anna is shaking her head. "This is my opportunity to get everything I have ever wanted in life."

Anna Maria lets the words hang a moment, but she can see there is no changing her mind.

"Fine. But . . . fine." She stands, takes a step toward the door. "Just know one more thing before you leave. If you want to change your mind, you can. This is your home. It is all of our homes."

Anna's focus returns to the hairs of her bow. But she nods, almost imperceptibly, once.

The small room smells even worse today, a mix of putrid canal fumes, warm milk, and feces. Paulina is pacing around the cot, a baby slung over her shoulder, patting its back and grimacing, while Anna Maria is midsentence.

"It's a fine plan, Paulina, you know it is. You have to come, it'll—" She has to sidestep as Paulina passes her again, her back flat against the wall. "It'll get you out of all of this," she says.

Paulina continues to pat the child's back. It vomits up a blend of milk and saliva onto a muslin cloth on her shoulder. She wipes its mouth dry.

"Paulina?" Anna Maria says, a little louder now.

"No." Her response is quick. It's the third time in this

conversation that she's said it. "I don't want anything to do with you or your ideas. Why will you not listen to me? Why will you not leave me alone?"

Anna Maria falls silent. She places the sheets she is holding down on the table, pushing aside piles of cotton nappies and pins to make space. "This is the music. The concert is three days from now at the Marcini Palace. Eight sharp."

Paulina continues pacing.

"Just think about it," Anna Maria says finally, her throat tight. "Not for me, but for you. Think about what it could mean for you."

Anna Maria tosses back and forth, throwing the thin cotton sheets off her body. She is lying rigid, facing the ceiling. Can't sleep, but not because she has been woken by drowning. Ever since she jumped in the lagoon, the nightmares have ceased completely. She cannot sleep because blood pumps fast through her veins, heart drumming at her ribs. She slides her violin toward her, plucks gently at the strings. The moonlight glints into her room, illuminates the deep reds and golds of her instrument. She rolls onto her side, nestling the violin into the curve of her body, and wills herself to dream of tomorrow.

On the top of the campanile tower, a gull opens its wings and falls upward, into sky.

A bee lifts off from the jasmine arches of the Marcini Palace gardens, following the trail of sweet scent through tall windows and into the palace, where its buzz and energy is matched by the feeling in the ballroom. It finds its destination: a bouquet of roses and jasmine spreading out across a long slim table against one wall.

At one end of the ballroom, a stage has been erected, seats empty, waiting for the *figlie* to take their positions. The chandelier in the middle of the room clinks gently, candlelight glittering on the walls. The sounds of laughter, of cheering, of gossip and rumor, circle among the crowd.

Anna Maria twists through the throng, dressed in a black satin dress, smiling widely, curtsying and shaking hands and looking deep into their eyes. "Welcome, thank you for coming, so good to see you," she says. A woman approaches with a quill and parchment. Anna Maria swirls her name across it, the sound of paper scratching beneath the nib.

The woman claps in delight. "A piece of you, a gift from God!" she breathes.

It is something she can take home and show her neighbors. Something she can look at in the depths of the night, when she wakes to the shadows. Now she can remind herself that she met Anna Maria della Pietà.

Anna Maria smiles graciously, moves further into the crowd of elites with their ruffles and their jewels. Let them touch her. Let them hug her and breathe her in and devour her whole. It's all part of the plan.

Elisabetta looks remarkable, wearing a deep purple gown with wide sleeves and a train. She greets her guests at the door, governors and nobles, philosophers and thinkers, poets and writers from all over Europe. Her teacher stands in the center of the room in black breeches, a white ruffled shirt, shaking hands, smiling, nodding politely.

Seeing him, Anna Maria feels a grip in her chest. She changes course, slips toward a quiet corner behind the ample frills of three ladies' dresses. Her eyes search the crowd. There's been no word from Paulina since their conversation three days ago, and no sign of her now. But there's still time. She could still make it.

Chiara is crossing the room, a pomegranate flower in her hair, another in her hand.

"From the famous Casanova," she says, smiling at her, tucking the flower behind Anna Maria's ear.

The petals skim Anna Maria's cheek. Let her be the angel they want.

"Are you ready?" Chiara says now.

"Almost. Gather the *figlie*, will you? And meet me in the salon in five minutes' time."

Anna Maria crosses the ballroom toward the ornate double doors, slips between them. She stands at the top of the wide, curving stone staircase that leads up from the courtyard entrance. Watching, waiting.

The clock ticks down, the excited rumble of conversation and clinking glasses muffled by the closed doors. Her heart begins to thud.

She has to come. She has to.

Anna Maria peers over the banister. Ivy winds up it, dancing in the breeze. But no sign of her friend walking up the steps, golden hair flowing over her shoulders.

Dread starts to ease through her. The concert is about to begin. But still Anna Maria stands. Still she waits.

If she doesn't come . . . Anna Maria won't even think it. She won't imagine what terrible reality Paulina might face once her milk is dried, her body useless to them. Anna Maria does the only thing she can think of and runs. Down the steps, toward the courtyard, past the marble pillars, and into the cool evening air.

She breaks out into the opening, her breathing hard, fast. She turns on the spot, alone, hope seeping from her bones.

And then a noise catches her attention. She looks sharp toward the canal.

There, being helped off a gondola by Sister Clara, is her friend.

The salon is a large oval room next to the ballroom. The walls are paneled with a navy satin. In the center of the room, two curving couches face each other. On them sit eleven young women who have been selected to perform tonight. The finest players in the entire orchestra. The twelfth, Paulina, is positioned on a chair in the shaded corner near the door. She seems exhausted and she won't look at Anna Maria, but she is here. It's all that matters.

Anna Maria stands at the front of the room facing them all, a huge mirror bearing down behind her. "I have something to say before we play tonight. Something I want us to remember."

The *figlie* watch her. Intent, focused.

"Each of us is special. We all have talents greater than most people could ever dream. We deserve our places here. Not because we are angels, or miracles, or gifts from God. Because we work hard. Because we care." There is nodding; Chiara is smiling at her. "In most places we'd be considered scum, spat on by the lowest of the low. Yet here we are, standing in the finest palace of all Venice with the crowds falling at our feet. That is the power and influence of our orchestra. If nothing else, think of this when you play tonight. This is our moment. This is our Republic of Music."

A hush falls across the crowd like a thick blanket. The *figlie* wait onstage in position. He is at the front, his red hair flowing across his shoulders.

Anna Maria waits for silence. The calm, the anticipation. And then she turns the handle. The crowd inhales as she emerges into the ballroom, takes the steps, crosses the stage.

He stands front and center with his back to the audience. An awkward smile, stiff, poised, ready to begin. She doesn't look at him as she takes the position of first violinist but instead at Paulina, directly across from her.

Anna Maria raises her instrument, guides her bow along the *A* string, leading the orchestra as they tune. The sound, though it is a single note, is astounding. Hundreds of years of musical innovation ring in her ears. She can hear the hollowed shell of the Arabic rebab, the twin strings of the Byzantine lyra. She can hear the medieval fiddle sing, the calm voice of the Chinese erhu. All the instruments that came before. Dreamed up, carved from trees, stuck with glue, adapted, played, adapted some more. Leading here. To Anna Maria, violin in hand, the liquid tone seeping through her body.

He holds his breath, mouth tightening as he waits.

She looks at him and nods. Sharp, quick. He lifts his arms. They lift their instruments.

A curl of red from the violins, a spiral of gold from the cellos.

And his face instantly drops.

Because this is not what he planned. This is not what he expected at all.

27

The baton swipes the air in jagged half movements. Though his arms keep conducting he looks only at her. Anna Maria's eyes bore through him, the colors exploding overhead.

This is a story told through music. Not only an Anna Maria composition but a *figlie di coro* composition. A collaboration, sketched on stolen parchment in her tiny Pietà room, woven by those who, just like Anna Maria, have been composing to the secret glint of candlelight for years. They play what it means to be a girl in this world. The fame and devastation, the fear and exhilaration, the rush of ideas and the crush of silence.

Beads of sweat form on Anna Maria's forehead, her arm starts to throb.

Enough, he is mouthing. *End this now.* He half glances to the audience, offers a weak smile to insinuate that he is in control.

Never, Anna Maria thinks. I will never stop for you.

Anna Maria's eyes flick to Paulina opposite, fingers fluttering up and down on her oboe. Like she knew she was being watched, her gaze meets Anna Maria's. She gives a small smile, one that sends a pulse through Anna Maria's chest. And then Paulina turns over the sheet, and she is focusing again. And now Anna Maria glances to her orchestra.

The *figlie* are a unit. Communicating with glances and nods, following Anna Maria's lead. She is on the edge of her chair, her spirit dancing as her fingers rush up and down the strings. The sound is more delicious than sugared dough, than melted butter, than honey dripped on bread.

His eyes shoot Anna Maria another warning. But the piece is building. The *figlie* change tempo so fast that someone gasps.

And, like a net thrown, the audience is captured. Barely a blink among them, they are twisted and turned through their emotions, guided on a journey by the sound.

The red is rising in his cheeks, his mouth pinched and tight. Still he conducts a piece he has never heard. What else can he do but pretend?

The *figlie* move the audience into the darkness now. Tumble them down a pit of scarlet and black, falling, clutching for the sides.

Anna Maria begins to smile. She thought the colors had been lost to the flames along with her ideas, but here they are, alive, vivid, erupting in her mind.

The *figlie* swirl back from the darkness into pinks and yellows. Anna Maria has to stop herself from standing, from following as they rise.

Butterflies. Hundreds, no, thousands of them. They take off from each individual shoulder, whirling through the air until there is no longer a flight of individual creatures but one throbbing, thriving unit.

Anna Maria draws her bow across the strings a final time. The air seems to thicken, a second of silence stretched, weighed down. Then comes the applause. The audience on their feet. *Bravo*, they are cheering. *Maestro, maestro, bravo.*

Anna Maria watches from the sidelines as he steps off the stage.

"Marvelous, *maestro*, just marvelous," a woman with an elaborately feathered skirt is saying to him.

"Your finest work to date," the woman next to her chimes in.

A man with gold buttons on his lapel squeezes between them, shakes his hand. "How do you do it, virtuoso, time and time again?"

More of the crowd flocks around him, hungry pigeons heaping praise and congratulations, slaps on the back, invitations to further events and performances, composing deals and parties.

"Thank you, Count, Countess . . . Your Highness! I did not know you were here . . . No, really, it is my honor . . . It was nothing," he is saying, "nothing."

And a titter, from a woman in a feathered gown. Directed not at him but at the rest of the guests at her palace. Elisabetta Marcini raises a Murano glass flute, clinks it with her circle of elites, and asks a question that will ripple on through the crowds and streets, hot and vivid as a flame.

"Are we certain he can handle those girls?"

Anna Maria tears her glance away. She slips quietly into the salon, prepares herself for what is to come.

The door slams open. She stands as he enters.

"You foolish child," he says, grabbing the handle and tugging the door shut. "You could have ruined the entire music program with a lark like that. You are lucky I was able to keep up appearances. And for what? The audience still thinks the music is mine!" He comes to a stop, his hands gripping the back of the couch opposite her.

"You're right," she says. "But that's not what matters."

His certainty shifts for a second.

"I know this is our work. You know this is our work. Heavens, maybe one day the world will know too. They will hear about the girls with missing fingers, the sockets instead of eyes, the pox-marked skin, and the 'P's' burned into our arms. They will know that we were here, that this is what we achieved. This music is the glory of our lives. I can live with that. Can you?"

"Can I what?"

"Can you live with knowing that these ideas are not yours alone? That one man does not make a history?"

"None of this matters," he says quickly. "I'm leaving, I'm going." He walks back toward the door.

"Away to Vienna," she says. "So I hear. And you're taking one of our youngest, most talented members with you."

"It is an opportunity—"

"It is a scandal. Living with a teacher, a man more than twice her age, when she is but thirteen years old. Her reputation will be in tatters."

He is turning the door handle.

"Tell me, *maestro*, is there anything you would not take from us?"

He rounds on her now. "I don't have to listen to this. You don't know what it's like. You know nothing of being poor."

She laughs. Quick, harsh, cold. "Perhaps you haven't noticed I'm an orphan—"

"An orphan who is handed her food every day, who receives her instruments and her education for free. You know nothing of growing up in the shadow of five siblings despite being the oldest, with barely a hunk of bread to go around. You know nothing of existing beneath a virtuoso father for whom I was never enough. I will not go back to that place, six of us around a splintered table deciding who would get to eat tonight."

"You want to advance your career, I understand that perfectly. But this isn't just about you. It is about the girl, about Anna."

"I won't go back to being who I was."

"And this is not the way."

His face changes for a moment. There is something on it like regret.

"I have always seen myself in you, Anna Maria. We both believe in excellence above all else. Stop this now. Do not ruin all that we have—"

"I'm nothing like you," she says calmly, certainly. "I would never do what you have done, sending girls away, taking everything from them."

"But you have already done so," he says. "To Cecilia, to Bianca. It is only as others were dropped that you were able to rise."

Something inside her contracts. She wants to say she had no choice, wants to say he made it so. But no. There is truth in it. The silence settles across her like a shawl.

She thinks he will leave without another word. But he pauses for a second, turns back a final time.

"Cast me as you will. But the truth is never so simple as we think."

The door closes, and she is drenched in darkness.

Sunlight filters through the branches of the tree in the courtyard and into her window. She slept so deeply it takes her a moment to hear the shrieks of girls running around the tree, the clatter of carts, the calls from the markets beyond the walls. The city is awakening. When she stands she feels lighter, like the air has shifted, like it no longer has such power over her.

She dresses in a dreamlike state, reliving the moments from last night. The sway of the audience, the perfection of the performance, the smile from Paulina. She meanders toward the refectory, hand gliding along the walls, the *figlie*'s music playing over in her head. She'll eat something, find the girl, Anna, speak to her again. Convince her to stay.

Sister Clara is on duty, standing by the entrance, squinting around the room, watching the girls.

"I'm looking for Anna, the young girl in the *figlie*, have you seen her?"

"Good morning to you too, Anna Maria," Sister Clara says, more bristly than usual.

Anna Maria waits a moment to see if she will say why, but there is nothing more, so Anna Maria adds, "Yes, good morning."

Sister Clara's face twists in disapproval. "The girl you mention left this morning. With him, to Vienna."

Anna Maria's gut clenches. They weren't supposed to leave for another week or more. After everything she said, Anna still left, still went with him.

"Did she say if she is coming back at all?"

"We don't house whores, Anna Maria, just their children. Surely you know that by now."

A bowl of fresh peaches and grapes lies in front of her at morning meal. She sits, starts to eat, barely registering the taste, the texture of the skins popping in her mouth, the chatter of the girls around her.

Anna was young, but she seemed strong, just like her at that age. Anna Maria hopes it can be enough. Has to trust that there will still be a chance to help her. That she will send word when she is ready.

The sweet juice dribbles down her chin as she takes a bite from the peach. And now a new thought pops into her mind. An opportunity, something she had never even considered, never thought possible. She is up, rushing back to Sister Clara, who looks up at her. "Yes?"

"The Master of Music role, is it open?"

"I believe so, yes. Sister Madalena is reviewing some candidates upstairs."

Anna Maria takes the steps two at a time. Three loud knocks, an "enter" from the other side, and she bursts into Sister Madalena's office.

"I have something to say."

Sister Madalena is at her desk, hunched over several piles of paper. As the door creaks shut, Anna Maria realizes she is not alone.

"Oh . . . excuse me, Signore," she says, shifting to her right to take in his large frame.

The man is immediately familiar. Aged, somewhat, since Anna Maria last saw him, his tufted eyebrows now white rather than graying, the lines on his face a little deeper, more pronounced.

"I mean, Governor Ciuvan," Anna Maria says. The same man who applauded her at her first concert, the same man who led her *figlie* audition and accepted her into its ranks at just thirteen.

His voice is croakier than she remembers, but it still has the nasal quality.

"*Maestro*," he says, offering her a formal nod as he lifts the black tricorn hat in his hand and places it back on his head.

"I'll come back," Anna Maria says, turning to leave.

Governor Ciuvan lifts his pale satin coat off the chair, tugs it on now. "No need. I was just leaving. As I was saying," he turns back to Sister Madalena, "we are going to struggle to fill the position at such short notice. Have those names to me by the morning, Madalena, not a moment later."

Sister Madalena gives him a curt nod, and the door closes behind him.

From upside down Anna Maria can read men's names, some details of their careers, listed in narrow lines on the thick piece of parchment on the desk. Sister Madalena looks at her like she is a dog freshly rolled in muck, wandered in off the street.

"So, what might it be that you want? Does princess need a more luxurious bedcloth? Another mirror to smash? Perhaps a broom to sweep up her own mess this time?"

"The Master of Music role. I want it."

Sister Madalena laughs. "Of course you do."

Anna Maria does not twitch. Sister Madalena puts down the quill she is holding, leans back in the chair, and crosses her arms over her chest. "Did you fall down, girl? Smack your head?"

Anna Maria stands firm. "I didn't, I haven't."

"It is a position for men—"

"It is a position for those who are capable."

"Well." Sister Madalena shakes her head. She speaks as if to a simpleton. "It's not up to me, anyway. You would need to convince the governors and— Where are you going?"

Anna Maria has tugged open the door and is running down the corridor before she can finish. The governor is at the top of the spiral steps, one hand on the banister, one foot jutted forward, about to descend.

"Governor, wait."

He looks at her in surprise.

"I need a moment with you and Sister Madalena. I will explain, please."

She can hear the tight satin of his coat rubbing against his shirt as he follows her back into the office. He resumes his seat in the corner of the room.

Sister Madalena raises her eyebrows, amused, awaiting what comes next.

"I want the Master of Music role," Anna Maria says, placing both hands on the desk in front of them. "I was the youngest ever member of the *figlie di coro*, I am a virtuoso violinist and a composer, and I make the Pietà a lot of gold. If you want the famous Anna Maria della Pietà to keep smiling and playing, you'll give me the role. You need me more than I need you."

Sister Madalena's eyes flick to Governor Ciuvan, who is listening, watching her, motionless.

Anna Maria continues, "I want to access my money. You will write down which bank it's in, any details I need. And I want absolute authority over the music program. I will pick the members of the *figlie*, I will decide what we play, when and where we perform. I will give the girls opportunities to compose. And in return, I will make the music program at the Pietà more famous and more powerful than you can even imagine."

She may never be credited. Her friends may never be credited. But she is part of a chain, she sees that now. She can be a better teacher than he was, she can create more opportunities than he did. She can continue that chain until eventually something shifts.

There is a beat, then another.

"A female Master of Music would be most uncommon," Governor Ciuvan says.

"I know that, but I am more than qualified and—"

His shaking head makes Anna Maria stop.

"I was not finished," he says. "A female Master of Music would be most uncommon. Then again . . ." Anna Maria breathes in, does not let it back out. "The Pietà has not known a talent like yours."

Sister Madalena is staring, unblinking, at the governor.

Governor Ciuvan stands, smooths down the fabric on his breeches, looks back to the two women in the room. "I will approve it."

Anna Maria finally lets out the breath she has been holding.

"You will?" Sister Madalena says, flabbergasted.

"A trial basis only. Three months. It solves our short-term

issue, wouldn't you say? We will have to see how she copes with the level of responsibility, with the demands of performing and teaching and composing too. The other governors will have to agree to it after that. You will see to the details, Madalena, and I will return in three weeks to check on progress."

When he exits the room the silence is thick, heavy. It looks like Sister Madalena has swallowed something large and uncomfortable. But Anna Maria can hardly believe it—Sister Madalena is taking a fresh piece of parchment, scribbling some words and numbers on it. Then she stands, extends her arm across the table, and shakes Anna Maria's hand.

"Welcome, Master," she says. "Now get out."

Anna Maria runs down the corridor, has to hop a couple of times to stop herself at the banister, to race down the steps. She is Master of Music! She is Master of Music! There is only one person on earth she wants to tell. She runs for the nursery, but in the entrance hall it's someone else she crashes into.

"Elisabetta? What are you doing here? Sorry . . . here." She picks up a roll of bread, knocked to the floor from the basket Elisabetta carries.

"And where are you off to in such a hurry?" Elisabetta says.

The words burst out of her. "I've been awarded the Master of Music role! Thank you, Elisabetta, for all your help."

"That is fantastic, Anna Maria. I'm glad I could be of use."

"I'm running to tell Paulina, she's not going to believe it—"

"Paulina is not here."

Anna Maria doesn't quite hear her, the words muffled beneath her pounding feet. "What?" she says, from the other side of the entrance hall now.

"She is not here."

"Well . . . where is she?"

"She decided to leave, early this morning. I arranged a boatman for her and the child. I'm sorry, I know this must be—"

Anna Maria walks closer. "Leave? To where? When is she coming back?"

A pause.

"She asked that I not say. But she is not coming back."

Anna Maria blinks, sinking against the wall. *She is not coming back.*

Elisabetta shifts the basket of bread to her hip, places the other hand on Anna Maria's shoulder. "She will find her way. There are families, good families, in need of a governess. Her musical skill will not be wasted, I'll make sure of it."

"She didn't want to see me?" Anna Maria asks quietly.

"I'm afraid some wounds cut too deep. Don't lose heart, Anna Maria. Leaving was a choice she was free to make. Your efforts helped her realize that."

A bird nestles on the windowsill outside. Anna Maria watches it for a moment, her throat tight. Then she says, "Why do you do it?"

"Do what?"

"Why are you helping Paulina? Why did you help me? I thought you hated me. It seemed like . . ."

Elisabetta sighs. Tugs the basket up an inch or two. "I did not *hate* you, Anna Maria. I found you . . . arrogant, perhaps, to be so expectant of my attention. But no, no, I did not hate you. I simply thought that you were safe."

A frown on Anna Maria's brow.

"You have such talent. Ever since that first time I saw you. Eight years old and playing on the chapel stage like God Himself was within you. You, I knew, were destined to succeed." She smiles sadly. "I help the girls who need it."

The high-pitched tones of some young girls singing filter down the spiral staircase toward them from the floors above. Anna Maria can feel them ruffling her hair like a breeze through leaves.

Elisabetta looks toward them as she says, "Of course, when I saw him with you, under that archway, I realized I had been wrong."

Anna Maria's mind reaches back to a hooded figure. Standing, walking away.

"And then you were on that street outside the tavern, and I realized you might lose it all and . . . well. I couldn't stand by and let that happen."

Anna Maria lets out a breath. She wants to hit the wall, to say that Elisabetta could have saved her, that there was no need for it to come to this. Anna Maria has lost everything she truly loves, everything but her violin, and Elisabetta has stood by and watched.

"You don't help the girls who need it," she says, the words bitter, sharp.

Elisabetta narrows her eyes, confused.

"The girls you funded for lessons at the Pietà, the rich ones, waiting there in their velvet cloaks to cut my class time. They did not need your help."

"Are you so sure?"

But Anna Maria will not listen. I needed you, she thinks, something heavy in her chest.

"Not everything is always as it seems, Anna Maria. Those girls came from money, yes, but grand families are not always good families. They can hit, they can scar. Music was a way to save them too."

But there is only anger coursing through Anna Maria's veins. The feeling floods up, speaks for her. "Why do you want to save anyone?" she hisses. "What good will it do you?"

Elisabetta pulls back. She looks smaller, childlike all of a sudden. She nods slowly. "You're right, of course. There is no saving me."

There is such sadness, such pain in her eyes, Anna Maria almost looks away.

"I had a daughter once," Elisabetta says now. "I stood at that hole in the wall, placed her down, walked away." It is an effort for her to speak, her voice stretched, strained. "She was a child of incest, born of brutality. Knowing her would have made it all too real. For years I tried not to think of her. But when my brother died—when I came to understand what had been done to me—something changed. I realized that to be parted from her was not what I wanted. I prepared everything, I was ready to return. But by the time I . . . by the time I came for her . . ."

Anna Maria lunges for the basket as the rolls fall to the floor. Elisabetta has to place a hand on the wall to steady herself. Tears spill down her cheeks.

"The room in your house," Anna Maria says, her voice a whisper.

Elisabetta nods gently. "Yes. It was to be hers."

Anna Maria moves closer. "I didn't . . . I'm sorry."

"I know I am no mother. But eventually I realized I had an opportunity with my wealth, my status. To help a little if I could. It certainly helped me to cope. It gave me a reason to get up, to get dressed, to keep going. To survive." She smiles, but it is a broken smile, one that makes Anna Maria's insides clench.

"It has become a life's work. But that is all it really is—survival. What you have—with your violin, with your compositions—that is what it is to truly live."

She straightens up, pats the tears away from her cheeks with two flat palms. "That is why I do this. For you, for Paulina, for the others. Because once I was a girl with no one too. I intend to leave this world a little more alive."

Anna Maria bends down, collects the tumbled rolls from the floor, hands the basket back to her.

Elisabetta takes it and nods, just once.

Anna Maria looks to her right, at the empty table opposite the entrance. She thinks then of the blue-purple flower delivery, so beautiful it was like they were blown from molten glass. Elisabetta standing, crying, clutching her waist.

"What was her name, your girl?" Anna Maria calls out as she walks away.

Elisabetta pauses, looking back. She smiles now. "Iris. Her name was Iris."

Her silhouette is strong, tall, as she walks through the Pietà gates and into the city beyond.

———

Anna Maria is at the end of the music room corridor when she stops. Lets her hands fall to her sides.

She had really believed. Really thought that returning here would fix things, that the plan would save Paulina, show her the way back to the *figlie*. But she has left. She is gone.

A curl slips from behind Anna Maria's ear but she doesn't move, doesn't push it back. For a moment she thinks she may crash beneath the surface once again, helpless as her lungs start to fill. But there is just silence. Just a quiet, true sadness.

She is not coming back.

Moments pass while the world around her continues to hum and beat. Then something else. Something that settles over her slowly, calmly, like a fine Venetian mist.

Paulina is not coming back, and that is her choice. This, like so many things, Anna Maria must learn to live with.

She walks quietly back to her room, spotting Chiara, Lorenza, and Angelica in the largest music room on the third floor, huddled over parchments, scribbling down ideas. The scene makes her smile, but she doesn't enter, doesn't make her presence known. There is only one place she wants to be now.

She clicks the door shut, lets the silence wash over her. Then she walks across to her bed, peels back her blankets, and reveals her violin. She crawls in beside it, scoops her body around its curving wooden frame.

"We did it," she says quietly, clutching it tight. "I'm the Master of Music."

The early light catches the sparkle. It skims off the canal, darts up to the Basilica, a million squares of golden glass glinting on its roof. And now the light jumps, travels through the patchwork of islands, knitted by bridges, woven with water. Off rooftops, shimmering against windows, rippling onto the lagoon, stretching out into the sky.

Anna Maria watches it from the doorway of the Banco della Piazza di Rialto, a sack of gold coins jingling in her hand, her violin resting at her feet. A chill breeze sweeps her cheeks and she lifts a hand to her mouth, takes the last bite of *frittelle*, savoring the smooth cream, licking the sugar from her fingers. Two meals a day of rice and pasta, fresh fruit, and meat have filled her body these past weeks. She feels strong, healthy.

She weaves through the streets, twisting between the market crowds, breathing in the smells of tomatoes and soil and salt. Then across the bridge to the Piazza San Marco and past the gilded dome of the Basilica, moving freely through the city as she has done every day since she took on her new role.

"Aren't you Anna Maria?" a child squeaks, his mother behind him, an arm on his shoulder.

"That I am," she says, bending down so they are eye to eye.

"Mother, it's her! It's her!"

"I know, dear." The woman is laughing. "I'm sorry. He says he wants to play like you one day. Here, would you?" She takes out a square parchment from her cloak pocket, turns over the shopping list, hands Anna Maria a small lump of charcoal. Anna Maria sweeps her name across it in elegant loops.

"Keep practicing," Anna Maria says, smiling as she walks away.

She follows the promenade, admiring the glitter of the lagoon, until the walls of the arsenal shipyard rise above her. She turns down a side alley, a line of white cotton shirts billowing above her head in the breeze. She knocks on a door.

It is just as she remembers, though it has been years since she was here last. The wide entrance hall, the huge golden-edged mirror, the violins rocking gently overhead and glinting at her from behind the glass case. It was the first place she was shown kindness and respect beyond the Pietà, a place she came when life was simpler, more innocent. This has always been, and will always be, somewhere she is happy.

He is aged, struggling to walk, but he still has the kind eyes, his face mapped with smile lines. "I thought you would never return," Nicolò says, taking her hands in his.

She is guided through the workshop to his office behind. A window at the far end is cracked open, the music of the city filtering in. But it's the far wall that makes her breath catch in her throat. There, pinned up and fluttering in the breeze, are parchments and clippings, reviews and summaries. Every one of them about her. The *gazzetta* from her first Pietà performance when she was eight, her first review, the announcement of her as *maestro*. Every moment of her career is here, in this place where violins come to life, carefully collected and preserved in her honor.

They stand quietly, looking at them. Anna Maria tries to dry her eyes with her sleeve, but Nicolò pulls a fresh embroidered cloth from his pocket, hands it to her as she dabs at her cheeks.

"I've come to buy it," she says, looking at him now.

"Your violin? But it is already paid for."

"I want to own it, properly own it. I have the money." She tugs the pouch of gold out from her cloak. "Can you see to it that my teacher is refunded, and the Pietà too?"

Nicolò smiles. "It will be done." Then he motions to her violin case, clutched in her hand. "Would you?"

"Of course," she says.

Staff gather in the salon of the violin shop, edging between the chairs, wiping hands on dusty aprons. Anna Maria stands in front of them, back to the glass case, violin held high. There is a beat, a moment, and then the notes start to course through her body, bow to string, fingers to wood. Until she is beyond, out there, with the music.

She wanders slowly back to the Pietà, sucking the salty lagoon air into her lungs, the first whispers of autumn in the wind. The violin—her violin—swinging in her hand. A man's voice singing opera floats down the alleyway to her right. The calls of the gondoliers join, mix with it, and now the tones of the shoe-shiners too. Blending, dancing through the air. A city of makers and creators, visionaries and dreamers. Her city. Their city. Their Republic of Music.

And with this thought come the colors. She watches them curl out of the open windows around her. Golds and reds, greens and blues, a thousand shades or more, each one thick and alive and glorious. And she is running. And she is chasing them, through the labyrinth, toward a future she does not, cannot know. But she is ravenous, and she is ready, and so she sprints faster, faster now, to the fresh manuscript book that lies on her desk, its pages deliciously, enticingly empty.

She tugs the colors to the parchment, lets them erupt from her mind, form the first notes of a piece.

And finally, when it is done, when her heart thrums in her chest and her hands are ink-stained and aching, she stops, breathes out, closes the book once again. Lets the last light of day ripple across the gold letters emblazoned on the front.

Anna Maria della Pietà.

A name, glistening in the darkness, ready, one day, to be remembered.

Author's Note

The Instrumentalist is a work of fiction inspired by true events from the life of Anna Maria della Pietà. An orphan born in Venice in 1696, she went on to become an international celebrity and one of the greatest violinists of the eighteenth century. Though little detail has been preserved of Anna Maria's work and life, I have tried to include as much truth about her as possible.

Before its economic decline and eventual fall to Napoleon in 1797, Venetians had enjoyed centuries of economic and political stability. A government ruled—a mix of monarchy, oligarchy, and democracy—rather than a dominant noble family or the Church. As Vanessa Tonelli writes in her thesis, *Women and Music in the Venetian Ospedali*, "Venetians lived in economic and political freedom, which allowed them to cultivate the creative arts like nowhere else." Though this was eighteenth-century Venice, Anna Maria and her orchestra of orphans were in many ways modern women too. They earned money; they had careers, educations, and dreams.

Anna Maria was recognized for her musical prowess at the Ospedale della Pietà at eight years old and was eventually considered a *maestra*, an honorific title of respect bestowed by critics and crowds from around the world. I have chosen to use the word *maestro* throughout The Instrumentalist, traditionally a male term, because my Anna Maria thinks of herself not as female but as simply the best.

It is likely that Anna Maria's mother was a sex worker, and

that Anna Maria would have been drowned in the Venetian canals, like many baby girls at the time, were it not for the existence of the Pietà. Anna Maria was a favorite student of Antonio Vivaldi, who both purchased a violin and composed music specifically for her. We know that she was a conductor and copyist, handwriting Vivaldi's music. If Anna Maria was a composer, nothing of her work has been preserved. She went on to occupy the position of *Maestra di Coro* (Master of Music) at the Pietà, a position for female orphans who showed extraordinary musical ability. She lived her entire life at the institution and died when she was eighty-six years old.

There is evidence to suggest that members of the *figlie di coro* helped craft the music we credit to Antonio Vivaldi, which I have largely worked into Anna Maria's story in *The Instrumentalist*. For example, in the book, it is Anna Maria who creates Vivaldi's *La Stravaganza*.

In the study *Women and Music*, Yves Bessieres and Patricia Niedzwiecki describe the Pietà as a "nursery for the virtuosos who provided Vivaldi with his 'musical material.'" They cite a letter from a Pietà student called Lavinia and write, "[Lavinia's] cantatas, concertos and various works had to be composed in secret and in imitation of Vivaldi's style." Here is an excerpt from Lavinia's letter: "You must understand . . . that I could not do otherwise . . . they would not take me seriously, they would never let me compose. The music of others is like words addressed to me; I must answer and hear the sound of my own voice. And the more I hear that voice, the more I realise that the songs and sounds which are mine are different . . . Woe betide me should they find out."

The *figlie di coro*, the famous orchestra of the Pietà, was widely regarded as the best in Italy. The girls and women who made up its ranks were given incredible opportunities. Vivaldi's *Juditha triumphans*, for example, premiered at the Pietà in 1716. It was created as a military oratorio, an allegory on Venice's fight against the Ottomans in Corfu.

Many of the *figlie* were proficient on multiple instruments.

They performed at concerts for kings and queens and rubbed shoulders with elites from across the world, some of whom even sent their children to stay at the Pietà and learn music from the orphan students. The *figlie* were often required to perform behind screens in balconies—heard but not seen for fear they would arouse men and entice them to sin. French lawyer and scholar Charles de Brosses famously heard the *figlie* play in 1739 and, in a letter to a friend, wrote, "They sing like angels, play the violin, the flute, the organ, the oboe, the cello and the bassoon; in short, there is no instrument, however unwieldy, that can frighten them." They were considered to be too intelligent to marry by many of the men of Venice.

Members of the *figlie di coro* were famously disfigured and disabled. Genevan philosopher and writer Jean-Jacques Rousseau wrote about them in his *Confessions*, stating "scarcely one of them was without some considerable blemish." He notes girls disfigured by smallpox and one who was blind in one eye. Other scholars have found examples of the girls missing multiple fingers and toes.

Giacomo Girolamo Casanova was born in Venice in 1725 and likely would have heard the *figlie di coro* play during his lifetime. His autobiography, *The Story of My Life*, explains many of the customs and norms of life during eighteenth-century Venice. While we think of him as a romancer, his book includes many disturbing events, including his involvement in the gang rape of a woman and his having sex with children.

Antonio Vivaldi was a remarkable violinist and composer. He was also an awkward and difficult man, with a shock of red hair, who suffered from an illness (likely asthma). While he enjoyed a period of popularity in Venice, he eventually caused moral uproar when he had his student, a girl named Anna, move in with him. Rumors and speculation continued to circulate of intimacy between them, so much so that Vivaldi himself wrote a letter denying the allegations in 1737. He spent most of his career at the Pietà, and it is said that he composed over 770 works in his lifetime. Scholars agree that without the Pietà and the *figlie di coro*, a breeding ground of talent to test ideas, his music would not exist today. We have a collection of disabled and disfigured female orphans to thank for the most famous piece of classical music on earth: *The Four Seasons*.

Vivaldi ultimately died alone and penniless in Vienna. He was rediscovered in the early 1900s, over one hundred and fifty years after his death, by scholars who saw that his work had influenced another musician—J. S. Bach.

Throughout the book, I have used real names of girls from the orphanage. Precise dates of events, like the publications of Vivaldi and Tartini's compositions, wars, and ceremonies have been amended for dramatic purposes.

I set out to write *The Instrumentalist* because the origin of some of the world's most famous music is different from what we know. At its heart are hundreds of girls and women. I hope it will encourage you to ask yourself—what more is there to discover? What genius have we not yet appreciated? History continues to be imagined. It continues to be written.

Acknowledgments

It takes so much, and so many, to bring a book into the world. And so I crack this novel into pieces: I share it with all who have helped.

To my dear friend Krystal Sutherland, I give the first note, the seed. This book would not exist without your friendship, support, and inspiration. Thank you for showing me what was possible. Thank you for telling me I belonged.

To my agent, Madeleine Milburn, and your entire brilliant team, thank you for seeing the potential in Anna Maria's story and in my work. I give you the sliced playing card, just as you gave it to me, for your guidance, vision, and belief.

To my editors, Alexis Kirschbaum, Carina Guiterman, Iris Tupholme, and especially Allegra Le Fanu, thank you for caring deeply about this story, for your expert feedback and suggestions. I give you Anna Maria's Venice in all its glory, a place as rich and brilliant as your minds.

Many assisted in my research: Vanessa Tonelli and her dissertation *Women and Music in the Venetian Ospedali*, Jane L. Baldauf-Berdes' *Women Musicians of Venice*, Michael Talbot's *Vivaldi*, and research by Micky White. Elizabeth Duntemann took me to the Venetian archives and helped me to find Anna Maria's records. Livia Soulstri helped with Italian translations. Much of what Anna Maria experiences was informed by Min Kym's extraordinary memoir, *Gone*. I give to you all the moonlight filtering through the dormitory roof, for helping me find the light in the darkness.

Acknowledgments

Thank you to the team at Florian Leonhard Fine Violins for showing me how instruments are made, and Jack Liebeck at the Royal Academy of Music for letting me sit in on lessons. Thank you to the students and teachers at the Conservatorio di Musica in Venice, the London Symphony Orchestra, and composers Dani Howard and Dmitry Sitkovetsky, for all your stories and wisdom. I give you the wonder Anna Maria feels when she first holds her violin. It is how I feel when I speak to each of you.

To those who read drafts: David Leipziger, Trevor Lewis, Alicia Ong, Louise MacBean, Jenny Cusack, Katherine Webber, Anna Russell, Alexander Palmer, Kim Ballard, Martin Seneviratne, Kieran Lewis, Arya Gibbs, Britt Collins; to Julie Fettingsmith, Noel Fettingsmith, Alissa Orlando, and Amanda Sperber, who came to Venice; and to my wider nest of friends and family, I'm so grateful to each of you for your encouragement. A special thanks here goes to Kiran Millwood Hargrave. I give you all the glittered gowns, the painted masks. And oh how we shall dance.

Mum, Dad—Judith and Lindsay Constable—I wish for everyone to have parents as loving and supportive as you both. Thank you for filling my life with music and color, and for every curiosity you helped me to follow. I give you the melodies weaving through each and every page.

And darling Owen. Thank you for your unwavering motivation and love, for late-night plotting sessions, for reading this book countless times, for never doubting everything I imagined was possible. Every day you make my world a bigger, more beautiful place. To you I give the colors.

Credits

Editorial
Allegra Le Fanu
Alexis Kirschbaum
Carina Guiterman
Iris Tupholme
Madeleine Milburn
Georgia Mcveigh
Rachel Yeoh
Saskia Arthur
Sophia Benz
Lauren Gomez
Zoe Kaplan

Sales
Brigid Nelson
Sarah Knight
Joe Roche
Fabia Ma
Lily Watson
Tomi Akintola
David Heathscott
Sarah McLean
Hattie Castelberg
Mariafrancesca Ierace
Rosie Barr
Ellen Chen
Joanna Vallance
Rayna Luo
Inez Maria
Emma Allden

Design
Greg Heinimann
Noma Bar

Audio
Tom Skipp
Emma Stephenson

Rights
Valentina Paulmichl
Liane-Louise Smith
Hannah Ladds

Production
Ben Chisnall
Beth Maglione

Publicity
Ros Ellis
Isobel Turton

Marketing
Beth Maher
Beth Farrell
Danielle Prielipp

Managing editor
Fabrice Wilmann

Copy editor
Sharona Selby
Beth Thomas

Proofreader
Martin Bryant
Tina Peckham

About the Author

Harriet Constable is an award-winning journalist and film-maker living in London. Her work has been featured by the *New York Times*, the *Economist*, and the BBC, and she is a grantee of the Pulitzer Center. Harriet was raised in a musical family, and *The Instrumentalist* is her first novel. It has been selected as one of the Top 10 Debuts of 2024 by the *Observer*.